BLAZE

Hope Bolinger

illuminateYA
f i c t i o n

BLAZE BY HOPE BOLINGER

Published by Illuminate YA Fiction
an imprint of Lighthouse Publishing of the Carolinas
2333 Barton Oaks Dr., Raleigh, NC, 27614

ISBN: 978-1-64526-052-3
Copyright © 2019 by Hope Bolinger
Cover design by Elaina Lee
Interior design by AtriTex Technologies P Ltd

Available in print from your local bookstore, online, or from the publisher at: ShopLPC.com

For more information on this book and the author, visit: www.hopebolinger.com

Brought to you by the creative team at Lighthouse Publishing of the Carolinas (LPCBooks.com):
Eddie Jones, Tessa Hall

Library of Congress Cataloging-in-Publication Data
Bolinger, Hope.
Blaze / Hope Bolinger 1st ed.

Printed in the United States of America

Praise for *Blaze*

Vivid. The perfect picture of the adolescent human condition that both entertains and empowers.

~**A. R. Conti Fulwell**
Author of *An Angel in the Distance*

Blaze peels back the curtains of our world's desires and reveals the beasts lurking behind. Packed with relevant topics and worldview, the story draws readers into a white-knuckle adventure where anything can happen—and anything can go wrong. Hope Bolinger delivers a fiery page-turner perfect for students and pyromaniacs, and shows what happens when we're called into the lions' den.

~**Caroline George**
Author of *The Vestige*

Hope Bolinger is a fresh new voice in compelling YA fiction that's not to be missed!

~**Michele Barrow-Belisle**
Bestselling author of Faerie Song Trilogy

When I heard that Hope Bolinger was writing a series of books taking the Daniel story and putting it into modern times, I knew it would be something special. And indeed, it is. Even though you know the Bible story, Blaze will keep you turning pages as you watch events unfold, as you cheer the faith of four brave students, and as you wait to see how Bolinger will tell the story next. Bolinger is creative, funny, and engaging. Blaze does not disappoint.

~**Linda Taylor, M.A., M.F.A.**
Assistant professor of Professional Writing, Taylor University

Bolinger has created a captivating academy world and engaging characters in Blaze. Readers will easily relate to the characters' struggles, and will find comfort in the humor and grace with which the characters navigate a never-ending slew of incredibly trying experiences.

~**DelSheree Gladden**
Author of *Invisible*

Hope Bolinger is a fresh new voice in young adult fiction. Teen readers won't be able to stop turning pages to find out what will happen to Daniel and his trio of friends in this witty, contemporary take on familiar Bible stories for a new generation. Blaze has something for everyone: adventure, relatable characters, themes of faith in difficult times, humor, and, of course, lots of fire.

~**Amy Green**
Author of *The Amarias Adventures*

In her debut novel, Hope Bolinger artfully delivers a witty and harrowing thriller. Blaze is the riveting account of friendship, faith and survival in the face of the fires of King's Academy boarding school. Whatever you think of your school, it's probably not as bad as the neo-Babylonian captivity that Danny Belte and his friends find themselves thrown into at King's. Bolinger has a gift for ingenious narration and fast-paced dialog with an imaginative and incendiary plot built on magnetic and luminous characters. Danny, Rayah, Michelle and Hannah are unique and infectious high school sophomores, but they face alarming threats, not only to their social and academic well-being but to their very lives. As the fires continue to be lit, their courage, resourcefulness and commitment to faith will keep you glued through each twist and turn.

~**Kevin Diller**
Associate Professor of Philosophy and Religion, Taylor University
Author of *Theology's Epistemological Dilemma*

In Blaze, Bolinger has developed a curious world where nothing is as it seems. Blaze is a unique twist on the classic high school drama.

~Amalie Jahn
YA author of The Clay Lion Series
and *The Next to Last Mistake*

Debut author Hope Bolinger entertains the young and young-at-heart with her YA novel, Blaze. She introduces us to Danny Belte and his friends and their struggles and triumphs of life in high school. But this book is so much more. Blaze is a contemporary twist on stories from the book of Daniel in the Bible. The way Hope threads allegory throughout the modern high school setting is masterful. Above all, Blaze is a fun, and can't-put-it-down, delightful story.

~Jennifer Hallmark
Author of *Jessie's Hope*

Dedication

To Daniel,

Tessa,

writing mentors past and present,

and all those faithful and unafraid of fire

Chapter One

A GIRL WITH BLONDE BANGS SWUNG AROUND A RUSTED locker and stopped Danny Belte to show him her phone screen. *What the—?* Danny squinted at the bright screen. His heart thundered in his chest as he made out the writing. His vision blurred as a familiar sensation of bile rose in his throat.

"So much for a non-stressful first day," he muttered.

He had Ms. Necho, after all, who graded harder than the law itself. Forget all those throwaway freshman classes like Earth Science and Spanish 1. Welcome to the world of AP tests and honors courses and a painful little thing called GPA, which turned any stomach inside out on itself. Especially his.

Not to mention a mother who was doubled over the wobbly kitchen table at home with a wrinkled report card from his freshman year, sobbing into the coffee-stained tablecloth, hoping and praying her little boy will pull off another 4.0 this year. Just like his older brother.

Just like his late father.

And there was the tiny little detail that they had a rival school that threatened to bomb Emmanuel Academy at least five times a semester. Not a big deal. They had more important things to worry about than their lives. College, for instance.

But with a heavy backpack slung over his shoulders, too many layers of pine-scented deodorant in his armpits, and a puffed-out chest, through the doors holding up crackling gray walls he had gone. All had been well with the world. All had been prepared ...

Michelle Gad pulled the device away and raised a pair of thick eyebrows at him. She smirked. There it was: the undeniable glow of victory that her latest piece of news had fazed one of her closest friends.

Danny scowled, shoved his fists into his pockets, and hunched his shoulders. A yellowing banner sagged over the sophomore hallway. Two frayed strings just barely clung to life at the edges of the sign that read in faded red letters, *Welcome Back, Students.*

What a way to start a Tuesday.

Inhaling the mixture of rust and mold, Emmanuel Academy's specialty cologne, he recalled seeing that same old banner dangling the first day of his freshman year. Emmanuel, after all, couldn't afford any better welcoming committee. The hordes of students with backpacks playing bumper cars in the hallway didn't seem to pay much attention to the fading sign.

"Well, Danny?"

He swallowed—the slamming lockers from other students blocked out the noise—and set his jaw. He looked down at his shirt front and picked a jet-black hair off it as if he hadn't a care in the world.

"Where'd you find it?" Although he kept his voice calm, his fingernails dug into his other arm. He wiped the white skin cells onto his shirt after one or two scratches.

"Girl's bathroom. Second stall." Michelle nodded down the hallway to a splintered blue archway over a worn sign of a female stick figure. In the past, Michelle had said the only thing worse than the moldy hallway smell was the aroma of ancient feces from the third stall. Had she ever caught a whiff of the men's room before?

"So what? That makes ten bomb threats from a King's Academy student in two years?"

Michelle released a loud sigh. She snapped a pair of scarlet talons in front of Danny's nose, drawing his attention to her reddening cheeks. "Pay attention to the handwriting. It's not a bomb threat."

He swallowed again and found his throat had grown dry. Calm down, Danny, just a stupid King's student. "Relax, Mitch. I don't understand how saying they're gonna 'burn Emmanuel Academy' is much different from a bomb threat."

Michelle frowned and gagged on something in her throat, mixing with the echoing conversations that bounced off the slate brick walls. "Oh, stop trying to act all calm about this. The picture scared you. I saw it in your eyes."

"Honestly! We'd have more of a chance of surviving a fire than an explosion."

"Don't get all optimistic on me. I know you see everything in a dark light, Danny."

Danny's lips twitched. "When the school pays the electric bill, I'll see things differently." A fluorescent light buzzed as if on cue, and a girl with neon socks bumped past Danny on her way to a classroom two doors down.

His friend sighed, squinted, and rubbed her talons on her bulbous nose. Another sharp exhale escaped her lips as she pulled a strand of dishwater blonde hair behind her ear and craned her neck toward Danny again. "You don't get it. The note said when they plan to set the place on fire. Check out the date."

"August 21, 2018. *Today.*" Not a big deal, not a big deal. He rubbed his sweaty palms against his pants.

Michelle raised her eyebrows again, one higher than the other. Her high heels tapped to an obnoxious told-you-so beat.

Dang it, Danny. He'd given himself away. He spun on his heel and twisted the battered lock on his locker, not paying attention to the combination. It squeaked as he spun it.

His friend tapped her plum-colored high heels against the ashen tile. "Well?"

"Sounds like a perfect way to kick off sophomore year." He rotated the dial again, perhaps with too much force as it let out a pained shriek.

A nearby huddle of sophomore girls in athletic wear shot withering glances at Danny, then turned back to their oversized soccer-team sign-up sheet posted on the wall.

"Why do they design every poster with Comic Sans?" Danny muttered.

"Wow, Danny, you sound chipper." Michelle picked at a pimple under her chin with her nails.

"You wanted me to be pessimistic. Welcome to the real me."

"Nice to meet you. Finally." She paused. "Should we head home?"

Danny faked a laugh. "Right. Even when I threw up my guts and gallbladder last winter, Mom still made me go to school that day. If I come home because of a fire threat, she'll send me right back."

Michelle's red lips formed an O to protest, but Danny held up a palm. He nearly smacked a freshman who had paused in front of his locker to consult a school map.

"Judah said King's students threatened the school at least once a week when he went here. He graduated twelve years ago, mind you."

"Stop trying to be protective and positive. I want the real Danny back."

"It's the truth. They were threatened way more than us."

"Yeah, they stopped reporting the threats after five years." Michelle paused and posed for a Snapchat selfie. Danny caught a glint of her silvery eyes in the blaring lights.

He placed a palm on her shoulder after she sent the Snapchat. "We'll survive."

She snorted, nostrils flaring. "Keep dreaming. And wake me when the real Danny returns."

A metallic whine, followed by the sound of a rattling door—as if the door could snap off brittle hinges at any moment—startled him into a jump. He whipped around to see a short girl hidden under a navy-blue bandana and a hunched back. She shoved the books into her locker and then crumpled on her knees as if she had no strength left to rise.

Danny hovered over her now-crumpled form, smelling a soft hint of cinnamon. Rayah.

"Hi, Danny." The girl chewed on her trembling lip and cast a wary glance at Michelle's phone.

"You told Rayah about the bathroom photo, didn't you?" Danny glared at Michelle.

"Freedom of the press," she mumbled, pupils glued to the screen.

Danny grumbled and offered Rayah a hand.

She slid her dark, icy fingers into his, and he hoisted her to her feet.

"Ray, whoever wrote it probably wanted to let off some steam when she lost to you in a soccer match."

A thin smile tugged at her cheek. "No. We haven't made a single goal this year. Earned the lowest score in the league."

"In that case, you should take up golf ... or cross-country."

"I know you're trying to be funny, Danny. To lighten things. But Michelle said the picture scared you too. Texted me when I was using the restroom." She shuddered. "A different one. In the senior hallway."

"Michelle's full of—I won't say it at a Christian school."

An upperclassman with a buzz cut growled as he skirted a group of girls huddling around an open classroom. Emmanuel had four hallways—a main one and three branching ones—all thinner than arm veins. Around the corner past the row of sophomore lockers, a large sticker of a white cross adhered to the front windows of the milky glass doors. The ends of the cross had yellowed, and the bottom of the sticker had flaked off in large patches. Now it just looked like a plus sign.

Rayah fidgeted with her cotton skirt. "Danny, you don't always have to be so strong. We all get nightmares. Even when we're awake." She gave a soft bob of the head and ambled over to Michelle. The girls stood looking down at Michelle's phone, their shoulders almost touching.

Irritated that Michelle had "won" this round of the argument, Danny clenched his jaw and shut Rayah's locker with a hard *thunk*. He returned to his lock, this time entering the combination with care, each turn amplified by a squeak. When he swung the locker open, a rotten cheese odor spilled out. The last owner must have left food on the top shelf for one week too many.

An ancient fabric-covered box on the wall boomed, and Danny jumped at the unexpected sputter of the speaker. He glanced over to make sure neither friend had seen. They hadn't.

"Attention, students." The voice came out shy and whimpering. "Principal Shiloh wants to issue a reminder that there will be no, quote, dilly-dallying, stealing of any school property, gum chewing"—Michelle slid a stick of wintergreen gum between her lips. She offered a piece to the other two friends. Both declined—"skateboarding in the hallway, venturing anywhere during class hours without a pass, vandalism of any kind, horseplay, loitering, profanity, and setting off firecrackers in lockers—due to the incident last year. Principal Shiloh's words." He added the last part in a morose note and switched to a chipper tone. "Have a great first day, Emmanuel!"

Michelle's plump lips formed a grin. "I love it when they make the assistant principal do the announcements." Her tongue flicked out green as if forming a wintergreen bubble. "He always sounds like anything he'll say will set his office on fire." Giving up on the bubble, she clacked her fingernail against the dark phone screen. "At least the poor little guy won't worry about needing to run the school. Thanks to Kim"—Rayah inhaled a sharp gasp—"the King's students'll destroy the place before the end of today."

The whites of her eyes suddenly bloodshot, Rayah scrutinized Michelle in horror. "What if *Ms. Shiloh* hears you?" Rayah placed so much emphasis on the name that she almost sounded harsh.

"If Kim expels me, *Miss Abed*, I'll attend King's Academy. Main requirements for the school: pull a golden goose egg out of my butt to pay their tuition."

Danny grimaced, envisioning what Michelle described. He imagined his friend's bulbous nose transforming into a beak. The mental imagery of his friend as a bird laying eggs reminded him why he never wanted to date her.

"You can join the other pyromaniacs at the academy." The image from her phone flashed across his eyes once more. He ran sweaty fingers through his tangled thornbush of inky black hair, which had fallen into his eyes.

Michelle snorted again, eyes rolling into her layer of bangs. "You confuse me with Hannah. She's the one who did the firecrackers in her locker last year, remember? Poor thing likes fire more than a caveman."

Danny winced at the words *poor* and *Hannah* paired together.

"Anyone seen her?" He was eager to change the subject from the threat. "Or is she gonna break her tardy record from freshman year? Should go to the Olympics for that—" His nerves jolted as the bell swallowed his final word with its earsplitting ringing.

Rayah's shoulders tensed as a teacher cradling a stack of papers ambled past her. "We should head to class."

Danny's chest relaxed as he followed Rayah in the opposite direction of the bathroom. But even if their classroom were right beside it, he would have walked all the way around the school just to avoid stepping in front of it.

🔥

Ms. Necho's dying voice reached its extent in the third row of her classroom.

Unfortunately, Danny sat in the fourth ... beside the fraying map of Israel on the corkboard all pinned up by red thumbtacks under a water-stained ceiling tile, the blot on it looking a lot like the letter F. So much for getting a good grade in this class if he couldn't even hear the teacher. Even Judah had gotten a *B* with Necho ... his mother had cried for a solid day straight.

Even worse for the students, Ms. Necho herself was not easy on the ears *or* eyes. Her squat, wrinkled body doubled over in a bowing position, much like the American flag dangling off a rusted hook on the wall. When he had passed her on the way to his seat, she had smelled almost as dusty and ancient as the room did. Perhaps Emmanuel sprayed everything in musk ... even the teachers. She wore solid-color jumpers, fabric thicker than her Coke-bottle glasses.

And whenever she spoke, her voice imitated a frog that sounded on the verge of tears. "The Babylonian exportation of Jerusalem's inhabitants"— her hoarse voice prolonged each *S*—"happened in three waves. For the first wave, King Nebuchadnezzar forced the elite young men of Judah to ..."

Danny jerked as a piece of folded paper fluttered onto his lap. He looked up, and Michelle nodded at him. Oh boy, here they went. He unfolded it and read, *Would rather die by fire or in this lecture? Perhaps my wish will come true.*

"They sent the most intelligent and choice hostages from Judah into a three-year-education in Babylon ..."

A gust of semi-cold AC from the musty vent tickled his neck. He shuddered.

He peeked behind to find Rayah glancing over his shoulder. He raised an eyebrow at Michelle. Then he crumpled the message into a ball.

Michelle bit her rosy tongue and crinkled her eyes.

Danny flicked his wrist and aimed the paper ball at the trash can by the peeling wood door. He missed ... by a lot. Stupid lighting in this school.

"Daniel Belte."

His mouth tasted like the dry Cheerios he'd eaten for breakfast. "Yes, Ms. Necho?" He leaned forward and cupped his ear to hear the sentence.

"Do not ever try out for the basketball team. No wonder they scored a losing record last year."

"Yes, Ms. Necho." His heart pounded in his temples, his vision in a slight haze.

"And visit Principal Shiloh when class ends to explain the halftime show you gave us. Returning to the lesson, the three-year education program took on four Israelites named—"

The wooden door creaked. A girl in a crop top, featuring a Japanese anime panda, and frizzy auburn hair trudged in.

Ms. Necho gaped at her, tongue bulging right behind her lips. She looked ready to catch a fly at any moment, a rather funny image. Nice way to take Danny's mind off things.

A dead pause enveloped the room while the AC unit gurgled as if it had an upset stomach.

The teacher collected herself and consulted the attendance clipboard on her desk. "Miss Hannah Shad, that top is elevated about four inches too high for dress code standards, and you have arrived forty minutes too late by any decent standard."

Hannah placed a rosy sheet of paper onto the teacher's chipped desktop. "Already went to the principal." Each note droned a monotone as if she were still waking up.

Ms. Necho snagged the paper and held it up to her nose the way Judah used to look at large bills when he cashiered for the local grocery store. Several moments later she set the paper down and jabbed a finger at the girl. "Sit. I cannot afford any more interruptions today."

Hannah slumped into an open desk next to Michelle with *David Wuz Here* scratched into the top. She propped her feet on the vacant chair in front.

"Detention on the first day?" Michelle whispered. "Did you want to break a record from last year or something?"

Giving up on trying to hear Ms. Necho's lecture and somewhat curious about Hannah's absence, Danny listened as best he could above the sputters of the AC unit.

Hannah picked at something in her teeth with her nails. "Actually, the attendance lady sent me to Jesse. Guess Kim's not in today."

"Feet down, Miss Shad." Ms. Necho paused from scraping the chalk across the green board at the front of the room. "You and Daniel can both visit the principal at the conclusion of class." She returned to her chalk work. "Now, Hananiah, Mishael, Azariah, and Daniel faced a lot of pressure to conform to Babylonian customs ..."

Hannah's clunky shoes hit the floor with a thud, and the loud thump caused Danny to jerk at his squeaky desk.

Ms. Necho glared at Hannah. When the death glower passed, Michelle leaned in to ask more questions. "Jesse? Assistant principal Jesse who sounds like he's always having stomach problems when he does announcements?"

"Turns out he's the same in person." Hannah leaned over her desk and pulled out a sketchbook from her beat-up pack. "The guy can't be over twenty-three. Incompetent as a fish climbing a tree."

Michelle flared her nostrils. "OK, Einstein, what happened when you arrived late?"

She flipped open to a page with a sentient flower using a scythe to decapitate a man. "I went to the office—papers piled everywhere—almost like he tried to build a city out of them." She pulled out a red pen to outline the blood in her sketch. "And the poor guy looked like he'd forgotten to do five projects that were due today. When I came in, he looked at me, frantic, so panicked. No idea what to do. So in a calm voice, I explained Kim's procedure: Let the kids off with a warning the first tardy day, and send an email to brendabarnes at emmanuelacademy dot org to put my name on the list of late arrivals."

Michelle's eyebrows furrowed into a blonde bridge. "But Kim's policy gives tardy kids detention no matter what."

Hannah hid a snicker behind her knuckle before returning to her drawing. "I also gave him a fake email address. No one named Barnes works here."

Michelle's mouth dropped open. "You didn't!"

Danny grinned. He wouldn't have the guts ... mostly because his guts were disintegrating inside him half the time.

"And he fell for it too!" Hannah whispered. "He fell for it like the walls of Jericho."

Michelle's eyes bulged just as the bell rang.

Desks screeched, and students bolted out of chairs to race out the door.

Ms. Necho rasped to the runners about a three-page essay due the next day. So the sophomore-year frenzy of homework began.

Danny swung his book-bag over one shoulder, headed out of the classroom, and followed the dim, flickering lights toward the principal's office. He felt a tug on his backpack and twisted around to find Hannah's hand, sporting chewed fingernails, wrapped around his other book-bag strap.

With a slight growl, he yanked it out of her grip. "Come on, Han. We should go. We disrupted class and everything."

"Rule follower as always."

"Look. If we don't go, Necho'll call the office and find out. Mom'll flip."

Hannah's chapped lips pursed. "Doubt Jesse can operate the phone, Dan." Her fingers made a lazy motion as if attempting to wave him over but giving up on the effort. "'Sides, rules are like families ... meant to be broken."

He winced.

Hannah turned and scuffed her feet down the dirty hallway, trailing behind Michelle and Rayah, who had advanced three door frames ahead.

A moment later Danny followed but stopped behind a group of five slow-moving senior girls who had decided to form a wall of linked arms as they meandered down the narrow halls. He passed several rows of aging corkboards overcrowded with sign-up sheets for various clubs.

Most of the papers had several staples jutting out and perhaps—if lucky enough—contained two names out of thirty available slots.

At the bottom, a burnt-orange piece of paper (half covered by the *Godspell* audition sign-up sheet) announced the lunch menu for the day. Danny's nose creased when he read the special: pork tenderloin. His mouth dried at the mention of the sandpaper meat. At least that's how his friends described it. As a vegetarian, he wouldn't know.

He was happy he had packed the PB&J, bread bleeding with grape jelly, in the tan paper bag atop his locker shelf. That is if the moldy locker smell hadn't seeped into his food.

"Yes, Mitch, I received your five billion texts about the writing in the bathroom." Hannah slammed her wobbly locker door shut.

Rayah jumped. Recovering, she wrapped her fingers around a Biology textbook.

Michelle released a sharp exhale. "I liked Jeremy's reaction better than yours, Hannah. He keeps messaging me in all caps."

"Jeremy is part of the *drama* club," Hannah said through gritted teeth. "And he cried when the water fountain stopped working in the hallway by the cafeteria. Do you trust his judgment?"

"At least be serious about this threat!"

"Deadly serious." Hannah smirked, her chapped lips lending a creepy note.

The smirk disappeared at a flicker of the dim hallway lights. Her head snapped away from her locker. She scanned the echoing hallway from left to right—Danny had never seen her move so fast. Despite the wall of sound from nearby conversations, Danny's heart pounded a timpani drumbeat in his rib cage.

He saw the back of Hannah's ruby nose ring when her nostrils wrinkled. "Do you smell that?" She didn't really ask so much as growl.

Michelle frowned. "What?"

Then he smelled it right as Hannah gave her answer.

"Smoke."

Chapter Two

A BURNT-RUBBER ODOR STUNG DANNY'S NOSE. Flashes of white lights danced to a tune of three shrieks on repeat. Everyone in the hallway froze, wide-eyed. They watched the fire alarm blast its death-pale beams, their shadows etching across the dull brick walls like the etchings of a crime scene.

Danny's cheeks flushed, and his heart beat so fast he couldn't distinguish one beat from the next.

"Move!" Michelle's voice broke the shadows out of their stupor. She rushed down the hallway in her thunderous high heels and turned right to bolt out the front doors, skidding along the mop-stained tile. In a blind daze, students followed her lead.

Hannah trailed at the rear of the crowd, her knuckles shoved into pockets. She strolled past the flaky cross on the front doors, and in the strobing of the bright beams of light, she moved as if she had time to kill.

Danny rushed next to her and scanned the crowd as it filtered through the tight doors. Looking for a navy bandana ... "Hannah, did you see Rayah go outside?"

No response.

He surveyed the heads once more. When he didn't see Rayah, he doubled back. He stretched out his arms to break through a cluster of students. He found an opening and rounded the corner toward the sophomore lockers. The stench worsened. No sign of smoke anywhere though. Oh, God, where was she?

He saw her huddled in a fetal position beside her locker.

"Rayah, get up! We need to go."

She remained still.

He crouched beside her, breathing heavily, and shook her shoulder with more force than he had intended. He tried another shake, gentler this time. No response. "Come on, Ray." He slipped his sweaty hand into her dry one and pulled.

Her limp body slumped against the outside of her locker.

His fingers released hers, and he scanned the narrow hallway for a teacher. The flashes of white light revealed no adults. "Where is every-one?"

No answer.

The burning smell intensified. Danny's stomach cramped as if some-one had plunked a stone into the acid building up in it. Bile rose in his throat, and his cheeks prickled with heat.

He glanced once more around the hallway, squinting his eyes to shield them from the harsh light flashes.

Shadows, like smoke billows, covered the gaping holes of door mouths—as if they were gasping in horror. The shrieking alarm sound-ed even louder in the face of their silent screams.

Not another human in sight now. He ventured another attempt to compel his friend to rise. He slipped his fingers into hers once more. *God, help me get her out of here.*

"Twelve steps." He grunted as her fingers slipped. He tried for a gen-tler voice, but heavy breathing and inhaling what smelled like the burnt wiring of a computer made it very difficult. "Twelve steps, Ray. That's how many it takes to reach outside. How many steps it takes to reach Michelle's unreasonably large nose."

Rayah's waxen expression melted. She stared at Danny for a mo-ment—dark pupils burning into his like a flame—nodded, and then stood.

He wrapped his arm around her, and they hobbled toward sunlight.

Danny counted thirteen steps as they bolted out of the glass doors. By this point, they were running past the crusty cross sticker and toward the parking lot. *Thank you, Lord.* The nausea passed as he breathed in the outside air. But it returned after a few seconds, as muggy air spilled into his lungs, choking him almost as much as the smoke indoors. So much for a cooler fall this year.

Ms. Necho stood over a worn picnic table that had been gouged by knives and marked up with graffiti.

He sprinted over to her, the brown grass crunching underneath his worn Nikes. Rayah's steps were a couple feet behind. "Where *were* the teachers?" His voice came out too forceful, at least for him.

The toad woman gaped, cheeks flushing a sunburnt red.

His heart hammered. Two times today he caused trouble with this teacher. Collecting himself and lowering his voice, he gestured toward Rayah, who panted behind him. "I found her huddled in the middle of the hallway. With the fire, you'd think a teacher would check to make sure all the students got out."

Ms. Necho's expression softened when she saw Rayah's fear-filled expression. She cleared her throat. "What hallway?"

"The sophomore one ... by the main doors."

"If any fire alarm goes off between classes, Principal Shiloh placed Mr. Peterson in charge of that hallway, and"—she scanned the sparsely wooded area by the asphalt, peppered with burnt brown grass—"I believe he took a sick day. Never showed up in the teacher's lounge this morning as per his usual routine."

Still suspicious, Danny peered down the row of faculty, attempting to spy the man who liked to sport ties with cartoon characters.

The teachers huddled over a patch of hot parking lot by a bowl-shaped pothole. The closest thing to Mr. Peterson was a man in a polka-dot bow tie swatting away a humming bee.

Ms. Necho's eyes bulged suddenly. "Besides her"—she motioned to Rayah—"did you see any other students lagging behind?"

Danny clamped his eyes shut, envisioning the empty hallway. "No."

"Quite certain?"

"I have a photographic memory, Ms. Necho."

Ms. Necho walked away and joined a group of teachers.

Danny and Rayah tried to find their friends in the mass of students.

Classmates huddled in unorganized clumps like billows of smoke around scrawny trees. Many had pulled out cell phones and taken selfies with the mud-colored brick building—the same hue as the lawn at the front of the school.

"What a great generation we come from"—Danny gestured toward the students—"taking pictures during an actual emergency." But what else was there for the students to do? Better to distract oneself with a phone or even a textbook than to drown in anxiety. Even his own hand inched toward his pocket that bulged with his phone.

Moments later, Rayah located Hannah and Michelle near a group of students huddled in prayer. They met them by a big blue trash can that reeked of warm, moldy food and was attended to by a handful of bees around the sticky liquid on the outside.

"Did they trample you?" Michelle yanked Rayah into a hug.

Rayah shook her head and buried it in Michelle's shoulder. She quaked, and her sapphire dress formed ocean waves.

"She panicked." Danny inched away from the trash can. "Fight, flight, or freeze. Freezing, the third and coldest option, isn't the best with a fire present."

Michelle glared at him. "I'm not sure whether to be madder at you for the terrible pun or the fact you're trying to be so lighthearted during an emergency."

"If you're not sure, then don't be mad at all."

"I saw you freak out, Danny, inside the building. You were just as paralyzed as Ray here."

Rayah let out a few hiccupping sobs, muffled by Michelle's cotton blouse, and Michelle patted her on the back as though she were an infant. "You'd think after practicing those fire drills once a month, even in the dead of winter, the students would know what to do in the actual situation."

"Doesn't help the alarm went off between classes." Danny swatted at his ear as a bee from Garbage Land hovered too close to his neck. "Normally, we line up according to whoever's class we were in during the drill."

Several minutes passed as they hovered in silence. The prickly grass scratched their feet as if it, too, itched to know why the first day of school must always end in disaster. A cluster of sparrows chirped overhead and soared over the soiled building, unaware of the worry in the world below.

The group of four moved away from the trash can and sat under a bony oak tree, where Hannah proceeded to decapitate heads of dandelions with her fingernails. With each murder, she kicked up the dirt, causing the air to smell of dust, just like Necho's classroom.

"Leave the poor flowers alone." Michelle swiped a talon at Hannah to remove the poor corpses. Hannah was quicker. "What did they ever do to deserve that treatment?"

"Nothing. Absolutely nothing." She continued to pop off the heads until none remained in her vicinity.

They watched as students continued to take videos of the building, perhaps expecting the school to explode into flames at any moment.

Although Danny could not rid his nose of the smoky smell of the hallways, no dark clouds rose from the building. Weird. Maybe the movies had it wrong when it came to building fires.

With a grubby hand, Hannah dug through her bag and pulled out a pack of cards.

"Seriously, Hannah?" Michelle asked. "We're going to play a game of cards when the school could burst into flames at any moment?"

"I mean it's either we distract ourselves with this or Danny makes another terrible pun."

"Fair."

Even Danny agreed. He'd rather not think about how much he had wanted to puke back in the building.

Hannah dealt even piles to the four of them for a game of "War."

During their freshman year, the four would often play cards during free periods on the crusty chapel carpet. They had often finished their homework early—or in the case of Hannah, didn't feel much like doing assignments at all.

After Hannah finished passing out the cards, Danny peeked out from behind his fanned cards to watch the activity on lawns infested by bees, thin tree roots, and dandelions untouched by Hannah. Most students had resorted to scrolling on their phones, but some had split open books from class. They were probably starting the homework assigned during first period. Not a bad idea. But he wouldn't be able to focus on the Necho essay with the backdrop of a burning building.

Nearby, an acne-scarred student who wafted a strong smell of co-conut sunscreen hollered into his phone. The interspersed voice cracks and whiny tone drove a spike into Danny's ear canal. "Come on, Mom! Pick up!" The student's pink tongue rolled over his silver braces. Moments later he slumped against a tree. "Voicemail again? Fine. Mom, the school caught on fire! I've been telling you for months about this place ... bad news. Tried telling everybody but no one would listen ..."

"Jeremy making more predictions about the future?" Hannah flipped over a card. She scowled at it. "Come on, another two? Why does this game hate me?"

Michelle raised an eyebrow. "He has a point."

"I'm a *she*," Hannah corrected her.

Danny hid his laugh behind his cards, which helped block the humid air from reaching his nostrils.

"I meant Jeremy." Michelle flipped over a seven of clubs. "He trusted me about the fire threat in the bathroom stall. Besides him and Rayah, no one else believed me."

No war occurred during the game until a couple rounds in when Rayah and Hannah placed down two queens. They each put down another three cards and overturned the last one.

Rayah, having flipped over an ace (the highest card), won another of Hannah's twos. Rayah took the cards with a shy sweep.

Hannah let out a deep-throated growl. "I swear this game hates me."

Danny overturned the king of hearts and glanced up at the shrill *doo-wee-oo* of a siren.

A ruby vehicle barreled down the street, zigzagging around the potholes. The students who had given up on waiting for the building to ignite returned to their cell phones to take selfies with the fire truck.

Danny's heart throbbed in his chest. He had to distract himself from what was happening to the school. He didn't want to know. Knowing would make him anxious, which would make him want to vomit. He returned his attention to the game.

Michelle, with a sweaty palm, had slapped down the king of diamonds next to his card. Dust sprang into the air and covered the cards. A wry smile. "Two kings down, Danny. That means war."

When the fire truck left, bouncing over the bowl-shaped pothole, the students remained outside in the muggy afternoon air.

The assistant principal approached the lawn in a disheveled shirt, the buttons in all the wrong places.

Despite the serious tone of the afternoon events, Danny's stomach bubbled with mirth.

He cleared his throat. "S–students and faculty, we p–postponed school for the rest of the day. P–please call your p–p–parents to arrange rides home for an early d–dismissal. Those students with c–cars here at school, inform your t–teachers prior to leaving." He then ordered everyone to line up behind their second-period teachers.

"Poor guy." Rayah cast a sympathetic look at the assistant principal as she followed a disorganized trail of students toward a teacher with a long beard. Emmanuel students were apparently terrible at fire drills and forming straight lines. But the state of Pennsylvania let them drive cars. "Terrible first day to go on the job if you ask me."

The assistant principal also, with a surprising lack of stutters, notified the teachers that none of the kitchen workers received any injuries from the cafeteria fire.

Ten minutes later, Hannah's father barreled down the parking lot in his rusted Honda Accord, making sure to hit every pothole in the lot before picking up his daughter. Michelle's mother must've also retrieved her offspring because she had also disappeared from the sloppy line of students for her second-period class.

A few minutes after Hannah left, Rayah—with heavy encouragement from Danny—plucked enough courage to trudge through brittle grass and ask her teacher if after-school sports would still meet.

Mr. Johnson, filing in a line of teachers to query the assistant principal, at last learned soccer practice would not take session. "Not today, because of the fire." Mr. Johnson shoved a pair of square glasses up his nose. "But you wouldn't have had practice anyway because Coach Anderson forgot you had one scheduled for today."

Rayah nodded. "He does that ... third time this season."

Apparently, Emmanuel excelled at hiring staff members as much as the students bested forming a straight line.

When Mr. Johnson finished taking attendance of the bus students, he told the line to sit on the lawn and wait as if he imagined not all the parents would arrive at once.

Cross-legged on the dry, itchy ground, Danny turned on the data for his phone as the school's Wi-Fi didn't work outside. It didn't work all too well inside, either. With an automatic swipe, he checked his social media accounts.

"Call your mom yet?" Rayah parked next to him, brushing the dirt off her skirt.

He shook his head, his mop of hair tickling the bridge of his nose. "No, she'll act like Armageddon came early. She's been on an end-times bent lately, and I want it to, well, end." No applause from Rayah. "Did you tell your parents?"

She bit her lip. "No, my dad hates this school. He wants to find any reason to transfer me to another place."

"Like where? King's Academy—and pay three times the amount of tuition? The closest school in Washington County is Lydia High. And that's an hour's drive away."

"Two or three hours on the bus." Her quivering chin bobbed up and down. "I know. Besides, they have a terrible academic reputation. My mom would throw a conniption."

What else were mothers for?

Both waited in awkward silence as the pleasant but untimely chirps of sparrows filled the sultry air.

Then Rayah's fingers fumbled with the zipper on her book bag. She pulled out her silvery notebook from Ms. Necho's class and scribbled with her mechanical pencil down the lines.

Danny pulled out his notebook from his book bag to start his own essay. But three lines in, he grew bored and sat, alone with his thoughts. Oh, happy day.

Heart pounding in his ears and breath growing shallow, he whipped out his phone again and opened his email, an automatic response ingrained in him from freshman year. Teachers loved to send messages. Not ones of love, though.

The emails in his inbox glowed the boring plain font, indicating Danny had read them. Except for one. His stomach burbled when he read the subject line.

"Rayah, ever heard of Edgar Rezzen?"

"Who?"

"Edgar Rezzen. Dude who sounds like his name came out of the 1800s."

"Is he from the 1800s?"

"No, he's some guy who shot me an email with the subject, 'Welcome to King's Academy.' He must've sent the message to the wrong person."

"Odd." She paused for a moment as a freshman girl shrieked and swiped at a bee. Then her mechanical pencil squeaked against the paper once more.

The email subject, for some reason, gave him more anxiety than the school fire. So he clicked off his phone and returned to the notebook. But the boredom. Oh, the mind-numbing boredom of the essay. This essay was going to kill him.

And curiosity, in the form of a restless heartbeat, pulsed in his temples. He rubbed his face and groaned. "All right," he growled. He pulled open the email again and clicked on the boldface message.

> **To:** Daniel_Belte@emmanuelacademy.org
>
> **From:** Edgar_Rezzen@kingsacademy.net
>
> **Subject:** Welcome to King's Academy
>
> Dear Daniel Belte,
>
> King's Academy has received your academic records and is very pleased with your application. We handpick the best and brightest in the country for our rigorous educational programs. Most high school credits transfer, so you would still be able to graduate within the next three years.
>
> Colleges across the globe seek graduates from our school and offer millions of dollars in up-to-date scholarships. Several of our

athletes are recruited by Division I schools such as the University of Pittsburgh and Temple University, to name a few.

King's Academy is pleased to offer you a full-ride scholarship, including room and board, for the next three years. Please schedule a visiting day with Ashley Penaz within the next three days, prior to the beginning of our fall term. I cc'd her the message.

Sincerely,

Edgar Rezzen

Danny's eyes wavered up and down the email, the phone's brightness turned up all the way in the harsh sunlight. At last, he understood the message.

He twisted around and tapped a finger on Rayah's shoulder blade.

She glanced at him, her fingers twitching over the essay.

"This will only take a minute." He waved his phone.

Her spine relaxed, and she placed the pencil on top of the half-done essay.

"Check out this email, Ray." He handed her the phone and watched her expression as she read. His chest felt as tight as if it were made of glass. If someone dropped him onto the crackled, potholed concrete, he would break. Why did he have to open the email? Now his heart was ticking faster than the National Debt Clock.

"Odder." Rayah's nervous fingers fiddled with her head wrap.

"I didn't give them an application, and no way in heck do I want to go to that school. They can spruce up the place in the email, but Judah knows plenty about the academy. You've heard the stories about what they did to him."

"Maybe your mom sent in your records." Long eyelashes bounced on her cheeks. "Every time we come over, she praises King's Academy."

"If so, she'll wish it was Armageddon."

Rayah nodded and craned her short neck toward her notebook. Once a bookworm, always a bookworm.

He checked his texts to distract himself from the email business and from the shrieks of freshman girls, helpless against an army of wasps.

Messages from his mom following the lines of *Are you OK???* and *Daniel Micah Belte, please respond!* swarmed his feed.

He swiped the screen to send a pacifying, *Doing fine. Don't worry*, but a light thump on his back caused him to drop the device before he could ask about King's.

He spun around and Rayah muttered a wide-eyed apology. "They sent me the same email."

He squinted at her phone. Rayah liked to keep the brightness low to avoid ruining her eyes, even in the sharp sunlight. The words of the email matched his to a T except the message opened with "Dear Marayah Abed."

"Man, they used your full Christian name. Aren't they pagan?"

"We both have parents who dislike Emmanuel. Maybe they sent in our records together."

Danny's rowdy phone buzzed in the grass. His skin prickled. "Mom, I swear, if you text me again …" He scooped up the device, wiping off the dust, but a note from Michelle blinked on the screen.

Did you find a weird email from the Academy? Just texted Hannah and she received one this afternoon.

His heart began to race again, but a funny thought crossed his mind. Hysteria, perhaps, in response to the school fire. "Hannah got an email from them? How?"

Rayah frowned when she peered at Danny's phone. "Maybe Hannah has been lying about her grade point average. Guess it makes sense. No one can receive a 'negative 4.0.' What if all our parents banded together to send us to King's?"

"Let's not jump to the impossible." He arched his back, in pain from not having a seat back. "Students here are jokesters. I would know. Someone probably sent a prank email to everyone at Emmanuel." His stomach released part of its tension at the thought of this. Maybe there was nothing to be worried about after all.

He decided to test the hypothesis. His legs carried him to a small sophomore parked by a clump of dandelions, ones Hannah hadn't managed to kill yet. Even from a gentle inhale, one could tell that she had doused herself in a little too much perfume that morning. Holding back a cough, he nudged her sunlight-warmed back with his index finger, and a freckled nose confronted him.

"Yes?" Her high-pitched voice dripped with irritation.

"Sorry. Name's Danny. Mind pulling up your inbox on your phone? We think some student sent a prank email to the entire school."

Her fiery eyebrows joined together, and she folded her arms. She shot him a wary expression but opened her email. "Nothing." Her furrowed brows matched his.

"Sorry for, well, nothing." He returned to his original seat and explained the awkward situation to Rayah.

"I mean, no one would fall for the prank if everyone in the school received the message, right?" Danny hoped. Prayed.

Rayah's lips pursed together. "It seems real, Danny."

"OK." He exhaled. "In that case, I think I'll just email him back. To let him know it's all a mistake."

She nodded. "Good idea."

"And that he should stuff it."

"Mmm, not a good idea."

"OK, fine. Just the first part."

> **To:** Edgar_Rezzen@kingsacademy.net
>
> **From:** Daniel_Belte@emmanuelacademy.org
>
> **Subject:** Re: Welcome to King's Academy
>
> Dear Mr. Edgar Rezzen,
>
> Someone made a mistake. I never applied to King's Academy. Thank you for the offer, but I wish to decline.
>
> Sincerely,
>
> Daniel Belte

He tapped the *Send* button much quicker than he had expected. Relief and fresh air spilled into his chest despite the muggy conditions. "Glad we put an end to that. Now if we can put an end to the end-times stuff, we can actually start stuff. Like homework."

"Do you really think so?" Rayah's hopeful tone crackled in the back of her throat.

"Ray, I refused a full-ride scholarship to a pretentious school. If the email wasn't a prank and they sent me an invite, they'll never reply again."

When Danny awoke the next morning, he had five fresh messages in his inbox. So the end times began.

Chapter Three

"GONNA FINISH THAT SANDWICH?"

Rayah shrugged and handed Hannah her half-eaten piece of bread, sopping with bananas and peanut butter.

Leaning over a stiff wooden chair, Hannah grabbed the sandwich and chomped into it. Only Hannah could eat at a time when the school—in all its burnt-tomato-smelling glory—could shut down at any moment.

And the administration had decided it was a grand idea to have students come back the next day. Bravo, American education system.

Letting out a gasp, Hannah lay down on the sloping ramp that led to the chapel stage. Facing the empty wooden platform with a vacant table and a cloth stained purple from grape juice, Hannah took another bite and swallowed. Strings of saliva stuck to the bananas.

"Did you forget we no longer have a cafeteria, Han? That's literally the only detail they gave about the fire, you know." Danny averted his eyes from the drool trailing off Hannah's lips, looking instead at the rickety ceiling fans, which wafted a scent of dust and Lysol to sidetrack students from the stink of the sticky carpet; then at the solemn navy curtains, which hung from the water-stained ceiling, highlighting the American and Christian flags in front of them; and finally at the cobwebs glittering in the corners of the cooled sunlight, streaming through the stained-glass window above the stage.

"Yeah, the enemy likes to strike the food supply first." Michelle's shrill voice yanked Danny's attention away from the window. "That's how King's Academy plans on forcing us to sign up. By starving us out." She shot him a long, penetrating look—perhaps one of triumph because she had been right about the fire—and then scrolled on her phone. "Not a terrible idea. I hear they import food there from fancy places."

"Dunno if what our school serves qualifies as an *edible* food supply." The ball was in Michelle's court now.

Her cheeks darkened almost to purple. "Either way, Hannah, you should've packed." Classic Michelle. Debating with someone else when she loses one fight. Bright political career ahead of her.

"Hey, I showed up to school on time." Hannah bent in half and spewed chunks of peanut butter onto the brown carpet. "I had to nix unneeded items from my schedule."

"Like eating?"

"Counted on Rayah's anxiety. She doesn't eat food when she worries. In fact, you all have a problem with stress and eating. Michelle overeats."

Michelle threw her crumpled brown lunch bag at Hannah.

Hannah easily dodged the toss and continued, "And Danny up-chucks everything."

Danny tore off a piece of vegan jerky with his teeth and swallowed the spicy snack without chewing. Cool air drifting through the AC vents chilled every part of him except for his tongue. "If you wait five minutes, I can throw this up for you too."

"He's gotten better about his stomach issues." Rayah fiddled with a rusty *103* seat-number placard that was dangling on a nail.

"Gather a crowd. We can sell tickets and get enough money for kitchen repairs."

Hannah raised her eyebrows. "How many times did you feel sick since yesterday, Dan?"

"Five, one for each email. It's a new record." He scrolled through his inbox, reading each subject line to the group: "'Welcome to King's Academy,' 'Extras if you join King's Academy,' 'Even more extras if you enroll today,' 'Scheduling your day visit,' and 'FAQ about King's Academy: read up before your visit.'"

And the conclusion: "Also had several nightmares last night, which didn't help either. Didn't throw up yet, though. Disappointing, I know."

A low whistle escaped Hannah's thin lips. They had a hard time hearing it amid the drone of the AC and other lunch groups clustered around splintering seats. "No vomiting, huh? Someone bring this brave heart a trophy."

Throughout his friendship with Hannah, Danny had hazarded many guesses on how she got to be so ... well, Hannah. His best explanation was a combination of a single dad and a handful of brothers—great for video-game nights—and an obsession with Tumblr and Hot Topic.

He ripped off another section of jerky with his teeth—another lava bath for his tongue—and pulled out his phone. The letter icon on the bottom right blinked with a fresh email message. Armageddon round six. He groaned and clicked the image. Nothing happened.

"You got another one from King's?" Rayah released the rusty seat placard, her fingers now rubbing up and down her dress.

"Yeah. Won't load, though."

"Emmanuel has as much decent Wi-Fi as it contains delicious food." Hannah forced the rest of the sandwich into her mouth. Her cheeks bulged.

Danny chewed on his jerky. "Wonder why they're so persistent. If they're offering free scholarships, they don't want us for our money."

Hannah shrugged. "Could be lots of reasons. High enrollment numbers, loyalty from alumni so they'll donate, so they can watch their rival school crash and burn. I could go on. You know I understand villains better than most other things."

That was for sure.

Danny chewed on his jerky in silence and rubbed his thumb against the crusty chapel carpet, landing on a sticky spot occasionally. Although disgusting, it kept his mind occupied.

He fixed his gaze on the one beautiful thing in the room—and in the school—the stained-glass window. The mural featured a golden lion—the school's mascot before they changed it to an eagle—amid a sea of blue. For some reason, the longer one stared at the art piece, the more the room smelled like fresh air instead of the trace hints of burnt tomato from the cafeteria.

"Guys." Michelle snapped a pair of talons at the group. The glow of the phone light made her eyes dance with conspiracy. "You'll never guess what Jeremy just texted me."

They could take a shot in the dark here: something to do with King's ... or his eczema, which he claimed smelled like rotting cheese. Danny never got close enough to find out. Neither one was a favorable discussion topic.

Fed up by this point, Danny hazarded several guesses that ranged from "Jeremiah discovered that he was a bullfrog" to "We're dreaming right now and, up to this point, lived our entire lives in a lie." He accompanied each of these with a snicker, but his friends only met him with blank stares and a moment of silence interrupted by a freshman in the front row complaining about how he'd packed expired Doritos.

Michelle spoke after the boy pelted a friend with a nacho-cheese chip. "OK, funny guy, this guessing game could take a really long time. How about I tell you? Jeremy went to ask the assistant principal if he could go to the gas station to grab some food because *some* of us"—she shot a pointed stare at Hannah—"don't mooch off others. Anyway, he overheard some ladies in the front office talking, and they said Kim left."

"Left for vacation?" Danny beamed. "Left as in died? Or left meaning the direction opposite of right?"

Michelle's eyeballs *left* for a brief moment behind squeezed-shut eyelids. They returned to glare at him. "She *retired*."

"You sure about this, Mitch?" Hannah eyed her and then Rayah's provolone cheese stick, which was handed over soon after.

Michelle bobbed her chin. "Deadly serious. She also pulled her son out of school and sent him somewhere else. I place a hard guess at King's Academy since she admires that place as much as Danny's mom. And don't you find it interesting how our principal runs the school for eleven years and just packs her bags—right after disaster strikes?"

Hannah's ribs expanded and contracted with a sigh, mirroring Danny's. Her already skintight T-shirt, today featuring an anime fox, clung tightly to her chest. She tore off a piece of cheese and popped the shaving onto her tongue. "Kitchen fire and disaster are worlds apart."

"We could've died. And she left under suspicious circumstances." To Michelle, a puppy wagging its tail could've been suspicious.

"Really, Mitch?" Danny's attention flipped between Hannah gnawing on the cheese stick and the freshman boy grinding the Doritos into powder with his shoes. "You don't think Ms. Shiloh caused the fire?"

"I wanted to draw our attention to a *significant* coincidence. Yes, mere chance that Kim *happened* to be absent yesterday even though she has a perfect attendance record. Sure, pure luck would have her hiring an incompetent assistant principal to drive the school into ruin after she leaves. Yes, happenstance she used to love King's Academy in the first half of her time here. A love for a vile school like that *could* perhaps drive someone to insane acts of devotion like pyromaniac tendencies—" She paused for effect and licked her lips. "Yes, a mere coincidence."

Michelle deserved an Oscar every day of her life. Danny envisioned the sawdust-fumed stage. Her mom did help with the local community theater.

Having her fill of theater, Hannah flicked the cheese-stick wrapper at Michelle, gripping the rest of the snack in her chewed-nail fingers. "Don't know why you didn't listen to Jeremy when he told you to sign up for the drama club." She tore off another cheese shaving and bit it, letting the bottom half dangle from her jade-tinted lips. "As for the rest of us nontheater kids, I think we'll stick to the cold, hard facts." She paused and then stared at Rayah's crumpled lunch bag slumping against a brick wall.

"Sorry." Rayah threw up her palms. "No more food."

A beam of cerulean light gleamed from the stained-glass window and landed in her palm. Her hand clasped into a fist as if desiring to grab the beam.

Squinting at the sapphire rays, Danny set down the almost-empty bag of vegan jerky, its fiery fumes still tingling his nostrils. "Kim or some academy student can burn whatever part of the school they like. Just leave this place intact."

A mutter of assent rippled through the group.

"The only thing Danny can't joke about." Michelle gestured to the room.

"They still plan to have chapel service on Friday, right?" Rayah whispered, her eyes big. "Even after the fire and all?"

Michelle, her dull blonde hair resting on her left shoulder, leaned toward Hannah. "Heard Kim attempted to do away with the chapel in past years. She didn't see the point in making classes shorter for it."

Hannah scooted away from Michelle. She was rather a fan of personal space. "Yeah, but she retired. We don't have to worry about her anymore."

They quieted, immersing themselves in silence and shafts of cool light.

For a moment Danny felt they had plunged into a lake. He leaned his head upon a thick, wooden folding seat and imagined gentle ripples massaging his hair. He relaxed and his abdomen pains subsided.

An icy, bright light interrupted the sanctuary stillness, followed by a sharp *ping*. An email notification blinked on his phone. He shoved the device into his pocket, curiosity pounding in his temples.

"Speaking of devils." Danny chewed on his cheek to distract himself from his itching fingers.

"Edgar?" Hannah smirked.

"Uh huh." He thumbed the fabric of his jeans when the sound of the school bell bounced off the walls of the auditorium.

Hannah and Rayah stayed because their sixth-period class, formerly in the room closest to the cafeteria, had relocated to the chapel for the late afternoon.

Danny rose and shoved his sweaty knuckles into his pockets.

Soft skin bumped his arm. Michelle linked arms with him. Unlike Hannah, she was a fan of physical contact. "Why don't you get this over with?" Her bangs bobbed as she nodded at the pocket that held the phone.

"I know what he'll say. He claims I applied and keeps 'improving' his offer. The guy gave me a free coupon to use the seniors' coffee shop, a sports pass to watch all games this year, and a season pass for the theatrical productions."

A cluster of junior girls in tank tops dominated the middle of the hallway.

Michelle and Danny broke apart their link, walked around the group, and joined together.

"Mitch, I just wish I'd never replied."

"Your fault for playing with fire," she said in a singsong tone.

He was a guy. What else did she expect him to do? "True. But if I don't answer any more of his messages, he can't do anything. Fires die if they get no fuel."

Despite the swell of chatter in the bottlenecked hallway, a muffled *ping* stung his ears.

Michelle stifled a snigger with her free hand and ducked under the chipped-paint entrance to the English room. A sign in golden letters above the wooden door read, *Never, never, never, never give up!*

"Dan, even if you don't feed him, Edgar doesn't seem to be running out of gas anytime soon."

The silver knife clattered against the plate and ricocheted to the circular rug on the floor. Danny bent down and scooped it, fingertips brushing dry bread particles the vacuum had failed to sweep. Returning to the dining table, he placed the knife against the chipped plate, eyeing the cat clock on the wall, the drooping plants on the kitchen counter-top, and then his mother.

"You mean you never sent them anything, Mom?"

"No."

"Hypothetically, you didn't shoot them a report card, or my social security number, or my second-favorite movie?"

"I don't think I know the last one, Danny."

"*Mean Girls*. We've been over this." He paused, wrinkling his nose at the bitter split-pea smell from his mother's end of the table. "We've also been over the fact that you're not going to tell any of my friends. Now back to the King's question."

"No, but I wish I had sooner." Asparagus juice dribbled off his mother's crooked chin. She wiped it off with wrinkled hands. "That Jesse Chin—your assistant principal—shot us an email a whole hour *after* the fire oc-curred and has refused to reply to any messages since. Then admissions has the audacity to ask for more money to fix the cafeteria—more money! I already give them ten grand a year. Do they expect me to pick up a third job?" She groaned and rubbed the dark bags under her eyes.

Danny's fingers fumbled with the oily knife, which had a bull en-graved on the handle. The sharp blade dug into a slab of vegan chicken. Steam wisped when he cut through it. *Tick. Thump. Tick. Thump.* The clock in the kitchen and his heartbeat beat in sync.

"Give Mr. Chin a break, Mom. Ms. Shiloh just retired, and the guy has a lot on his plate." Danny struggled to maintain a calm voice as he wondered how Edgar got his email in the first place if his mom didn't send King's anything.

"She *what?*" Globs of green soup splashed onto the circular table.

Goosebumps rippled up Danny's arms.

"We received no notification of this!" In a rapid motion, his mother flicked up her arms, bumping the low-hanging light over the table. It swung in circles. *Tick. Thump thump. Tick. Thump thump.*

"We found out today." Danny reached forward to stop the light, burning his fingertips. "Can we please return to the emails from King's?"

"Sure, sweetheart. Schedule a visit anytime next week. I don't mind driving over there."

Tick. Thump thump thump. Tick. Thump thump thump. The scent of the split pea soured his stomach. "Mom, no. Please listen to me. They must've directed the message to the wrong person. We never applied."

"Their mistake, our gain." Her tongue siphoned soup off her chin. "Daniel, they offered a *full-ride* scholarship. That would put ten grand toward a new kitchen table." She wobbled the legs back and forth until they creaked in agony. "Heck, we could purchase a whole kitchen with that money! I always cherished the idea of granite countertops."

Great. She could also make his gravestone granite if she sent him to King's. He braced his hands on the table and rose, his chair skidding back and his ankles knocking against the creaky seat.

"Daniel Belte, you haven't finished."

He turned back to look at her. Her chipped fingernails motioned to his plate. "Agreed. Give me one minute."

He escaped the soup scent, rounded a wooden door frame with etchings from where his dad used to measure him and his brother—Judah had always been taller at every age—and padded up emerald-colored steps. Chocolate-colored splotches and stains marked the corners of each stair.

The door to his bedroom moaned, and Danny's shaky hand slid open a desk drawer. His fingers clasped the only item: a gritty fishhook. He slammed the drawer shut.

He galumphed down the stairs in his ratty sneakers, around the measurement wall, and back to the round table. The fishhook gave a dull *ding* when he tossed it on the table.

His mother's cheeks blanched, and her twisted chin quivered. She shuddered and blinked tears away.

"Finished." He crossed his arms.

A silvery tear spilled from her bottom lid. She put her fingers to her lips and choked on a sob.

Immediately he felt guilty for causing her to cry. Even though her face flooded as easily as the Nile, his chest ached with regret every time.

When her quaky voice reached an understandable level, she whispered, "Dan, forward me Edgar's email address. I will put an end to this tonight."

The clinking of dishes and sniffles contaminated the kitchen for the next ten minutes.

Danny apologized. Guilt over her tears caused hot wax to drip in his chest, so he sought peace in his room. He unfastened his laptop and directed Edgar's address to his mom. Collapsing into his musty pillow, he let out a sigh of relief and stared up at the *Gladiator* movie poster clinging to sticky tac on his ceiling. Fire's out.

Forcing himself to rise again, he pulled the navy comforter from his bed over his knees and placed the warm, humming laptop on his knees. He started another valiant attempt at the Necho essay when footsteps thundered up the stairs.

A creak. The ghost that resembled his mother—chalky cheeks and leaden, bagged eyes—stumbled into his room. Perhaps she was ready for the granite gravestone before he was. Her bony fingers crushed his wrist.

"Mom, what's going on?"

The silent figure yanked him out of bed—knees in a sudden chill as the blanket fell off—and dragged him by his arm down the stairs.

He passed the kitchen—*Tick. Thump thump thump thump. Tick*—and entered the family room. "Mom?"

The phantom thrust him onto the couch. Foam that peeped out of the holes in the argyle pattern swallowed him. The gaunt figure motioned to the television. Tangerine and marigold. Bright colors ignited the screen, and the familiar scent of a burnt computer filled Danny's nostrils ... even though it was happening miles and miles away.

"Mom?"

"That's your school, Daniel." Smoke billowed in thick clouds against the backdrop of an inky sky. "That's Emmanuel."

Chapter Four

"THE CHAPEL WASN'T DAMAGED." MICHELLE TAPPED her fingertips on the glass coffee shop table. "And a couple of the classrooms at the other end of the building are fine too." She tilted her head back to swallow the last gulp of a vanilla cappuccino. "Necho's classroom is toast though."

"A shame." Hannah smirked.

The acrid aftertaste of black coffee lingered on the roof of Danny's mouth. Soft jazz trumpets did little to soothe his ever-quickening pulse. Shouldn't have drunk coffee, bad for the anxiety. "Any idea when Chin'll open Emmanuel—"

The whining of a grinding machine cut Danny off. The pungent drip coffee then punched him in the nose.

He shouted over the machine, "Think we'll be able to graduate within the next ten years?" and found himself yelling in the sudden quiet. He avoided the stares of customers in wooden chairs and focused on a low dangling light above their table.

Clack. Michelle plunked the ceramic cup onto a side table where Hannah's feet rested. "Better luck in finding a new school." She wrapped her index finger around the cup's handle and then eyed the empty chair next to Hannah. "For those of you who were wondering, Ray couldn't join us because her mom wanted to research some schools in the area. Thanks, Dan, for asking your mom to drive us, by the way." She saluted him with the dove-painted mug. "Mine leaves work by five."

More like she left work around nine. Working all those long hours at the theater. He was surprised her mother even picked her up after the first fire.

Before Danny could reply, the shriek of the grinding machine began again. Even after that died down, the chatter from students squished into chairs nearby took a while to reach a reasonable level.

"Mine usually goes till five too"—Danny hunched into his stomach to stop the searing pains—"but she took today off. Afraid I'll burn the house down with her gone. Or worse, I'll watch an R-rated movie." He feigned a gasp.

Michelle heaved herself off the chair, bumping into a group playing checkers behind her. "Gonna grab one of those chocolate croissants. Anyone want anything?"

A chocolate croissant sounded good. Danny rose to join her.

"All right, then." She shimmied the opposite direction of the checkers players, inching around a group of girls snapping photos of their coffee. "I might ask the guy up front to turn up the heat. Even though it's a hundred outside, it's freezing in here."

The goosebumps on Danny's arms agreed.

Michelle marched offbeat to the tune of a brassy trombone, skittering around students in glazed wooden chairs and low dangling lights in every direction. Her quick steps clashed with the sluggish blares of the instruments. Always moving at the speed of light. No wonder. Her dad had coached track at Emmanuel for five years.

She waved to various classmates in the café. She knew half the student body, from the guy in glasses scalding his thumb with coffee to a stocky girl shrinking in a corner by a bookshelf. Danny didn't recognize any of them but waved awkwardly anyway.

As Michelle ordered the pastry at the wooden counter, a barista with a wave of ocean-blue hair fidgeted with a cup. A snakelike tongue flicked over his puffy lips. Both tongue and lip had piercings. "Sorry, don't have any of the croissants left."

"Blueberry muffins?"

"Gone."

"Those old-fashioned donuts?"

"The new fashion, apparently." His lips flapped as he laughed at his own joke. When he received a blank stare in response from Michelle, the cup wobbled back and forth in his nervous hands. "Sold out, sorry." The mug slid from his fingertips. By luck, a patch of carpet underneath the register caught it with a thud.

Michelle rubbed the bridge of her nose with rosy fingers, face reddening. "OK, do you have *any* pastries left?"

He rubbed his red neck to the sound of a low trumpet blare. "We still got the lemon scones if you want those."

She wrinkled her nose. "No—thank you. Can't stand citrus anything. Not after Dad's attempt at lemon bars ... he left out the sugar."

The *thank you* shocked Danny for a moment, but then Michelle had worked concessions at a softball field last summer. After that, she treated any worker with as much kindness as a Michelle could muster ... so not much, but more than most customers.

"Just perfect!" Michelle heaved a theatrical sigh. Danny dodged the checker group as they returned to their seats. "Can't get an education or a pastry."

The AC tickled Danny's neck when he returned to his seat. Oh, yeah. Michelle was supposed to ask about that.

"Guess we'll fix the first one of those problems so we don't have to hear you complain." Hannah's run-down sneakers slipped off the table. She uncurled her spine, rose, and lumbered toward a bulletin board overpopulated by business cards.

Curious and feeling a bit claustrophobic in his group's tight corner, Danny followed. "Trying to find something?"

"A school."

He frowned. "A school? What's wrong with Emmanuel?"

"It doesn't exist anymore." A lazy thumb flicked a neon green card. "This one looks nice."

"Freedom Obedience Academy?"

"Yeah, Mom says I'm terrible at compliance."

"Hannah, dogs go to that school."

"Woof." Frizzy red hair curtained a chapped-lip smile.

A shadow hovered behind him accompanied by the distinct tapping of Michelle's high heels.

"Lydia High." Hannah pinched a purple card.

Danny squinted at the blurry ram logo. "Too far."

"North Sussex."

"Awful place. Colleges refuse to touch it. So do health inspectors."

"Armenia Elementary."

"Hannah, we went there for kindergarten."

"Meede Media."

"Only if you want to pursue a degree in film."

Michelle finally voiced her opinion. "And you're a fan of horror movies and anime, Han, so I doubt you have the refined taste of those students."

Hannah lobbed her arms into the air and sighed. "I'm trying to decide who's harder to please, Mitch. You or your parents."

She ripped a goldenrod card off the board and clapped it into Danny's palm. With a withering glare at Michelle, she bumped into the table with the cloth checkerboard.

The two players sighed and one tossed down a red chip. "I give up."

Ignoring him, Hannah collapsed into her chair and rested her feet on the table.

Danny glanced at the card for King's Academy. A golden lion outlined in black glowered at him. The pupilless eyes. Daggers for teeth.

Hannah dangled Michelle's cup on her pinky. "You have either that or homeschool, Dan."

"I choose homeschool." The thought of spending more hours than necessary with his mom annoyed him. But maybe that could help heal his relationship with her. She was never quite right after Dad died three years ago.

The cup slid off Hannah's finger.

Danny lunged forward and caught the mug and reset it on a coaster. *There you go, little guy. Stop trying to break so much.*

He returned to his seat and felt his pocket vibrate. Mom? He palmed his phone with his icy hand and read the text. He frowned. "Thought she wouldn't come for another half hour."

"Our ride's here already? We just sat down." Michelle picked at something under her nails with the Lydia business card, then swung a large bag over her shoulder, and placed the coffee cup on the counter.

An employee scooped the mug into his hand.

"Sorry about this, guys." Danny grimaced. "I remember she said she'd come around four thirty." He glanced at his watch to make sure he got the time right.

Michelle returned to her seat. "Maybe she has an appointment she forgot about."

A loud smash of pottery colliding with the tile floor met a saxophone solo on the radio. The worker who had dropped the mug swore. Another rushed to grab a broom to collect the shattered pieces.

The bell to the shop dinged. His mother began speaking before all of her was inside.

"Come on. Come!" Her auburn bob haircut frizzed. Strands jutted out in random directions. "I should've picked you up half an hour ago."

"I know our family has never been great at math, Mom, but—"

"No time for that, Daniel. Tell your friends to pile into the car." The serpentine chin disappeared behind the door.

Danny mouthed an apology to his friends.

Michelle shook her head and bolted for the door. "Do what your mom says. If you think fires are dangerous, they've got nothing on an angry parent."

"Mom, you missed the turn for Michelle's neighborhood." He rubbed a thumb under his nose to block out the Mom-van smell: a combination of smelly shoes, wet floors, and food left for years underneath the spotted carpets.

"We need to run an errand first. Hannah, dear? Please take your feet off the dash."

The shredded sneakers complied and slumped to the floor. A low growl emanated from his friend's throat. Hannah twisted her neck and pitched a glare at Danny.

He threw up his palms to catch the dirty look. Her fault for calling shotgun.

She sighed and rested her thin arm on the windowsill. Golden light spilled through the glass as she reached for the nob on the radio.

Click.

Thunderous drums beat out of the radio speakers, causing Danny's quads to pulsate.

Gonna tear down your walls with fire and hate!

Hannah's chin bobbed along with the beat. Such nice, calming lyrics.

'Leven years of waiting, I will avenge.

Gonna rip out your heart and seal your fate.

Enter your house on a horse named Revenge!

Click. His mother's chipped fingernail dialed the nob. A pop station with a strong, staccato rhythm broke, broke, broke, broke, broke the air.

B–b–b–b–betrayed by my own kind!

N–n–n–never saw you coming, baby.

W–w–what was yes, now becomes a maybe.

Oh, how could I be so bl–i–i–i–ind?

Click. An opera swelled in the muggy car. Hannah stuffed her fingers into her ears and gave a soft moan. Danny now wondered why people never used this type of music as a torture device.

Yes, yes, he deceeeeeeeeeeeei–ved me

Yes, yes unfaaaaaaaaaaaaithful to me

He be–a be–aaaa, be–a betrayed me.

Deceived me. Betrayed me.

Disloy–oy–oy–oy–oy–al to—

Click. The music died.

"Never have any good music on the radio nowadays," his mother muttered.

Hannah removed her fingers from her ears and shot Danny an odd look. Either anger or confusion. She was the hardest of his friends to read.

Wasn't always like that. He rested his chin on his sweaty fist. In elementary school, she had liked to wear dandelion crowns and make them for all the teachers. Even for Mrs. Dunlap, who was allergic to dandelions and had to go to the hospital for two days. Then came the divorce. Now she ripped up every dandelion she saw.

Hannah plunged a hand into her tatty beaded bag, for which only one strap remained and half the beads now needed a home. A pair of earbuds found their way into her small ears. Her chin commenced bobbing to an inaudible tune from her phone.

Danny peered out the window. A cloudless sky begat a gorgeous, cerulean backdrop. Golden heads of wheat in a field bowed under the scorching August heat. The brittle necks of some were snapped. When his mother's car whizzed past, the severed crowns collapsed in a pile onto the brown grass.

Cold sweat beads formed on his lip, and his warm legs shifted uncomfortably on the leather seat of the car. "Mom, do you mind turning on the AC?"

"Yes, I mind."

"It's the approximate temperature of H-E-double hockey sticks."

She hated the use of the word *hell*. Yet still managed to be obsessed with Armageddon. Weird.

"The car needs some more gas, but we won't run into a station until we make the trip home. The errand's about ten miles away, no time to drop off your friends until after it's done. Roll down your window if you want to cool off."

He clicked the black button on the side of the car door. The window logo on it had been scratched into oblivion. Warm, thick air spilled in. The scent of manure clogged his nostrils, and, thus, the window rolled back up.

He exchanged an odd expression with Michelle, who fanned herself with her hand. They attempted a conversation about her upcoming tennis match to keep their minds off the heat. And his mother's odd behavior. Well, odder than normal.

"Coach scheduled practice for tomorrow because he canceled it the day the cafeteria fire happened. But half of the girls on the team can't drive, so I don't know who all'll show up."

"Uh huh. Interesting." It wasn't interesting.

The discussion tapered off due to the overwhelming silence in the car. Michelle whipped out her phone, and her thumbs rattled a quick message. A *ping* sounded from Danny's pocket. *Do you also feel like everything we say sounds like a secret? Did something happen to your mom?* the text read.

He met her eye and shrugged.

She nodded and chewed on her sweaty lip. Anxious thuds of Michelle's heels against the muffling carpet filled the car.

Danny peered out the window as a distraction again, but after two minutes of seeing wheat fields, he gave up. Thanks, Pennsylvania, for the lack of things to see. If states were Halloween candy, it'd be licorice.

A sigh. He probed a zipper on his backpack and pulled out a deck of playing cards.

"War?" He flashed the Ace of spades on top of the pile at Michelle.

A smile split her worried expression. "Ready to lose? Or should I go easy again?"

He didn't know how anyone could "go easy" on a game of chance. "Shuffle and find out."

The jumbled cards created small breezes when Michelle rearranged them—the closest they'd come to AC that day. She split the deck in "half" and handed him the larger of the piles. "Gave you a few extra ones, champ." She winked.

He smiled. Michelle liked to give the other players an unfair advantage. Made her feel better when she won against greater odds.

Danny's senses deadened once the game commenced. No anxious thoughts plagued his mind until his mother's shrieking voice awakened him.

"Michelle, you put fingerprints on my windows! I cleaned those last Sunday."

"Cleaned" operated as a relative term. Whenever some sort of bug smeared the glass in a suicide attempt, a yellow residue remained for five years straight.

"Sorry, Ms. Belte." Michelle withdrew her hand from the pane and poked Hannah in the back.

A pair of small eyes glared at her and petite fingers tore the earphones out. "Yes?"

"Doesn't that minivan look like the car Rayah's mom drives?" She gestured to a dented van that sported olive-green paint.

Hannah shrugged. "Yeah?"

"Yes! I recognize the license plate." Michelle rolled down the window and threw a frantic wave at the rusty vehicle. "Hi, Rayah!"

The ancient minivan yielded no reply.

Danny's mother commented that Rayah probably didn't answer because "a truck would have whizzed by us and torn her arm to bits if she put her hand out the window like you did, Michelle."

When Michelle shut the window, Danny flipped over a king of hearts.

"Wonder what she's doing out here?" Michelle smoothed down her static hair that stuck to the light on the ceiling, home to plenty of dead bugs. "Rayah's mom."

"Her? What about us?" Hannah cast an expectant look at Danny's mom.

Michelle overturned a king of diamonds. "Same face, this means war." She placed three cards down and turned over the last one: an ace.

Danny followed suit, but right before he looked at the final card, something shiny glittered in his peripheral vision.

Two golden lion statues, one on each side of the road, stood on pedestals with dagger claws outstretched. They bared horrible teeth. Behind the beasts, a concrete sign with gilded lettering declared an unapologetic *King's Academy*.

No. "Mom, turn around."

She didn't reply. Danny glanced at his lap and saw the final overturned card: a two.

The king of diamonds had won.

Chapter Five

DANNY'S HEART RACED AND A SUDDEN lightheadedness seized him. The spinning in his head slowed, and he focused on breathing. With the rattle of an overworked engine, they rolled into a parking spot.

When the car stopped, Danny clasped a palm onto the edge of his mother's seat. Sweat kept his fingertips stuck to the seat. "Mom," he tried to keep an even tone, "you promised to put an end to any King's Academy business. You sent an email yesterday. This doesn't look like a kept promise at all."

She unclicked her seat belt. It made a distinct zipping noise as it whipped against her door. "Last night I *planned* to do so. My laptop was sitting on my knees when I turned on the news. Halfway through typing the message, that awful image of your old school appeared. Oh, it was terrible, Daniel! I kept picturing you inside that building, your body consumed in a billow of smoke! Glare at me all you want, but when you become a parent, you'll understand."

Seeing how his friends' moms and dads treated them, Danny hoped at that moment never to become a parent.

With a puff of dark exhaust smoke, Rayah's green van chugged into the spot by Michelle's window. The large, rusty dent in the passenger seat door had been caused by Rayah when she pulled in too close to the wall of her house's garage. Her parents had yelled at her for two hours straight that day. For a little dent. She paid for the damages too. No wonder she was scared all the time with parents like that.

Mom continued. "I figured Chin would cancel classes today—considering the fire destroyed three-quarters of the school—how much harm can a tour of the academy cause?"

"A lot, Mom." Danny rubbed a finger under his wet nose. "Did you forget what happened twelve years ago?" There was no way that God meant for them to attend King's.

"They had a different principal then."

"Do fishhooks mean nothing to you?"

Her crooked nose wrinkled. "Fishermen exaggerate their tales."

His cheeks and forehead blazed with fire. "Did Judah?"

Her icy blue eyes, the hue Danny shared with her, widened in the rearview mirror. Her tongue grazed her lips. Her face softened. "If you still love that pile of rubble more than this place by the end of the tour, you can continue to attend Emmanuel, OK?"

He searched her expression for a moment. Nodded. It was gonna be hard to love rubble, but there were plenty of things harder to like. Like taxes, death, and anything Benjamin Franklin said.

He swung open his door. A wave of heat overwhelmed him.

Already body odor was overpowering Danny's pine-scented deodorant, and a fretful Rayah awaited them on the blacktop. Her raven hair sported a golden rose instead of her usual head wrap. She flashed a feeble grin, sweaty lips trembling.

Jumping out of the car, Michelle engulfed her in a hug and linked arms with the shaking girl. "Stay by my side." She jabbed a finger at Rayah in a matronly way.

As much as Michelle grated on Danny's nerves, he appreciated how she liked to play the role, as she called it, of "the mom-friend." No wonder she felt the need to do so. They all had pretty messed-up moms. Maybe it was a requirement for the American experience.

"Thank you," Rayah whispered.

Attempting to add humor to the situation and to keep his mind off the impending tour, Danny offered his arm to Hannah, who leaned against the hot metal car.

Her nose scrunched and eyes narrowed. "Not a chance, Dan."

"You won't accept my call to *arms*?"

"Danny, stop talking."

He shrugged and ambled beside her, keeping a healthy distance. The smooth charcoal pavement proved a sharp contrast to the road at Emmanuel.

Hannah's pace matched his, slow to the point of being almost motionless, unlike their other friends, who had already spanned the parking lot.

They probably wanted to get the tour over with as quickly as possible. But the group waited—his mother in particular—with enormous patience for the two to catch up.

At long last, they approached a gate with two golden lions, one flanking each side like gargoyles. In the distance, a faint *bwomp* of a tuba sounded, mixed with the drone of a dying clarinet. Pubescent squeaks carried through the air even this far away. Through the goldenrod bars, tall brick buildings cast shadows twice their size.

He craned his neck to see a pattern etched on top of the smooth, clean skyscrapers—at least, skyscrapers compared with Emmanuel. Painted golden lions, teeth bared in the glistening sun, followed a trail from one structure to the next. Danny realized he had uncurled his spine to make himself taller, towering enough to reach the windows on the first floor of any building. This wasn't a school. It was a city.

Once, during freshman year, his choir class had traveled to Pittsburgh University to sing in a competition. They fared worse than the ancient library in Alexandria had in the great fire that destroyed it. Only there had he seen buildings—skyscrapers really—larger than the ones he saw now at King's.

The whistling of the wind through the buildings was accompanied by a piccolo solo far off in the distance. The wind through the gates carried with it a sweet breeze wafting the scent of a freshly cut lawn, which tickled Danny's nose. So much for the dry brown grass at Emmanuel.

Five feet out from the gates under a yellow-leafed beech, a group of four boys played a game of Spikeball. The tallest in the group, who had a thick neck and beard, smacked a yellow ball into a circular net with his palm. It bounced and walloped an opponent in the chin. Clutching his jaw, the victim muttered a few words Danny wouldn't repeat with his mother present.

"Dean!" The injured player swore again while the brute cackled. "Stop taking cheap shots, man. I know you can aim better than that."

Hope we don't meet too many Deans here.

The speaker by the gate gargled something that could've been English. Mom clicked the black talk button and shouted, "What?"

"Name and reason for visitation."

"Belte family for the campus tour." She glanced at his friends and Rayah's mother. "And the Abed family."

Michelle's arms gathered Rayah up in another hug. "Guess that makes us sisters."

Danny raised his eyebrows at the scowling Hannah. "Guess that makes us—"

"Not related." She hugged her sides so tightly the circle anime bird pattern turned into an oval. "And never will be."

The gate clicked and swung open onto a cobblestone path lined by thick, leafy trees almost as tall as the buildings. No dirt lived in any crevice of the road, and the even stones seemed to propel his toes toward a large, creamy building despite his wishes. He felt as if someone had plunged a fishhook into his navel and pulled so he could not do anything but trudge on. Clean-cut grass bordered the path. A gracious wind bounced off the rippling lawns to Danny's nose. It smelled so green he couldn't believe the plants were real.

Thwack. Augh. Danny's left temple throbbed. He winced and twisted his head toward the path. A yellow ball bounced off his ankle and tumbled into a patch of grass.

The tall owner with the thick neck, Dean, scooped it up with frying-pan-sized hands. He smirked at Danny, lips twitching in such a merciless way Danny wanted to bolt on the spot. "Accident." An eggshell smile flashed in the midst of his crimson beard.

Danny tapped his temple with his forefinger, acting cool. "Not a problem, hardly felt the hit."

Dean's smile faded back into the shadow of the tree.

Danny's steady heartbeat increased. Wrong answer. *Keep walking, keep walking ...* he was still staring. *Keep walking, keep walking.* His cheeks flushed, and he shifted his gaze back to the cobblestone path, praying that would be his last encounter with the Spikeball player. He stared at Michelle's purple heels bouncing up the stone hill toward the rosy building.

Danny's group reached the double doors at the front. Each bore a golden knocker in the shape of a lion's head. His mother's quaking fingers slid into the teeth of a lion knocker. But before she could tap the beast against the polished portal, the doors opened.

"I was afraid we would have to reschedule." The thunderous voice rattled Danny's bones, the sort of tone that would never need a megaphone to project in a football stadium. The words emanated from a six-foot-four figure with a square jaw and broad shoulders who had restrained his long brunet curls in a ponytail. His long fingers smoothed down the front of his black suit before he shook the hands of the touring group. Two amber eyes twinkled at Danny when the man clasped his hands in an iron grip.

Danny cleared his throat, but his words came out feebler than planned. After all, whose voice could compete with thunder? "Daniel Belte, sir."

"I know."

He smelled like incense and Danny had to hold back a cough.

The man drew himself to his fullest height on the top step and addressed the group with a precise, loud voice. "Although my birth certificate reads 'Edgar Rezzen,' most students here refer to me as 'Ned.' If you call me Mr. Rezzen, I glance over my shoulder for my father, who used to lead this school. So, please, Ned will do." An amber eye winked at Rayah.

To Danny's surprise, and perhaps dismay, she didn't shudder. Maybe that's how Ned planned to get everyone to join the school ... by wooing them. Well, he wasn't Danny's type.

Ned bellowed a good-hearted laugh and clapped his palms together. They made a sound that resembled tree bark cracking after an axe blow.

"We can take the loop around the campus. It surrounds the perimeter, and most of our running students take advantage of its size."

To run away from him, sure. Why else?

Ned commenced a backward walk, like a tour guide, as he spoke to the group. Even down the sinfully smooth steps. Yet he never checked behind himself to make sure he would avoid a fall. When they reached the path, his gliding feet stamped as if he were extinguishing a spark from a fire.

His long arm motioned toward a spiraling tower at least five stories high. As with all the buildings on campus, artists had painted golden lions, corkscrewing to the top. A clock tower in the distance tolled one low note to indicate fifteen minutes past four.

"Our Lebab Language Center to your left, folks. Or, the LLC. The gentleman with the construction plans wanted to make the LLC three times the size of the building you see today but lacked the funding."

Danny arched his back to obtain a full glimpse. All that money for a thing that looked like a pencil. Glad to know the school used their finances well.

"Inside, we nurture one of the largest linguistics programs for a high school in the country. Students can select from twelve foreign languages."

His mother bobbed on her heels and clasped his shoulder. "Did you hear that?"

"Yes, Mom."

"You've always excelled at languages."

Ned continued to the next building with his effortless moonwalk. They passed the only cluster of unimpressive buildings on campus and the only non-red buildings at King's, yet he said nothing about them. The builders had formed them out of a dull-gray brick, and they looked a great deal like an afterthought compared to the rest of the King's Academy city. Especially because they didn't have a single lion painted on them.

Mrs. Abed raised a timid hand decorated with glittering nails. "Mr—Ned." She paused, apparently unused to saying first names of authority figures. Like mother, like daughter. "Will we stop inside any of those?" She motioned to the dreary buildings.

Ned guffawed, hand clutched to his stomach. "The dormitories? I would love to but students move in this week. Trust me. Once you get shoved against the wall by a mini fridge and futon, you will never want to do it again."

Seemingly satisfied, Rayah's mother folded her hands and stepped back onto a heart-shaped stone without another word.

Unsatisfied, Danny squinted at the dormitories. Pretty sure there was more than one reason why he wouldn't let them in there.

When Judah attended Taylor University, some of the academic buildings had been impressive, but his dorm, Wengatz, had lacked AC, space, and privacy. Maybe they had made changes in the last twelve years. The tour guide who had taken his family across campus there had never let them into the dormitories either. A strange, as Michelle would call it, coincidence.

"In complete honesty, we could visit." Ned spied a straw wrapper on the ground, scooped it, and shoved it into his pocket. "But I have a difficult time watching the parents say goodbye to the students. I have a son at Pittsburgh, and even though he's entering his fourth year, each goodbye still hurts."

Mrs. Abed's bottom lip quivered, and she wrapped Rayah in a hug so tight that Rayah opened her mouth to get a breath of air. "I feel the same way, Mr. Ned."

"After my son's freshman year, I made sure to give the parents plenty of time before they had to say goodbye to their children. We allow them to stay on campus for up to a week. And they can schedule a visit any time during the year … if it doesn't conflict with any major school events."

Mrs. Abed's fingers combed Rayah's glistening hair. "I appreciate that, Mr. Ned."

A shriek escaped Michelle's lips, and Danny jumped. "I've never seen so many!"

Heart attacks? Danny clutched his chest. His heartbeat was outdoing the sound of a large drum off in the distance. Perhaps the marching band was practicing today.

Michelle gestured to twenty tennis courts, comprised of red clay, four hundred yards in the distance. Thwacks of rackets colliding with green balls added a steady beat to Michelle's wobbling back and forth on her feet. She gazed at the fresh gold-and-red uniforms, and Danny recalled how she often complained about the "hand-me-down-excuses-for-a-jersey" Emmanuel provided.

Ned nodded toward the tennis courts and smiled. "Yes, I admire King's athletic programs. We require students to do at least one season of a sport here. Colleges approve of student involvement and have given many of our kids here full rides, a rarity this millennium."

A wiry hand clasped Danny's shoulder. His skin prickled. "Daniel, did you hear that?"

"My ears are still working, Mom."

"You've always excelled at sports."

Michelle sprinted to the fence surrounding the teammates. Along the way, she slipped off her heels as they got stuck in a patch of mud. Claws clung to the wire as she stood on her tiptoes, trying to capture everything. At this rate, his friends would all enroll by noon.

In a way, he felt terrible about blaming Michelle. Her father always hounded her about getting a full-ride scholarship based on athletics. And no recruiter would come to Emmanuel to watch a terrible tennis team play on a court that smelled of pot—a remnant left behind by some neighborhood kids who borrowed the fifth court during non-practice times.

A Frisbee whizzed past Danny's ear, and a beautiful girl in a billowing scarlet skirt caught the disc. When she turned to run back, he noticed half her hair had been shaved like a soldier's buzz cut. The girl vanished from view.

Michelle returned. "That girl on the first court, the one with the braid, has perfect form on her kick serve. I keep asking Coach for tips to improve, but he says, 'Sorry, but my low salary package only covers drills in practice. If you want to upgrade to premium, please pay me another $20,000.'"

They curved around the loop and a golden water fountain. Michelle extolled its beauty, but Danny thought it rather tarnished in certain areas. They meandered past several buildings, including an auditorium three times the size of the chapel at Emmanuel.

Ned elaborated on the magnificent art programs at King's. "We urge students to participate in at least one type of art here at the school. Like in athletics, students rise to the occasion."

Here Rayah questioned Ned about whether King's offered a program for graphic design, an area that she bested.

Ned assured her they had the fifth best graphic-design team in the nation for high schools. They had even beat the renowned Meede Media in several competitions.

Rayah sealed her lips. But her twinkling eyes scared Danny. He had only seen them do that when she was happy.

Danny's mother said nothing about him always excelling at the arts. Mothers can only lie so much.

They ambled by a beautiful garden surrounded by a wall of well-manicured hedges and weeping willows dancing in the light, billowing breeze. Fresh lavender scented the air, and the place tasted like warm sunlight.

Try as he might, even Danny couldn't find a flaw with this stop on the tour or even anything really funny to say about it.

Ned glanced at the array of shrubberies with a reverent expression, square chin softened by the golden sunlight. He looked a lot friendlier in this place. He said nothing about the plot of land, and the group continued onward.

When they spotted their starting place in the loop, one lone, unnoted building remained. An aroma of beef drifted from inside the ruddy bricks.

"Bad day to skip breakfast." Michelle clutched her stomach.

Rayah, her mother, and Danny jerked their heads into enthusiastic nods.

Sweat dribbled down Ned's forehead. He toweled the sweat and his greasy hair with a clean handkerchief from his pocket. "I should hope so! Our dining commons—what most schools call a *cafeteria*—is just inside those walls."

Four of the group members ogled the mess hall as if they had never seen a building.

Danny's pocket declared a soft *ping*. He pulled out his phone and squinted in the harsh sunlight to read a text from Hannah.

Hear that, Daniel? You have always excelled at eating.

He flashed his friend a smile. Not the best usage of the rest of his month's data, but worth it.

Her chapped lips cracked a similar reply, and she winked.

Ned loosened his tie and fanned himself. "Hot out here, huh? Let's usher ourselves inside for an early dinner. Also, don't worry about paying." He nodded at Mrs. Abed, who had already reached into her purse to retrieve a wallet. "King's will cover this meal."

Michelle—whose love language was food—led the pack and lumbered toward the garnet-colored doors.

Ned's long strides managed to surpass hers, and he swung open the door for them. Everyone filed past him, Danny in the back.

Right when Danny ambled by Ned, he heard, "We haven't had a cafeteria fire in about ten years."

Chapter Six

BEEF JUICE SLOPPED OVER MASHED POTATOES AND spilled onto the floor, the scarlet tablecloth, and Hannah's plush leather chair.

Danny jumped up, his attention torn from the hanging plant right above their table. Hannah's tray had slipped. What could Danny say? At least Hannah excelled at something: making a mess.

Everyone at the table reacted, spoiling the gentle jazz piano music playing overhead with shouts and exclamations.

Hannah nonchalantly grabbed a napkin.

Danny reached for his to help clean, but a large hand waved for both to stop.

"Allow me." Ned rolled up his sleeves and stood from his seat at the table. He walked over to Hannah's spot, and his gentle voice of thunder asked her to move.

With an eye roll, she obeyed.

Ned's knees cracked when he kneeled on the floor. He scrubbed with a cloth napkin, and Danny offered his chair to Hannah because hers was soaked.

She waved him off with Band-Aid-wrapped fingertips. "I'm fine, Danny. Save your gentlemanly stuff for Rayah."

What did she mean by that?

Hannah pinched her brass-colored miniskirt in a mock curtsy and selected a seat next to Danny's mother, who had a fist clutched to her chest at the sight of Ned's act of service.

"Finished!" The principal stood, head inches away from the dangling plant, and beamed at the table.

Hannah grumbled. "You didn't have to do that, Ned."

Everyone else, except Danny, agreed but in coos of admiration instead of Hannah's disdain.

The principal's square chin shook. "Not a problem! I love to fix messes."

Forks clattered against scarlet-and-gold plates. Everyone but Danny and Hannah pestered Ned with questions ranging from academic difficulty to mealtimes at King's Academy.

Danny avoided joining in by forcing garlicky mashed potatoes into his mouth. They tasted all right—he hadn't eaten breakfast—but not as good as he had expected for King's. In fact, if he were to eat these gloppy potatoes again, his stomach would sour as it always did with half-baked food.

Due to their unfortunate habit of eating too fast, Danny and Hannah completed their meals within five minutes of the discussion starting. Sideways glances and pocket *pings* served as distractions from social interaction.

"Daniel, dear?" Mom cleared her throat and glared at his phone. "Did you hear Ned's question?"

He tore his eyes away from the glow of a text. "Sorry." He placed his device on the table near the soggy brown spot from Hannah's spill. "Could you please repeat it?"

Heartily, the thunder laughed. "Not a problem. My wife, Amy, tries to drag me away from social media any chance she gets. I must check my inbox twenty times a day. The school has sinfully impeccable Wi-Fi." He snatched a glass of grape juice, tilted his head back, and drained the cup in one fluid motion. An ice cube clicked inside his mouth against his teeth until it melted.

Danny's own tongue chilled.

"Speaking of emails"—Ned's long fingers straightened his charcoal tie—"mothers, would you mind if we moved our conversation to one of the booths over there? We have unfortunately boring business to discuss."

Their impending deaths at King's Academy did sound terribly dull.

The corners of Ned's lips melted into a pouty Scrooge frown for a second. Then it was replaced with a row of teeth.

The three adults collected their trays and vacated the table. They went to the other side of the dining commons and disappeared under the shadow of a hanging wooden lion.

Danny and his friends waited. The occasional clanging of plates and rowdy chatter from surrounding diners littered the peace. How loud would it sound when all the students arrived for the year?

Moments later Michelle cleared her throat. "Ned seems—"

"Horrible? Sleazy? Arrogant?" Hannah stuck a Band-Aid finger into her mashed potatoes and swirled it across the plate.

"Nice."

Nice? Then again, Rayah said her dad was "nice." *Nice* put a bruise on her arm in sixth grade for getting a *B* in science.

"Nice as in pleasant?" Danny swallowed water to drown the garlic taste in his mouth. "As in polite? Or nice as in wants-to-make-you-thrust-your-thumbs-into-a-paper-shredder?"

Michelle siphoned a spoonful of mashed potatoes into her mouth. "Clearly the third definition," she replied, spewing globs of spud slime.

"Great"—Hannah flicked a glob of potatoes at Michelle—"for a second, I thought you had meant *nice* as in actually nice."

"I do."

"How ... nice." Hannah punctuated the word with a cruel smile. Danny exchanged a quick glance and smile with her. Glad to know the divorce was good for one thing: the elimination of her filter. She could say what everyone else was afraid to.

Michelle blushed a furious pink yet said nothing. She jabbed her fork to arrange a mound of mashed potatoes into a mountainous shape. Then she fiddled with the peas to make little lines radiate from the center like rays of a pearly sun.

Seeing how dark her cheeks had grown, Danny sensed an impending outburst. He gazed at his empty plate, clasped it, and rose. "Anyone else want me to take their empty plates to the conveyor belt?"

"How can you say he isn't nice?" Michelle exploded, flinging a pea.

Danny inched away in the direction of the conveyor belt. "Any plates?"

"He gave us a nice tour, Hannah!"

"Last call for *los platos*."

Michelle slammed her palm against the table, and Rayah flinched. "Sit, Danny. I know you hate conflict, but you started this one with your stupid definitions of the word *nice*."

Despite himself, he parked in the leather dining chair and stared at the tablecloth.

"If you enjoy Ned's company so much, Mitch," Hannah growled, "you should join the mothers meeting in the booth! You all could be contestants on *The Bachelor* or something with the way you're doting on him."

Michelle kicked the table leg, causing the plates to rattle.

"Who said I wanted to attend King's?" Michelle glared at the other three members of the table.

Danny continued to stare at the tablecloth until Hannah slapped her palm against it. "Come on! 'Ned, I wish I had tennis courts that large!'" Hannah straightened her spine and mocked Michelle's shrill tones. "'Ned, it's amazing that everything doesn't smell like weed or feces here.' 'Ned, does King's always breed this many cute boys?' 'Ned, kill my parents and adopt me.'" Her U-shaped neck stooped again.

"I never said the last one!"

But she wished she had. Couldn't really blame her with a dad who took away her phone for a month when she lost the tennis sectionals last year.

Michelle's eyes rolled behind curtained bangs. A sigh escaped her lips, followed by a sharp inhale. "Fine, I'll prove to you that I don't want to go here. Danny, you have a photographic memory. How many buildings did we pass on our tour?"

He furrowed his brow. What did this have to do with anything? "A billion."

"Danny, be serious."

He clamped his eyelids and visualized each landmark they passed. "Twenty, I think."

Michelle snapped her fingers at Rayah. "Hold your fork in place. And, everyone, take your spoons off the table."

Although perplexed, the friends did so while Michelle stood. She gathered all the cups, plates, forks, and knives and assembled them in the center of the table in the shadows of the hanging leafy plant. For the next two minutes, without a word, she placed each dish in a circular formation. Danny watched, mesmerized. Some cups and forks clumped close together. Others drifted far away from the nearest neighbor. She finished and thrust her hands onto her hips.

Danny wasn't a fan of modern art and didn't want to tell her it wasn't his favorite piece at the museum.

"Each one of the dishes represents a building on King's campus. Did I organize the dishes right, Danny?"

He nodded.

"All right, tell me, Mister Snapshot Memory, of all the landmarks we explored, did Ned ever mention a chapel?"

He frowned and imagined the campus layout again. "No."

"A church of any kind? A synagogue or mosque? Any religious organizations or clubs in the area?"

"None."

Her eyebrows raised, and she looked hard at Hannah, who had developed a sudden interest in a girl shoving her cup repeatedly against the ice-machine nozzle, which didn't appear to be working. Goodness, he had never seen Hannah lose a debate. *History in the making, folks.*

"We may not have a kitchen, a cafeteria"—Michelle gestured at Rayah's fork, which apparently represented the dining commons—"or most of our classrooms at Emmanuel. Half of our lockers have more inky marks than the black mold developing on the ceiling of the girls' locker room. But *we have a chapel.* We attend a safe place where we can declare, 'One nation, *under God.*' Not 'under fire,' 'under terrorist threat,' or 'under fear of death.' Yesterday, the chapel survived the fire. I would rather burn inside that chapel than bask in the AC of this *dining commons.* Long as the sanctuary stands, I attend Emmanuel."

Danny felt a firm clasp on his shoulder—almost like someone had dropped a bag of heavy rice on him. He jumped and whipped around to find Ned. Adrenaline throbbed in his chest. Had he heard what Michelle just said?

The square jaw stretched into a smile. "How did you enjoy the meal?"

Guess not.

"Very … nice." Hannah smirked at him.

Everyone's chins nodded. The mothers emerged from behind the principal. Mom beamed at Danny, crooked chin quivering. Bet she had already signed him up for this school.

Ned stooped over the table and placed each dish into an organized pile. He grimaced when he finished. "Messes show up in my nightmares." He rubbed his neck and collected the dishes to place them on the conveyor belt. Meanwhile, the mothers sat and exchanged odd expressions with each other and then the kids.

A thunderclap sounded behind Danny, and he whipped around to find Ned rubbing his palms together.

"These ladies and I just engaged in a wonderful discussion. I would love to continue the dialogue with each of the students here in my office." Amber eyes glittered at Danny. "Would you like to join me first?"

Danny's heart leaped into his throat. He couldn't swallow. Why him first? Hannah and Michelle were braver. And he could make a break for home … could get there by sunset if he ran. But, no, he was first. To follow his mother's desires or choose a burnt building instead? Michelle's speech about Emmanuel's chapel filled him with a hint of courage … just a hint.

Danny rose to alleviate the height difference between himself and the principal. It did little to help. The buildings and teachers all must be tall here. Probably something in the water. "With respect, sir"—he winced at the words that would follow—"I have an idea where you want to go with this. I appreciate your offer, but I decline."

"Daniel!" His mother's eyes flickered like a flame in the ambient cafeteria lighting. He avoided them.

Ned held up a long finger. "Thank you, Ms. Belte, for your concern, but we ought to regard in high esteem the decisions of students." He regarded Danny gravely. "My offer expires in one week, should you change your mind before then."

Danny returned to his seat, his face burning.

Thunder rumbled at the rest of the group. "Will anyone else accompany me to my office?"

With a fervent jerk, Hannah shook her head.

"No." Michelle's cheeks reddened when she gazed at the towering figure behind Danny. "Thank you," she added and slid down her seat, rendering half of herself invisible.

Six heads swiveled and landed on Rayah, who had her head bowed toward her lap. Shaking fingers fiddled with the gold rose clip in her hair. She pulled the accessory off and analyzed it.

"Rayah?" Her mother rubbed her glittering nails on her daughter's shoulders. "Would you like to follow Mr. Ned to his office?"

Rayah exchanged nervous glances with her mother, her friends, and the flower. The clash of dishes on the conveyor belt and the soft piano notes accentuated the silence. She watched a cluster of girls, all in soccer uniforms, place cups onto the mini treadmill that led inside the kitchen for cleaning. Inhale, exhale. She placed the rose clip onto the table and turned her attention to Ned.

"Unfortunately, I must turn down your offer, Mr. Rezzen."

Rayah wore *brave* well.

Mrs. Abed clasped a fist to her lips to stifle a sob. Danny's mother rose and engulfed her in a hug. What else were mothers for?

Ned's "soft" voice reverberated behind Danny, causing him to shrink. "I will not hide my disappointment, but I cannot change your choices. I have another tour group waiting for me at my office. Do you remember where the cafeteria's entrance is?"

"The *exit*?" Danny jerked his chin at a green exit sign hiding behind a dangling lion. "Yes, I remember." The forcefulness of his reply surprised him. Not often did he speak to an adult this way. First Ms. Necho, now this. Danny boy was changing.

A palm tapped against the back of his chair, and then pounding footsteps diminished in the distance. The softer they grew, the more Danny's tight chest released. When the steps silenced, he breathed at last.

As the group left the cafeteria, the mothers marched five strides ahead of the teens. Walking beside Rayah, he noticed tears brimmed in her eyelids.

"That was brave"—he nodded back toward the cafeteria—"what you did back there."

Her chin trembled. "I was going to follow him to his office, but I kept thinking about Michelle's speech. I'm sure my dad will tear me apart later, but I had to say *no*. For the chapel."

"Same. Sorry about your dad. You can stay with us tonight if you're worried about him."

She shook her head. "He hasn't hit me in years."

But Danny had a feeling this was a lie.

Heat overwhelmed them when they stepped outside, and his skin prickled. In Danny's peripheral vision, he spotted a cluster of parents and students by the stairs to Ned's building.

A soft *ping*. He grasped his phone and a new email blinked at him. No way. Before he opened the message, a pair of amber eyes glittered in the margins of his vision. He glanced at Ned, who was immersed in conversation with a father who had a cell phone glued to his ear. Danny's gaze returned to his own phone, and he swiped open the message. His heart did a backflip when he read the subject line.

"Rayah, look at this email!"

Michelle gave a hammy sigh. "Can't Ned take a hint?"

"He didn't send it. Emmanuel did."

"Emmanuel?" Michelle cocked her head to the side. "What did they say?"

"Classes start again tomorrow."

Chapter Seven

DANNY YAWNED IN THE HUMID MORNING AIR AS A goldenrod school bus rolled up to his driveway. A backdrop of a scarlet sunrise bled into gray storm clouds. What a day. The sort of weather English teachers and writers would soak themselves in. Halfway in the bloody sun and the other half in the raindrop mist.

This climate reminded Danny of when he was three years old and Judah would take him fishing at Jordan Creek. Judah had recited the old mantra "Red sky in morning, sailors take warning." After that year, his brother had never wanted to fish again.

"Get ready, sailors," Danny muttered as the bus door creaked open.

Stepping onto the bus, Danny caught a whiff of the driver's Monster energy drink—the scent of liquid PEZ candies—as he ambled past the front seat. He was met instantly with the odor of sweat and Tootsie Rolls, which were stuck to the floor of the second row. He preferred the energy-drink scent.

Only half the usual passengers sat on the bus. Maybe they had slept in. The bus did seem to be picking people up much earlier than usual.

He slid in next to Rayah, who sat on the wheel hump toward the back. In an automatic motion, he reached toward his back to move his book bag onto his lap, but he grasped nothing.

"Did you forget your backpack?" Even in the dark bus, beads of sweat glistened on the surface of Rayah's neck. Her normally navy-colored head wrap looked black in the early morning light and was tilted to the side.

"I put it into the storage closet in our basement after I saw the school fire news Tuesday night. We keep all our suitcases there. I figured, hey, if Mom homeschools me, I won't need this for a while."

"That sounds reasonable."

"But when I heard Emmanuel opened its doors again, I went down there this morning to grab the bag. Not only did my backpack go missing, but all the suitcases disappeared."

"Odd." Rayah rubbed her sweaty lip against her dress sleeve.

"Bet the rapture came and we missed it."

"Don't joke about that. And your mother would probably come back and take you up to heaven with her."

"Scolding all the way." He morphed his voice to match his mother's, "You should've read *Left Behind* instead of *Harry Potter*." Standing, Danny leaned over Rayah and gripped the clasps on the window, pulling it down. Warm air leaked in. He sighed and closed the window.

Rayah stared at a smashed ladybug on the pane. "Any other ideas as to why the stuff went missing?"

"Cleaning, maybe? Mom said she wanted to tidy our house for a while, but at six in the morning?" Danny shook his head. "I swear Ned's cleaning habits rubbed off on her." He paused. "How did your dad react when he heard you wouldn't go to King's?"

"I don't think Mom told him. He got back late from work last night."

Danny let out a sigh of relief. He had been worried about Rayah's safety all throughout the night, wishing he'd insisted that she stay with them.

At the next pickup spot, the bus's brakes shrieked, and everyone lurched forward. The driver, Zeke, liked to wait to employ the brakes until the last minute. A forty-year-old's only way to live life on the edge.

"Had no idea how early Zeke would arrive this morning." Rayah indicated the man in the driver's seat with the static mane. "Luckily, I got up two hours before my alarm. Couldn't sleep after yesterday's tour. That, and my mother sobbed the whole night because I refused to enroll at King's."

Danny's eyes narrowed. "The email said how early Zeke would come. Didn't you read that?"

"We have spotty cell signal in our house, so I never saw the message. Any idea why they changed the route?"

He explained Zeke would chauffeur the students to another building until Emmanuel was repaired. Heaven knew how long that would take. But the distance to the new location was much farther, hence the earlier arrival time. The parents and student drivers received an address with the name of the location: Sparehouse Warehouse, a discontinued warehouse that used to contain spare parts for computers.

Danny jerked forward again as Zeke collected his final passenger, Jeremy the senior.

Jeremy grabbed the top of his shirt and fanned himself. "Zeke, would you mind turning up the AC? It smells like wet feet in here. Feels like we're inside a shoe too."

Here's to hoping Sparehouse had lots of AC. Had to with all those computer parts, right?

Zeke shut the doors. "Sorry, kid. We're going to run out of gas if I try to cool down the vehicle."

The senior continued to waft air with his T-shirt and sat.

"Weird." Rayah pulled her gaze away from the yellowing window. "Zeke never picked up Rachel."

Danny recalled the girl with the weeping willow tresses who sat across the aisle from them and always wore the smell of a house with one cat too many. She had missed the bus loads of times. Rachel slept in at least three classes every day their freshman year.

Just in case, he scrolled through his contacts, found Rachel's number, and shot her a quick text to let her know about the new bus route. She, like Rayah, may not have access to a decent cell signal. It seemed all of Pennsylvania was stuck in the 1800s in that matter.

With a jolt and a rattle of the engine, the bus surged onto the highway. Tires collided with the rumble strips every five seconds. Danny focused on the scenery in the tangerine morning glow, trying to ignore the vibrations his legs felt and the queasiness building in his stomach. He recognized the golden heads of wheat they had whizzed by the other day for the tour. Maybe Sparehouse was in the same direction as King's.

He zoned out for a few minutes until Rayah's palm slapped the window. "You don't think ..." She licked her sweaty lip. "Where is he taking us?"

Dreadful possibilities pounded in his brain. Stay calm, Danny. Rayah and Michelle like to jump to the worst conclusions. Stay calm for her.

"Other places than King's Academy are on Carchemish Road." He gestured to a burger joint at the end of an exit. "They had to find a building large enough to fit our student body. You saw us trying to squeeze into the café."

Rayah stared at the damp, mildew-scented floor. She pried open her lips, but a *ping* from Rachel distracted Danny from her answer: *Sorry! I just got up. I don't remember getting an email from Emmanuel, but I'll check my inbox.*

The bus swerved to the right, and Danny collided with Rayah into the window. When he caught his balance again, his phone *ping*ed once more: *Nothing here ... you sure one of the seniors didn't send a prank message?*

A soft gasp departed from Rayah. Danny glanced up and spotted a golden lion statue out the window. Right in front of the King's Academy sign.

Zeke pulled into the bus lot, which was a lot bumpier than the parking lot his mom had driven into the other day. The number of potholes rivaled the ones in Emmanuel's parking lot. The rattling Emmanuel bus squeezed into a space between Meede Media and Hevenin High vehicles, neither of which had a layer of dust caked upon them like their own bus.

Zeke clicked open the squeaking doors, but nobody moved. He spun around in his chair, adjusting his baseball cap, which had turned a darker shade because of sweat. "Don't everyone get up at once."

No one got up at all. Out of pure instinct, Danny placed his arm on the seat in front of him to bar off Rayah, not that she planned to bolt out of the chair anytime soon. But he had to protect something.

"Come on, guys. I have another job that starts in half an hour." Zeke tapped his wrist. "Please leave."

Jeremy stood and gripped the emerald seat in front of him, which had several holes. His fingers dug into the fabric as he glared at the driver. "Zeke, turn around. They gave you the wrong address or something."

"They emailed me the place, and I plugged it into my GPS." Zeke waved a phone with a map. "You can take it up with Chin when you meet him inside. Now scoot."

Jeremy's fingers dug as deep as the green fabric would let them. "Ridiculous." He released his grip and swung a huge backpack over his bony shoulders. "I'll call my parents to come pick me up."

He marched off the bus and into the wheat field, armed with his cell phone. For the first time in about a week, it appeared he had reached his actual mother instead of her voicemail because Jeremy's "Praise the Lord! Mom, you'll never believe where Zeke dumped us ..." came through the thick glass windows with surprising clarity.

Not a soul budged for the next minute and a half, all stewing in the steaming bus as if they were animals waiting to cook. Danny shut his eyes tight and prayed a desperate prayer.

After that time passed, Zeke sighed and clasped the doors shut. The engine coughed as he turned the key to start the bus.

Rayah and Danny let out sighs of relief.

"Were you praying for the rapture?" Danny rubbed his sweaty palms against his pants.

"Uh huh." Rayah wiped a trail of snot from her nose. "You?"

"Like my life depended on it."

Zeke said, "If you don't want to go, I won't force you," right as a frying-pan-sized fist knocked against the front doors.

Once again Danny barred Rayah with his arm, fingers grazing the cool metal wall.

Zeke shut off the bus and swung open the doors, and heavy feet thumped up the stairs to the bus. Not again. A large rock plunked into Danny's stomach.

The brute Dean gazed at the inhabitants of the bus with twinkling eyes, as if each were a wad of cash. His chin twisted toward Danny for a moment, and his grin tore like a knife up his red beard.

"May I help you, son?" Zeke glared at the boy in the Guns N' Roses T-shirt.

"The principal sent us to escort the students to the football field for an assembly," Dean spoke in a high, gentle voice. Like the tone a nurse uses before giving a child a painful injection.

Rayah jumped when someone banged their knuckles against her window, followed by a deep guffaw.

Danny peered out and a handful of boys roughly matching Dean in size and weight stared at him. He glanced at Zeke, hoping the man would tell Dean to skedaddle.

Zeke shrugged and thrust his arm toward the students. "They don't want to go."

Dean gripped the driver's seat and leaned down to his eye level. "Do teenagers ever want to attend classes?"

"Whatever." Zeke sighed. "Time means money. So if you can get them off here fast ..."

Dean winked at Zeke and paraded to the back of the vehicle, each step sounding like wet thunder. He shoved up the red emergency exit lever, and the back door of the bus swung open.

A shrieking alarm, similar to the fire-drill screech, sounded. Men built for football clambered onto the bus, climbing like massive gorillas. With strong grips they snatched passengers out of seats, saying, "Don't want to be late the first day, sweetie," and "You'll like the new Emmanuel. Now get up."

By the time they reached Danny's row, he had thrown his whole body in front of Rayah as a barrier, but Dean grasped fistfuls of his T-shirt and forced him out of his seat. "Welcome to King's Academy, Princess." Spittle from Dean's lips landed on Danny's nose. He smelled like alcohol. Dean dragged him to the back of the bus and shoved him out into blinding tangerine sunshine.

Ugh. With luck, he landed on his feet, and without luck, his momentum pushed him into another King's Academy student. He shoved Danny into a single-file line that headed toward the entrance gates.

Gravel crackled underneath his feet. This was nothing like the smooth cobblestone paths from the day before as patches of mud and stone glued themselves to his shoes.

He tried to crane his neck back to see if Rayah walked behind him, but a King's senior monitoring the lines grabbed a fistful of his hair and forced him to look forward. Even though he obeyed, the student continued to pull. He winced at the fiery pain. He knew he was overdue for a haircut but would rather not get it this way. When they reached the gate, the student released him to talk to the speaker at the gate.

Danny whipped around and found Rayah with her knees and hand bleeding.

"Didn't land on my feet." She nodded toward the bus lot.

He wanted to wrap her wounds right there but feared the student who had pulled him by his hair. To obey or to protect his friend. *God, what do I do?*

Although desiring the latter, the gate clicked open before he could so much as kneel to inspect the scrape. They could get her cleaned up when they reached a stopping point.

The captives marched forward, making a sharp left toward the football field. Instead of the squeaky trill of a clarinet, silence hovered over the area, give or take the interspersed chirps of sparrows ... who, like all birds, seemed unaware that the world sometimes stopped its movement for a heartbeat before a disaster.

They cut through the grass. This patch seemed a lot yellower than the lawns he had passed the other day. Along the way he stepped over mangled frogs, some with body parts dismembered, and others, unrecognizable masses.

He shuddered.

"Happens when they mow the lawns." A student with a lip piercing nudged a frog with his toe, the juices staining the shoe. He grabbed another fistful of Danny's hair. "And will happen to you if you don't keep your eyes forward. Saw you looking at the girl behind you when we were at the gate."

The walk to the field seemed to take forever. Good thing his book bag was gone that morning. His back would've killed.

Slumped soldiers trooping in front of him fiddled with their backpack straps. Some slid them up and down every place possible on their shoulders. Others resorted to cradling the bags in their arms after giving up on their backs.

Danny wished he could carry Rayah's backpack in his arms, considering she tended to stuff the poor bag more than Hannah stuffed her cheeks with food. But the kid with the lip piercing had just released his hair and kept eyeing him. Danny decided not to risk anything. Not under such a careful watch, at least.

At long last, they reached the stadium. The arena itself covered the same surface area as his old school. The golden words *Lions* and *King's* marked each end of the red end zones, and a painted lion's head bore jagged teeth at the center of the field. They filed their way toward scarlet stands. Another mass of students already sat in neat rows, unusual for a group of teenagers. Already the stadium capacity doubled the population of Emmanuel.

In a sea of blonds, he spied a burning bush of red hair belonging to a very grumpy-looking Hannah. He thought about waving to her, but the puffy-lipped senior kept giving him the stink eye.

As he trooped up the stairs, gripping the metal bar, the distinct clunk of heels against the metal bleachers caught his attention. He followed the sound and found Michelle on the top row with her large cheeks buried in her fists. She reminded Danny of a depressed squirrel.

One of the King's students leading the pack stopped halfway up the bleachers and motioned with a snake-tattooed arm for the Emmanuel troops to park in a row littered with popcorn containers and Gatorade bottles. He made sure to shove those who did not move fast enough. No one moved to his liking.

After ducking under the snake-tattoo thrust, Danny sat next to a curly-Afro junior in front of him who went by the name of July. Danny's seat felt wet from the humidity. Rayah was seated on his other side as she nursed her bleeding knees and hand. Before Danny could offer his shirt to stop the blood, July dug into her one-shoulder bag and pulled out a Band-Aid in a yellowing package. Rayah accepted it gratefully and plastered it on one of her knees.

"Want to use my shirt for the other knee?" Half of Danny's top was off when he finished the question.

Rayah shook her head. "Keep it on. We don't want to draw attention to ourselves." She used her dress to absorb the clotted blood of her knee and hand.

He pulled the shirt down, wrinkling his nose at his body odor. Should've put on more deodorant that morning. As Rayah stoppered the blood, Danny twirled around to focus on some of his other friends in the stadium. With a subtle wave, he tried to get Michelle's attention in the top row, but she remained motionless. He dug his phone out of his pocket to text her, but someone snapped her fingers, and Rayah nudged him. Danny looked up at a King's student, her hand outstretched.

"No cell phones during the assembly."

Now that was too far.

They passed a large plastic bucket down the row with a white *Cell Phones* label slapped onto it.

"We will return them to you after the assembly." The low voice belonged to a female. Danny recognized the girl with half her head shaved from the Frisbee game the other day. "But if we catch you with your cell phone during this meeting, we'll drop it off the top of these bleachers onto the concrete. Got it?"

They got it.

Piles and piles of weary travelers loaded onto the bleachers, always marching in single file. Finally, when the last straggler, who used crutches, hobbled into his seat in the first row, at least a thousand students must have sat in the stadium.

Feedback from an amp pierced the icy morning air, and the nervous chatter died down.

A tall man with curly hair in a ponytail marched to the center of the field and stopped right in the mouth of the lion. Even from far away, one could hear the thunderous voice of Ned. "Sorry for the abrupt start to your morning. We ran a bit behind schedule and wanted to speed up this process. Welcome to King's Academy."

Great welcoming party. Wish he could stay longer, but he was late for class.

Ned cracked a good-hearted smile amid his thick beard, and then his expression melted away into stone. "My name is Mr. Rezzen. I will be addressed as such and by no other name. Now you might want to listen well for these next five minutes. Your very life might depend on it."

Chapter Eight

DANNY WIPED HIS FOREHEAD WITH THE BACK OF HIS hand as Ned's speech continued. Of course, Pennsylvania would decide to be Florida today.

"New students, over ten different schools are represented in this section of bleachers alongside you." Ned paused, scuffing his dress shoes on the football turf. "But I want you to forget whatever high school you arrived here from because you attend King's Academy now. Might I add, all of you received a scholarship—about half with full rides." A glint of the rising sun caught his eye as the principal stared in Danny's direction.

For some reason, the man's whole being—his tall stature and burning eyes—struck fear into him. Danny pulled a sheet of his wet hair to cover his face. Head snapped down, he continued to listen.

"Because we underwrote a significant amount of the costs for you to join our student body, we expect you to follow the rules even closer than your colleagues who pay full price."

A sudden murmuring of the King's students in the other bleacher sections hushed as Ned jabbed an index finger into the air and swung it in a circular motion.

This signaled the King's students on the outside of the bleachers, who ran to the field to grab stacks of thin paperback books. They then passed them across the rows until a small forty-six-page booklet with a lion emblem on the front slid its way into Danny's hands. Bold lettering declared: *King's Academy Handbook*.

Danny flipped through and held the book inches away from his eyes because of the miniscule writing. At least the fresh paper smell relieved him of the sweaty scent of the stands.

Minutes after each student received the school rules, Ned spoke again. "I trust all you newbies can read. We would not have offered you a spot here otherwise. Do yourselves a favor and read through that rule book. Because if any of you violate a single regulation, we *will* expel you."

The thought of expulsion caused Danny's heart to beat faster for a moment. If he tried to go to another school afterward, they would submit inquiries about why he had been kicked out of King's.

In the handbook, decrees such as *no chewing gum in any academic building* seized his attention. He glanced over at Hannah, who gnawed on an impressive wad of gum, causing her cheeks to bulge. Could they expel her for that?

"And"—Ned combed fingers through his beard—"an expulsion from here means dismissal from any college of your choice. Believe me, if you cannot survive King's Academy, we will ensure you will not be able to even attempt to anywhere else."

The first email from Ned had mentioned King's connections to high-profile colleges. Michelle had at least two Ivy League schools in her top ten places to go. If the school expelled her, goodbye Yale.

The transfer students in the stands exchanged glances that ranged from dubious to frightened. Rayah, unsurprisingly, occupied the latter category, and Danny wished he could offer a word of comfort. Mouth agape, no words trickled off his tongue. For the first time in months, he had nothing funny to say.

"No further information to cover, but my student assistants will call out your names based on your housing." Ned gestured at no person in particular. "When they call your name, go to where they point on the field, and after that, wait for the rest of the names to be called for your house. Then someone will lead you from there."

Before they began the roll call, the King's students passed the *Cell Phones* bucket back through the rows. As it weaved around, various students complained about "no cell reception" and "the service at a fast-food restaurant is better than here."

When his sweaty fingers wrapped around his own warm phone, he clicked the power button. Sure enough, *No Service*.

The girl with half her head shaved called names in alphabetical order for a girl's hall by the name of Suanna. Rayah, having the last name

"Abed," was called first and stood with two large spots of purple blood on her blue dress from the scrapes on her hand and knees. She, along with Michelle, Hannah, and about twelve others, stepped down the loud, metal steps and formed a single-file line at a ten-yard mark. Turns out, King's Academy students were somewhat better at lines than Emmanuel's. Probably because they were paying more tuition and they actually had a chance to learn such things. After Hannah slumped at the back of the line, the half-hairless student marched them around the corner and behind a row of trees.

Three hall calls later (Hawkins, Borgen, and Kading), Dean approached the chain-link fence in front of the bleachers with a clipboard, which was swallowed by his beefy pink hands. "Names for Phrat River: Gabe Adams, Daniel Belte ..."

When Danny passed Dean on his way to line up behind Gabe Adams, an albino boy in a white hoodie with a Los Angeles Angels logo, Dean's gaze followed him amid the list of names. Heat burned on Danny's face. Dude, why? Why did Dean keep staring at Danny? He was not that pretty. Even after Dean reached "Joshua Zariah," he had not glanced another direction.

"Let's go, cupcakes." Dean slapped Gabe's hoodie with his clipboard. "You're gonna fry in that thing."

With his large feet stuffed into black jungle boots, Dean led the line of troops out of the stadium. They cut through the grass again, past the disfigured frogs, toward the LLC, angling right toward a dull-gray brick building. Unlike the tour, thick trees did not line their pathway to the dorm. Danny yearned for shade to cool his hot neck and back.

They curved around to the back of the hall, far from any visitor's view, and off-white words made of metal on the water-damaged outer cement wall spelled out *PH AT RIVER*. The *R* in *PHRAT* must have fallen off some time ago. Either that or the heavyset students felt unrepresented.

Not a single window appeared anywhere on the building, and there seemed to be only one door into the structure—in the back. Danny realized why he hadn't noticed this before. The large evergreen trees shielding the building from the view of the touring path probably aided that.

In front of the smoky-hued door, a boy with a puffy eye sealed shut shuffled several packets in his hands.

Now Dean turned to look at him. Maybe Dean had a thing for staring at ugly dudes.

The guy with the puffy eye stepped out from a cement walkway that led from the dorm to the path and craned his neck to find the line had wrapped around the building. A long-drawn sigh escaped his lips when he returned to the pathway. "Anyone missing?"

Dean consulted his clipboard. "Not now ..."

"Did Ned recruit a whole country?" An exasperated groan.

"We have enough room, Duke." Dean slapped Duke on the back. Harder than Duke probably expected because he lurched forward into Gabe. "'Sides, I doubt half'll make it through the first two weeks."

Danny's blood chilled. Did the school have a crazy-hard academic reputation or something? It was sophomore year, after all.

Duke raised his eyebrows but said nothing in reply. He swiped a key card from his pocket, and the door gave a sharp *ding* followed by a *click*. Serving as a doorstop, Duke motioned with a quick wave for the students to come inside. "The number on the packet is also your room number." He slapped a packet on the chest of each student as he entered.

After a manila envelope with the number 207 slammed into his rib cage, Danny stepped inside onto a hard concrete floor littered with soda cans and moldy food.

Humidity and heat overwhelmed him on entry. Guess they had no AC in this dorm. Just like Judah's place at Taylor University. The stuffy air stopped Danny's breathing for a moment. His face beaded with sweat in the humidity as he inhaled deeply, adapting. Every breath smelled warm and musty.

He shadowed Gabe down a narrow hallway. Danny gripped a sweaty yellow railing and forced his way up several winding flights of stairs, figuring all the 200s would be on the second floor, just like Emmanuel's classrooms. An eternity later he reached the door to the second level, flung it open, and skimmed each door until he landed on 207. Sweaty hair stuck to his cheek, and his fingers fumbled to brush it out of the way. He wiped his hands on his pants to jostle the doorknob. Locked.

Clammy knuckles knocked once, twice ... After the third try, he consulted the envelope Duke had handed him. Peering inside, he located a key and plugged it into the door. He swung it open, but the dark, windowless room offered mere shadows of clunky wooden furniture against the fluorescent hallway lights. The thick scent of warm, stale beer drifted into his nostrils and got stuck in his throat. Smelled like he had some fun roommates ...

Danny groped the wall of the room, which had the texture of chilled—nearly wet—brick, until his fingers fumbled around and found a light switch. He clicked it on and hesitated after entering the light's wan glow.

How did all this get here? By the third bed, the one without covers, in the squat room lay a pile of suitcases and bags—including his book bag. *Oh, right. Mom.* Guess the rapture didn't happen after all. Shame.

Danny kicked away piles of dirty clothes and beer cans to get to his bed, closest to the wall and the only one not stacked. He shoved aside one of the suitcases, a ratty one missing a wheel, to sit on the stone-hard cot. Leaning his heavy head back, he tried to get a glimpse of the room. Of dark dried-glue patches on the wall from sticky tac, of the circular smoke detector on the ceiling that blinked red, of the wads of dirty clothing partying in every crevice of the room. There wasn't much to see.

Overturning the manila envelope, he dumped the contents onto the bed: a student ID with his freshman yearbook picture from Emmanuel—oh, the terrible haircut—a campus map, his semester schedule, a Welcome Weekend list of events, and a King's Academy quick-facts sheet. To distract himself from the heat and abrupt turn of events, he perused the final item:

KING'S ACADEMY QUICK FACTS

1. King's Academy was founded in 1859 when oil discoveries drove visitors to Carchemish.

2. More than 45% of our students have a 4.0 GPA or higher.

3. Every student is required to participate in an art and a sport. Additionally, students have over 117 different clubs and activities to choose from ...

"So we got a princess and a bookworm in our dorm."

Danny glanced up to find Dean and Duke with their necks in the doorframe.

Danny's heart leaped into his throat. *Oh, God, please no.* Anything but rooming with them. The one-eyed dude and the other dude who keeps staring.

Cracking a smile, Dean swaggered over to Danny's bed, ignoring the fact he trampled on a pair of pants and an empty ramen packet. Dean leaned over and snagged the rulebook Danny had received on the football field.

"Bookworm, do yourself a favor." Dean ripped the handbook in half and tossed it into an overstuffed trash bin, which caused crumpled tissues to spill out and litter the floor. Lovely room arrangement they had going. "We break a lot of rules and things here, starting with everything you read in there."

Duke stifled a snicker and proceeded to collapse on the bottom bunk on the other side of the room, scrolling on his phone. Sweat had glazed him so much his self-cut tank top had darkened to almost black.

Dean thrust a clammy hand in front of Danny's nose. How did even his fingers smell like beer? "Name's Dean, and you have Duke over there. You got a name, or should we just address you as *Princess*?"

"Danny." He shook the hand, finding it difficult to maintain a firm grip with his sweaty fingers.

"Another *D*. Dean, Duke, and Danny. You'll fit right in here." He turned to Duke, who had not once glanced up. "Think we oughta give Princess Danny a tour of the room?"

Duke shrugged. "Who would take any interest in something so small?"

"Ask the girl who visited you at 2 a.m. last Monday."

Duke chucked a beer can at Dean, who dodged it with ease.

Then Dean encircled a firm grip around Danny's arm and forced him to stand. "Let's take a tour around the den, Princess."

Glad to see his new pal was giving him a choice. "The den?" Danny cast a glance at Duke's lower bunk bed, expecting a lion to spring out from the shadows.

"Yeah ... no windows and they lock the door from the outside after curfew, so it makes you feel a bit like a wild animal from a den. We have lots of nicknames for things around campus." He stared at his pants for a moment. Danny didn't want to know.

"The door has no inside lock?"

Dean moved to the door and showed him the inside and outside handles. To Danny's dismay, only the outside knob had a keyhole ... a really banged up one, at that.

But what if a student needed to escape? What if a tornado drill happened, or Dean was forcing him to learn his nicknames for things and Danny needed to get away from him?

"Yeah, they lock up the doors at curfew, which is midnight." Dean jabbed a thick finger at an orange sheet on the door listing meal times and curfew. "If they catch a student outside their room, they supposedly give them detention or something. Wouldn't know. Never been caught."

"Besides"—Duke's throaty voice piped up—"they gave each of us a key. We've found ways to sneak around the—"

Dean shushed him and jerked his head toward a smoke detector on the ceiling.

"—never mind."

Danny stared at the smoke detector. Had Ned hidden some sort of recording device inside? Like *1984*, the book they had read for his freshman literature class. Ned was Big Brother.

The larger roommate, Dean, left the door ajar and approached the back wall. "You'll see we have a blank canvas here. Duke used to have a Black Sabbath poster." He motioned to a spot with yellowed sticky-tac marks on the white brick. "But humidity caused the thing to keep falling down."

He slapped a beefy palm on each bed in succession, forming a sweaty handprint on each. "Mine, Duke's, yours. Usually one of us would take the one on the floor and make you take top bunk, but the bed smells like urine, so."

Ah, nice roommates.

"We keep it in that order," Dean continued. "Only you and your visitors can stay on that bed over there."

Visitors? Yeah, Danny was not letting any of his friends in here to meet these guys.

Dean pointed out three sets of drawers, desks, and shelves, making sure Danny knew which ones he could access and the off-limits areas—nearly three-quarters of the room. On all the desks and drawers, including his, Danny spotted piles of soiled underwear, socks, and candy wrappers. He couldn't wait to show his mother the room.

Dean and Duke had very strict rules about socks and doorknobs, which "regulations" they seemed to insert into every part of the "tour." The two roommates also pointed out a heating vent by the bunk bed, which they claimed never kicked on during the winter.

"The last people who came here tried to vacuum out the thing." Duke made a sucking noise. "At least forty dead spiders from those vents. I think someone found a rat in theirs once. The ancient things stopped working twenty years ago ... so we've heard."

Glad to know King's used their finances as well as Emmanuel.

Dean motioned to a water pipe, browning at the ends and hanging right next to the fire alarm on the ceiling. He warned Danny not to hang any of his wet clothes from there.

"The dryers downstairs only work half the time, so you'll be tempted." He peeled off his sweaty shirt and tossed it on a pile of chip wrappers. "Besides, you'd have to take a five-mile hike to reach the nearest laundromat, and they have strict rules against leaving campus."

They also mentioned a few vending machines that existed in the laundry room on the bottom level and a study lounge at the center of each floor.

The thought of bottled water from a vending machine caused Danny's throat to dry as he swallowed. He thrust his hands into his pockets. No spare change.

"We have only one closet, and Duke seems to own all of the thrift store, so unless you can cram a nice suit in there, stay away from that. Any questions?"

Danny couldn't think of any. Even if he had, his throat had grown so tight from fear of Dean that he decided not to venture one.

"Then you should probably check your Welcome Weekend schedule. I think you have an event in about fifteen minutes."

The laminated pink sheet, sticky and wet from the steamy room, read, **11:00**, *Boys' physical skills test. Girls' test will follow at* **11:30**. *Location: Hadad Track-and-Field.* **Wear athletic apparel. 12:30** *Luncheon with parents. Location: Dining Commons.*

"The football field you just came from is where you're going to do the skills test." Dean tapped the paper. "They ran out of room to build a track separate from the football stadium when they constructed the school. If the principal would knock down his stupid garden, we'd have room for it."

"Do you run?" Danny inched as far away on his bed from Dean as he could.

"The school or track?"

"Is that a *yes* to both?"

Dean shrugged. "No one here likes the word *no*."

Danny stripped off his sweaty clothes and rummaged through another suitcase to pull out a crumpled T-shirt and running shorts. He dug through a blue bin full of footwear, which smelled a great deal like vinegar, attempting to locate a pair of tennis shoes. Another suitcase contained a bag of school supplies and his Bible. After digging through all his bags, which were in a complete state of disarray—Mom must've rushed to pack these—he couldn't find any tennis or running shoes.

With a slight hint of pity, Duke offered to lend a pair of his. He handed over white-and-black Nikes with holes in the sides. Without a complaint—at least, not one spoken aloud—Danny stuffed his size-thirteen feet into the size-eleven shoes. His toes bunched up but he managed to walk around the room in them.

Just before he exited, a large hand clapped his shoulder. His skin recoiled.

"One more thing: if you have any complaints against the academy—or against Ned"—Dean jerked his chin up at the smoke detector on the ceiling—"don't do it in here. We had a roommate last year with a large mouth. The guy didn't last long."

With a roommate like him? No kidding. Danny cast a wary glance at the fire alarm, then at Dean. He nodded and left the room.

Chapter Nine

"NO AC IN YOUR DORM EITHER, HUH?" DANNY NEARLY tripped on a rock kicked up by Levi's crutches.

"Worse." Levi panted, sweat dripping from his crewcut hair. He paused, wiped his hair on his brawny right shoulder, and continued hobbling. "They ... turned ... heat ... on."

Out of pity, Danny left the rest of the conversation alone so Levi could breathe. Rattling rasps and coughs interspersed their crunching steps.

It had taken Danny several minutes to retrace his steps to the football field. After wandering past mangled frogs and patches of yellowing grass, he had spied the student on crutches from Ned's meeting in the stadium earlier. Not wanting to be alone on such a foreign campus, he joined him as the classmate exhaled heavy breaths traveling down a gravel hill on sticks.

Danny had introduced himself, and through gasping breaths, the other managed to get out a wheezing, "Le–vi." Each syllable required an inhale. Levi's spiky hair dripped with sweat onto his rosy forehead and down his nose like a faucet.

Part way through the walk, Danny took off Duke's shoes due to fiery pain in his cramped feet. Even after shedding his soggy socks and stuffing them into one shoe, his feet ached as they trod upon the jagged gravel.

At long last, they reached the stadium, passing the red-trimmed gates with billowing signs for various business advertisements. An *Up on a Pedestal: Custom-Made Statues and Large Art* sign bulged with a gust of warm wind.

A clump of boys was huddled on the starting line of the red track. Levi and Danny joined them and stopped amid the sounds of chattering and complaints about moving-in experiences.

"No time to unpack." A boy with red-colored contact lenses massaged his shoulder. "Mom just dumped everything from home into the dorm room."

"The place smells like garbage." Another, in a blue bro tank, crinkled his nostrils. "My roommates tried to fit two futons into that room. Must've forgotten to measure the dimensions because there's no way they'd fit. One gave up and just burned his outside."

So that would explain the fiery scent that reeked outside Danny's dorm when he had left for the track. That seemed to be the solution to everything at King's. Burn everything.

Amid the grievances, Danny watched as Levi slumped onto his crutches like a dead man's body draped on a railing. Poor guy. He scanned the area for a drinking fountain to point Levi toward. Nothing by the announcement booth with a painted white lion on the front. Nothing by the squat building with weathered signs by the stands for restrooms.

Nothing at all.

Instead, on the field, he noticed something that looked a great deal like an obstacle course. Hurdles, horizontal training ladders, a shot-put ring, along with several other stations, sat in a perfect oval on the turf.

A piercing sound hit the air.

The disgruntled cluster turned around to find a fat man in a striped shirt and a skeletal woman in a pencil skirt approach. The large man's cheeks puffed as he blew into his whistle again, face white from the sunscreen he hadn't rubbed well enough into his face.

The woman in the pencil skirt allowed for a thin smile to stretch across her bony face. "Good afternoon, new students. For those of you who can't read name tags, mine says, *Ashley Penaz*."

Incredible. Never would've guessed.

She flashed a white badge pinned to her suit jacket. Unlike everyone else on the track, Ashley did not have a single trace of sweat on her. Probably worked in an office with AC.

"Ned—Mr. Rezzen"—she paced back and forth like a drill sergeant—"asked me to recruit every one of you. I hunted through report cards, standardized tests, and scholastic awards to see if each student here would make a good fit for our rigorous academia."

The man in the striped shirt stifled a yawn behind a fist, smudging sunscreen on his hand.

"However, we expect you to excel beyond academics here." She glared at the man. "As you may know, we require every student to participate in one sports season each year and at least a semester of an art program."

The woman shoved a pair of glasses up her nose and smoothed her hair, which was in a severe bun. "We can let feeble talent in the arts survive because we have plenty of behind-the-scenes positions that do not require a high aptitude."

Danny. Definitely Danny.

"*But* we do not tolerate poor performance in sports."

As if on cue, a *fah-lap* of wind hit an advertisement for a physical-therapy service five miles from campus. The noise appeared to jolt the group.

Ashley continued, "Granted, while you may not—and as we expect, will not—achieve playing time on varsity, we have plenty of colleges that recruit from our school. If our junior varsity third string has even one player with a physical defect, that could discourage a recruiter from offering a scholarship."

Out of the corner of his eye, Danny saw Levi wobble on his crutches. The poor student's knees trembled as if someone had set them to vibrate.

Ashley did not seem to notice. "In fact, five years ago, a representative from Pittsburgh U attended a game for our worst team in basketball, junior varsity fifth string. We had not informed them of this fact, and they considered recruiting a player. Then the player started wheezing."

Levi panted, tongue lolling out.

"And because he had a full-on asthma attack, Pittsburgh refused to send another recruiter to one of our basketball games for three more years. We *will not* let that happen again."

With a stiff arm, she gestured to the man in the striped shirt, who stuffed his phone into his athletic shorts. "Meet Coach Velin, who leads the cross-country and distance track teams—all five of them. Today he has set up various activities for you to complete in the next half hour. Failure or poor aptitude in one or more of the stations could result in expulsion."

Expulsion. Danny's heart raced. They couldn't expel students for being bad at sports. And if they did, what would King's tell the other schools? "You can't take on this student. Can't throw a hammer far enough. We want our students to have the arms of Thor."

Ashley turned to Coach Velin.

His voice was reedy and far less impressive than Ashley's. "Single-file line." Coach approached every student with an injury, only three in number: a boy with his arm in a sling, another with his leg in a boot, and Levi.

After sending the first two home, Coach Velin asked Levi what sports he played.

"Football, sir. Linebacker."

"Anything else? A large guy like you?" Coach's feeble voice dripped with the same hope Danny felt for Levi. The guy looked like he lifted. Put a ball in his hands, and he could do anything.

Levi shook his head and Danny felt his heart plummet for him. "At Lydia, we went year-round. Drills and two-a-days on and off seasons. Coach would never let us join another sport."

Coach Velin squinted at him. "And that injury looks like it has a few months to go. How long do you need to be on it?"

"Twelve weeks." Levi swallowed hard.

A long sigh passed through the coach's lips, and he wrenched his head toward the two others he had sent home. By now they had reached the gate at the end of the stadium. "Go join 'em then."

"Please"—Levi arms shook as they clutched his crutches—"my mom saved for five years to get me into this school. I can try another sport in the spring."

"We don't like a gamble here." Coach Velin folded his arms over his thick chest.

"I'll excel at academics and run an event in track. No one pays attention to the guy in the eighth lane."

Ashley's cold voice broke in as she consulted her phone. "Your GPA stands at a meager 3.95, Levi. We have plenty of 4.0 students who would love to take your spot."

After another minute of pleading, Ashley and Coach Velin grabbed each of Levi's arms—attached to his crutches—and forced him to hobble three-quarters of the way down the 100-meter stretch.

Danny's cheeks burned just watching this. The injustice of it all ... Levi was no Rayah, but he still had to protect him somehow. Without thinking, he lurched forward, fists balled, but something encircled his arm and pulled back.

A guy in green track shorts yanking at his arm swore. "What are you doing?" He released, and Danny stumbled forward, almost colliding face first into the scarlet track.

Danny gestured to Ashley and Coach as they reached the gate. Levi was hobbling past the billowing sign. "Can't just let them get away with this crap. Someone has to tell them to let those students back."

"Dude, they work for King's. Their consciences died years ago ... burned up like cigarettes."

Burned up like everything else here. "Is anyone gonna stop them?"

Awkward silence. The responses varied from stifled snickers to glances anywhere but in Danny's direction.

The athlete in the green shorts approached Danny with his jaw clenched. "Don't play with fire here. Shut up and you might just be in the half of recruits who survive."

Dean had mentioned that half the newbies leave by the end of two weeks. Made sense.

Ashley and Coach returned, and the group watched Danny.

Although his face flushed with fury, he remained still. Rule follower at heart ... and he hated himself for it. He shook his head, feeling at odds with himself. Coward.

"Now that we have all the defects out of here"—Coach Velin nodded over his shoulder at the gate—"let's see how you all do with the physical tests." He paused and glanced at Danny's bare feet. "Son, you might want to put on those shoes in your hands. We have a mile run as the first event."

"Two sizes too small." Danny wiggled his toes.

"You don't have another pair?"

Clearly. Didn't he see them on his feet? "Left them at home."

"Go get them then!" The coach made a vague motion in the direction of the dorms.

Danny's chin shook back and forth. "No, that's *not* home. Besides, I can handle four laps without shoes."

The polyurethane track bit into his soles in reply. As the sun grew hot, so did the crimson lane. At least it wasn't gravel.

Coach Velin shrugged and rubbed a pair of fingers over large eye bags. "Your choice, your loss." He licked his dry lips and blew into the whistle. "To the starting line."

Ratty, ragged, and ripped clusters of shoes along with a pair of bare feet made their way to the white line at the 100-meter mark.

Danny kept his eyes on the track to ensure no one would step on his feet, but the other runners—several from Emmanuel—yielded a bubble of space for him. He tossed Duke's shoes onto the turf, and they landed a few feet away from the horizontal ladder set up for another event.

"You will run four laps as quickly as you can." Ashley's cold voice barked from behind a phone screen. "I will tell those with the slowest times to go home. I would say do not land in the bottom ten or even twenty, but that would discourage you from running your best. For all you know, we may just keep five of you. Coach"—she nodded at the man—"give them the commands."

Equipped with his stopwatch, Coach Velin raised his arm into the air. "Runners, take your marks."

Shoes squeaked when they bounced against the track, students jumping up and down.

Danny tried a few times but found this stung his feet. Instead, he lifted his knees to his chest one at a time.

"Set."

All the racers leaned forward as if trying to peer into a dark cave, into a den.

Jagged rocks sunk their teeth into Danny's soles. Right as he reconsidered slipping back into Duke's shoes, Coach Velin's "go!" and the shrill stopwatch *beep* sounded.

In a daze, Danny picked up his legs and sprinted to catch up to the runners who had advanced several strides ahead. He had passed them by the time they reached the 200-meter mark and led the race when he whizzed by the starting line for the first lap.

Coach Velin called out the runners' times whenever they completed a loop. "Fifty-seven seconds." The time announced when Danny passed him.

By this point, Danny's sides and feet seared. He swallowed and found his mouth tasted like blood and bile. Went out too fast. He added ten seconds to his second lap and started to run on his heels as opposed to the balls of his feet to ease the prickling needle pain in his soles.

Five runners passed him in the third lap. Now his calves exploded with blistering heat. His neck stooped, the weight of his head seemed to be the only thing propelling him forward.

Ashley snapped her fingers at Danny. "Pick it up, Barefoot. Remember, I may only keep five of you here."

Was he willing to give up college and the future for the sake of stinging feet?

As the sixth runner flew in front of Danny, he inhaled a sharp, dry breath and broke out into a full sprint. Lactic acid pumped in his legs with each stride, and sweat burned his eyes. Burned his lips. Burned his tongue.

But he ran.

He glided past the six runners, past the white starting mark, arms behind him as if they held a bar attached to a train cart. As he passed Coach Velin and heard the faint "4:11," he collapsed on the turf and hurled his breakfast ... tasted like rancid Cheerios. His contribution to King's Academy. They were welcome.

The clip clop of heavy feet, followed by desperate gulps of air informed Danny the other leaders of the pack had just finished their race. One kneeled by him and dry heaved.

Meanwhile, Danny nursed his feet, which had imprints of the track in the soles, with one hand and massaged his throat with the other.

"Where did you learn to run like that?" The coach's pencil-thin eyebrows raised.

His throat burned as he rasped, "I have an older brother." He thought it served as an adequate explanation.

He, along with ten other runners who had crossed the finish line in under six minutes, hobbled into the restroom by the bleachers to find a water source even if they had to dunk their heads into a toilet. They found three porcelain sinks, which had chipped and developed weird spots, and dipped their heads under the faucets. Although the water had a brownish tint and muddy taste, no one minded.

When they returned to the track, they discovered Coach Velin had sent anyone with a mile time of eight minutes or higher home.

Having about fifteen minutes left, Coach Velin directed them to five stations: the shot put, hurdles, horizontal ladder—for high knees and, honestly, a break for Coach Velin from having to evaluate the students—push-ups for one minute, and a sit-and-reach station, which measured flexibility.

Danny did well at the shot put, at least compared to his predecessor, who threw incorrectly and almost hit Coach Velin's toes with an eight-pound ball. Coach Velin did not give that student a second try.

Because he had long legs, Danny jumped over the hurdles with ease, even having terrible form, and the high-knees station gave him a nice break to chat with Gabe, the albino Phrat River resident, who had run the mile at a time of 6:03.

In fact, Danny excelled at all the stations except for the last one, where he had to straddle a plastic sit-and-reach board, each bare foot in a placeholder. At the base of his feet and beyond lay a ruler that measured up to six inches. He bent forward to reach as far as he could, but his hands barely scraped the one-inch mark. Pain spiked in his groin and calves.

After another try, Gabe, who was serving as his monitor for the activity, clucked his tongue. "You just aren't flexible."

"I get it from my mother," Danny joked. Half-joked.

Gabe chuckled. "Sounds about right. OK, monitor me next."

Five inches later, Gabe and Danny, along with twenty or thirty others walked out of the stadium, passing a group of girls about to start their testing at 11:30. Danny thrust a weary thumbs-up at Rayah, Hannah, and Michelle with one hand while carrying Duke's shoes in the other.

All strode out of there like heroes who had won a great battle. All, now, King's Academy students.

Chapter Ten

STOMACH GROWLING FROM THE PHYSICAL TRIALS, Danny shoveled warm mashed potatoes into his mouth the second he set down his tray in the dining commons. With his cheeks packed with white globs, he chugged two cups of water in ten seconds. Mouth still dry and now reeking of garlic, he rose to refill his glasses.

His mother cleared her throat above the soft piano music. "The line for a drink is thirty people deep. Why don't you stay a while?"

At King's or the table? Neither option sounded ideal. He slumped back into his seat and scooted farther away from his mother, still mad at her for sending him to King's, at least as wide a berth as two inches would give considering fifteen people packed around the small circular table.

His mother shifted in her seat and pressed her elbows to her sides, away from the neighbor with a unibrow next to her.

Sweating into the hot leather seat, Danny bit into a cantaloupe slice, the closest thing to a drink on the plate. The sweet juice cooled his parched throat a bit.

"I thought you had a water fountain on your floor." His mother winced at his slurping noises.

He dropped the gnawed fruit onto his plate. "We do, but none of the drinking fountains in Phrat River have worked since last term. The custodian was in the restrooms for an hour today, so we couldn't bring our water bottles to the sinks."

"What about the sinks on other floors? Certainly the cleaning people work one bathroom at a time."

"The first-floor one flooded this morning, and the line for third stretched longer than the one for the soda machines over there." He gestured to the queue that now wrapped around five columns and past a pasta-bar station, which had a dangling lion next to a hanging metal bowl of noodles.

His mother waited in silence, drawing her spoon through Alfredo sauce and fiddling with peas. "I must say"—she formed a smiley face with the sauce—"you have the kindest welcoming party here. When I arrived this morning with your bags, a group of senior boys *insisted* they take up all your luggage to your floor. Of course, I took them up on their offer."

No wonder they insisted. With all the beer cans that littered the floor and the fact it smelled like a club, she would have freaked out seeing the state of the room.

"Who wants to travel with heavy bags up two flights of stairs?"

"In a dorm without AC." Danny swiped a hand across his clammy forehead. No use, the sweat came right back.

"Yes, yes, I'm sure they'll get that fixed soon."

Yeah, fix it as fast as it took them to fix their family. They'd have air conditioning in twenty years at Phrat River.

"Danny, you should have seen how insistent those boys were about carrying the stuff into the dorm. They even convinced Michelle's father to take her things to the room. That man has a heart of iron, you know."

"He does have hemochromatosis." Danny twisted around and caught Michelle's eye at a table toward the back corner of the dining commons.

She sat underneath a dangling pot and next to her lanky father, who often bore a ghostlike appearance with dark shadows under his eyes. But for once, instead of a somber expression, he wore a toothy grin and a bellowing laugh. The look looked odd on him. Like a clown smile plastered onto the grim reaper. Jerking her head at her dad, Michelle made her fingers into a pair of guns and pretended to shoot herself in the temples.

Danny nodded. If only.

"And"—his mother's crooked chin quivered with excitement—"your principal gave the most wonderful welcoming ceremony after a delicious brunch here in the dining commons."

Yeah, he also sent home students on crutches. Stellar guy. Danny swallowed, his throat burning and garlicky desert dry. "Mom, let's talk about something else."

"The man ran through every and any procedure King's Academy has from curfews to the number of colleges that visit every year."

The piano music switched to a minor key. "Mom."

"He answered every question the parents thrust at him. Believe me, we had quite a few. He gave the most authentic and sincere replies."

The notes began to play faster. "Mom."

"Why, Danny, he has the safest campus here out of any other school I've ever visited, more secure than most universities."

And faster. "Mom!"

"You'd have to hire ten expert arsonists and *hope* one of them could *maybe* light a candle with his precautionary measures."

And faster. Danny slammed one of his empty cups against the table so hard that even through the tablecloth it made a loud *clunk*.

The rest of the table paused their activities and glanced in his direction.

Whoops. Didn't mean to draw a crowd. Back to a major key and slow, soft notes.

The chatter resumed, joining the cloud of sound permeating the whole dining hall.

He stared at his mother, who blinked at him several times, not seeming to comprehend his outburst. Danny didn't understand it himself. Anger burned in his gut, from the physical trials, from his roommate situation, and he had to release that fire somehow. And there didn't seem to be a joke that he could crack ... the whole situation didn't feel all that funny.

"I just—I just want you to go to a good school, Daniel." Her lip trembled. "A good school. A *safe* school."

Back and forth, his fingers slid the cup from one hand to the other. Speaking of stellar guys, look at yourself. Can't say two words without making your mom cry. A twinge of guilt stabbed him in the abdomen. "Sorry, Mom." He scooped both glasses. "I need to get a drink. I'm dying of thirst."

Without casting a glance behind to see his mother's expression, he rose and joined the ever-growing snake of a line.

"Don't feel bad, Danny." Hannah picked the yellowing grass up with her toes and tried to toss the clump into the air. After a few failed attempts, she gave up and slumped her head against the side of the girl's hall Suanna. Poor little grass assassin. Too tired even to murder a lawn today.

On the rocky road near the girls' gray dorm, colorful bikes zoomed past. Hannah kept pitching dandelions at the cyclists—perhaps hoping the wheels would catch one and cause the bicycle to stop working—but the weed caps always fell a foot or two away from her, nowhere near the gravel path. As the bicycles passed, a fresh spray of dust and rocks fell over the group.

"To get away from my dad, I faked a massive migraine." Hannah brushed off the dirt and collected dandelion ammo into a pile. "Mitch would have killed her dad if they hadn't called for a parent assembly five minutes before two o' clock. Would've killed her mother too if she wasn't working a retail shift today. I had a butter knife ready for Mitch, but those cafeteria cutters can't slice through anything. Probably for good reason."

Reason number one: a girl named Hannah.

Michelle blew at her sweaty bangs to get them off her face, but they refused to move. A pungent scent of sweat and musk wafted off her, and Danny's nose wrinkled. For the love of all smells warm and vanilla-y, didn't she have time to clean up?

But the line for showers after the boys had returned from their physical test had been long. The girls most likely had the same situation. He had rushed through rinsing in the cold water, which bore the faint scent of mildew.

They had given the girls half an hour *less* to get ready. Bravo, King's. Girls definitely take much less time to prepare themselves than guys.

After his own shower, he had begun to set up his room. Besides adding the covers to his bed, which he knew he would end up kicking off in the heat, and stuffing a few piles of T-shirts into drawers, loads of suitcases and boxes remained unopened still. He'd even had a few minutes to open his Bible and read Psalm 88.

Apparently that still hadn't been enough time for Michelle though.

"What bugged me most about the whole encounter"—Michelle swiped her bangs with her fingers—"is the fact my dad wouldn't believe anything I told him about the dorms or the physical examination. 'No, Mickey!'" She dropped her voice down to a lower register. "'No one would ever send a girl home because she arrived in a wheelchair,' 'Nice try, Mick, but I doubt they would physically drag a student out of the track because she threw a shot put two feet. Honestly, where do you get these ideas?'" She pressed her face into her palms and let out a wild groan.

"Your theatrical past didn't help, Mitch." Hannah plucked the heads off dandelions, smudging her fingers in yellow. "Of course he thought you exaggerated."

Michelle shot Hannah a dirty look before pressing a water bottle to her lips and draining half its contents.

"So I take it you all passed the physical test?" Danny shifted his position against the wall of Suanna, brushing rocks and a littered water bottle away from his backside. He ducked a little to avoid the glaring sun peeking from behind the gray building. It was an exact copy of Phrat River, except with different lettering on the front. *SUANNA*, all letters accounted for.

"Yeah, you should've seen Rayah run the mile. Under six minutes!" Michelle winked at Rayah, who buckled her head into her chest.

She busily scanned her handbook and pretended to no longer listen to the conversation. Never had been one for recognition. When she won the spelling bee in third grade, she had hidden under one of the auditorium seats while the audience clapped for her.

Michelle unscrewed the cap to her water bottle and took another gulp. "I barely made the nine-minute minimum, but I play tennis, so that requires sprinting, *not* long distance."

"Nine minutes?" Danny whistled. "Man, you girls have it easy."

Michelle glared at him. "I will pretend you never uttered that sentence."

He would, too, based on the gaze of death coming from her eyes.

"They sent three-quarters of the girls home." Hannah flicked the dandelion heads at Rayah. "Kind of wish I had failed the test so I could go back to Emmanuel."

Rayah set down the handbook on her knees, her eyes bobbing back and forth with eyebrows raised and eyes wide. "We no longer have that option."

Hannah catapulted a dandelion into Rayah's face, smudging dirt on her fingertips in the process. She wiped her hands on Rayah's dress. Great manners. She should meet Duke and Dean.

"Sure, we can." She smirked as Rayah yanked back the skirt. "I spotted loads of bike racks in front of the halls, plenty without a lock. Emmanuel lies—what? Ten or fifteen miles away?"

'Course Hannah wanted to leave. Quit when anything got harder than level one of PAC-MAN. He glanced at Michelle. All right, Mitch. Shut down the idea.

Instead, Michelle glanced at the top of the Suanna dorm, where a few sparrows let out high chirps. "The sun's still up for a long time. We could make the journey in the light."

Whoa, coming from the girl who's been practicing the A-C-T before A-B-C?

Rayah tossed her handbook at Hannah, crushing the remaining dandelion grenades and astonishing all parties present. "Read that." Voice still somehow ever-gentle. "If you leave the premises without permission, Mr. Rezzen can blacklist you from any college. Even those who flunked the physical test today will forever have a bad note from King's Academy just because they failed to run a mile in time."

Hannah's Band-Aid fingernails dug into the ground-dandelion-and-dirt powder and piled it on top of the handbook—perhaps to give it a proper funeral.

Rayah lurched forth and snagged the book away, wiping off the filth.

"Maybe *you* should read it." Michelle hugged her sides with her arms. "For instance, one rule says if we drop below a 3.5 GPA, they will expel us. *Us*, as in just the transfers, not the students who have always gone here. They have set us up to fail no matter what. We might as well quit now and return to Emmanuel."

Danny squinted into the sun, searching for an answer. Blinking away blue spots, he discovered nothing.

"Where is this coming from?" He rubbed his eyelids. "Mitch, your parents will kill you if you can't get into a college. Besides, aren't you the girl who likes to play games with the odds against you?" She had given him an extra-large pile for War, after all.

"There's a difference between improbable and impossible, Danny." Michelle sighed. "I have a feeling we're dealing with the latter at this school."

"When did that ever stop you?"

"I guess when I tried track last year and learned that some things, no matter how hard you try to fight them, can't be beat."

At Emmanuel, her dad had urged Michelle to join the distance runners. Dead last every time, she had stayed hours after practices to perfect her form and chisel down her running time. Halfway through the season, she'd barely made a dent in her personal best. The only thing she had ever quit halfway through. Her dad had refused to talk to her for two weeks.

A group of chattering girls in soccer uniforms ambled past the group to the other side of the building. Such a rancid stench of sweat and body odor fanned from them, they made Michelle smell a great deal more like vanilla. The door on the corner of the building beeped as they slid a keycard through.

"If you leave, where will you stay?" Danny gestured to Phrat River. "I doubt your parents will welcome you with open arms after you turn down this scholarship. Remember how your dad acted in the dining commons, Mitch?"

Michelle bit her lip, tapping the ground with her purple heels, causing clouds of dust to form. Her foot stopped bouncing, and her eyes lit up. "Jeremy. We'll stay with him."

"Jeremy?" Danny frowned.

"You know, the kid with acne. Wears drama on his sleeve. Once wet himself when he had to dissect frogs his sophomore year."

Danny held up a hand. "Yes, I know him. But, Mitch, Jeremy's house? Of all the people!"

"Why not? I saw him get off your bus earlier when my dad dropped me off. I think he escaped the morning assembly. And his mother leads my youth group. The woman's basically a second mom to me."

"Did you ask him if you could stay?"

She wiggled back and forth as she pulled her phone out of her tight rear pocket. When she had retrieved it, she wiped the screen with her fist to get rid of the sweat and tapped the phone several times. After a moment, she growled. "Great cell signal, my butt. I haven't had a decent signal since the second I entered this school."

"Got any data?" Hannah rolled onto her back, staring at the shapeless clouds.

Michelle shook her head. "Dad likes cheap cell-phone plans." She typed a text message to Jeremy and stood with her phone raised high above her head like an official at a track meet about to fire a pistol. The sweat stains on her armpits turned her orange blouse to a near red. She stood on her toes, not elevating herself much higher because of her heels. "Come on, come on." She groaned.

"Yeah, what gives? It was working just fine when we toured this place." Danny sighed.

"Two guesses. One: When all the students moved in, the cell signal couldn't support us all. Two: Ned intentionally crippled it." Of course, conspiracy-theory Michelle would say that.

Danny drew a tree in the dust and then smudged it away. Even after he had finished, Michelle still persevered in her attempt to reach satellites in the heavens.

"Aliens got your signal by now." Danny rubbed his warm neck. The sunburn was spreading.

Michelle's custom "sent message" sound, a gush of wind, announced itself from her phone. She exhaled a sigh and collapsed onto the ground.

"Now we wait for his response." She cradled the phone in her lap.

So they lingered. Five minutes … six … By the time they reached seven, Hannah had grown impatient—as Hannahs tend to do—and left for her dorm.

She returned a few minutes later with a deck of cards, Michelle's. "War, anyone?" She shuffled a deck of clear, thick cards.

"Those the waterproof ones?" Danny asked.

Hannah uncapped Michelle's water bottle and dumped it on the stack of cards.

He hoped they were the waterproof ones. Droplets splashed onto the dust, forming small pools of mud. The cards only retained dew.

Rayah sighed and wiped the cards with her dirty dress and returned them to Hannah unscathed.

To avoid the stream of sludge snaking his direction, Danny scooted backward into direct sunlight. The air smelled the way rain does when it hits pavement, earthy and stale. "Those are Michelle's cards, right? I remember she got them for Christmas two years ago. Did she lend you her key so you could get into her dorm?"

Michelle palmed her forehead while Hannah dealt the cards, causing water droplets to hit whomever she launched a card at. "We forgot to tell you." Michelle sighed. "They placed us in the same room, 315 Suanna. We thought they did the same for everyone from Emmanuel until you described your roommates."

"Another excellent reason to leave." Hannah tossed the last card in the deck at Rayah and fixed her own pile. "They sound like my mom ... a little bit too high on life."

Michelle stood once again to wave her phone around. At last it *ding*'ed.

She sat again, whipped out the device, and beamed at the glowing screen. "His mother started to prepare beds," she informed the group. "They say it'll be a tight squeeze, but they have a room for us three girls and an air mattress in Jeremy's room for Danny."

Oh, boy. Lodging with Jeremy. The perfect dream.

Fans of cards plummeted toward the mud.

Her phone buzzed once more. "He says to meet us at Emmanuel because he lives much farther away. I'll text him when we arrive there."

Hannah, with a speed quicker than Danny had seen her move during the first Emmanuel fire, disappeared behind the building for a moment and returned with two bicycles: one red, one gold.

For a moment he considered the opportunity to go home. So what if future colleges asked him why King's had expelled him? They could take the case to court if they wanted to. But remember what happened when his family had tried to get the courts to listen about Judah? Did plenty of research then, Danny. The school had a team of lawyers that could knock down any case.

He drew another tree in the dirt. Where would he go to school? Would Jeremy's mom homeschool all of them? Because that's the only choice he had, and the woman already worked a full-time job. Even if she didn't, she was taking care of Jeremy. And that *was* a full-time job.

"Could only hold two bikes at once." Hannah parked the stolen vehicles against the dorm by a brick with a naughty picture carved into it. "Be back in a minute with the other two."

Better not play with fire. Besides, Mom wouldn't let him back home if he left here. And Jeremy's mom shouldn't have to take care of four extra kids. He couldn't be a burden like his mom. He just couldn't.

Danny bolted up. "Hannah, only take one. I'm not going."

"Grab none." Rayah's nervous fingers fumbled with her damp head-wrap. "I'm staying here."

The group glanced at Rayah, eyes wide and faces slack.

She cleared her throat, voice tight. "Who knows what my dad would do if I left here? Even in the safety of Jeremy's house, he can find me."

At this point, everyone took a sudden interest in their shoes.

"Valid," Michelle answered at last. "We won't bug you anymore about it, Rayah." She rounded on Danny. "What's your excuse?"

When he presented his defense, both Hannah and Michelle folded their arms over their chests.

Hannah growled. "In a day or in a month, Danny, they'll send you home eventually."

"Agreed." Michelle stood next to Hannah, towering like the King's buildings. "Might as well beat them to the sucker punch. They probably invited Emmanuel students just so they could humiliate them."

They waited in silence. For a moment Danny wanted to forget all his responsibilities and join the girls. But then again … rules. His mother. Poor Jeremy's mother. His future.

And Rayah … Rayah, he had to stay to protect her. Without a close friend from Emmanuel, the school would eat her alive.

"Coming?" Michelle kicked up dust with her heels.

Another long pause.

"Enjoy burning up in the dorms." She grabbed a bicycle, straddled the seat, and pedaled away. Hannah followed and craned her head over her shoulder for a moment to say, "See you after they expel you."

Rayah and Danny watched them ride all the way down the bumpy gravel road and disappear.

Chapter Eleven

A POUNDING AT THE STALL DOOR FORCED DANNY TO hurl his lunch of mashed potatoes and peas into the toilet. He meant to rasp, "Be out in a minute," but, instead, more vomit came. He was leaving all sorts of contributions for King's today. He needed to pace himself.

This time the rapping at the door came in a gentler register. Accompanying it was the giggle of a toy ghost that held a plunger out by the third sink. "You OK in there?" The voice belonged to Duke.

Danny heaved in response. Another knock and Danny twisted around one more time to click open the stall door before revisiting the bowl to retch, coughing what tasted like old pizza. The sour smell of the sick contents intensified in the hot, humid air of his dorm.

A warm hand clapped his back. On any other occasion, he would have appreciated the gesture of comfort, but now his skin burned.

"The school food does that to you." Duke released his grip. "Wait till they take away the nice stuff they give to the parents. I never left the toilet for three days during my freshman year."

Yay. Looked forward to it. Danny hardened his abs as another bubbling monster shot out of his stomach and into the john. This time only hot bile came out.

Duke left the bathroom. A few minutes later someone came in. Behind Danny the water turned on from a faucet. Must've been the third or fourth one because the sound-activated ghost let out a high giggle. After shutting off the faucet, the person set something beside him that sounded like plastic hitting tile.

Danny looked over and found a blue cup with nearly clear water, albeit a slight yellow.

"Had to rinse the thing out a few times." Duke's knees cracked as he bent down on the dirty brown tile. "Believe I drank something sticky in it before, but Dean just ran out of dish soap, so I had to make do with hot water for a cleaning agent. Drink. You lost a lot of fluid."

Danny obeyed and tipped his head back, letting the cool water run down his scalded throat. He choked a little because it tasted the way beer smelled, but he forced himself to swallow half the cup.

Two minutes later, he vomited the contents.

Duke clucked his tongue. "Guess your stomach refuses to keep anything. I'd suggest a hospital, but the closest one is forty minutes away. Not to mention the principal allows students to leave only if they put in a request of absence two weeks in advance. Unless you're dying ... and even then he might not make an exception."

Danny's stomach boiled again. Dying didn't sound so bad at the moment.

Duke concluded with. "So I would say go to Nurse Nintin."

"Where? Where do I—" Danny struggled to force out each word.

"Take a right from the administration building toward a little white shack. A seven- or eight-minute walk. Now if you don't mind ..." Duke dumped the rest of the water into the bowl, flushed the toilet, and motioned for Danny to move out of the stall. "The other two stalls stopped working, and the occupant in the last one hasn't left in the past twenty minutes."

Ah, figured there was a catch for why he was being nice. On all fours, Danny crawled, palming the sticky floor. He caught a pleasant view of an ant congregation underneath the graffitied urinals. With his legs still in the stall, he turned around and rasped, "Thanks."

"Don't mention it"—a frowning Duke slammed the door and kicked out Danny's feet—"to anyone."

As Danny forced his way down the stairs, doubled over, he ran into Gabe.

The kid palmed the sweaty wall, his hand just above a laminated sign for open-house hours. "Want help?"

Gabe draped one of Danny's arms over his shoulder, and the two tottered down a gravel path onto a cobblestone one.

Duke's predictions of their ETA came up a bit shy considering it took them twenty-five minutes to reach the building instead of seven. This owed to Danny's faltering, staggering steps and the fact he had to stop on the side of the road to dry heave three separate times.

Glad they were not timing him on how quickly he got there. Would've been expelled by now. Danny apologized after the third time, but Gabe seemed unfazed by the delay.

"Would rather help a friend than attend a meeting about the campus's history."

Mind still fuzzy, Danny recalled a vague image of the Welcome Weekend events. He had missed the new-student orientation meeting about King's legacy. A shame.

After forever, they reached the squat shack's white double doors painted with bared-teeth lions in nurses' hats. All the sounds of students flicking Frisbees and others stringing the elastic of hammocks against thick trees sounded like echoes … miles away.

Danny had begun to hyperventilate, and his vision darkened as he dove into the doorknob. A frigid burst of AC did little to aid his skin prickling as with fire ants. He tried to slow his breathing, and the black halo around his eyes disintegrated into blurry vision. Each breath tasted sterile and cold—the flavor of fluorescent light—like every waiting area in a doctor's office. He forced himself to focus on the blurry elements of the room. Old medical magazines on a short table, a dangling TV playing *Family Feud*, tissues and hand sanitizer on the receptionist's desk … no use. He still had to vomit.

Gabe rose and pestered the front-desk worker for something Danny could puke into. With a visible eye roll, the receptionist handed over a bucket.

Moments later, Danny hurled into it.

"That covers the 'Why did you come here?' question."

The clean-shaven receptionist, with a low yet very snarky voice, eyed Danny with his nose held high. Probably tired of dealing with parents all day. His mother refused to let Emmanuel give him most medications. Multiply his mom by a thousand, and that was what the receptionist had to endure during Welcome Weekend. Poor guy.

The receptionist handed the patient a clipboard, pinched by two well-groomed fingertips. He held the clipboard far away from him as if the thing threatened to bite his whole arm off. "Your paperwork." A thin-lipped smile curled up his thin cheeks. He couldn't have been a day over thirty.

Danny grabbed the papers and the blue pen with a shaky hand, which the receptionist ignored as he returned to his computer. Danny's trembling fingers spilled the ink all over the sheet. "Should I fill out these questions without an adult?" he whispered, trying not to open his mouth too wide because of his rancid breath. "I don't turn eighteen for another couple of years."

Gabe shrugged and readjusted himself in the maroon plastic chair. "From what I've heard from my roommates, King's Academy never has had a perfect record when it comes to the law. Lucky they got a good team of lawyers. Just answer the questions so they can fix you."

Ah, like they'd fix their AC problem, too, huh?

Danny scribbled his way through various check boxes. He handed the finished sheet back to the receptionist, who issued an insincere "thank you" before facing his computer once more.

Ten minutes later, a kinder nurse in baggy turquoise scrubs and huge spectacles with bug eyes called out his name.

Danny leaned over to tell Gabe he could leave. He didn't want to be a burden. But instead of saying anything, he puked, covering both himself and his new friend in vomit.

Dang, Danny. How much had he eaten?

The nurse waddled back on thick legs to fetch two pairs of patient gowns. When she emerged through the wooden door, she handed Danny a faded sky-blue one and Gabe a white one with charcoal polka dots.

Gabe stared at the garment. "I'll fit right in with the cows back home."

Danny's lips twitched.

"You'll have to excuse the small selection." The nurse's voice sounded like she had swallowed a gulp of helium. "We've had so many patients come in for heat stroke or food poisoning today. Vomiting, like your friend over here. Oh goodness, so many outfits to wash ..."

They slipped into the gowns in the waiting area and pitched the foul-scented clothes in the lobby trash can. The receptionist flared his nostrils at them but said nothing.

The nurse led them back to the farthest room on the right. Danny had to use the wall with its various medical-cartoon posters as support, clutching his vomit bucket in the other arm. Its sour smell was enough to make him want to vomit again on the spot. Passing a scale and a measuring stick on the wall, they ducked into a room with beige paint and a burlap curtain in the middle of the room.

Danny situated himself on a bed with a paper covering. The nurse stuck a thermometer under his tongue and waited. She pulled the device out after it beeped and tutted under her blue mask. "101.4, and that hot dorm won't help you any."

She asked Danny to list his symptoms for her, and he struggled to do so without vomiting. Nurse Nintin, or so read her plastic name tag, poured him a cup of water that, unlike the drinks in the dorm, bore no tint. "Drink that in small doses"—she tapped the rim with a gloved finger—"since you have difficulty keeping even liquids down. From the sound of it, you drank that cup your roommate gave you too fast."

He probed the cup's contents with his tongue. Tasted cool and a bit like the paper cup she put the liquid in. Minute by minute, he allowed for more and more water down his throat.

Nurse Nintin waited ten minutes, and when he did not send the water migrating back into his bucket, she pulled a bottle of Pepto-Bismol out of the cabinet. "Today during one of the meetings, the parents signed medical consent forms." She poured the bubblegum-pink liquid into a small cup. "My receptionist reviewed your papers, and your mother complied with the use of Pepto-Bismol—the only medication she agreed we could give you. My oh my, your mother had the most unbending form out of the bunch."

"We've never excelled at flexibility." He laughed and regretted it because of the aftertaste.

His mother usually believed in toughing out sickness instead of using medicines of any kind. Once a doctor spent twenty minutes convincing her to let them administer numbing medicine for surgery on the ACL he had torn playing rec basketball.

"I can't give you any other medication." The nurse swung open a cabinet and sighed at the plethora of orange bottles. "At least not over-the-counter ones because this building just operates as a mere school nurse's office. Surely you had one back at whatever school you came from?"

He nodded, thinking about the dark, ramshackle room that smelled of urine and dust. Visited that room plenty of times thanks to his mother's tough-out-every-sickness-at-school mantra.

Danny tipped his head back, emptying the cup of its sweet contents. A rosy residue remained after he drank it.

"The Pepto should kick in in about twenty minutes." Nurse Nintin shut the cabinet and peeled off her gloves, tossing them into a bin. "If you still struggle to maintain your liquids within twelve hours, come back here, and I will phone an ambulance. The fever shouldn't last longer than a day, two at most. Let me know if it persists after that. Otherwise, I need to ask the pair of you to scoot on out of here. The office closed at five, and that was twenty minutes ago."

No wonder the receptionist was so rude. A prickle of guilt stabbed Danny in the chest.

Gabe and Danny thanked Nurse Nintin for her help. When they arrived at the front desk to sign out, the receptionist seemed to perk up considerably when he heard they would depart.

"Feel better soon." He already had his satchel swung over his shoulder, ready to bolt.

Right as the door clicked shut behind them, Danny's stomach seared in pain. Here they went again. He doubled over and knelt, palming the itchy grass and heaving again. His labored breaths caused the dust on the ground to rise, filling his nostrils with the dry, dusty scent.

A group of students playing a game of catch with a football paused when they saw the two boys in hospital gowns and moved their session to a stretch of hills nearby.

"I think they're jealous of our fashion choices." Gabe made a gentle tug at Danny's shoulder. And then another one, stronger this time. "Dan, should we go back?"

Danny looked up through the nurse-lion screen doors to watch the receptionist flip a sign in scarlet lettering: *Closed.*

The sick ex-patient flopped onto his back, wondering how the sparse clouds in the sky could spin so fast.

Gabe shook Danny. "You OK?"

He tried to nod, but the back of his head bumped into something dome-like—an anthill? A prickling sensation scuttled up and down his body at the thought of thousands of insects crawling on his skin. "This nausea problem goes away." Danny's chest relaxed when the itchiness ceased. "It always has."

Gabe parked next to him. "Dan, we go to a school that you can't escape. I have this horrible feeling nothing could go away from us, even if we ran a four-minute mile."

Danny hardly remembered the journey back to his empty room full of beer cans, or why he jerked awake with his chest soaking and cold. Two pairs of arms encircled his before he received answers to his questions.

"Morning, Princess," came a voice belonging to whoever gripped his right arm. "Two in the morning to be exact."

The two guards dragged him into the hallway, where he bumped into an Emmanuel sophomore. The guy's hair and shirt were drenched. Did someone dump a bucket of water onto him? Why?

In a stupor, he shook his head. We could've used that water treatment a couple hours back after the physical trials. These King's folks aren't very timely.

Although the strangers released their holds, they forced Danny to keep moving forward by jabbing him in the back with a heavy stick—baseball bat?—as a groggy Dean's voice barked at him. "Keep walking."

What did he think he'd been doing? Hula hooping?

They rushed down the concrete steps and out the doors, meeting five more Emmanuel students, who had two escorts each.

The King's students herded them into a ring, and the group made its way past the golden water fountain, still glittering in the pitch night, by the auditorium, and toward shadows of leaves and vines that resembled a garden.

Even in his dazed state, Danny recalled how the principal seemed to enjoy this landmark the most on the campus tour. He scanned the area for any adults. None. At least, he couldn't imagine he'd see many roaming around at two in the morning.

Everything smelled wet, miserable, and a bit like fear as someone in the group had peed himself.

"Line up!" Dean thrust a satchel from his shoulder onto the grass. The bag landed with a loud clunk. The noise jolted Danny awake. Oh, crap. (He didn't think "crap.")

Within seconds the cluster formed a single-file line full of trembling guys in front of a plant that appeared to bear leaves the size of Danny's head.

"We have a tradition here whenever Emmanuel students stay on campus, inspired by an ancient Assyrian practice, thanks to our Ancient History teacher Mr. Sarong."

"Guy's taught here for twenty years," a voice, sounding like it belonged to Duke, underneath a hood added. "He looks like a walking tombstone."

Even in the darkness, Danny saw the whites of Dean's eyes roll into his head because of the interruption. "Yes, they've met old people before. Anyway, we adopted this custom from the Assyrians any time we have visitors from the other side of the tracks. Sometimes Emmanuel stops by for state cross-country meets, and they stay overnight in the dorms or for speech-and-debate tournaments. Whenever any group of *Emmanuelites* drops by, we make sure to leave at least one student with a parting gift."

Thumps from Dean's army boots clashed with the night choruses of cicadas and nocturnal frogs. The world was wide awake for a nightmare. Dean paced, crunching fallen leaves from the garden under his boots. "For you non-history buffs, the Assyrians used this particular practice whenever they took someone captive. Seeing our school represents a sort of prison, we found this tradition to be rather fitting."

He bent down and fished for the heavy item inside the bag. Danny shivered, having a terrible idea he knew the exact contents. When Dean's hand stopped rustling, he grabbed the item, paused, and gleamed at the group like a ravenous wolf. "By some good luck, they sent us twelve Emmanuel students today, so we have a wider selection to choose from."

The empty bag crumpled to the ground as Dean pulled out the mystery item. The soft glow of a nearly full moon illuminated a thick fishhook in his beefy fist.

Danny's blood iced. *Oh, God.* Vomit lodged in his throat, but he choked it down.

Besides the difference of a few inches, it almost presented a mirror image of the souvenir Judah had acquired during his last visit to King's Academy. Shiny, jagged, thick.

Danny was trying desperately hard to think of something funny to distract himself. But his head was devoid of all jokes. There was nothing funny about this. This was serious.

Deadly serious.

Dean scanned the crowd for a victim, and his gaze stopped at Danny. Danny scanned the scenery for something to shield himself from the horror about to ensue. In the dark, there was nothing to look at. *Wake up!*

The boy with the hook stepped forward in a deliberate motion.

Oh, God. Wake up now!

But the hooded figure gripped Dean and pulled him back into a huddle. The two whispered back and forth for a few moments, a great deal of it being a heated argument amid the shrill of the cicada chorus.

What seemed an eternity later, Dean's silhouette nodded. He slunk toward Danny but angled to the right before the two met toes.

If Danny wasn't his intended victim, then who?

Out of the corner of his eye, Danny saw the boy standing next to him in an Emmanuel golf-team sweatshirt quaking so much one would have thought he was experiencing a seizure. Even in the darkness, Danny recognized the boy from the monthly *Emmanuel* magazine. Almost always they featured a picture of the student, even long after golf season had finished and often accompanied with an appeal to donate more money to the school.

He was the son of Emmanuel's ex-principal. Any damage done to him would mean a direct blow to their old school.

Dean tilted his head to the side and surveyed the wobbly target. With clawed fingers, he gripped the boy's chin tightly to hold him steady. "Students of King's Academy!" Dean announced in a loud voice, perhaps trying to drown out the whimpers coming from his intended sacrifice. "Let's make ourselves fishers of men."

Then he drove the fishing hook into the boy's nose.

Chapter Twelve

"HATE HIM OR NOT, YOU HAVE TO TELL Mr. Rezzen what happened last night." Rayah's whisper echoed in the atrium.

Danny dodged the question and bumped into a table with a cluster of students in orange improv-group T-shirts. He apologized, wiped his eyes with his fingers, and motioned to a booth with a well-crafted sign. Blinked once, twice to see it clearly. "Would that cover the required art credit?"

Rayah stared at the orange sign-up sheet on the table for a moment. "Graphic-design class? I believe so."

Good, her mind was off the fishhook incident. "Put your name down, Rayah. You're the only reason the student council stopped using Comic Sans font back at Emmanuel."

A sheepish smile. She scribbled her name on the sheet and gestured to another booth that hooked her interest: robotics club.

As she hunched over the table with free pens, the smell of cotton candy pulled his attention. Over his shoulder, he spotted a student from the initiation last night reaching with a shaky hand for a bag of the blue candy.

Ugh, couldn't anyone stop reminding him of last night? His thumbs rubbed the large bags under his eyes. They had grown into such heaping satchels that they persisted in reminding him of the sack that carried the fishing hook. No matter how raucous the hum of conversations in the math-building atrium, he couldn't drown out the victim's shrieks when the hook had plunged in. Or the black blood that spurted out against the backdrop of night.

"Thank you for joining the team!" A girl at the graphic-design table with a nasal septum piercing—*why did it have to be in her nose?*—and purple streaks in her hair waved to Rayah, pulling Rayah's attention away from the robotics-club booth.

The graphic-design student handed both Rayah and Danny fliers. They tucked them away in folders full of twenty or so other handouts from various organizations they had visited. The two ambled at a slow pace, each feigning glances at the tables for the school clubs and class electives.

Ducking under a banner, they sat with their backs to a wall beneath a staircase, away from most of the crowd. A strong buttery scent from the engineering club handing out popcorn fanned from a display case nearby.

Rayah eyed the passersby and dropped her voice so low even Danny struggled to hear it. "Figured you would rather talk about the incident in private."

He'd rather not talk about it at all, but he thanked her for thinking of him. "I doubt Ned would do anything even if all eleven students came to him about the hazing." Danny hoped this would put an end to the discussion. "Minus the twelfth, who could maybe phone him from the hospital."

"Still, you should give it a try."

"Ray, the tradition has lasted at least twenty years. Ned must know about it by now and doesn't care."

Her knees nestled in her chin. "Secrets have lasted longer than that in history." A moment's silence sent her rummaging through her folder to pull out the orange sheet from the graphic-design class. She squinted at the paper.

"Says I have to take it either fifth or eighth period. I can't quit English at fifth. I have it with you, after all ..." She nodded at Danny.

He understood. He would rather take his classes with someone he knew too.

"Eighth period I have a study hall. I don't mind dropping that. My parents always wanted me to overstuff my schedule, but maybe I should check with my advisor. Any idea where I could find her office?"

Danny consulted his school map and found the advisor Ms. Hani in the administration building. The same place Ned worked.

Rayah slid the orange paper back into her ballooning folder. "I'll visit her after we grab lunch. But before that"—she pointed at Danny—"we need to sign you up for an art and a sport since we're required to do both here."

They faced the atrium with its arching streamers, its carnival-food smells, and clustered booths. Students moved through each one like clogged arteries, each little blood cell bumping into another one.

"Track and art-appreciation class. Got it."

"Danny."

"What? I can run and I can appreciate."

"I would appreciate it if you put your name down for graphic design."

He scrunched his nose at her. "Art and I don't get along well."

"You're great with computers!" Rayah untucked her knees. "Better than the entire Emmanuel population. Remember? The IT guys would come to *you* when the teachers had trouble with electronics. And we'd have yet another class together. We must stick together in a place like this."

Danny's forehead creased. Rayah had never argued this much in her life. Something about the atmosphere of the school seemed to change ... everything. Maybe it was something in the water.

He rubbed his neck. "Fine."

She delivered a near-silent squeal and squeezed his arm. A smile threatened to erupt on her face. "Thank you! The only other girl in that class I know lives on my floor ... and she stole my clothes and towel when I took a shower."

Wow. Glad to know there was gender equality when it came to cruelty across campus. Go twenty-first century. "Remember, Ray, you want to *convince* me to join this class, not sprint as far away as possible."

A shy laugh. "You'll meet plenty of other charming Suanna neighbors in classes we have together. One likes to pick at scabs—and not her scabs. Try not to sit in front of her ... or next to her ... or anywhere near her. Another enjoys spoiling milk for a week and then planting the moldy drink in someone else's room when they forget to lock the door. Oh! And we have one who ..."

Her soft voice evaporated as Danny curved around the speech-and-debate-team table. On a golden overlay tablecloth, a trophy in the shape of a goblet seized his attention. The golden bevels in the rim were reminiscent of the chalice that used to live in Emmanuel's chapel before someone had stolen it. They never did find the culprit. He eyed the trophy with slitted eyes and pursed mouth.

A kid in khakis and a sorrowful expression waved at him from behind the golden bowl of the award. "Hey, want to sign up to surrender every Saturday of your year to visit a cold school at 6 a.m. where you give four speeches"—his voice cracked about ten times—"but win nothing because other competitors take this club too seriously?"

"You should really go into advertising." Danny laughed, mouth still having a terrible aftertaste from the other day.

The sallow youth shrugged, his suit jacket sagging. "The debate students who really sell the club left for lunch and deserted us. All that's left are the dramatic-interpretation students."

The group that huddled behind the table all wore gray faces and hunched necks. How had they managed to have their souls sucked out so early in life? Hannah would be a great puzzle piece for the group. Wow. He missed her. Never thought he'd say that ... or, er, think that.

"I'll think about it." Danny gave a thumbs-up to the student at the booth. Yeah, probably wouldn't give it a second thought after this.

"Don't!" The speech student's bloodshot eyes bulged. "Thinking leads to dangerous things."

Rayah and Danny squeezed their way to the track-and-field table, where the coach managed to bully Rayah into signing up for the girls' team after telling everyone at the table and in the near vicinity about her quick mile time. The girls' distance coach, a pear-shaped woman in her fifties, joined in the urges.

With each prod, Rayah sank deeper and deeper into herself until she threatened to melt into a puddle. Served her right. She forced him to sign up for graphic design.

Rayah signed her name. Then she hid in the neck of her dress like a turtle as the coach announced to the whole atrium, "We have the fastest transfer on the girls' team!"

Rayah pressed her palms to her cheeks as she shuffled quickly to leave the atrium. The third-grade spelling bee all over again.

"Look at her go." The female coach jabbed a scarlet fingernail in Rayah's direction. "How fast those stubby little legs move!"

Embarrassment. E-M-B-A ... did the word have one *R* or two? Glad they stopped spelling tests after middle school.

Taking Danny's arm, almost as if she wanted to use him as a shield, Rayah bolted out of the atrium toward the dining commons. Into the harsh sunlight and heat ... out of the noise. Rayah didn't slow down until they had given the Seleucid Center for Mathematics building a wide berth.

On the way to the dining commons, every tree on campus wore a hammock of some sort. Several had two or three, and the weaker trees bowed inward on the brink of collapse.

Far away enough from the club convention, Rayah's brisk walk transformed into a lazy stroll when the warm sunlight hugged their skins. Everything smelled green and good in the world.

When they reached the rosy dining building and cracked open the doors, a cool, sterile wind gusted out of the red doors.

Danny shivered in the burst of air conditioning. "No place has the right temperature here, does it?"

Rayah agreed.

Pungent odors, a mix of burnt chicken and second-day split-pea soup, greeted their entrance. Danny stifled his nostrils with an index finger. "Duke was right. When the parents leave, so do the decent cooks."

"I hope they pick out caterpillars from the lettuce, unlike the Emmanuel chefs."

However, their venture downstairs revealed they did not pick out any critters from the salad because no such commodities existed. In fact, even after spending ten minutes weaving through lines under various dangling lions, Danny spied *no* fruit or vegetables. At least, nothing fresh.

"I would suggest the apples." Rayah gestured to a basket of Red Delicious, which had the appearance of wax fruit. "But I bit into one of those this morning. Rock solid."

"Any other plants?" Danny's voice came out louder than he expected. They no longer played the soft piano music.

She bit her lip. "I saw green beans, but they mixed them with bacon, so that fails to fit your vegetarian diet."

"Any entrees without meat?"

"They mixed meatballs into the pasta, taco meat in the Mexican line, pepperoni pizza, and baked chicken. I believe that covers all the stations."

Danny scooped a warm orange plate into his hand. It still had food crusted on the rim from incomplete washing. "Mashed potatoes for a meal again, I see."

His stomach simmered in reply. Sorry, pal. He patted his abdomen. The school had to have other students with health issues. They'd serve more fruit and vegetables tomorrow. He hoped.

He slid into a hard seat and banged his plate on the table. This time the cafeteria seemed to forget about tablecloths. The population in the freezing room had declined a great deal from the day before. And the bright, cheery voices belonging to parents had disappeared behind the sunken cheeks of hungry students.

Rayah took a seat beside him and dug her knife into a chicken drowning in ranch dressing. "Suppose we leave." Her knife ceased after ten slices through the tough poultry meat.

"This cafeteria?" Danny glanced up and realized they'd removed the hanging plants. Now it was just a wooden ceiling with all its cracks and spiderwebs displayed for the world to see. "Know of any other places to eat? One of my roommates has a stash of Pop-Tarts. Not that I would survive if I took any from him."

After tasting the pungent potatoes, which the kitchen staff had infused with spicy red-pepper flakes, he tilted back his chin and drained his water cup. Guess cafeteria food stayed the same no matter where you went, even under the guise of "dining commons."

A knife hit the plate with a soft chink. "No, Danny. Suppose we *leave*."

He choked. Coughing and pounding his fist against his rib cage, he felt his face and neck flush. "What? Rayah, think about your dad."

"Either this school *or* he is going to kill me, Danny. I'd rather go down with a good meal in my stomach and not worry whether someone is going to plunge a fishhook into my nose."

"First, you become more talkative after Hannah and Michelle leave." He interspersed some words with hacks and hard swallows. "Then you want to risk never going to college after this school expels you for leaving the premises."

Rayah flipped open her overstuffed folder and pulled out the handbook. The lion vector looked a scarier sort of red in the low lighting. "Did some light reading last night and discovered all the ways they could make us leave this school. For instance, if a girl wears a sleeveless top—expelled. If a student breaks curfew, poof—gone." She flashed both hands like a magician talking about a vanishing act. "A student prays in class—he or she doesn't have a prayer for college."

She drew a finger over the rule in the handbook as if highlighting it. "Even if we follow the rules, they break easier than a family, Danny. And who knows if last night's initiation is the only one?"

Danny shuddered.

Rayah glanced at the rulebook again and sighed. She shook her head. "Never mind. You're right. My dad would kill me if I left. And I can't give up on college … not yet." Her dark eyes burned into his. "But we need to put an end to the hazing before it gets to Suanna … or strikes your dorm again. If you don't take it to Mr. Rezzen, at least inform the police."

"How? My cell phone that has no service here? Even if they did pick up, what evidence do we have?"

"Twelve witnesses." She rose a little in her seat, looking taller than when she stood. "You could get all of them to testify. Twelve witnesses with one in a hospital."

"Yeah, and Kim's son said he got into a fishing accident. Dean threatened to do more damage if he told the doctors the truth."

"Put him in a court. What will Dean do? Stick fishing hooks in all the juries' noses?"

Wouldn't put it past him. He held up a hand and the light died in Rayah's pupils. "Say we managed to convince all witnesses—very frightened witnesses, mind you. Dean threatened all of us—to pull together a court case."

"But—"

"And say we could somehow convince a jury with no evidence and far more testimonials from King's Academy students who participated in the initiation—remember they outnumbered us two to one. Even if those factors magically worked themselves out, tell me, Ray, where will we find the money for legal fees?"

Rayah slumped.

"Sorry." Oh, the chilly guilt in his gut. "It's just ... my family went through this once before. Believe me, we wanted to fight it with everything. But the folks at Emmanuel have nothing to give. And the people at King's have an incredible team of lawyers."

"I know."

"My family researched past court cases. King's always wins. Either financially or just with better legal protection. And it's not just King's. Plenty of schools in America get away with crap like this, or at least what we found in our research."

"But"—her bottom lip trembled—"what about students who have graduated? Didn't any of them have horror stories to tell?"

He lifted his shoulders in a shrug. "The hazing ceremony is for Emmanuel students only, and until this week, most Emmanuel students didn't attend this school. So I don't think any graduates from here ever had to deal with that."

"But they had to handle other things, like illegal surveillance methods. What about cameras and speakers in our rooms? One girl was trying to cover her fire alarm with a towel to prevent King's from spying on her."

"All hearsay, Ray. Again, no evidence. Even if a graduate took something to court, King's has enough dirt on a student to convince their future college, or future employer, to get rid of them if they try anything in court."

Her jaw shook as it dropped. "So even after we graduate, we carry these burdens with us our whole lives?"

"Unfortunately, yeah. Sucks doesn't it?"

Rayah nodded, lower lids brimming with tears.

Great move, Danny. By instinct, Danny placed a hand on her shoulder, but she shook her head at him.

The clanging of forks on plates held the conversation for the next few minutes until Rayah wrinkled her nose at the tang of week-old ranch and said, "Even if we can't sue King's, we have to have a say in what we eat. You sure you don't want to talk to the head of the cafeteria about this food?"

His abdomen burned after he swallowed the next gulp of potatoes. Acid reflex scalded his throat behind a refrain of stomach growls. He had already turned her down about the initiation thing and made her cry doing that. Maybe if he said *yes*, he wouldn't completely ruin her day.

"Tell you what, Ray." He gestured to his tummy. "We'll let this guy do the talking for me."

They questioned their way through six different workers until they finally received an answer about where to find the dining-commons manager.

"Down the hall, past the restrooms, and to your right." A disheveled worker dumped a pile of warm plates onto a rack. The poor guy caught his finger under some of the dishes and swore. Rayah and Danny offered to grab him ice from the drink machine, but this made him curse them and all their families and anything else he could name at the moment, waving his purpling, crushed finger.

"Maybe some of those words he used have a different meaning here." Danny swung open a wooden door into a carpeted hallway. "All the four-letter ones were probably synonyms for *love*."

"Pretty sure those words mean the same thing everywhere you go."

They found themselves in front of an office door with the nameplate *Fred Coriander, Director of Food Services*. Bent blinds hid the window that peered into the room.

Danny pressed his ear to the door and heard a deep voice. Danny whispered, "We have located a life form."

Rayah peered at the window, eyes flitting to the nameplate, to the water leak in the ceiling in the shape of a pepper, and then to Danny. "On a phone call, you think?"

He tapped a knuckle against the door, but no one on the other side answered the knock. Next he tried the handle, twisting it slowly. To his surprise, the knob turned.

"Not locked."

Rayah's fingers twitched. "Maybe we should wait a few minutes."

Despite her suggestion, he cracked open the wooden door to peek inside. A balding man, Coriander, sat behind an untidy desk, papers everywhere. This reminded him of Hannah's description of Jesse's office back at Emmanuel.

In front of the desk, leaned back in a chair, a puffy eye came in and out of light as the shadows of a ceiling fan waved over it. Duke.

"Multiple complaints about you, even though we stuck you with the dishwashers, away from the students." Coriander flipped through a packet of papers. "Even one about pouring dishwater on a girl's head."

Pouring buckets on people's chests, dishwater on girl's heads, what was with these guys and improper use of liquids?

"Don't need the lecture." Duke sunk into the chair. "Get plenty of those from the Catholic mom."

"Dishwater, Duke! On her head!" The man palmed a large, sweaty forehead. "Does that not constitute at least a firm talk with your manager?"

Duke wiped his hands on his red cafeteria apron. Guess he worked here. Never mentioned it. Probably hoped Danny didn't know.

Judah had scrubbed dishes at a town buffet one summer and often lied about his job when church members asked what he did for work. "Oh, mow lawns here or there. Lots of landscaping," he would answer. "More respectable," he would add aside to Danny with a conspiratorial wink.

A *bang* against the table caused Danny to jump. Fist against a stack of papers, Duke rose from his chair.

"Fred, you try to stop yourself when the students insult your family. She called my sister a—" He stopped as he noticed the beam of light from the cracked door illuminating a lion paperweight at the desk.

Right as he spun around to see the intruder, Danny shut the door and hurried Rayah out of the dining-commons building.

Oh, please say he saw nothing! His puffy eye had faced the door, maybe his eyesight didn't work with that one.

How had Duke's eye gotten to be like that in the first place?

Danny shook his head. Not a priority. They needed to get out of here before he came after them with a butter knife. Or worse … a fishhook.

"What did you—?" Rayah began.

"Just go." He panted, ushering her down the steps outside. "Go, go, go, go, go."

Now was Danny's turn to run away from a building, just as Rayah had earlier. When they had gotten far enough away, they stopped and checked their schedules and praised heaven that the next event read *Ice Cream Social.*

"In this heat and with that terrible lunch, I would eat frozen snails." Rayah fanned herself with her palm, armpits drenched in sweat.

The ice-cream social was set up at a handful of tables in front of the golden water fountain. All of the campus showed for the event as evidenced by the line that wrapped around three buildings.

Rayah and Danny joined the back of the winding queue and inched their way toward the tubs of sweating ice cream on the plastic table coverings. If he imagined hard enough, the air smelled like Neapolitan. If he didn't imagine, well, it smelled like BO and too much cologne from the group of guys in front of him.

"Why did we bolt so fast from the dining commons?" Rayah smeared a palm across her sweaty upper lip. "If we waited another hour, this line could be half the size."

Danny peered over his shoulder. Twelve more students in shorts and tank tops had marshaled behind them.

"Saw my roommate in there," he whispered.

"In Coriander's office?"

"Yeah. And I hope he didn't see me. Because if Duke recognized me, I'll join Kim's son in the hospital. He participated in that hook initiation, you know. He picked out the victim for Dean."

Rayah shuddered. "Do you have someone else on your floor you can stay with? Kind of like when you offer your house to me when you're worried about my dad?"

Up at the tables, a freshman screamed. A Styrofoam bowl of ice cream had landed on her flip-flops and oozed a brown soup of dairy. She clapped a hand to her mouth and let out a laugh.

"Gabe mentioned something about a futon when we walked back from the nurse yesterday." Danny watched a squat junior dash inside through glass doors. "But I doubt his other two roommates will want me there every night. We have hardly enough space for two people in those rooms."

"Since Michelle and Hannah left my room, I would offer, but having boys stay in a girls' dorm—"

"Is against the rules." Dean was a big fan of breaking that one.

She offered a shy smile.

Behind them an uproar of protests commenced, which Danny tried to ignore. Still, he picked up objections such as "back of the line!" and "who said you could cut in front of thirty-some people?"

He winked at Rayah. "Speaking of not following rules." She failed to see or hear this because she had spun around. Her eyes grew wide and her mouth dropped open.

He turned on his ratty sneaker heel to find Hannah and Michelle marching in their direction past the snaking line. They came back?

"What are you—?" Danny began but Michelle shushed him, then silenced the crowd behind her, many of whom had persevered in their protests.

"In a minute! We'll move to the back after I show them something." Michelle thrust her phone in Danny's face. The back of her hand wafted a campfire aroma. "Press play."

He did. He and Rayah watched the screen as smoke poured out of a decrepit building.

Oh, God. Danny, wake up.

Tangerine tongues of fire licked the windows and crawled up the bricks on the little screen. Five seconds in, Michelle clicked pause.

"What did you make us watch?" Danny's knees buckled.

"Emmanuel's chapel." For once in her life, Hannah looked frightened. "They burned everything."

Chapter Thirteen

"WHAT ABOUT JEREMY?" DANNY ASKED MICHELLE, who was busy testing the strings on her tennis racket. "I forgot to ask you yesterday, but why didn't he pick you up from Emmanuel? Too busy practicing Shakespeare monologues or something?"

Michelle's talons fiddled with a loose string. It clicked when she popped it back into place. Rayah listened as she picked at mud in her cleats. Hannah flipped through a comic. "His mom became uneasy about the whole affair about five minutes after she said we could stay. Didn't read the text from Jeremy until we arrived at Emmanuel."

"Uneasy?" The sound of tennis balls clinking against the fence overpowered Danny's question.

"The third Emmanuel fire sent her over the edge, and she said she couldn't take the two of us in. Jeremy called us and said to make a life for ourselves at King's Academy. 'Bad things often lead to great things,' he said, or something crappy and philosophical."

"The way the bad cafeteria food led to a great visit to the toilet last night?" Danny clutched his searing stomach.

Michelle continued, "Fortunately Rachel picked up when we called and let us stay the night with her."

He stared at the tennis court. The billowing scarlet windscreens blocked his vision of the King's players inside the red courts. Even with those out of the way, life-size pictures of the seniors in red uniforms lined the front of the fence. An image of a blonde girl in French braids and sea-green eyes had a bulging head in the warm wind.

Michelle followed his line of vision and smirked. "She's the one with the really good kick serve."

"I don't know what that means."

Michelle rose to practice "ground strokes." Her racket *whooshed* every time she swung the head. "We weren't gone too long, so I doubt anyone noticed." She paused her drills to swing her racket at a buzzing wasp.

"You saw no suspects at Emmanuel?" Rayah strapped the Velcro to her shin guards. The soccer tryout field was only a hundred meters away from the courts. "Or did anyone leave behind any evidence?"

"Besides the spray-painted sign that read, 'All of you deserve to go here' outside the school? No."

Rayah frowned at the green layer of grass caked on the bottom of her cleats. "I wonder what 'here' meant."

"They meant *hell*, Ray." Michelle's bangs swayed in the light afternoon breeze. "When the fire department came, they said the chapel had burned for quite some time. For all we know, the culprit might've left hours before we biked there."

"You talked to a firefighter?"

"Read it on an online newspaper, Danny, our only outlet to the world. When you see a building on fire, you don't stick around and wait for someone to show up who you can talk to."

A neon green ball soared above the fence and headed for Rayah, who had begun rolling up light-blue socks over her shin guards. She ducked, and Danny tossed it back over to the player behind the windscreen.

"I think we should hazard a guess at who could've set Emmanuel on fire." He swallowed a bitter aftertaste from last night's ice cream. It was far less sweet this time around. "If we let them go, they could target any of us here." Already freaked out about the initiation, he didn't need to worry about an arsonist running around campus. The image of Rayah in a burning building once again plagued his mind. He couldn't let that happen to her ... or to any of his friends.

Michelle rolled her eyes. "Like that's going to happen."

"Don't you worry you'll wake up to a burning dorm? The doors only have locks on the *outside*. You know I'm not straying far from possibility."

Frowning, Michelle took a sip from her green water jug. Her sunscreen wafted over from several feet away. Hot day in hell.

"Let's see." Droplets spurted out of her full mouth. Suanna must've had dark water because it came out brown. "Who do we know at this school that despises Emmanuel?" She spread out her arms to indicate everyone.

Hannah licked her thumb to flip a comic-book page. "Still think Kim did it."

The woman whose son had a fishhook in his nose?

"How—literally how?" Michelle turned to re-wind the blue grip on her racket. "Have you heard any news about her lately?"

"Dunno." Hannah shrugged. "Just have a gut feeling. My gut never lies, you know."

Michelle snorted. "Sure, it won't when you're sixty and it realizes how much fried food you've eaten throughout your life."

Hannah waved the comic at them. "Trust me, I know villains."

Because she acted like one ... the *dink* of a tennis ball against a fence caused Danny to jump.

"Kim's really upset that Dean stabbed her son in the nose." Hannah flipped another page. "She had wanted her precious little thing to attend this school. Without a septum and with a good amount of hospitalization, that won't happen for another year."

"You're giving me good reasons for why she should set fire to King's, not Emmanuel."

"Give me a better guess than her, Mitch." With a slow swipe, her thumb grazed another page. She was definitely not reading the book at this point.

"Rather obvious." Michelle stepped farther up a sloping grass hill. "Ned."

Danny bit his cracked lips. Not a terrible suggestion. He seemed more probable than Kim at least.

The comic book settled on Hannah's lap with the hero on the cover, Blacklash, hanging upside-down by his golden whip. "Ned? Seriously?"

"The school burned right around the time he recruited us to attend here. Coincidence?" Michelle slammed her racket down but nailed herself in the leg. "Augh!" She buckled to the ground and nursed her shin.

With an eye roll, Hannah returned to her comic book. "Correlation."

For several moments, Michelle gaped with her eyes shut tight as she gripped her leg.

Finally, through gritted teeth, she said, "Thoughts, Rayah? You agree with me, right?"

Grass stuck to Rayah's fingers from her clawing it out of her cleats. "Too early to hazard a guess."

Good ol' Rayah. She'd make an excellent politician if she didn't have a conscience.

"You hazard everything else." Michelle threw a dismissive wave and returned to her shin. "What about you, Dan? Do you think Ned set Emmanuel on fire?"

Before Danny could answer, a high-pitched squeal came from the door that opened into the tennis courts.

"Babe, you came!" A girl in a flaxen French braid and lilac tennis dress swung open the whiny metal door and collapsed into the thick arms of Dean on the concrete slab in front of the courts. The girl with the kick serve ... whatever that meant.

"'Course I did. I love watching you play." Dean kissed her forehead, then her neck, then her cheek, then her lips ... then the two made out for the next several minutes, only stopping to take gasping breaths.

Ah, young love. Danny gagged, and his three friends wore various shades of disgust on their faces.

Suspect three: Dean. Liked to stick fishhooks in people's noses. Danny wouldn't put it past him to set a school on fire. Ding, ding, ding. They had a winner.

"Got a couple culprits in mind." Danny tore his gaze away from the couple to Rayah's red bench with *D+V* carved into it, scar white. He nudged Rayah, tapped his nose, and gestured at Dean, who had given his tongue an overtime shift.

Rayah shuddered. She swung her dirt-scented soccer bag over her shoulder and muttered something about heading over to the field. She disappeared, unnoticed by anyone but Danny.

"What all'll happen during your tryouts?" Danny asked Michelle, who was doing toe touches and other useless exercises.

"The process may work differently here"—right toe, left toe—"but at Emmanuel, Coach had us do some warm-ups where he determined our skill level. Then he pitted us against those with similar abilities. If you lost, you played the next player below you. Won, you played up."

"Sounds fair."

"Fair?" Her face reddened as she reached for both toes and missed by a significant margin. "Sure, if you call sabotaging tryouts so his daughter can play first singles, the top position, we can go with that word ... *fair*."

Got it. *Fair* and *nice*. Two words that could no longer be used around Michelle.

A whistle trilled within the chain-link fence behind the windscreens.

Dean's girlfriend unsuctioned her lips from his, making a gross slurping sound. "Gotta go, babe." She kissed him once more, turned, and left. Her French braid received so much treatment from his fingers, it had merged itself into one tangled knot.

Danny slid off the bench, which remained marked by his leg sweat and moved alongside the court, the only flank without a windscreen blocking his vision. Too bad, no benches here, just rocky ground camouflaged by tufts of long grass.

Dean appeared to have had the same idea and squatted on the same hillside as Danny.

A tanned woman who appeared to be the coach herded the team into a circle around a red court. She addressed the group with an adenoidal voice, which made every word sound as if it journeyed straight from her beaky nose. "Name's Coach Gilga, and we do not have time to go around the circle and introduce ourselves." She motioned to the fifty-some players standing in the ring. "So we'll skip that."

Wow, she seemed nice.

"Second, most of the players here have already had a proper tryout a few days ago. Step forward if you just enrolled here."

Michelle and two others took a step inside the loop.

Coach Gilga tutted at the group. "They gave me a rather decent line-up before you showed, you see. Tell you what I plan to do. To make tryouts go fast so we can get back to our regular season schedule, I'll have you compete in a match against one of our current players."

The coach paced around the ring and tapped the shoulders of three players, one of whom wore the tousled French braid.

Smirking, the three players entered the ring.

Dean stifled a snigger and spotted Danny's puzzled expression. "The coach just chose the top three players on the team. My girlfriend is number one." He gestured to the girl in the lilac dress and messy braid.

"You three will challenge one of the players I selected." Coach Gilga twirled the black whistle string around her finger. "If you win, you take her place. Lose, and we stick you in the JV sixth string, our lowest-ranked team. Understood?"

The three challengers nodded.

Coach Gilga whistled at Michelle and motioned her forward with a finger. Michelle obeyed as the coach scrolled on her phone.

"Emmanuel transfer, correct?"

"Right." Michelle arched her shoulders, ignoring the glares from the King's Academy players.

"I'll put you on court one with Julia Mesh." She motioned to the girl in the French braid. "You'll play an eight-game set." The coach paired off the other two newcomers and marched over to the chain-link fence and pulled out three canisters of tennis balls.

"What sort of tie breaker should we play if we get to one?"

The coach clicked open one of the canisters, which made a fizzing noise like a soda can. "You won't reach a tiebreaker. I promise." She shoved the canister into Michelle's sweaty chest and left the court to sit under the shade of a pavilion on a hill adjacent to the courts.

Danny swiped the sweat on his lip and choked on the muggy air as Michelle began her warm-up.

Every forehand she sent Julia's way, the number-one player slammed the ball back with impressive speed. To Julia's dismay, however, Michelle returned most of the ground strokes with equal velocity.

Dean, who had been leaning back at the beginning of the warm-up, now hunched forward with his hands pressed against his lips and his forehead creased.

When they finished their practice serves—during which Michelle seemed far more impressive than Julia—Coach Gilga whistled Julia over to Danny's side of the chain-link fence.

"Hit to the corners, Julia. This girl doesn't like to run. Use those wide angles."

Wait a minute. Could she give the player advice during tryouts? That didn't seem fair. Or nice, really.

Gilga sent Julia away, and Danny expected her to call Michelle over for some guidance. Instead, the coach ventured to the second court to pep talk the next player through a gap in the windscreens, her whistle bouncing on her chest every step of the way.

Julia spun her racket to determine who would serve the first game.

Michelle had once discussed this in one of her numerous attempts to explain the puzzling game to Danny. "There's a label on the butt of the racket. After you spin it, it could read one way or another. Like a heads or tails coin."

"*P* or *D*?" Julia held up the Prince racket. Danny imagined the butt of the racket had a *P* for Prince on it.

"*P.*"

Julia spun the racket, and it landed on the court with a clatter. She knelt and the light from her face disappeared. "It says *D*. My call." Ah, *D* for Dean. How perfect.

"Won't you let me see it?" Michelle squatted as if trying to get a look at the racket herself. "In all my matches, the opponent showed me the racket butt."

Julia's lips sagged. "Tell you the truth, it looks like a *P*. The sun messed with my vision, and the butt's a bit scuffed up." A nervous laugh. "Your call, I guess."

"I'd like to serve first."

Julia froze for a moment, eyes unblinking and mouth slightly open. Her voice came out small and tight. "Sounds good. I'd like this side then." She pointed to the other half of the court away from the sun.

The girls traveled to the appropriate areas, and Michelle bounced the ball seven times. She squinted up into the blazing sun. "Love–all."

How interesting *love* is actually zero in this game, Danny mused as his friend aced Julia on the first point. Love must mean nothing at this school.

Michelle won the first three games, whereas Julia only scored three points total throughout. Even Michelle's dad would've been proud of some of the winners she'd hit.

During their water break, after Julia had flipped the scorecards to show 3–0, Coach Gilga whistled her over. Julia's neck rolled back, and she let out a guttural sound of annoyance. Still, she hustled to the chain-link fence.

"Did you run her all over the court?"

"T–trying!" Still catching her breath, she tilted her head back for a gulp of water, which spilled all over her face. "She returns everything like a freaking backboard. Keeps racing toward the net. You know I mess up when an opponent does that."

Gilga's visor swayed back and forth in disapproving jerks. "From now on, any ball that comes close to the line is out. Every other serve is a double fault, understood? Otherwise someone from Emmanuel is going to take your place."

Danny balled his fists. No way. He clenched his hands so hard he felt himself shake.

Julia nodded and rubbed a towel over her sweaty forehead. She sprinted to the other side of the court and rattled the ball against the ground with her racket. "0–3, love–all."

They should change it to hate–all.

Although Julia clapped in a wicked-fast serve, Michelle returned it to the opposite corner of the court where Julia couldn't reach in time. The enemy player froze in her footsteps, stared at the line, and held up an index finger. "Out!"

Of course she did.

Michelle cocked her head. "You sure about that?"

"It went way out." Julia hit her racket against the ground five inches behind the line. "I saw the ball hit here."

Another serve. Another excellent return … another out. And another. And another.

So the next two games went. At the next water break, score 3–2, Coach Gilga called Julia over again. "In those last few points, I saw her hit safer shots—too far into the court to call them out. You need another strategy if she keeps it up."

"I did see her go for more net shots."

"Next time she sprints to the net, take her out." The coach smacked her leg, palm print staying for seconds on the sunburnt skin. "You can't outlast her, so see if you can injure her."

Danny's face flushed. He rose, fists tightened until his knuckles whitened, nails boring into his palms.

Dean snapped a pair of fingers at him. "Leave it alone, Princess."

"You think I'll stand by while she—"

"One injury is better than two." Dean slowly thumbed his nose. His septum. "Don't interfere. You'll regret that decision."

Despite himself, pain in his nose from imagining what Dean could do to him in his sleep caused him to sit in the grass once more. Coward.

For the next two games, Julia slammed every shot she could whenever Michelle approached the net.

Coward, coward, coward.

Julia struck a bull's-eye when, during the last point of the second game, she walloped a ball into Michelle's eye. Michelle clapped her palm on her face, and Julia feigned shock and surprise.

"So sorry about that." She bit her lip and twirled the end of her braid in her fingers. "You OK? Score was love–40 before this point, right? Means that puts me at 4–3, correct?"

"Yes." Michelle's voice cracked, on the verge of tears.

With a jaunty strut, Dean's girlfriend swaggered to her water bottle and inhaled generous gulps. Coach Gilga rushed over to give a high five through the clinking fence. "Atta girl! Keep it up."

Enough of this. So what if he lost his nose? Things smelled terrible on this campus anyway. And Michelle's eye was gonna go if he didn't do something.

Danny rose and whistled for Michelle to meet him at the chain-link fence. Palm clasped over her bad eye, she shuffled in a slow, defeated pace.

"You know nothing about tennis, Dan." The warm spit managed its way through a fence hole to Danny's eye.

He wiped it away. "I know that the coach keeps telling Julia to call good shots out and to hit you when you come to the net. Really nice lady, don't you think?"

"Great!" Michelle thrust her hands up in the air, revealing a nasty shiner on her eye. She reached down and rubbed her face with a white tennis towel, covering the bruise once more. "A biased coach, so I can't ask for a line judge because she'd call everything out anyway."

"True ... But you figured out Julia runs like an awkward ostrich and plays poorly when players approach the net. Use that somehow."

Michelle jerked her finger toward her eye. "And get another one of these?"

Eye for an eye. Danny saw Julia break away from her meeting with Coach Gilga and bounce a ball on her way to the service line.

"Michelle, you have to win this match. What'll your dad do if you don't make varsity? There goes your full ride."

Biting her lip, she sighed. "I don't know if it's possible, Danny."

"You always play card games with the odds against you. Think of this as War."

Michelle thought for a moment. "You're right. She does run like an awkward ostrich."

"Now go out there and ... and, dang, I don't think I have an ostrich pun at the ready."

"Oh, darn. A shame." Michelle chuckled. "All right. I have to do this or Dad won't talk to me for weeks. Not that that's necessarily a bad thing." She straightened her spine and sprinted to receive one of Julia's paltry serves.

"If your girl wins, you lose, Princess." Dean flicked a rock at Danny as he returned to kneel on the rocky hillside.

Danny hugged his knees and tried not to think about the excruciating pain of a fishhook in his nose.

Chapter Fourteen

WHEN JULIA DECLARED *LOVE–ALL*, SHE MEANT IT WITH all her heart. With her bright white shoes scuffed in red court clay, tennis dress a deeper shade of purple from sweat stains, and the score 5–4 in Michelle's favor, Julia served every shot with pure hatred.

Love–all.

A furious Julia, with snot dribbling from her nose, sprinted to the net. Michelle lobbed the ball over her head. It hit the court and then the fence by the pictures of seniors. Julia's portrait received a dent in the nose.

Love–15.

Julia served double faults, whacking each one into the net, coupled with strings of unrepeatable words.

Love–30.

Michelle passed to Julia's weak backhand, and the girl slammed it into the chain-link fence, causing Danny and Dean to jump.

Love–40.

A now-sobbing Julia, rivers of charcoal mascara gushing down her cheeks, missed a ball Michelle returned, proceeding to completely whiff her swing. Then she smacked her racket against the court five times, spraying bits of clay before she crumpled to her knees to sob.

Game.

Arm outstretched, Michelle waited at the net to shake Julia's hand.

Hiccups and coughs interspersed Julia's moans. She assumed a fetal position and her wracking sobs showed her rib cage through the tight tennis outfit.

Glad to know people at King's took losses like champs.

Eventually, Julia rose and gripped Michelle's hand hard. When they shook, Michelle's jutting fingers looked like Julia was trying to break Danny's friend's hand. "Good game."

When Julia released her crushing hold, Michelle shook her hand back and forth to reintroduce a proper blood flow. She beamed at Danny.

Joy welling up inside him, he threw a pair of thumbs up and offered a cheek-splitting grin. Totally worth the nose piercing he was going to get from Dean later.

Julia flew out of the gates and into Dean's arms. As he rocked her back and forth on a plaque for a late-coach from the '40s outside the courts, he mouthed something to his roommate.

Although Danny did not understand most of the message, he read the words "kill you" somewhere in the dispatch. His heart leapt into his throat for a moment, but he focused on Michelle's smiling face when the match had ended. Worth the pain. Worth the pain ...

Michelle joined Danny outside the tennis courts. She collapsed into him, giving a sweaty hug. When she released, they met up with Hannah, who was still engrossed in her comic book, by the benches.

"I went to Rayah's tryout." She jerked her head at the empty soccer fields. "The coach placed her on JV second-string, but she seemed fine with the decision."

"Must be nice to have parents that don't pressure you to do well in sports." Michelle collapsed on the bench, sweat streaming down her body. Danny seated himself beside her.

Hannah scooted away from Michelle's stench. Sunscreen only did so much. "Mitch, you don't mean that. No one wants Rayah's parents."

Michelle's cheeks flushed. Clearing her throat and clicking a string on her racket with her thumb, she relayed the highlights of her match to a disinterested Hannah.

As she did this, Danny absentmindedly watched a pair of high heels and a pencil skirt stroll up the cobblestone pavement with surprising ease. He looked up and recognized Ashley's skeletal face from the physical trials a few days before.

What was the principal's assistant doing here? He rubbed his sweaty lip on his shirt.

Now about twenty yards away, Ashley scanned the area: the wooden pavilion with golden lions painted on the border, the billowing portraits of seniors, the benches ... and stopped there. She wanted them?

Ashley marched toward them onto the rocky, grassy hillside partway through Michelle's description of an overhead smash she had mastered in the 6–4 set.

"You three." Ashley snapped her bony fingers at them. "Follow me."

Danny's blood chilled. Called to the principal's office before school started. Good to know they were kicking things off right.

Michelle blanched, smile vanishing. "Should I let my coach know first?"

"Follow me." Her stern gaze wavered for a moment. Then she marched down the path.

The three shadowed her, Michelle deflating and looking short without her heels.

The bench outside Ned's office was hard and hit the spine in all the wrong places. Like a church pew, just in time for the last day of Welcome Weekend. Danny imagined this was the only Sunday the office would be open for business.

Trying to adjust their seating positions, the three friends squirmed into awkward postures.

Danny doubled over with his palms on his knees. He focused on the drone of phones ringing once, twice before Ashley picked them up. He studied the dangling plants at every corner of the check-in room, including small succulents in clay pots on the check-in desk right by Ashley's nameplate. Finally he strained to feel the bitter AC wafting through the vents. No use, still nauseous.

While Ashley tapped her fingertips on the keyboard, Michelle channeled her fear through her tapping feet, the crimson carpet muting the noise. Hannah hid behind a comic book, but she remained on the same page as if frozen.

"What are you fazed about?" Michelle jabbed her in the ribs with her elbow. "I thought you said you hated school."

Licking her thin lips, Hannah shrugged. "Emmanuel detentions were one thing. Expulsion is something else. I need to get into college." Hannah needed a high GPA to attend King's in the first place.

Danny said, "You always talked about how stupid you thought college was. How ridiculously expensive and all that. When did that change?"

A Keurig coffee machine clicked, groaned, and sputtered, filling the room with the aroma of coffee.

She shook her head, burying it farther into the comic book. "I can't be like my parents. Neither one made it past high school, you know."

"Mr. Rezzen will see you now, Daniel," came Ashley's call between sips. Several mugs sat next to a K-Cup litter on her desk.

Shaking, Danny approached the door and knocked.

A grim "ENTER," belonging to the principal, came out like clear thunder even through the thick wooden door.

Danny opened the door, and Ned's face softened when he saw him. Danny held his breath, hoping.

"Dan, the man I wanted to see." Ned's beard covered most of the grin. "Go ahead and shut the door."

He did so and choked a little on the strong scent of incense permeating the room. He had to squint to catch an outline of the principal since the dark, pleated curtains covered most of the window. Even without those, the leafy plants on the windowsill blocked out the remaining sunlight.

Ned dug into a glass bowl situated by a cyberbullying poster. He tossed Danny a mint. "Take one. My wife bought one of those large containers, and I need to get rid of these."

Danny tore open the wrapper and popped the sweet into his mouth. "You called me?" He tossed the candy cover into a silver trash bin.

"Yes." Ned motioned to his laptop. "I have had quite some trouble with this thing since early this morning, and an Emmanuel source says you have a particular savvy with computers."

The pressure that had built itself up in Danny's chest outside the office released. "Sure, let me peek at it." He slid into a plush crimson chair in front of the desk.

"My computer won't connect to the Internet." He handed the computer over to Danny after typing in the password. "Got a number of emails I need to send out today." Ned leaned back in his chair, hitting a bookshelf behind him with it. "But I left my cell phone at home. I could always have Ashley look at it, but, you know, confidentiality and—oh, done already?"

Danny returned the laptop to Ned, the King's Academy logo sticker staring at him from behind the screen.

"Just reset the router. Give it a few minutes. Teachers at Emmanuel had this problem all the time."

Ned puffed out a sigh of relief and fidgeted with his scarlet-and-gold tie. "Thank goodness for that! You know, this computer just about runs the school." A thunderous laugh, a pause, and then two fingers reached forward to adjust a crooked succulent pot, out of line with the five others on the desk.

"This morning, for the life of me, couldn't access the outdoor cameras nearby the Asger Science Center. Missed a group of vandals spray painting the side of the building." He clawed his fingers. "Slipped right through. Now I'll have to scroll through hours of media to find the culprits."

"Outdoor cameras?" Danny surveyed the items on Ned's tidy desk. A picture of the principal and a younger boy—his son?—with a fresh-caught fish stood out. The quality of the photograph rendered it about ten years old.

Ah, fishing. Fishing hooks. Didn't want to think about that.

Ned swung the laptop around to show Danny the screen. He clicked different boxes on the side, and videos played on the main screen: outside the dining commons, outside the math building, and outside the Suanna dorm.

The videos played without sound. At Suanna a girl laughed with a wide mouth, but no sound of mirth came out of the computer's speakers.

"I had no access to indoor *or* outdoor today! And only this computer can view these videos."

Outdoor cameras, huh? Wonder if he had one where initiation took place. By the garden.

All morning Rayah had bugged him to talk to the principal about this. With Dean threatening him at the tennis courts, it couldn't hurt to expel his roommate before he caught another victim with his hook.

"Sir"—he cleared his throat, mouth full of a bitter taste—"do you have a camera outside that large garden we passed on the tour?"

"*A* camera? Got ten out there. If a fly touches that garden, I'll go outside and electrocute it."

Danny's heart throbbed in his throat like a bouncing tennis ball. Perhaps the principal had evidence of the initiation after all. In that case, goodbye, Dean.

"Sir, would you remind viewing the tapes of the area just outside the garden? The first night of Welcome Weekend. Around two in the morning."

Ned's eyes narrowed in the darkness of the room. "Anything, in particular, I should watch out for?" He moved the succulent again.

"You'll know it when you see it."

Danny left the dark office and went back into the bright fluorescent lights before he received permission to do so. A gutsy move, but asking the principal to review the tapes probably crossed a line anyway.

Rayah had joined the group on the bench outside, the odor of sweat and grass smeared all over her. A path of dry mud led from the front of the office door to the pew.

"You left a snail trail, Ray."

She glanced at him sheepishly. "Tried to wipe them off on the carpet outside. Cleats trap everything though."

He squeezed into the seat, meant for maybe two-and-a-half butts.

Brows furrowed, Michelle asked him how the meeting went, but when she discovered the principal needed Danny to fix his computer, she deflated.

"I can't turn on a computer to save my life." She buried her red face into her palms. "Wonder what he wants us here for."

Danny shrugged his shoulders, then asked Rayah about tryouts.

"Not terrible." Her whisper had a hard time outdoing the ringing of the office phones. "He, the coach, had me play goalie against some of his best scorers, but no complaints here. JV second-string seems like a nice group."

"Did they call you to the office too?" Michelle bit at a hangnail on a finger that was already bleeding.

Rayah shook her head. "Wanted to meet with my advisor about dropping my study hall for the graphic-design class, but she's on a call." With a muddy finger, she pointed two doors down from Ned's office.

Hannah flipped the last page of her comic, sighed, and started over.

"Michelle, Hannah, office." Eyes glowing from the reflection of her computer light, Ashley jabbed a finger at the office door.

Maybe they addressed every student in the same way here. Just to freak them out over nothing.

Back at Emmanuel, the ninth-grade English teacher used a similar tactic. He once, with a stern face, yanked Danny's arm and pulled him into the disinfectant-scented lounge just to tell him that he had earned a perfect score on the test. Danny's heart still pounded for an hour afterward that day.

After Ashley called the names of his two friends, she clutched a loud brown paper bag and vanished around the bend. Lunch break.

Michelle and Hannah shared a wary mien and shuffled to the office door, the latter far more reluctant than the former. The same cold "ENTER" answered their knock. They swung open the door and disappeared.

Danny and Rayah sat in silence for a moment.

"You fixed Mr. Rezzen's computer, Danny?"

Danny doubled over because his back hurt in the hard seat. "Yeah, he wanted access to the Internet and outdoor cameras. So he can spy on us and all that. I made sure to ask him to review the tapes from the initiation like you suggested."

He craned his chin up at Rayah, his long hair tickling his nose. She greeted him with mouth open. "Outdoor cameras?"

"Mm-hmm. He's mounted them everywhere. We could have our own reality show if we wanted. Although no one would watch it."

"Oh."

"So like I said, I took your advice and told him to review the tapes of what happened during initiation night."

She clutched her knees and rocked. Heat radiated from her skin.

What had he done?

"By everywhere"—she drew a cleat through a mud clump—"do you mean outside the dorms, by the school gates ... everywhere?"

"Ray, the word means the same thing *everywhere* you go."

She shook, stone-brown eyes blinking. "Dan, this is bad."

He blinked. "How? He'll catch the initiation guys in the act. I may actually survive tonight if Dean goes home."

Rayah smoothed her dirty hands on her green soccer shorts. "I didn't mean that ... Dan, Ned has cameras posted outside Suanna, correct?"

"He toggled that one in his office, yes."

She pressed her fingers into her temples. "Do you remember two of our friends spoke about breaking the rules and left minutes later on bicycles ... and they did all this in front of Suanna, *where he has cameras?*"

Danny's heart stopped. After muttering quite a few expletives, he chewed on his cheek until he tasted blood. "Ned saw them leave campus. He knows they broke one of the major rules and called them into the office to expel them, didn't he?"

Rayah clutched his hand, squeezing hard. "Do you know if those cameras had decent audio? I'm hoping they didn't catch the conversation at all." She rubbed her temples. "Except Michelle isn't known for being quiet."

"The cameras can't hear a thing." He shut his eyes. The silent camera images in front of Suanna flashed through his head. "Pretty sure he uses no audio for the outdoor ones."

She stared at him for a moment, drew her dry tongue over her chapped lips, and nodded. "Be right back." Rayah released her grasp and approached the door. Before Danny had a chance to ask her intentions, she had knocked and disappeared into the office.

Alone on the bench and with his dangerous thoughts, Danny scrolled through the messages that had all come through at once during a moment of a strong signal on his phone.

MOM: Tried to schedule an appointment, but they advised against students having much contact with parents so you could adjust well (at least for the first few months). That would explain why I haven't heard from you.

MOM: Miss you and love you!

JEREMY: Hang in there! Praying for you all back here!

MOM: Miss you!

JEREMY: Hey, I left my inhaler back on the bus. You didn't happen to grab it did you?

MOM: Love you!

JEREMY: But seriously. I almost died today. You sure no one has my inhaler?

MOM: All right, Daniel. I know they said you can't contact us much, but this is ridiculous.

MOM: Call me.

MOM: Still miss you.

MOM: Still love you!

Danny sighed and sent a *love you and miss you too* message in reply. Without much of a surprise, the text didn't go through.

Ten minutes later, Rayah emerged with her face sunken and her body trembling with a new earthquake.

"What did you—?" Danny began.

"What I had to do." She collapsed on the bench and buried her face in her palms.

Hannah and Michelle trailed behind, each with wide eyes and lifted brows. Ned's door to his office banged shut.

"What happened? Did he expel you?"

Michelle's bangs swayed when she jerked her head. "No. He didn't because Rayah told him she gave us the idea to leave campus."

Danny clapped a comforting hand on Rayah as sobs wracked her small frame. "Did he expel her from King's Academy?"

Chapter Fifteen

"MISS ABED, TELL ME WHO AUTHORED *THE CLOCKWORK Orange*?" Mrs. Burgess, a dumpy woman with several chins, slapped a pointer stick on Rayah's desk.

Anthony Burgess.

Rayah shrunk, looking to the wall for clues. The posters of diagrammed sentences and thick blinds over the windows did little to help. "I do not know."

Mrs. Burgess leaned in closer to Rayah's desk, her strong perfume giving Danny a headache. "I suppose I shouldn't ask you who penned *The Handmaid's Tale*."

Danny mouthed "Margaret Atwood" to Rayah, but his friend's wavering eyes alternately fixated on and wandered from the teacher.

"No, ma'am."

"Did you do the summer reading at all from the textbook, Miss Abed?"

Rayah rubbed her hands against the bottom of her desk and pulled them away fast. Gum, most likely. "I'm a transfer, ma'am. We didn't hear about the summer reading."

"Be that as it may, other transfers in my previous classes seemed to know the material, so I will not accept that excuse."

Because all other transfers, other than those from Emmanuel, received the homework assignments during the summer.

Although Ned had not expelled Rayah, he had gifted her with a month's worth of detentions and blacklisted the girl among the King's Academy teachers. Nice guy. All the professors placed Rayah in the front row of the classroom even though they allowed other students to pick their desks. Danny and Rayah's English instructor targeted each literary question at the poor girl. Rayah excelled in every academic pursuit ... except for literature.

"Miss Abed"—Mrs. Burgess used her desk to support her weight—"in my classroom, we have a three-strike system, and only one chance remains for you. Tell me the name of the dystopian novel Ray Bradbury wrote in 1953."

Rayah's jaw sagged but no words trickled off her tongue.

"I expect you to know this information for the test in a week. Answer the question."

Rayah cast a helpless glance at Danny.

He lunged forward and scribbled *Fahrenheit 451* on his notes, but a harsh *thwack* of Mrs. Burgess's pointer hitting her desk made him flinch.

"Five seconds, Miss Abed."

Fahrenheit 451! Why couldn't Rayah read his mind?

"*1984?*"

Danny's chest deflated.

"That answer took away all your participation points for the day, Miss Abed."

Rayah's jaw quivered.

"I would also like to remind the class that classroom participation counts for thirty percent of your grade. So the zero in the grade book for today should already be detrimental to our transfer's grade."

Danny raised his hand and responded to her questions incorrectly so he, too, could lose points for the day. When the question "who wrote *Crime and Punishment?*" came along with the drone of the AC, Danny's hand flew up, as if trying to catch the tile ceiling and harsh lights. "Dr. Seuss."

Mrs. Burgess eventually caught on and refused to direct any more inquiries his way.

Other teachers followed suit. They shot hard questions at Rayah. When she failed to give the right answer in time, she lost all her points for the day. Furthermore, the teachers graded her papers harder than they did other students'. She and Danny had a similar punctuation mistake for their history reflections. The history teacher had taken one point off Danny's paper and five off Rayah's.

"Back at Emmanuel, the lowest grade I had in a class was a 97." In the hallway of the math building, her entire body shook when they passed a glass display case with photos of those on the Principal's Advisory Council, which Danny stopped to look at. "If this keeps up, my GPA will drop below a 3.5, and they'll expel me. Then what's Dad going to do?"

What sounded like a bag of potatoes dropping to the floor pulled Danny away from the photos. He glanced over his shoulder at Rayah, who had slumped onto a bench near a pair of energy-drink vending machines. He joined her.

Rayah sniffled and scrunched her face like a person trying desperately not to cry. "I think I'm breaking, Danny. I can't fail these classes ... I can't."

He wished he could take her place ... Danny swathed her in a side hug. Her arms quivered, the scent of cinnamon faintly wafting. He sucked in his cheeks, unsure of what to say, and pulled in his feet because they kept tripping students that drifted too close to the bench.

Then he had an idea and plucked at Rayah's dress.

Her neck straightened as she glanced at him.

"We have free period next. No teacher gives you a bad grade for that."

Her trembling lips curved downward, tears forming a sort of lip balm when they cascaded over her mouth. "We still have three more classes, two of which don't have anyone from Emmanuel."

The bell clanged, cranked up five times louder than the one at Emmanuel. Its round, pompous tone reminded Danny of the clock tower in the middle of campus and in his town square.

Once his English class had visited the landmark for their study on John Donne poems, about the way bells had been used to signal the death of a community member.

Rayah drew in air, breath rattling. "Maybe I should complain to someone. The teachers are all clearly trying to fail me."

Send not to know for whom the bell tolls.

He licked his lips and found a sulfuric aftertaste spilling out from within his mouth. Forgot to brush again. "Mmm, maybe not, Ray. I mean, who would you talk to?"

The hallway had a strange, metallic echo now that its inhabitants had disappeared.

"I'll write a letter to the superintendent."

"The superintendent?" Danny lowered his voice so the cameras could not overhear him. He wasn't sure if the indoor ones, like the outdoor ones, had sound hooked up or not. "Bad idea. You don't have a clue who's in that office. For all we know, Ned's father could run the school."

"Mr. Rezzen." She tossed a rare glare at him. She had done the same when Michelle called Kim by her first name. "And, no, he doesn't."

"OK, say you write to the superintendent. What will Ned do when he sorts through the mail the students send to the outside world?"

"Sorts through the mail?"

"I know. He's like a professional stalker or something. Should've chosen a different career path."

"No one can ransack the mail, Danny. Once I put it in the mailbox, it's a federal offense to tamper with the envelope."

"True, but will a school like this care?"

She leaned her head against the vending machine, glancing at painted equations just under the exit sign at the end of the hallway. "Might as well try anyway."

It tolls for thee.

Deciding to escape the building for free period, they rose from the hallway bench. The two ventured to the gardens because Rayah wanted a lungful of nature.

"The concrete ceiling seems like it could crush you at any moment." She shuddered as they passed through the glass doors of the math building into the warm sunshine. "You'd think we had entered a mine or cavern in there."

Or a den. The Seleucid Center for Mathematics, with its dim cave lighting, emitted such a gloomy atmosphere, one could not help but feel like a prisoner. Not to mention the building wafted strong whiffs of bologna, an unsavory scent among most sensible humans. And vegetarians.

A few seconds into basking in the sunshine, the bounce had returned to Rayah's steps. Her weight appeared to become lighter and lighter until the mere breeze tugging her skirt against her ankles threatened to blow her away. Off the beaten sidewalks onto the grassy path, Rayah broke out into a full sprint toward the garden, yards and yards away.

Danny peeled off his hoodie with clammy hands and caught up to Rayah inhaling balmy air.

Rayah froze when she reached the entrance to the garden, eyes closed for a moment, a smile crawling up her cheeks.

A weeping willow swayed at the gate, its laughing branches bouncing in the wind. Graceful and green and good, the garden seemed to operate in its own time zone. While the rest of campus appeared fixed like concrete, the garden swayed and billowed like a play parachute. One would have thought they were looking at an underwater orchard if not for the earthy scent of soil as opposed to a briny ocean tang.

"It seems ancient," Danny said.

The ferns lining the edges of the garden bobbed.

"Kind of reminds me of the chapel, you know?"

"Yes."

Amid a soft breeze and the sound of wind chimes dangling off a wooden post, echoes of the shrieks from the unfortunate soul with the hook in his nose filled Danny's mind. Oh, joy. More flashbacks. He shuddered despite the eighty-degree heat. Why did they do initiation in front of the garden?

Rayah slipped off her shoes and Danny followed suit. They left them by the dancing willow and entered. For some reason, the action felt proper ... and right.

"Sorry if this reminds you of that night." She avoided his eyes, thumb grazing a bright-orange hibiscus petal.

He followed her lead and touched the soft flower. "Better to create good memories in the same places as the bad."

After all, when his dad had died at home, bad memories sprouted like thornbushes everywhere. Every green carpeted step and every rusty kitchen hanging light carried a painful burden. The same wouldn't happen here. Not in this beautiful, unfunny place.

He buried his nose in a flower that had a very faint, sweet smell. "Some thorns have roses, you know." He had a sudden idea. "Ray, what do you think about starting our own Bible study?"

In their bare feet, tickled by long strands of smooth grass, they continued down a winding path that carried itself in whimsical spirals.

"Danny!" Rayah's eyes glinted. "That's a wonderful idea! I could really use that. I can't take much more of this school. When?"

"I dunno. I'll figure it out after talking to Han and Mitch."

Around one bend a glittering brook poured over smooth stones. Rayah pointed out some golden koi fish. Another corkscrew led the two toward a bush cut somewhat like a lion. The shrubbery needed a considerable trim because its bloated body of leaves had started to resemble a bear. One tiger away from an "oh my."

"Why is the school obsessed with lions?" Danny brushed his hands against the bush and shivered at the barbed texture.

Rayah shrugged, sapphire dress tugging at her legs in the wind, making her look like she was wearing a jumpsuit. "King's Academy ... king of the jungle. Makes sense, doesn't it?"

"Nice symbolism. And you said you're terrible at literature."

"Lucky guess, I guess." A modest smile curved up her cheeks. "You know you're far better at the subject. Our English teachers always hounded you to write a book."

"Already tried. Only got through twelve chapters."

"I still think you should try to finish it."

"I don't think I'm bitter enough to be an author." Yet.

They passed another green lion around another spiral and found a thin figure huddled on a stone bench. Ivy crawled up the edges of the marble seat toward a cross-legged Hannah, who hunched over a sketchbook. As she jabbed her scarlet marker across the paper, she glanced up at them. "Skipped class too?"

"Too?" Danny raised his eyebrows at Hannah. "You mean to tell me Rayah has to deal with her point-taking teachers to save you from expulsion, and you turn around and try to get expelled again?" He plucked a leaf off a bush and crushed it with his fingertips, smudging them green.

"Our teacher never showed up for this period. So we kind of did our own thing. Most students opted for a second lunch or ran back to the dorms."

"Oh." His cheeks warmed. "So ... do you come here often?"

Hannah stuck the red marker behind her ear, forgetting to put the cap back on. "Been here a few times. Reminds me of a park I saw a lot growing up, except the park had lots of dandelions instead of whatever the heck these flowers are. My parents walked together there a lot until ...." She plucked the marker out of her hair, which had formed a crimson squiggle on her ear, and returned to her drawing.

Rayah walked beside Hannah. She paused before parking. "You want a seat, Danny?"

Next to Hannah when she was on a murder bent? No thanks. "Ladies first."

"What a nice drawing of a ... bamboo plant ... killing a panda." Rayah grimaced.

"Thought blood made you squeamish." Hannah slashed the white sheet with more red.

"Did you join an art class for your required credit?" Rayah looked away from the gory sketch, taking a sudden interest in a blue jay perched on a thorny rosebush.

"Nah, I joined the speech-and-debate club. Their dramatic-interpretation team sold me on the idea."

The image of a sad student in khakis flashed through Danny's mind for a moment. Sounded about right. Danny shifted back and forth on his feet. "Why don't we check out the rest of the garden, Ray? We only have twenty minutes before next period, and I'll bet we still miss half this place, based on its size."

Rayah winced and massaged her calves. "I'd rather stay here for a while longer. Soccer practices have beaten me up this past week."

Hannah frowned at her bamboo assassin drawing. "Since when are you one to complain about anything?"

Danny said, "Didn't you hear me say that all Rayah's teachers are taking away participation points from her for not knowing answers?"

Rayah melted into tears when he brought up English class.

"Dagon! They broke Rayah," Hannah said when Danny had finished.

He tilted his ear toward his shoulder. "Dagon?"

"An Assyrian god. I figure since the people here like to take the Christian God's name in vain, we might as well get back at them somehow. I was originally going to use a god from a modern religion, but Michelle told me it wasn't politically correct."

Ah, couldn't have that, now, could they?

Rayah lifted her head, streams of fresh tears forming rivers on her dry skin.

"I have to write a letter to the superintendent." Rayah's lips trembled. "Never have I felt so angry in my life. I don't feel like myself anymore. Hannah"—she gripped the skinny girl's elbow—"you agree with me, right? I need to notify someone. The teachers are going to kick me out for not knowing who Margaret Atwood is."

Hannah blinked at her shoes. Perhaps she also hadn't a clue about the identity of Margaret Atwood. "To be honest, Ray, you may need to listen to Dan on this one. A girl in my science class texted a friend about how much she hated the school. Two days later, they expelled her."

"B–but"—Rayah's wet lips stuttered over the words—"'gainst the l–law to ... t–tamper with letters ... m–mailbox."

A fresh wave of tears overtook her. "B–but"—the snot on Rayah's lip slurred her words—"if I d–don't write to someone, they'll expel m–me soon. With all the p–participation points the teachers k–keep taking!"

Rayah continued to sob as sparrows chirped nearby and the deciduous leaves in the garden sighed as they bled orange and red.

"Play it by ear." Hannah tapped her ears, one of which had a chain running from the lobe to the top. "Parents have no way to reach their kids because of the bad cell service and crippled Wi-Fi—which conveniently stopped working once the parents left. And the school makes them schedule appointments on weird, select days. Want to bet how parents will try to contact their darlings next?"

"Letters?" Rayah sniffled, wiping her arm across her nostrils.

"Uh huh. And we can tell if a letter's been read by someone else before. They'll tape the envelope closed or something."

Danny's phone dinged with ten fresh messages from his mother. At last, the cell service had drilled through the school's gates.

Hannah jerked her head at Danny. "We can also take a wild guess as to whose mother'll write a letter first."

Sure thing, three days later, Danny received a letter in his campus mailbox. He jostled the stubborn lock and pulled it out of the 4 × 4 in. box. The envelope was taped closed. Creeper Ned at his finest.

He unfolded the paper and squinted to read all the lines, which had been obscured with black marker.

Dear Daniel,

I miss you terribly back home. You never answer my texts or calls, hope you change this habit by the time you go to college. ███████

███

███

███

The other day, however, I received a note from your principal about your academic success in the first week of school and your savvy on computers. This warms my heart. ████████████████

███

█████████████████████████████ *and have a wonder-* *ful week. Hope to hear from you soon!*

Love,

Mom."

Danny showed Rayah, sitting next to him, the letter, and she clasped her hand over her mouth when she read the bowdlerized note.

"But can't students show juries letters like this as evidence?" She leaned her head against the Suanna building, crunching brown leaves in her fingertips. "That people in King's are dodging the law?"

"You could argue anyone could've opened the note and crossed things out. I did that in fourth grade when Marcie wrote me a note saying she liked me."

"Poor Marcie."

"Yeah, poor Marcie, whose parents make six figures each. But as for this note, we have no proof of who specifically did it."

"If we can't reach the outside world and let them know what happens here, how are we going to survive?"

Danny sighed and grabbed his own brown leaf. "I wish I knew."

Chapter Sixteen

THE TEACHERS STOPPED TAKING OFF PARTICIPATION points from Rayah by the end of the week. By the time she passed her English test with an *A minus* (one of the two *A*s in the class, Danny receiving the other one), even the stubborn Mrs. Burgess didn't shoot any more questions Rayah's way.

In fact, for all four friends, campus oppressors seemed to loosen their reins. Danny, for example, was allowed back into his room after a week's banishment. Dean had—after the tennis-tryout fiasco—placed a gray sock on the doorknob every night Danny came back to the dorm. Knowing he couldn't enter the room during those occasions, he had crashed on Gabe's Goldfish-Cracker-crusted futon and endured the locomotive snores of the other two roommates.

When Dean and Duke finally admitted Danny back into the room, both seemed rather chipper. Duke never mentioned seeing Danny in the cafeteria when he was meeting with Mr. Coriander, and Dean once even offered him a smile.

"Beautiful day outside." Dean tapped the wall where a window should be.

Danny frowned. "Uh huh."

"But if you ask me, it's really hot. Almost like a wildfire could break out any moment."

Well, it was still summer, Dean. That was typical for weather patterns.

"Hope the tennis girls don't burn up at their match in this heat." Dean fanned himself with a stack of papers on his desk. "Julia's sick of this hot weather. And when she complains, I get sick of her."

"Well, the hot weather's going away soon."

"We'll see." Dean smirked at him and kicked a beer bottle as Danny left the room.

What was that all about? They never talked about the weather. Well, they never talked about anything.

On his way to Suanna, he met with Hannah underneath a green tree whose tips bled scarlet. In the shade, she had a stack of papers held to the ground with a rock—what looked to be her speech pieces involving death, depression, and dark topics.

"Depression and I have been friends since eighth grade"—she grabbed the top paper on the sheet, tearing it because of the rock—"after the divorce and all. I feel like I'm competing in a duo round, where two competitors do a speech together, with depression as my partner."

Glad to see she was still as chipper as ever.

Two thick fingers tapped his shoulder. "Ready to go?"

"Sure, Mitch. Warning, though. My stomach's not one hundred percent. I might not make it to the courts."

"It's fine. You've seen me win a lot of matches. And going against a hard team today … I'd almost rather you didn't watch."

Even Michelle garnered a lot of success on the tennis court, despite her coach's attempts to deter her progress.

"Lose a match and we'll let one of the lower players challenge you," Coach Gilga would warn. "Julia's serve is perfection. If you fail, we'll have you play her again."

Michelle had yet to lose.

"Isn't that ridiculous?" She was dressed in her full tennis team uniform, and her golden skirt swished as she plodded on the sidewalk. "I win every match and Coach still threatens me!"

Danny muttered in agreement and clutched at his burning stomach. Wished he'd taken a Pepto tablet. His mother had made him a medical kit, filled with prescriptions she wouldn't allow the school nurses to administer to him. But his roommates had stolen most of the medicine in the set.

Michelle eyed Danny as she smoothed her pin-straight hair into a ponytail and adjusted her tennis bag latched onto her shoulder.

"I agree with Rayah." Michelle squirted a white patch of sunscreen on her chest and rubbed it in. "You should talk to someone in the cafeteria about vegetarian options. You can't keep eating mashed potatoes for every meal." She moved her tennis bag again. "Rayah, Hannah, and I have also gotten sick from the food here."

He considered returning to Mr. Coriander's office, but he blanched when thinking about seeing Duke in full uniform behind the cracked door. Dagon, he hoped Duke hadn't seen him.

Pain spiking again in his gut, he moaned. "If they send someone home because they complained about King's Academy over text, what would happen if they insult the food?"

"Fine, stay safe."

"Sounds like a plan."

"Hannah told me she wrote your eulogy for when you die from malnutrition. Says she made it nice and morbid. Your mother'll love it."

"Right—after what happened to Dad—I know it would kill her."

In the distance, the campus clock sounded a death knell.

"So what are you going to do about it, Danny?"

"Nothing. I don't want to be expelled."

"There are worse things … I can't think of them right now, but there are."

"I won't die from mashed potatoes, Mitch. That's ridiculous."

She paused her step on the cobblestone, and her balloon nose sniffed the air. "Isn't it a bit too hot for that?"

Actually, by this point, it was in the sixties, so it wasn't exactly too hot for anything. "For mashed potatoes or dying?"

She glanced over her shoulder and her eyes widened. "That." A shaky index finger pointed in the direction of the large garden.

In front of the garden, a small fire and something bent and misshapen lay in front of the boogying willow.

Michelle frantically unzipped and peered into her bag, digging through the contents. A sharp gasp. She pulled out an old badminton racket and some tennis balls. "What …? Oh, Dagon, no. Please, no." She sprinted, breathing heavily, toward the scorching mystery item.

Danny passed her and stopped five feet short of something that had been white that resembled—

"My tennis towel!" She clutched her sides, out of breath, and collapsed on her knees. Then she cried, "And my racket. Oh, Dagon, my racket!"

A dented piece of metal with cut strings lay beside the fiery cloth. Michelle cradled the broken bits in her palms. Danny kneeled beside her, feeling the curiously intense heat of the burning towel and an uncertainty of what to say.

Michelle rocked on her knees, eyes watering ... from the fumes? "What's Dad gonna do when he finds out?"

The way he skimped on money, nothing pleasant.

"I broke the strings on my extra one in a match against Lydia," she sniveled. "Just the tennis girls knew that happened. No one else."

"You think one of them did this?" Danny envisioned Julia, the girl with the French braid and her mouth suctioned on Dean's.

"Julia?" Michelle seemed to read Danny's mind. "No. Girl's terrified of anything like that after she lost her cat in a house fire. I learned this at the tennis-team bonfire she refused to attend." When Michelle had met him the morning after the bonfire, she had still smelled of smoke.

"Maybe she convinced someone else to do it. Like her boyfriend." Dean had threatened him after tryouts. Maybe he had gotten his revenge at last.

Then the odd conversation about the weather he had had with Dean that morning popped into his head. "I think he hinted something about a fire." He relayed the events to Michelle. "I'm guessing that's where the badminton racket came from."

"Sounds about right." Michelle wiped her face. "Forget Ned. I'll bet your roommate set fire to Emmanuel too."

The tennis racket clanged as Michelle tossed it aside onto a patch of dirt. "Dunno what to do, Dan." She stood and dragged her toes toward the sidewalk. "Our match starts in an hour, and you sort of need a racket to play."

"You could borrow someone else's racket."

Michelle scowled. "I mean, I could"—she sighed, shoulders, body, everything sighing—"but the kind of racket you use affects your whole game. To switch rackets just before a match against a top-level team ... I wouldn't expect you to understand."

It pained him to see her so dejected. "Remember War, Michelle. You can beat unbeatable odds."

"I know. But you get tired after fighting a lot of battles."

There was nothing else to say ... nothing funny, at least.

Not feeling well and worried about the match, Danny left after he escorted a morose Michelle down the grassy hill to the courts. He wanted to stay to support her, but the stress of watching the match would cause him to puke.

When he reached the sultry dorm, he threw up on the hallway carpet before he made it to the restroom. His retching for five minutes drew Duke out of the room and behind him to utter the comforting words, "Three weeks and you still vomit everything up? Do you have the stomach of a regurgitating bird or something? You eat like it."

Between heavy breaths and shadows crawling under his eyes, he managed to get out "vegetarian" and "diet" before throwing up again.

"There any way we could ... add vegetarian options to the ... cafeteria?" Danny's arms wobbled as his head spun. He tried to focus on the fire-drill procedures poster on the wall next to the men's room. Far off, an electronic ghost giggled after someone flushed a toilet.

"That why you tried to come into Fred's office that one day?"

So he had seen him. Guess he didn't mind after all. Otherwise, Danny would have no septum by now. He nodded. Everything in Danny burned in the rancid hallway.

Duke stretched out an arm and the tips of his fingers, apparently to comfort Danny, not daring to inch closer to the pool of vomit surrounding the sick sophomore.

"Listen, pal. I do have a lot of connections with those who order the food, one being Dad. But I've had students come to me with lactose problems, the gluten-free fad, everything. The principal hates when we use more of the budget to buy healthier options. If I convinced my dad to order something different, I could get expelled. Family's too poor to put my education at risk."

Danny coiled into a fetal position at the onslaught of abdominal cramps. Dying seemed a lot more realistic now. What a horrible way to go. As he rocked back and forth, an idea occurred from a lesson at youth group, three months back. Something about a handful of men refusing a banquet suited for a king. "How about this, Duke ..." Danny grunted. "You convince your dad to order vegetarian food for me and three other friends."

Duke opened his mouth to protest, but Danny continued. "And we'll have a control group, like in science class, to compare ourselves with. Have four other students who have the same BMI as us eat the food in the cafeteria."

The roommate rolled his one good eye. "How long would you keep this up before the principal catches on?"

What would be enough time? Mom lost weight within half a month when she started going to the gym. At least she claimed she did. "At the end of, say, fourteen days, have the school nurse decide who looks healthiest."

"Can't be two weeks." Duke noticed some puke on his arm and walked to Gabe's dorm, bent, and rubbed his arm on the welcome mat. "The principal tracks our expenses like a hound. How about a week?"

"Too short. Compromise at ten days? My mom has tried diets for that long." Not that they ever worked. He grimaced. War, Danny. War.

Duke returned to his seat on a vomit-free area of the carpet. "Fine, ten. What if Ned catches on anyway? You should see him with those number sheets ... scans them like a dictator."

"You can just say you're conducting a science experiment."

"Me? Do science?"

"Extra credit for physiology? You ranted to your girlfriend the other day about how the professor tried to fail you. I have a friend who can forge signatures well." Hannah. "So she can write you a 'teacher's note.' Worst-case scenario, I have a knack for computers and could send an email from the physiology teacher's laptop."

A red tongue slathered Duke's lips. "Ned'll still be upset about the money, science experiment or not."

"I can pay him back for the meals, giving him the money from my summer job scooping ice cream." Chills gave Danny goosebumps on his arms. "Worst case, tell him I forced you to do it and threatened to keep you out of the room if you refused."

Duke rubbed his face, making half of it turn pink. "You mean that I'm sick of you barfing and stinking up the dorms every day? All right. But only because my girlfriend found a caterpillar in the lettuce bin last week and was upset the rest of the night. On our anniversary."

Danny thrust a shaky fist into the air. Yes!

"What if Nurse Nintin chooses the control group as the healthiest?" Duke looked to his right at a Health-Center-hours sign near the lounge full of torn-up couches.

"The food stays the same, and I visit the doctor for some heavy medication." Good luck with that. And all the restrictions Mom imposed in doctors' offices.

"What if she says your group looks the most fit?"

"You tell Ned about the experiment—remember, you can say I ... forced you. And explain why we need healthier options."

"Yeah, what am I supposed to say when he asks me that?"

An image of Michelle's dad popped into his head. The man was the only reason Emmanuel offered some semblance of fruit in the cafeteria so the track athletes would stop getting sick from the unhealthy options. "So his students can win more sports. More sports won, more money for the school."

"Sports ..." Duke scratched his chin scruff like a philosopher. "All high school administrations like that word."

Danny unrolled himself from the fetal position and stuck out his hand. "Deal?"

"Deal. But I ain't shaking that hand." Duke's nose wrinkled.

Danny made a wry face, withdrawing his arm. "OK, deal."

At the first of the ten days, the school nurse measured each candidate at the Health Center for a baseline to track their progress over the next week and a half. The three girls and one boy chosen as the "carnivore" group weighed nearly the same as Danny and his friends, BMI fluctuating by mere half numbers. Nurse Nintin handed each subject a purple calorie-tracking sheet and warned them not to stray too far from the recommended 2,000 per day. Hard to do with all the fried food.

To ensure they conducted themselves in an honest manner, Nintin paired each with a student who would monitor their food intake for the week. Duke volunteered to accompany Danny, but when they entered the dining commons, he sat as far away from Danny and his friends as possible.

Danny followed him to the tables by the tinted windows. "What gives? I need you to keep me in check this week."

Strings of boiled brown beef dangled in his open, chewing mouth. "Duck back into the kitchen. They have your plates ready and already portioned 2,000-calorie meals for your day." Greasy juice spilled down his chin. "You don't need a monitor this week."

Not complaining. Rather not spend more time with the roommates anyway. Danny followed orders and stooped under a blue stanchion rope that separated the kitchen doors and the food court.

Several workers in plastic hairnets dashed from a cold metal table to a silvery metal oven and toward something else metal. Steam from one of the boiling pots on the metal stove wafted a convincing whiff of burnt tomato soup.

Danny tapped a worker in square-rimmed glasses and had to shout amid the clangs of various pots and pans.

She squinted at him for a moment, nodded, and motioned at four plates covered in plastic wrap.

He stacked two of the plates on top of the others and carried them out of the kitchen, stooping under the blue rope again. His ears seemed to sigh with relief when they no longer endured the clamor of the kitchen.

He joined his friends, all absent monitors. They must have abandoned his friends like Duke had Danny. No one cared about the experiment.

The steam had fogged the plastic wrap. Tearing it off, his eyes widened at the array of colors on the plate.

Hannah gave a low whistle. "Never thought I'd be happy to see a type of vegetable that wasn't candy corn."

"Carrots!" Michelle's tongue glazed her lips. "Yellow peppers and—oh!" She inhaled the sweet scent from the steaming plate. "Dagon! They put asparagus on there. I thought they banned anything from VeggieTales at this school."

"Who would hate singing-and-talking animated vegetables?" Rayah ogled the steaming broccoli heads. The steam flew up all the way to a dangling lion with a chef's hat.

Danny slid his plate toward himself, the sweet perfume wetting his nose. "They hate anything having to do with religion here, Ray. Duke says his chemistry teacher stuck a kid's Koran over a Bunsen burner when he caught the student reading it in class. Claimed it was an 'accident.'" Funny. A lot of "accidents" happened here.

Rayah gave a solemn nod, glanced over each shoulder, and bowed her head in prayer. Chin curved over the tangerine plate, Rayah didn't notice a group of King's students near the drink-dispensing machine staring at her.

Moments later Danny realized their attention was on the plate of vegetables and not the praying friend. "Starting to get worried people at King's have a staring problem." He motioned for Hannah to look at the cluster by the drinking machines. "Dean, the principal and his cameras, now them."

"Well, we are very attractive." Hannah had stuck a yellow pepper on her tooth.

He impaled seven different forms of produce onto his fork and slid them onto his tongue. The sweet, warm juices flowed down his throat.

Rayah's neck craned back up, and she skewered a fork into a soft vegetable. "How did your tennis match go yesterday? Wanted to come but we had a soccer game. Coach sat me out the whole time, but we won."

Danny's spine rippled for a moment. Caught up in the experiment, he'd forgotten to ask Michelle what had happened in the match without her racket.

Michelle chewed her food for five seconds, swallowed, then responded with a clipped, "Won … barely."

Danny and Rayah pressed her for more details, and without fail she cracked a dramatic smirk and leaned back into her crackled-leather chair. She relayed the events of finding her tennis towel burning by Ned's garden—"Dean did it, no doubt"—and the dreadful discovery of her bent racket.

"The extra ones Coach had, weighed, like, five tons." Her arm slumped to her side as if she held a heavy carpet bag. "Took me a whole set to adjust. Luckily, my opponent lost her momentum and I got the next two. You know, Emmanuel students have more patience than anyone. We can endure a lot of heat."

"So no challenge match with Julia?" Danny eyed a circular clock on the brick wall toward the back. Michelle's story had consumed twenty minutes.

"No challenge match and a fuming coach. Looked so mad, you would've thought she and Dean *both* planned to dent my racket in the first place."

Maybe they had. Who knew?

Sweaty bangs stuck to her forehead as she jerked her neck to the side. The firelight of conspiracy once again danced in her pupils. "Bet we just solved the Emmanuel fire mystery."

Hannah growled. "No, we didn't."

And they were off to the races.

"Any evidence to the contrary?"

A strained sigh from Hannah. "The coach had a decent roster before Emmanuel students showed up. She had no motive to burn our old high school. Again, Michelle, I know villains. They need strong motives."

"Sadism. I call that a motive."

"I've been researching speech pieces about sadists. Read about twenty of them and your coach doesn't fit. Try again."

Michelle pounded a fist against the table. "OK, maybe not Coach but how about Dean? Pretty sure he set fire to my towel, Hannah. *Set fire.*"

"So could any other kid who lights up behind the dorm buildings. I could list ten I saw this morning alone."

Jangling silverware hit the table as Rayah's shaking arms pierced the air in a motion of surrender. Her voice came out soft and trembling. "Dean, Mr. Rezzen, Ms. Shiloh—who cares? Even if we discovered who set fire to Emmanuel, who could we contact?" She lowered her voice even more if possible. "We already have to be careful about what we say here."

Silence from the others. Various bits of gossip from the choir kids' table and a stifled yelp of a boy as another student stuffed ice cubes down his shirt filled the pregnant pause while the friends gnawed on vegetables.

Danny found his meal had grown cold and not quite as fragrant as before.

Michelle set down her fork, and her shoulders heaved up and down. "Ray," her voice came out slower and calmer than ever before, "we're discussing this because if we figure out who burned Emmanuel, we know who to watch out for."

Rayah reached forward to grab a brown napkin from the dispenser to wipe a tear trailing down her cheek. "With all the respect in the world, our dorm rooms lock from the *outside*. Even if you know who did it, they can still trap you in your sleep, setting fire to your beds at night."

Listen to her. She'd never been this upset before.

"Just gotta make it to Christmas break." Michelle pounded her fist against the table with each word like a heartbeat. "They send all the students home for half of December. If we make it to then—"

"If"—Rayah interrupted, surprising everyone—"we survive the next few months without getting hurt, we still return for the next term. And the next. If Ms. Shiloh, Dean, or Mr. Rezzen caused the fire, they won't go anywhere in our remaining three years of high school."

The group stared at their plates, apparently no longer hungry. Even Hannah.

Michelle sniffed and forced a mouthful of broccoli. "Eat." Her fork scraped across the plate. "We may not have safety, but we need to win this experiment to at least get decent meals."

Hannah's nose ring disappeared as she wrinkled her nostrils. "Don't see the point." Her nails scratched a dent in the round table. "Little guys versus a big school. And everyone's pitted themselves against us. Say we have better BMIs than the control group in ten days … maybe Ned won't care. Maybe Ned will expel us for trying to eat healthy in the first place. Why does it matter?"

Ice pumped through Danny's veins.

The word "War" seemed to cross Michelle's lips for a second and then, "Eat. That's all we can do for now. Eat."

Ten days later Nurse Nintin remarked at the contrast between the two groups. The "carnivores" each had a weak, wan hue to their skin and various health problems. Left lots of fried food-scented contributions for the academy in the toilets. The nurse even gave Danny's group bonus points when she discovered he had not vomited in the past eight days.

Fourteen days later, various shades of yellows, emeralds, and scarlets painted the food-warming bins in the cafeteria buffet. The dining commons was not prepared for the influx of lines around these featured dishes, and the bins emptied fast, leaving the disgruntled workers to fill them with expired fruit.

"Since when do teenagers like vegetables?" one grumbled as he dumped syrupy peaches into a tray that had once held snow peas.

No one touched them.

Three weeks after that, the cafeteria finally managed to order enough vegetarian entrees to appease its consumers. Greasy foods disappeared from the menu, and the entire building smelled like steam and slight sweetness. Whenever Danny sensed the clammy aroma, he kicked his leg to ensure he wasn't dreaming. He half-expected to awake one day and find himself facing nothing but piles of mashed potatoes for meals, but the gooey globs of white disappeared from the menu during the following weeks.

"It matters." Michelle's voice was just a hint louder than the piano music drowning the dining commons. She scooped a spoonful of orange peppers onto her plate. "Every victory matters."

Chapter Seventeen

"I ONCE PERFORMED *GREEN EGGS AND HAM* AS MY dramatic piece, turning Sam-I-Am into a serial killer." Hannah stabbed watery eggs in the dining commons with her fork. "Much more fun to lose than to take this club seriously."

Goodness, Tumblr had done a number on her. Hannah had begun her speech competitions in October, proceeding to earn herself the lowest scores in every round—an "accomplishment" for the borderline sociopath girl. Once a confused judge marked her at second place in a round, and she returned to her dorm furious. Poor thing. Glad to know Emmanuel students took wins well.

A few more triumphs materialized for the other three friends as well from late fall to early winter. Michelle and Rayah finished with winning seasons, the former playing all matches, the latter none. Both were happy with the series of events. And Danny excelled in all areas of academics. Often he earned Rayah's rare jealousy in English class.

"How does symbolism come so easily to you?" This question, whispered in the middle of class, lost her participation points for the day.

Feeling bad, Danny forfeited his points by standing on his desk and spreading out his arms, gladiator style. "Are you not entertained?"

She wasn't.

Danny even did well in graphic design, his supposedly worst subject. While winter approached, Jack Frost masticating the noses, ears, and toes of the students in dorms where the heaters broke, the teachers grilled the high schoolers full force with last-minute projects and tests before midterms.

Danny's graphic-design teacher made no exceptions. "For the last project before exams, create in Illustrator a design that represents school spirit." His nasal voice carried well over the lack of heater noise in the chilly computer lab. "I expect you to apply the various skills we've learned along the way, such as creating vectors and using Photoshop. You can read the guidelines in the sheets I handed out to you."

Such projects took Danny hours to complete, so he lingered in the white-walled lab long after hours to create his vector of a lion. He hoped it would be a spitting image of the one that once had been in Emmanuel's chapel. That part of the Emmanuel campus deserved a memorial. It had been the only safe space for some people, like Rayah.

Hannah joined him in the Lysol-scented room. "I have nothing better to do and don't want to stay in a cold dorm with girls who hate video games." She leaned back in her fabric chair to glance at the American flag hanging over a list of computer-lab rules. "You should come to my speech tournament this weekend."

Danny clicked the wrong button and moved the lion's eyes off its face. "Whoops."

"I'm transforming *Goodnight Moon* into a suicide note for my speech piece this week." She snapped forward and thumbed a purple flash drive someone had left behind. "This'll make the fifth childhood book I've ruined. You should see me perform the masterpiece."

Danny rubbed his eyes, which had begun to hurt from staring at the bright screen for so long. "As fun and insensitive as that sounds, Han, something tells me this project'll take up most of my weekend. Shoot." He had dragged the lion's nose onto his feet. An unpleasant reminder of Dean's sweaty sock stench drifted in the back of his mind.

"Come on." Hannah banged her hand against her keyboard. "You and Rayah practically live in the academic buildings. Mitch says poor Ray hasn't left her English classroom since the teacher announced a surprise test on Thoreau."

He highlighted the various shapes and formed them into one.

"At least take tonight off, Dan." A *wabba-wabba-wabba* noise came from her bright screen as she commenced a game of PAC-MAN.

Their youth group used to have a number of old video games in the blue-carpeted basement of the church. The teens would spend the first fifteen minutes socializing and playing games like Dig Dug and PAC-MAN. Danny held the highest score in Tetris. Ah, the good old days, when they were young.

"It's Friday." Hannah's PAC-MAN swallowed a cherry. "Drink a soda, turn your music up a notch, burn down this building. Sky's the limit."

"I really miss church."

Hannah sighed and slumped in the squeaky rolling chair. "You know, you and I have very different ideas of how to have a good time on a Friday."

He turned away from the screen, squinting in the dark, the room lit only from a window at the end of the room. "Not Friday, Sunday. Tell me you miss services at least a little."

Her PAC-MAN collided with a pink ghost and disintegrated. "A bit." She rolled her eyes. "Youth group and stuff like that. But Pastor Paul, like all feature films, needs a lesson in shortening his messages. And the coffee in the foyer tastes awful, period."

"I miss the worship band up front. Derek had a wicked talent for the drums, remember?"

"Tastes like watered-down socks."

"Derek?"

"No, the coffee. Keep up ... or stay behind."

She was entertaining. He'd give her that. Maybe she should do the humor category in speech.

To take a break from his project, he minimized Illustrator and clicked on the web browser. The Internet icon remained motionless for moments while the mouse's arrow caught itself in an endless blue hamster wheel.

"The Internet versus Danny!" Hannah pretended to hold a microphone to her lips like an announcer. "Who will win in the endless battle?"

"I want to check the church website. Paul puts up his sermons every week."

Hannah clicked her tongue amid the *gabba-gabba-gabba* of the PAC-MAN munching little dots. "You've tried this website *how* many times this semester?"

A red **X** flashed on the screen followed by a *Web Page Blocked!!*
"Of course." Danny exhaled noisily.

"Ellie, a girl from my computer-applications class, tried to look up Tibetan Buddhist mandalas. She really likes to draw them. The website blocked her. Mandalas are in coloring books, you know."

Danny refreshed the page five more times and sighed five more times. Some battles were not worth fighting. Finally, he closed out of the Internet and returned to the lion vector.

"Nice blue background you have going there." Hannah's eyes glowed with blue PAC-MAN ghosts dancing across her screen. "Reminds me of the stained glass in the chapel."

His lips curved up at the ends. "The project said to make something school-spirit related. I've got plenty of it for Emmanuel."

"Man, the rule follower starting a rebellion. Sounds like every stinkin' YA novel."

A spiraling noise followed by a *blop, blop* served as a coroner for the third death of PAC-MAN. Inhaling deeply, Hannah said in as dramatic a voice as she could muster—just above monotone by any other standard:

> "Goodnight, PAC-MAN.
>
> Goodnight, PAC-MAN's tomb
>
> You really hit the sack, man."

Her voice changed from solemn to stoic, as if someone had used her throat as a faucet to drain all color as she quoted the rest of the book and then stuck out her tongue, made a gagging noise, and slumped over her chair, feigning death.

Bravo, Han. He was clapping, way down on the inside.

The large bags under her heavily lined eyes made the act even more convincing, and her pale skin read sheet-white in the dim lighting of the room.

Sitting up moments later, she winked at Danny. "A sneak peek."

"You just showed me the death at the end. Doesn't that spoil everything?"

She shrugged and nodded to her screen, which blared *Game Over*. "Death sells."

He toggled through various shades of goldenrod, trying to decide whether he wanted a lighter or darker hue for the mane.

"Shadow me, Dan."

"I think your eye bags do a good enough job at that."

"At the speech tournament, I mean. You went to Michelle and Rayah's athletic events. Well, this is my sport. Watch me be terrible at it."

He leaned back, and his chair squeaked. Since when did Hannah get this pushy? "Switch personalities with Michelle or something? You almost sound clingy."

She raised fiery eyebrows at him and pinched her mouth closed. "This school changes people, Dan. Rayah now has a temper, you had more anxiety attacks this semester than in your whole life, and, yes, I want my friends to watch me in an event I waste ten hours every Saturday doing. Happy? Now pick a freaking shade of yellow and come to the tournament tomorrow."

"But, Hannah—"

"Come on, Dan. My parents don't give a crap if I place in these tournaments or even if I finish high school. I want to know at least someone cares about something I don't really care about."

"What, speech and debate?"

"Me."

Yikes. He winced, squinting at his guideline sheet to distract himself from Hannah's burning gaze. At least six hours to go on this project. But Hannah deserved to have someone watch her. Decisions, decisions.

He sighed. "I really want to support you, Han. This is just the craziest time of year homework-wise."

"Fine. If you want something in it for you, I have a piece of Emmanuel at these tournaments you do not want to miss." Her voice leaked a Michelle-like conspiracy. "A three-letter word."

The only three-letter words that passed over Danny's eyes were well-favored by his roommates, and he did not imagine Hannah would suggest the same to him.

"D-O-G." A stray calico mutt used to wander the woods by Emmanuel.

Hannah palmed her forehead. "Try again."

"P-O-O, Michelle was obsessed with our bathroom the first day of sophomore year."

"Seriously?"

"W-O-O, as in *woo*!" He thrust his fists into the air in mock celebration.

With an iron grip, Hannah clenched her fingers around his wrists and thrust his arms down into his lap.

"Never mind, this game will take forever to play. It's Kim, Danny. K-I-M."

"Yes, our old principal from Emmanuel. And?"

"She goes to the speech tournaments. She's one of the coaches for King's Academy. Leads the original orators, the heathen."

His forehead furrowed. "OK, Kim did retire from Emmanuel before the place burned. Maybe she left because she got a job at King's."

Hannah glared at Danny. "True, Danny, but we have three main suspects for who destroyed our old high school, including Kim."

"Right. And right now we think it's Dean."

"We could gather evidence at the speech tournaments to narrow down whether she caused the fire or not."

"*You* could." Automatically, his hand gripped the mouse. No, Danny. He'd done enough graphic design for today. It *was* late.

"Yeah, and Michelle will just take me at my word even though she suspects Dean did it. Right." She sighed. "Everyone in the group trusts you the most because you look at all the facts. If you came with me to the speech tournament ..."

"I could confirm the information." Should've lied earlier in his life. Having people not trust you had its own particular benefits.

Hannah's eyelid twitched at him in a half-hearted wink. "Exactly."

He saved his design, then pressed the power button on the monitor, the computer letting out a death knell of *doo-wee-doo*. The dying of the light filled his chest with massive stones. So much work to do. And they'd have to wake up early. "Fine, I'll go." Only because he supported the other two at their events. It was only fair.

Ah, fair. What a word. "But we have to be careful." He grabbed his book bag and scooped it onto his shoulders. "If Kim's a pyromaniac, she knows where we live."

"We'll be fine. Stop worrying."

Might as well tell him to stop breathing. "Just sayin'. Don't play with fire."

Her smirk faded with the disintegrating of PAC-MAN on her screen. "We live at King's Academy—one of the closest places to hell on earth. We can't escape fire here."

Very early the next morning, Danny cupped his hands on the cold tournament-bound bus and breathed hot air into them. He doubled over, teeth chattering. "Han, you think we could ask the driver to crank up the heat?"

"Clarence says the vents haven't worked since last season."

"Clarence? Did the 1800s name him?" First Edgar Rezzen. Now this.

Hannah, in her wrinkled suit jacket and pencil skirt, ignored Danny and nodded at the sallow youth whom Danny had met at the speech booth. Instead of khakis, he wore a bright-scarlet suit jacket and pants to match—you could even tell the color in the 6 a.m. darkness—and an expression in which the skin on his face seemed to reach for the floor like pulled taffy.

Hannah unfurled her crusty *Attack on Titan* blanket and offered Danny one-fourth its length. Generous for her. Mildew perfumed the worn-out cotton fabric, reminding him of the scent of the old Emmanuel buses. At least King's buses smelled like pine air fresheners. The flames on the design exaggerated the icy-hot feeling in Danny's toes, and the fact he saw his cloudy breath in the murky lighting added to his chill.

"Howdy, Clarence." Hannah nodded at the glum speechie, the nickname for anyone who competed in speech events, in the crimson suit.

Clarence let out a theatrical moan that outdid the rusty motor on the bus. "What piece of eloquent literature do you plan to botch today?" When Hannah replied with *Goodnight Moon*, his throat gargled like a sink's garbage disposal. "When we wall-talk, stay away from me. You already ruined *The Very Hungry Caterpillar* three weeks ago."

"People should be aware of binge-eating disorders." Hannah stifled a snicker behind a bluish finger. "All the other drama pieces cover serious issues too, you know."

A dramatic sigh from Clarence and a glance out the window at the deep amethyst sky, the sort right before a sunrise strikes. Red in the morning, sailors.

"Still have no idea how you got Kim to allow you to practice a different piece each week." Clarence, shivering, folded his arms over his chest.

Wait, did Kim also coach Hannah's category? Danny nudged Hannah. "Kim?"

"You know, the ex-principal from Emmanuel. The one we're trying to catch for arson."

"Hannah, be real."

"She's on another bus. Probably doesn't want any of our Emmanuel stench on her."

The student in front of her waved an extra-large box of Pop-Tarts, which they passed up and down the rows. The two friends each grabbed a shiny silver treat and dispatched the box to Clarence, who refused to look away from the windowsill.

Danny peeled the crinkling wrapper as Hannah spilled crumbs on the blanket. "Han, what did Clarence mean by you practicing with Kim? I thought you said she coached a different category. Original oratory, right?"

He bit into the Pop-Tart and the tang of artificial strawberry exploded on his tongue. As he swallowed, his stomach soured upon the "breakfast's" entry. Not the healthiest of foods.

"She does coach a different category," came Hannah's thick voice, full of frosting. "But because we have so many students in the dramatic and humorous categories, they sent some of us over to her."

"So you do practice with her?"

"Nope. I told the drama coach I would rehearse with Kim, and I told Kim I worked with the drama coach. Therefore, I can do whatever the heck I want on Saturdays. How else do you think I can get away with turning *The Rainbow Fish* into a story about communism and *Where the Wild Things Are* into a tale about clinical lycanthropy?"

"Never heard of that disorder."

"Where humans act like animals. Got my inspiration from Bible class at Emmanuel. We heard the story about when Nebuchadnezzar starts acting like a bull, fingernails growing like spikes."

He grimaced. "Hannah, maybe you shouldn't handle these issues so lightly."

"Says the boy who makes a joke during every serious situation."

Fair.

Hannah slinked underneath her blanket, a warm phone glow illuminating the flames on her *Titan* blanket. Before they left the school, the coach had issued a warning no students could use their phones for the duration of the trip, probably because this upcoming school had better service. More of a chance for students to tell their parents what really happened at King's. Hannah, however, as always, broke brittle rules and left this one without exception. Each one had to be treated equally, after all.

An eternity later, after passing streams mid-freeze and deciduous trees mid-death, they arrived at the tournament school: a small brick building with a gray archway at the entrance right across from a concrete path that led to the American flag.

Danny tapped Hannah on the head, and she flung the blanket off, stuffing her phone into her pocket. Static electricity sent her frizzy hair springing in all directions despite her lax attempts to collect the madness into a bun.

A brisk wind stunned Danny's eyes and nose when he stepped off the bus. His ears froze and nostrils hardened, smelling crisp snow and cold alternating with expelling enormous clouds of vapor. Danny sought refuge in Hannah's blanket.

Reluctantly she offered him a small sliver, which just covered his left shoulder. Thanks, Han. Helped so much.

Underneath the backdrop of a fiery winter sky, they crunched through unpaved sidewalks into the building.

Chapter Eighteen

A HOT MADHOUSE. HUNDREDS OF STUDENTS IN SUITS stood an inch away from the brick walls, lockers, and closed doors, talking to them. Shrieks from a dramatic girl in a tight cobalt dress and popping noises from a duo team in matching outfits, along with the sounds of hundreds of simultaneous, different speeches, served as a harsh contrast to the hushed stillness of the outdoors.

Well, it was a much better alarm than the one that woke him earlier.

"Wall-talking." Hannah flipped off the blanket and absentmindedly dragged it against the wet yellow tile. "Every speechie practices once or twice in front of a brick wall before going into rounds." She patted a patch of wall with a plaque for a wrestling championship title in 2006.

A duo team swooped into that spot and began a dramatic rendition of *Charlotte's Web*.

"We love the walls here." Hannah stared at the aging brick with affection. "They're excellent listeners."

He wished she could've brought a wall with her to overhear Kim's conversation. He stifled a yawn. It was too early to be up.

The team marched into a cafeteria full of overflowing tables and a faint whiff of donuts being sold nearby. Each circular seating area had book bags, dripping coats, and scattered papers from a variety of schools. Danny heard a King's student mutter something about "never arrive on time" and "only the early people get tables."

Flustered, one of the King's coaches ordered the students to shove aside the other schools' stuff to make room for their own. Glad to see they were taking the high road here. Dozens of King's students collected armfuls of coats and dumped them on other bloated tables.

Five tables—out of twenty—later, the coach said, "Good enough." He handed out colorful sheets to each competitor as some of the boys peeled off their suit jackets. Too hot in here even for winter.

Hannah received a scarlet paper with the heading of *Dramatic Interpretation* and a list of evaluation criteria such as eye contact and professionalism.

"We hand these to our judges each round." Hannah flipped through three sheets, one for each round. "I try to get low points on everything listed here."

Danny frowned at a television hanging above their table, displaying the lunch menu for the week. "Why want to lose so much, Han?"

"Because it's more fun. You need something amusing when you deal with all the serious stuff at King's. You of all people should understand. And since I can't access Tumblr at King's ..."

Not necessarily a bad thing.

"Practice your speeches against the wall." One coach with a bald patch in the middle of his head slid into a yellow cafeteria chair. "One of our buses ran late because a debater forgot to set his alarm this morning. We should see those students in about ten minutes."

Hannah gave Danny a long look. "Kim's bus."

"We can spy on her later. We should be good at stalking. We go to King's."

"Yes and no. In ten minutes, they post rounds. And Kim often doesn't stick around until the bitter end. I hoped to eavesdrop on her during this time, when she usually trashes Emmanuel, King's Academy, or both."

"You know this how?"

"She takes a lot of phone calls on Saturday mornings. Always eight o'clock on the dot." She glanced at a digital clock, which read 7:50, on the wall next to the television. "I try to wall-talk near her to hear."

"Well, worst case, you can skip your first round."

"If it comes to that, I can. *If* she takes the phone call inside and not on the bus."

Hannah staked out a small patch of brick by a rusty drinking fountain and presented her speech for Danny, who squatted near the damp floor. Never had he seen such a melodramatic version of the story about a bunny wishing various objects in his room *goodnight.*

Turning the ten-page book into a ten-minute piece, Hannah infused sound effects such as car crashes, skydiving accidents, and a weird, breathy *huh-uh*, which Hannah explained meant a transition between characters or time segments. She wasn't very good at sound effects, and most of the noises sounded like an asthmatic kid wheezing. Like Jeremy without his inhaler.

She rasped, clutching her throat, as the last word of *everywhere* before collapsing.

At the conclusion, Hannah clasped her hands against her hips. "Not bad, huh? Let's try it again."

Danny excused himself to use the restroom. He was gonna see that speech three more times today. Could only take so much of a suicidal bunny.

"Good choice, using the bathroom." Hannah gestured at a male cartoon that led to an alcove on the right. "The rounds last an hour each."

Oh, joy. He passed by an original orator wearing too much perfume and red heels. She was telling an orchestra-concert sign all about the woes of schools' lack of funding for art programs.

Skirting the right corner, he froze. Stepped back.

In the small nook by the restroom stood a large woman with hips wider than life and dark-chestnut hair. Her emerald one-sleeved dress draped like a royal robe.

Kim.

Ear glued to her phone, she hadn't noticed the small shadow lurking around the corner. "I don't care if you have to blame Jesse, Lilah. We need to get these people off my back."

Danny glanced at Hannah, who had immersed herself entirely in a machine-gun sound effect. Deciding not to disturb her, he pressed his temple to the brick, and like the wall, he listened.

Kim bore such a deep voice the only one deeper than hers that came to Danny's mind was Ned's. "You forget, Lilah, all the reasons they keep pinning that fire on me."

His chest froze. His heart thudded against the warm brick wall.

"Oh, you really need me to refresh your memory? Very well. Remember how the school board planned to fire me this year—the whole reason I resigned early? Stupid, really. We cycle through those boards every three years, so this shouldn't have been a problem."

No wonder she was at Emmanuel so long. No one had a chance to fire her in time. Bravo, Emmanuel school system.

A sharp sigh. "But one little genius started the investigation his first day in. They thought I liked King's too much and didn't have the school's best interest at heart. After I burned that one student's paper, every parent wanted to watch me boil."

He couldn't deny it. Jeremy had submitted a proposal to Kim about changing the nature of chapel services. During the first semester of Danny's freshman year, the services were wishy-washy sermons with outdated worship songs. The paper had accused Kim of being the main culprit in this, and she had burned the document on the browning school lawn—a fire hazard, really. The months' worth of detentions Jeremy received afterward earned her no sympathy with the parents, either.

"Second, I physically burned that paper. Means I have a track record with fire."

Danny swallowed a bitter taste. So much for the strawberry Pop-Tarts.

"Third, I hate the guy they chose to replace me. What better way to ruin Jesse's career than letting it blaze before his very eyes?"

Far away in the cafeteria, a deep voice bellowed something about "round postings." In Danny's peripheral vision, Hannah disappeared behind doors into the recesses of the lunchroom.

Kim paused for a long time before speaking again. "Listen, Lilah, they have many other reasons to blame me, but I need to go soon. They're having me judge a Congressional debate round. Whatever you do, try to direct their fire at Jesse. Heaven knows he smokes like a bomb. Blame it on a dropped cigarette. Or on his mental instability ... the job became too much for the guy. Stuff like that."

The shuffle of hard-heeled footsteps coming his direction caused Danny's heart to pound.

He raced back to the cafeteria and ran into Hannah, who had elbowed her way through a group of dramatic students crowding around a yellow pillar with round postings.

"Did you spend ten minutes in the restroom?" She shoved past a boy in braces and khakis. "Or where else did you go?"

"To hell and back." He relayed the conversation on the way to Hannah's first round.

"One nation under God, indivisible, with liberty and justice for all."

"I hate we have to do this stupid pledge every day," someone muttered.

The science teacher, hovering by a display case of a taxidermied rat, motioned for the students to sit, and chitchat commenced.

Today had been deemed a "study day," which meant two things: (1) The teacher had given up on lesson plans for the semester, and (2) the students would not, in fact, study in that formaldehyde-perfumed classroom.

Thick fingers tapped Danny's shoulder.

He spun and faced Michelle, placing his palm on his lap when he realized it was still on his chest from the pledge. Felt extra patriotic today.

"Tell me you recorded Kim's conversation on your phone"—her fingers rapped against the black table—"at the speech tournament."

"No, my phone was in the cafeteria."

Her lips sagged. "Why didn't you sprint back to the cafeteria to grab it? Now we have no evidence to use against her."

"Sorry, Mitch, they told the students to keep phones away in bags, and I had no time to go there and back, anyway. The phone call lasted maybe two minutes."

"Well, when we go home for winter break, you can't give your little spiel to the police without a recording. No one will believe some sophomore kid against the testimony of someone with a master's degree."

They wouldn't get to stay home for long anyway. The four friends had had a previous opportunity to leave during Thanksgiving break. But the school, to prevent most students from journeying home, offered to host a Thanksgiving feast for any of the parents that let their children stay over break "for students to have extra time on campus to relax and prepare for upcoming exams." How sweet and unsuspicious. Danny's mother, who never said *no* to a free anything, of course, attended the banquet held in the dining commons, which, by coincidence, happened to put out the best food they'd seen all semester.

However, because December encompassed so many religious holidays, and the school most likely did not want to provide fourteen free meals for all the December holidays, the teenagers earned themselves a two-week break from the academy.

With a heavy sigh, Michelle buried her nose in a biology textbook with a frog on the cover. "Just saying, the recording could've been our chance."

"Even if we had evidence, she'd find a way to burn it. I felt unsafe around that woman the whole speech tournament."

The fact that five people had given speeches on house fires didn't help. Nor did the burning-hot classroom in round two, which stunk of smoky, old heaters blasting on high.

"I swear"—Danny glanced over his shoulder at a snake pressing itself against a glass case in the back of the classroom—"when I graduate, I'm going to school in Siberia, where it's nice and cold and where no fires break out."

Michelle sucked in her bulging cheeks. "Even though I'm annoyed you don't have a recording, I guess it doesn't really matter in the grand scheme of things. Hannah says King's might fire Kim soon."

"Really?"

"Probably nervous when they caught on to her arson record. If they do fire her"—she picked up an audition pamphlet for *Julius Caesar* that was on the table and scanned it—"I have a feeling she'll send a few King's buildings up in flames. Plenty of evidence with all the video cameras at this school."

Danny muttered assent and returned to his customized English study guide, where his eyes glazed over the symbolism section for the nine works of literature they had covered in class. In complete honesty, he had only added that portion for Rayah. The poor girl had burst into tears no fewer than ten times due to the amount of material on the exam. "Forty percent!" Tears had stained her class notes. "Mrs. Burgess knows I can't pass her tests to save my life." Nice guy that he was, Danny shared his notes with her via Google Docs—when the Internet worked.

He could do symbolism in his sleep. Time to move on to the main-theme portion.

Half-dreaming, he read the section in a lull, dazed by the sweltering heat in the classroom. "*Fahrenheit 451* explores the main themes of censorship, where the characters cannot own or read a book." Like one of the teachers burning a student's Koran? "It also talks about ignorance versus knowledge and how each comes with consequences. Furthermore, the book discusses the benefits and harms of technolo—"

"Daniel Belte."

He looked up and saw Ashley hovering in the metal door frame. "Meghan Dietrich, Alex Grater, and Claudia Trajan, follow me to the office."

His heart wobbled in his throat. What adventure awaited him now? Danny swung his bag over his shoulder and shadowed Claudia, the girl with the curly-headed bob. He was rather sure he recognized her thrice-pierced ears from his graphic-design class. She was the girl who liked to pick scabs, not her scabs. Charming woman. Should go into dermatology.

Without an explanation, the group trooped outside into the bitter cold, cheeks flushing an instant ruby. Everyone, except the pin-straight Ashley, hunched into their stomachs to keep warm. They stomped through foot-high snow, slipping on icy cobblestones, into each academic building, collecting students along the way—all from his graphic-design class. When the group nabbed Rayah, she pressed herself into Danny for warmth—due to having no body fat.

"Why didn't they call us to come over on the announcements?" Her teeth chattered. "They always do the pledge over the main speaker."

He hadn't thought about it. "They pulled us out of class five minutes before the period ended. Maybe they didn't have enough time to tell the announcers."

Along the way to the main office building, Danny needed to rub his wet nose on his shoulder but couldn't with Rayah leaning so close to him. When they passed through the double doors with the lion knockers, Rayah released herself and soaked in the heat while Danny wiped his nostrils against his hoodie.

Ashley instructed the group to "stay where you are" and passed the front desk. Bony knuckles rapped against Ned's office door, and she disappeared inside.

"Notice anything about this group?" Danny nudged Rayah.

She breathed into her palms, massaging them. "All from our graphic-design class."

And Bingo was his name-o. "Any guesses as to why he called us here?"

Before she could answer, Ashley returned, shadowed by the towering figure of Ned. For some reason, he looked a great deal smaller today. Perhaps the fluorescent lights tricked Danny's eyes, but the principal's hair appeared thinner, and his face had paled to a chalky hue, like the dramatic-interpretation speechies. Or a ghost. Not much of a difference, really.

"Good morning, students." His deep voice sounded like a gravestone, cold and hard. "I would have invited you all into my office, but it would've been a disaster to try to squeeze thirty-some teenagers in there." The man's hard, bloodshot eyes surveyed each member of the group.

"Yesterday, I received a disturbing email with a photoshopped image. We have evidence that the JPEG came from one of our school's own computers ... sent during your graphic-design class period. We only have one computer lab, and no one was absent from your class that day." He folded his arms behind his back and paced like a military general.

"One of you sent me the email with the image, but I can't figure out the meaning of it. And your teacher informed me you do not have assigned seats, so we cannot pinpoint which student forwarded it from a particular computer." Strides stopped right in front of Danny. Ned's scarlet tie dangled toward the carpet.

"If the student who sent the email would kindly come forward and explain yourself, we can set the rest of you free for your next period."

The members of the group exchanged glances, but no one moved. A phone in the office droned for four rings before Ashley rushed in to pick it up.

"Very well. I will now give the students of this class a chance to interpret the picture for me because the disturbing image kept me up all last night, and I would not like a repeat tonight."

Claudia combed fingers through her bob, staring at the popcorn ceiling. "Show us the image and we can figure it out for you." Her head jerked at Danny. "Heard this kid aces every symbolism test in his English class."

Ned eyed Danny, face full of amusement. He shook his head. "Nice try. But I want you to decode the image *without* seeing it."

Without? Why not ask them to lick their elbows or do ten other impossible things?

Unpleasant murmurs rippled through the group.

"Describe the sketch then." Claudia's fingers picked at a scab on her arm. "If you don't want us to see your email for privacy purposes, at least paint a picture for us."

"No descriptions either." With a slight smile, Ned rubbed his shoes on the carpet as if he were squishing a bug.

Members of the graphic-design class exchanged open-mouthed, wide-eyed expressions. If this was a joke, it was rather unfunny. Danny would know.

"No one?" Ned's eyebrows raised. "Very well. This group has twenty-four hours to either come forward with an explanation of the image or a confession of sending it in the first place. If you didn't send it to me but are able to figure out what the picture means, I will reward you. Failure to decode the picture will send each and every one of you home with an expulsion by second period tomorrow."

Of course. Wouldn't expect anything less.

Without another word, the principal turned on his heel and slammed the door to his office, which boomed in everyone's ears.

Chapter Nineteen

"NED TOOK *NONE* OF THE SUGGESTIONS THE STUDENTS gave him?" Gabe rubbed a pair of fingers through his white hair, wrinkling his nose at the vents in the Phrat River lounge. They had collected so much dust, it looked like they were covered in fur. A urine smell didn't help the picture—reportedly from an out-of-sorts student who, two days back, mistook the vents as a urinal.

"Not one," Danny said. "Someone suggested a bomb threat to him during lunch. Another said the picture contained gory images of his family. Lots of nasty, disturbing stuff, none hitting the mark. Even Hannah would've been grossed out." Well, maybe not.

Danny's smattering of study guides sitting at the leg of the crackled-leather couch illustrated how his brain felt at that moment. Unable to concentrate on his computer screen, he slammed the monitor shut and sat cross-legged on the lounge chair.

Gabe rubbed his neck, angel tattoo half-hidden by the eggshell-white hoodie. "You have no idea who sent the image?" Shivering, he tucked himself into his hoodie.

"Professor Plum with the rope in the kitchen. That's all I got."

Gabe shut his computer, the blue glow no longer highlighting his reddish eyes. "I wish I could help you, but billions of images are on the Internet. Unless he's disturbed by cat photos, my help just dried up." He rubbed his chin. "And the school cell signal is really weak. Even if we tried to search the Internet for answers, it could take all night."

Abdomen burning from a new wave of nausea, Danny gnawed on his hangnails. A sharp sting from the bite, burgundy blood ... and still queasy.

"I wish I could turn myself in and let everyone else off. I want to protect them all, you know? Protect Rayah ... " Danny sucked his bloody finger and glanced at a photograph of the golden water fountain behind him. Each lounge on campus hailed a different campus landmark. "But then Ned would ask me to describe the image to see if I was lying or not."

"Expulsion either way." Gabe stooped to gather the papers on the floor into a single stack.

Danny nodded, tucking his chin into his neck. "Can't believe tomorrow's my last day here. Washed up at sixteen."

"Maybe not." Gabe clacked the stack of papers against a round table. "You're a Christian—you lead that Bible study every week. Why don't you pray about the situation?"

Sounded like another way of saying *couldn't help him*. Pray and hope, and something magical would happen. Every Christian's perfect excuse for doing nothing. Skeptical and frustrated, he said a quick prayer, while looking up toward the water-stained ceiling, that ran somewhere along the lines of you-won't-listen-to-me-but-please-fix-this.

Danny had experienced a somewhat tumultuous spiritual existence during this semester. Lack of a church didn't help, and although he had finally started a Bible study in the Phrat River lounge, only Gabe and his other three friends showed up for it. Not exactly a mega church.

However, the worst part was prayer. Prayer felt like conversation with a brick wall, just like the competitors at the speech tournament. But this brick wall wasn't listening. Prayers for quelling anxiety and puking episodes, prayers for easing tensions with his roommates, prayers for the teachers to stop picking on Rayah ... relief pleas, tears-soaking-the-pillow nights, wishes for insomniac episodes to end, appeals to get through another day: all unanswered. Or the opposite of what he asked for. The way his panic attacks intensified. Or the reply he hated the most ... W-A-I-T. Often followed by a *no*. Prayer worked as well as school did for Danny's stress levels.

He tilted his head back to glance at the clock hanging beside the photograph of the fountain. "Crap."

"What?"

"Five minutes before curfew. The monitors'll come up any minute to lock the doors to the rooms."

Gabe bolted up and by reflex rushed to his room. His footsteps stopped at the welcome doormat. "Staying with us again tonight?"

"Probably." Danny envisioned the holey brown sock dangling from the doorknob to his room. Third night this week. Wonder which girl it was this time. He'd lost count.

"Hurry up, then."

Danny's fingers fumbled with the laptop, flipping it open. "I'll follow you in a minute. Just gotta call my group project members for English to let them know why I can't present tomorrow ... because I won't be attending King's after second period." It wasn't a group project if someone wasn't dropping the ball.

Gabe's jaw sagged as if he wanted to say something. Sealing his lips instead, he curved around the hallway and vanished as a door softly clicked shut. Gabe's roommates often went to bed early.

Fingers flying against time, Danny logged into his email and clicked *New Message*. However, he paused partway through his draft when he realized a bold, unread letter inhabited his inbox. He clicked out of the draft to see who had sent him an email at such a late, freezing hour.

God had replied.

Danny sat shivering outside the doors to the building at six thirty, nostrils inhaling the stale, cold scent of winter on the front steps. It turned out that the building that housed Ned's office opened at 7 a.m. Ten minutes later Danny heard a pair of heels tread gingerly on the glassy sheets of ice that paved the sidewalks.

"We often call cops on homeless folks who sit at our doorstep." Ashley Penaz smirked, face frostbite red. She sipped a steaming cup of coffee in her gloved hand.

Danny's legs jittered up and down. "Wh–when does Mr. R–Rezzen arrive?" He buried his head in his legs.

"In fifteen minutes." Ashley punched a key from her jingling set into the door and swung it open. She cast a glance at him. "Come inside." She jerked her head in the general direction. "You look two shades colder than a 'Blue Christmas.'"

He staggered into the dimly lit building and parked on the bench outside Ned's office while Ashley flicked on the various lights. Each let out a dull buzz and flickered every handful of minutes. His frozen fingers hurt with the rapid switch of temperature from the outdoors. He fumbled with his ice-cold laptop, trying to type his computer's password for a good minute.

"Want any coffee?" Ashley clicked a K-Cup into the Keurig coffee machine.

"No, thank you. Stuff always shreds my stomach." Everything does. Glad the school had healthier food, though. Helped a little. Just a little.

The machine groaned as it brewed the coffee, filling the room with a warm, earthy scent.

Meanwhile, his knees bounced up and down, laptop shaking on his legs.

Five minutes passed ... ten ... fifteen ... and then a loud moaning of the heavy doors signaled the entrance of the principal.

Before Ned could say a word, Danny bolted up. "I didn't send you the email, sir!" Mmm, not the best start. Danny had rehearsed it in his head about twenty times before this.

With drooping purple eyebags, Ned looked at him like someone who had just woken up from a terrible dream. His face remolded itself with a smile and crinkled eyes. "Neither did half the world, it seems."

"But I do know what image you received. A mysterious sender forwarded me the message last night." His shaking finger clicked on the newest inbox letter.

The subject line read, *Fwd: This will happen to your school.* The body of the memo contained a picture of Ned from head to toe in a suit, sitting on an office seat like a king on a throne. It was rather obvious, to those inside the graphic-design class, that the image had undergone a Photoshop makeover with the light curving in odd places and the edges of the shoulders wearing patches of white from the editing room. But the edits themselves made it obvious why the portrait perplexed the principal.

For one, the editor had colored Ned's head a King's Academy gold.

The next part of the body, the chest, wore a silver layer of paint over his sports coat. And a bronze belt sagged into his tucked tummy. Iron-clad legs followed, the same color as the iron sword Judah had hung in his room, which he'd bought off a friend. A really, really sketchy friend.

Oddly, the photograph concluded with crackled feet, shoes half-shod in a brittle clay and the other half the same iron as the legs.

"Half the puzzle." Ned pressed his fingers to his lips, warming them with his breath. "But you still owe me an explanation for what the picture means. Otherwise, I won't get sleep for another month."

And Danny wouldn't get an education for another lifetime. "Burned my brain half the night. But then I remembered a lesson from youth group that reminded me of this. Also, I'm not terrible at symbolism, so I'll give it a shot." He inhaled, blinking his dry, bloodshot eyes.

"First, the artist put you on a chair that looks like a throne, acknowledging your authority as head of the school. Speaking of heads, they made yours gold, one of the most precious metals out there. We call the best eras golden ones, after all. So the person who sent it wants to make it clear that you do a good job leading the school."

"Buttering me up gets you nowhere."

"Hate dairy, always have. As for the silver chest, we know no one picks a silver engagement ring over a gold one. At least, not sane people." His mother did have a silver wedding ring. And she had picked it out. Figures. "That means someone or something of lesser value, a weaker ruler will take over here after you leave."

The lines on Ned's forehead creased as he passed by Danny to sit on the bench. "Rather large jump."

"Not really, Mr. Rezzen. You see, Emmanuel experienced terrible principals since day one, and they just got worse and worse. And the subject line of the email gives a pretty clear indication this has something to do with the school."

"Not too shabby." Ashley tilted her head back and drained the rest of her coffee. Right as she did this, the phone began to clang its *bah-lah-lah-lah*. With an eyeroll, she picked it up.

Danny flipped the computer to face Ned on the bench.

Ned rubbed his dry hands together. "What about the other metals in the picture? Next one looks like bronze or brass or something."

"Bronze." Danny's great uncle had received a bronze medal in the Olympics several decades previously for race walking. "And bronze is a lesser metal than silver, iron lower quality than bronze, and so on until we get to the feet, which barely seem to hold themselves up. I'm guessing that's the last guy to lead the school."

The principal tore his fingers through a tangled knot in his beard and stared at the bright screen for a long moment. Danny held his breath, growing ever more aware of his rapid heartbeat.

"It's not exactly a pleasant message ... at least, not for whoever will take my place after I leave King's." Ned sighed, rose, and approached a potted plant on Ashley's desk, an aloe. He stroked the spiky leaves for a moment.

Then with a thump and a spin in his heavy shoes, he faced Danny. "But somehow the explanation seems to fit all the puzzle pieces together." He eyed the large golden watch on his wrist. "Before the deadline, as well. I suppose I ought to reward you for the effort."

Worth more than gold, the prize came in the form of a position on the Principal's Advisory Council. Lame as the name sounded, the rank entailed meeting once a week in the principal's office with a cluster of well-to-do students, who made suggestions to Ned on actions he should carry out. Not that Ned ever followed their advice. But it looked nice on a college application.

When asked if he had any other requests before joining the group, he asked if his friends could also be appointed to the council. With their help in the food experiment, it was only right to give them the same opportunity.

🔥

Ned allowed Hannah, Rayah, and Michelle to join the student council, which tended to lord its responsibilities over school activities and fundraisers, like school-wide bake sales with suspicious-smelling brownies. Duke said you could barely taste the chocolate in them. And they had a certain influence over the Advisory Council's decisions.

Michelle appreciated this change of pace because she had several improvements in mind for the school. "Fix the busted water fountain in Seleucid, which tastes like blood. Get rid of the possibility of expulsion for chewing gum in class ..."

Although Rayah viewed the new position with uncertainty—the soft-spoken girl had never led a group before—the only one disappointed in the shift of rank was Hannah.

"I hate government. Why would you make me a part of the system?" The student council chipped away at her five o'clock hour on Tuesdays, the prime time to prank unsuspecting freshman dorm rooms by leaving wads of wet toilet paper by them or to play PAC-MAN in the computer lab. But Hannah tended to be disappointed about everything, and she would get over it.

Fuzzy heather cardigans with a King's Academy emblem, a pristine glass water bottle with a lion logo, and a $2,000 scholarship accompanied Danny's new position. Considering he attended the school on a full ride, the extra two grand landed in his mother's bank account.

"Seems rather over-the-top." Hannah flared her nostrils at the dining-commons meatloaf, which smelled like dog food. So much for the healthy food. "Any English teacher could have given Ned an explanation of the *deep meanings* behind the picture and earned another two grand. Heaven knows their salaries need it."

Could explain why Mrs. Burgess and so many of the others were so cruel. Michelle's coach at Emmanuel had refused to do his job well because of his low salary.

"Ned seems to think it was worth two grand." Michelle raised an eyebrow as she swigged a cup of orange Gatorade. "If I was in his position, I might think so too."

"Seriously?"

"Use your brain for a moment, Han. Dan just told Ned any new principal who comes after him won't be as good. Read any history book. Kings like to hear stuff like that. *Alexander the Great* isn't the exact name someone wants to hear when they ask, 'Who will take over after me?'"

Hannah stabbed her meatloaf and appeared disappointed when the knife slid through the spongy food.

Michelle sneered. "You just don't like the fact Danny's promotion took away your Tuesdays. Heaven knows why you hate student council so much. They accepted your proposal to form an anime club in the spring."

"Still … I think Dan must've used more butter than my aunt and her famous mashed potatoes to get a bonus like that."

"So what if he got two thousand bucks? Why do you care?"

"His mom is probably going to pay for his college. Guess whose won't?" Hannah jabbed a finger at herself.

Yikes. He wished he could convince his mom to fork over the two grand to Hannah. But even if she allowed it, Hannah would refuse. Too proud.

Buttering up seemed to be more of a problem from the other members of the Principal's Advisory Council than from Danny. For instance, during the first meeting, a girl named Valentina—the president of the student council—with large eyes and an overdose of vanilla lotion, arrived with a steaming cup of black coffee for Ned, his favorite brew.

Another, Lawrence, with an unfortunate spider vein crawling across his forehead and temple, complimented the principal's son's performance with the Pittsburgh Panthers basketball team. "If they were a part of March Madness, I'd put them as my number one on my brackets." One could barely catch his wink in the dark lighting of the office. "'Course we got months until that arrives."

Of course, all the members unloaded requests on Ned following these chirps of admiration.

Valentina, after stroking a manicured nail on Ned's picture of his son, took a firm stance on extending curfew hours.

Danny held, with definite certainty, he had seen Dean with the girl before.

As for Lawrence, he wanted cell phone use to be allowed in class.

Ned ignored these requests but all of Danny's were slated for action.

Danny's first suggestion—to allow all straight-A students a choice to opt out of one exam—out of six or seven—passed.

Tears sparkled in Rayah's eyes when she learned she no longer had to take the English final. "I'd spent all semester earning that A." She cried into her palms, letting the tears stain her study guide in free period. "I thought the exam worth forty percent of the grade would tank me for sure."

Other students unleashed their appreciation for Danny via a clap on the back down the hallway or a mailbox full of censored notes from admirers. Even Duke, who unbeknownst to Danny had a 4.0, offered various kindnesses such as handing Danny his last zebra cake, a rare frosting-filled delicacy, and urging Dean to only steal the room away once a week. Dean, who paraded a sturdy 2.3, refused.

It was only fair.

Ned also accepted Danny's second proposal to ban the maximum amount of times a student could use the restroom during class—one teacher allowed students only one hall pass a semester—a particular gift for Michelle, who visited the bathroom ten times a day.

When Ned allowed both of Danny's suggestions to go through, Hannah cried foul, as Hannahs tend to do. "Something seems off. Danny could say he wanted students to recite Psalm 119 and wear Emmanuel T-shirts, and Ned would allow it."

"Come off it." In the Phrat River Lounge, Michelle's long fingernails tore through the old bathroom passes with a clean, satisfying *rip*. She shivered. "Just got goosebumps. But that could be because it's freezing in here."

Danny shrugged. "We could always have Bible study in your room, you know. It smells less like a boy's bathroom in there."

Hannah waved at the group to return to the original subject.

Michelle sighed. "Ned gave in to Danny's advice because he has other students' interests at heart. We all know why Valentina wants to extend curfew hours. A four-letter word."

"Mitch!" Danny imagined the sock on the doorknob.

"I meant D-E-A-N. Dean." She dumped a load of bathroom-pass confetti, bright-pink and blue, at Hannah's feet.

The other ignored the contribution as she bled a scarlet pen, underlining various passages of *The Giving Tree*. For her final speech tournament before Christmas break, Hannah planned to transform the bittersweet story into a cautionary tale about narcissism.

"Don't get me wrong. Students appreciate Danny's input. I'm not complaining about not having to take one of my exams." Danny glanced over his shoulder and watched her underline a passage at the bottom of the page of her book.

Danny frowned at the clock. Five till the end. So much for actual Bible studying ... "Why worry, then? We have way too many other things to be concerned about. Impending death, college, and most importantly ... prom in the spring. Surprised they let sophomores go. That's not usual."

Hannah finished painting flames around the boy in *The Giving Tree*. "Listen, Mitch. Danny is making so many decisions for the school, he might as well be the next principal."

"It was only two."

"Within a week, and it's two more than Valentina and Lawrence combined."

"He'd make a better principal than Ned." Michelle's voice had lowered, and she eyed the ceiling for a camera. Just a smoke detector and a stain that looked suspiciously like a curse word.

"Exactly!" Hannah slammed the book shut. "Danny said the principals who would follow Ned would be even worse. Don't you think if Ned noticed the students liked Danny's suggestions, he would reject them? No Saul likes a David, you know."

"Get to the point."

"Argument, Mitch, is Ned probably has something more sinister going on. No one would agree with Danny like he did unless they had a strong reason. Our friend doesn't have a problem with buttering up. The principal does."

Michelle stared at her tapping mauve heels for a moment as they thudded against the carpet. Against a clementine-sized tear that went right to the concrete. Her eyes ignited with conspiracy. Off to the races again.

"Keep an eye on Ned and Kim. Something tells me each placed a piece of wood in the Emmanuel fire."

Chapter Twenty

"DROP THE BAG OFF IN THE DINING ROOM." Rayah rubbed her shoes off on a mat covered in snow. The black cursive *Welcome* had grown worn over the years. "Any farther into the house and my mom will smell it."

Christmas break had started before Hannah's final tournament ended. While she attended that, the rest of the friends had traveled home for Christmas right after their last exams at four o'clock. A dirty, pungent laundry bag swung over his shoulder, Danny boarded the cold Emmanuel bus with Rayah. King's had decided to let Zeke take the old dust-miser for a spin because too many King's buses were shipping students home.

When they sat on the cold, torn seat, Danny wrinkled his nose at the stench from his bag. Rayah didn't say anything but she did grimace the whole ride. Might as well bring the laundry home since the washers didn't work at King's. Either that or scare away any admirers from kissing him under mistletoe by the pure stench of his bag. Clearly the first reason, but hey, 'tis the season. They had reached Rayah's stop, where they disembarked. Her small navy-blue house glistened with icicle lights and a warm glow. Trumpets blared a soft *Have Yourself a Merry Little Christmas*. Danny glanced at his watch, which read 5:01. Just in time.

They had crunched past ten cars jam-packed on a nearby driveway and by the sidewalk—apparently another neighborhood party. All the passengers thereof were likely too full of spiked eggnog to recognize notices about parking too close to white-and-red fire hydrants and mailboxes with ruffed grouses painted on them.

Rayah's driveway, however, was free of cars and wore a fresh blanket of snow. Had he read the time wrong? His watch showed he had not. Guests always showed up half an hour after these things started, anyway.

A wall of music and warmth had hit their frozen ears upon entry into the house. A wail from Ms. Abed indicated her presence far off in the kitchen. Rayah's suitcase hit the floor, and she sprinted down the hall and to the right. This was followed by her mother's stifled sob and "Oh, my baby girl. My sweet baby girl."

Danny smiled, wide and warm, and rounded the left corner into the dining room. Albeit snug, the small oak table displayed fine china on lacy doilies. Cinnamon and evergreen scents from burning candles flooded his nostrils in the dark, cramped room. He slumped his smelly bag on a frayed carpet, a hint of guilt building in his chest for placing something so ugly in such a beautiful room.

He headed for the kitchen, where Ms. Abed finished dicing cucumbers on a glass cutting board. Rayah helped place them in a row on a vegetable tray for the soon-to-arrive party guests. Everything smelled fresh from the cool, crisp cucumbers to something sweet and warm baking in the oven, caked in years' worth of grease.

"How did exams go, Marayah?" Ms. Abed moved onto carrots next, wiping her hands on her nice red dress.

"Fine, I think. Nothing too hard."

The knife made a clack every time it hit the cutting board. "Trevon showed me his report card today. Cs in two classes. What's he going to do when he hits high school? At least the grades aren't permanent in seventh grade."

Rayah's paused mid-scrape of the carrots into a bowl, eyes widening. "Did Dad see it?"

"No. He's at his apartment throwing his own Christmas party. Now don't remind him of your brother's report card when he visits on Christmas."

"Of course not."

Danny's cheeks flushed, overhearing this from his corner of the room. Rayah's parents had been separated for two months. Thank God. He offered to help dice vegetables, which Rayah refused.

"You're our guest, Danny." She wiped the carrot juice off her fingers with a blue-striped dish towel. "Now, go relax. It'll be your first chance to do that all semester."

Feeling useless, he resorted to popping a few dipped vegetables in his mouth. Tangy ranch mixed with a sweet cucumber at the back of his throat. Nothing quite like home-prepared food.

"How soon will your mother arrive, Daniel?" Ms. Abed's voice carried poorly over the draining water in the sink as she sprinkled her hands.

"Five minutes, tops. Surprised she hasn't arrived yet. Woman makes Michelle seem late."

Michelle always got to class five minutes early even though the students had a full ten minutes between periods. Once, for her first job interview, she arrived an hour and a half early, to her dad's chagrin as he drove her under the impression she would interview earlier. Her phone conversation, or nervous breakdown, with Danny consumed a good hour of the time she waited in her dad's car to venture inside. It was for a fast-food restaurant.

"Will Michelle join us as well?" Ms. Abed motioned to a white refrigerator tucked between the oven and the wall. It was covered with pictures of Rayah and her friends. "Or her parents?"

Danny shook his head. "Stomach bug. Poor thing ran herself ragged for midterms."

"I think her parents had to work too." Rayah reached for the peppers on a counter stacked full of receipts and torn-open letters. "Her mom works retail when she's not at the theater."

Ms. Abed clucked her tongue. "Poor thing. Bless her soul during the shopping season."

"Well, she has to feed five kids somehow."

"Three of them still in college, no doubt."

Yikes. No wonder Michelle's parents jumped at the opportunity for her to attend King's for free.

Rayah nodded. "Lucky most have good scholarships for academics and athletics. All of them have 4.0's. At least, what Michelle has told me."

And why Michelle felt so much pressure to do well in school and sports. His gut soured for not realizing this before. Every one of his friends hoisted the world on her shoulders.

To pass the time between now and when the guests would arrive and let his stomach get the better of him as he always did, Danny piled a small green plate with every food in sight. A mountain of pasta salad—all speckled in black olives and grape tomatoes—and peppered cucumber slices, vegetable kabobs, stuffed mushrooms, and Ms. Abed's famous holiday fudge littered the small disk, which just fit his hand.

Saliva pooling in his mouth, he collapsed on a couch with an awful yellow pattern, probably from the '90s, in the family room, and Ms. Abed set a coaster on a chipped coffee table for his drink.

Guests wafted through the front door like December snowfalls: hardly any, then all at once.

At 5:20 a crooked chin belonging to his mother trembled when it passed through the hallway doorframe. She spotted Danny on the couch watching a game of basketball. He saw her in his peripheral vision amid the chatter and the crowd booing at the Cavs as they scored yet another point. She rushed over, stooped, and enveloped him in a hug full of stifled sniffs and way too strong a peppermint-scented perfume.

Oh. This felt awkward. Julia-running-like-an-ostrich awkward.

"Tried to schedule a day to visit you, Daniel. So, so many times." She released him to wipe her nose. "They offered me every excuse on this planet. Such a shame your cell phone also had terrible reception there."

Their conversation, like a blizzard, seemed to last forever yet bore a cold, aloof tone. He wished it wasn't like that. He really didn't. Maybe in a few years, they would warm up to each other. It tapered off and he returned to Lebron in his yellow jersey. The same color as the couch.

Finally, his mother excused herself so she could help Ms. Abed frost the two hundred Christmas cookies for the twenty-some guests who would attend.

Rayah, who had been sitting on the opposite end of the couch in a Santa-red Christmas dress, nudged Danny and nodded at his mother. "She cares a lot about you—broke down into tears once a week because she missed you so much, according to my mother."

A lump formed in his throat at this news as he swallowed the cold pasta salad. It tasted like dust going all the way down. "Trust me, Ray, I know. If anything, King's Academy brought me and Mom closer than before. She hasn't hugged me in about a year." Granted, he didn't exactly try to reach out either. Like mother, like son.

Rayah glanced over her shoulder at the two mothers in the kitchen, the Santa hat's pompom on her head bouncing on her back as her chin turned.

Crow's feet clawed at the mothers' eyes as they belted hearty laughs. Danny's mother had smudged green icing all over her hand from an uncooperative cookie. Cheerful cackles came from Ms. Abed as she swung open a drawer for another dish towel. This one, argyle patterned.

Danny allowed for a smile. Mad as he was for her sending him to King's and going crazy when Dad died, he had to admit, all moms deserved to be happy. Especially his.

When enough visitors arrived, Ms. Abed announced they would partake in a white-elephant gift exchange underneath the shedding, sweet-scented tree. Danny had forgotten this Abed Christmas party tradition and wondered if anyone would accept dirty laundry as a present. Fortunately, Ms. Abed was prepared for the unprepared and had wrapped an extra five gifts under the tree for anyone who had forgotten.

Rayah unpacked—quite literally—a white elephant. The stuffed animal's beady eyes caught a glint of the dimming lights on the squat tree in the family room. She named the animal "Holly" and endured Danny's jokes for the next five minutes about how they "needed to talk about the elephant in the room." What a trooper.

Danny tore open reindeer wrapping paper to find a package of toilet paper. He sent up a secret prayer of thanks that Hannah would not arrive at the party for another hour because she would have (1) unleashed the toilet paper upon some poor neighbor's yard and (2) invented several jokes involving his gift, of which his mother would not have approved. Before the hour expired, he stuffed the toilet paper into his dirty laundry bag and rejoined the party.

But on his way back, Hannah crashed through the front door with a swift, cold breeze and fresh snowflakes in her static hair. "You got back early."

"No one placed on the team." She shivered, lips blue. "So we left before the awards ceremony." She popped off her ratty sneakers at the front door, and the floor mat stained with melted slush.

Tell him she didn't give her speech in those. He glanced over his shoulder to see if Rayah had noticed Hannah's arrival. Rayah was busy nuzzling Holly in her chin.

"Sad to say you missed the white-elephant exchange, Hannah." Not really all that sad but he was saying it anyway.

She shrugged, her suit jacket slinking off her shoulders. It got caught in the wreath on the door. "One of the judges gave me first place during one round. Probably felt sentimental around the holidays."

Like Danny, Hannah headed straight for the food. She forced five unfrosted sugar cookies into her mouth and approached Rayah with bulging cheeks. Rayah had her finger wrapped around Holly's trunk when Hannah motioned for both to regroup in another room.

The three of them huddled in the dark living room, illuminated by a fireplace glow. Danny wished they could shut the thing off. Had enough flames for a lifetime.

Hannah chewed along to Michael Bublé's "White Christmas." She gulped and then said, "Ned couldn't have set Emmanuel on fire."

Danny licked his salty, sweaty lip and scooted farther away from the fireplace. "How do you know?"

"Overheard Kim chatting during our wall-talks. The woman hates working with anyone and would never join heads with someone as dominant as Ned. She liked Jesse because she could wipe her feet on his doormat face."

His face did have a natural knotted quality of most doormats.

"Did she say so?" Rayah hugged Holly to her chest, fingers stroking the hexagon-patterned carpet. "About not wanting to work with Ned?"

"She mentioned something about trying to get the man fired."

Danny shrugged. "With the incident that happened to her son, I don't blame her."

"But the board turned against her. Ned, after all, stuffs their pockets a great deal. Now her job is on the chopping block."

Drama, drama, drama. The fireplace popped and sizzled. "So how do you know she burned Emmanuel on her own?"

"*Besides* the information from the last conversation you heard, Dan?"

"Yes."

Hannah's bloodshot eyes gazed into the warm fire. "Because she said, 'If they fire me, I'll fire them ... the whole school. The thing'll burn ten times brighter than Emmanuel.'"

Oh.

"Chestnuts roasting on an open fire ..." hummed softly from the speakers. All the three friends could do was stare at each other.

January frost coated King's Academy upon their return. Ice glazed the trees, making the brown bark appear to have been forged out of glass.

In Danny's room, the heater had sputtered its last by the third of the month, and even Duke's space heater emitted pathetic, sporadic bursts of warmth. Both in and out of the room, Danny donned thick gloves, a scarf, and a hat. Never mind what he had said about wanting to live in Siberia. At this point, it almost seemed better to be burned alive than to freeze to death.

Matter of fact, the only heated item on campus was the news of Kim's sacking. The messenger, Hannah, bore the dispatch when returning from the second speech tournament for that semester.

"Everyone wondered why she didn't show up the first week, but we put two-and-two together by this tournament."

Despite Kim's threats, nothing on campus had caught on fire. Yet.

All four friends engaged in a flurry of activities the first week of the fresh semester. Already meeting once a week for student government, three of the four also participated in spring sports that started workouts in January.

Hannah joined the girls' lacrosse team. It began weight training in an alcove above the gym with barbells weighing more than Rayah. "Makes the most sense for me to join lacrosse," she panted. Hannah had joined the group in the dining commons afterward, sweaty from one of the training sessions. "My sport lets you hit people with sticks."

The boys' lacrosse team joined the girls for these pre-season workouts, and through Hannah, Danny discovered Duke played for the boys with netted sticks.

"He can lift two times my weight." Droplets of sweat mixed in Hannah's broccoli-and-cheese soup.

Both liquids smelled about the same, anyway. That's nice. "I know he used to lift his girlfriend before he broke up with her."

She let out a sigh, which disturbed Danny. At least for affairs with Hannah, this troubled him more than usual. "Too bad he wrestles with the wrong crowd because he looks an awful lot like a character from my *Fullmetal Alchemist* fanfic."

Danny hoped that this character was one she either killed off or found to be very, very ugly.

Michelle auditioned for the play *Julius Caesar* per Jeremy's request for her to pursue theater. According to a red sheet attached to the front of the auditorium doors, she got a small role named Calpurnia, the wife of Caesar. The character was haunted by prophetic dreams about Julius' impending death and warned him to stay at home during his doomsday, The Ides of March. In his natural state as a husband and a man, he ignored his wife's advice and flaunted himself in the streets anyway, proceeding to earn thirty-three stab wounds. Way to go, pal.

"Thirty-three?" Hannah frowned at the script, which Michelle perused during a Bible study session. "Even for me, I call that overkill."

Nontheatrical Rayah and Danny began track workouts for meets that would start in March.

The girls' team was full of common sense, like Calpurnia, and did all their exercises indoors, taking laps around the school hallways. Sure, they stunk up the place with sweat, but at least they were warm.

The boys' team followed more in the footsteps of Caesar. And Danny wasn't feeling very Roman that day. Shirtless and with rather skimpy shorts, they ran circles around the school grounds outside, the crunching snow causing freezing water to seep into holey tennis shoes.

Coach Velin had the team assemble outside Ned's office building. The man donned a red-and-green striped shirt, and his reedy voice carried well in the barren cold. "Campus has a mile diameter, meaning one lap will be over three miles. So about a 5K. I expect you back here in twenty minutes. Go."

Ninety-some runners in the cluster hustled, clouds of cold air trailing their breaths. As they ran, Danny glanced at his chest and realized his skin had faded to a purplish-blue. Do as the Romans do. So die young?

They passed by a soccer field, now invaded by the girls holding lacrosse sticks and wearing eye goggles fogged by the cold. The boys' team sat off to the sides, and Danny spotted Duke with his helmet in his lap, shivering. What's he staring at? Why does everyone at this campus like to stare at things?

Duke's unwavering eyelid, not including the puffy, swollen eye, never blinked. Duke kept his gaze transfixed on one of the girl players. Danny followed the roommate's line of vision and spotted Hannah slapping a player on the head with a stick near the goal.

Stay away from her, Duke. She's too good for anyone.

The athlete whom Hannah hit promptly crumpled to the ground and refused to move for a good minute. This was followed by a coach's shrill whistle. Hannah tore off her eyeglasses and stared the coach down with pure loathing.

"What do you mean they don't allow for that in the girls' leagues?" She thrust up her red, frostbitten arms. "Fine, place me on the boys' team, then!"

Atta girl. She did have a handful of brothers, after all. Her whole life was a boys' team. That came out weird.

Danny pumped his arms up and down and forced himself to breathe in the sharp, wintry air. Fists clenched, he brushed past Gabe, who always managed to sprint upright as if his abdomen never gifted him with cramps, and led the pack. Stomach and abdomen burning, he stuck his chin to his chest and focused on breathing.

A gasp followed by cursing caused him to snap his head up. A runner pointed to some sort of dark-gray cloud in the distance. A terrible stench of tar punctured the crisp smells of the outdoors.

Danny turned his head. Plumes of smoke rose somewhere across campus, hidden by a grove of trees. The pine trees wrapped their branches around each other like a huddle of conspirators. A huddle of Michelles.

"Smells like asphalt." One of the runners rubbed a finger under his dripping nose.

"It's not asphalt," commented another. "It's a certain kind of smell trees give off when they're burning. My dad likes to chop down firewood from our backyard. We learned our lesson the one year we burned an elm. Smelled like crap." He didn't say "crap."

The group diverged from the cobblestone path and sprinted through a gap in the trees toward the source of the smoke: Ned's garden.

Oh, crap. Danny's heart plummeted to his feet as he came to a stop, out of breath with sweat beading on his forehead. Hannah's haven during first semester and Ned's favorite spot on campus was now disintegrating in flames.

Flailing and aflame, the weeping willow branches danced in a red-and-yellow frenzy to snuff out its burning head. The once-green garden sleeping under blankets of snow was now forced alive and awake in hot black-char misery. Half its inhabitants had been reduced to ashes. The other half, the creepers up the stone walls and the once-budding flower trees, looked on at the inferno, each awaiting its turn in the fiery furnace.

The perpetrator stood accused at the entrance, barefoot in a patch of snow and shaking from the cold and perhaps a bit of madness. Her quivering hands held a lighter in one and a large jar of lighter fluid in the other.

Kim Shiloh dropped both and crumpled to her knees, sobbing.

Chapter Twenty-One

BY THAT FRIDAY, THE *ACADEMY HERALD* FEATURED A news story about Kim's arrest for arson.

Staff Member Fired After Fire

Kim Shiloh, speech coach at King's Academy and former principal of Emmanuel Academy, found herself in a police car after she set fire to the campus gardens. Her arrest charges include suspicion of arson in the infamous Emmanuel Academy fire back in the fall. When asked about these charges, Shiloh refused to comment. When asked about details for the events, police refused to comment.

"A lot of information that gave us." Michelle flung the paper onto the dining-commons tables and dug a spoon into her yogurt and granola. "If you ask me, none of the students who write this paper should pursue journalism. One contributor misspelled *ceiling* on page four. How?"

"Takes talent." Hannah reached for the paper and flipped to the comics.

Inconsolable, Ned had also refused to comment on the damage inflicted on his garden. He hid in his office and canceled the Principal's Advisory Council meetings for the following two weeks.

"Poor guy." Rayah picked at some undercooked eggs with her fork. "Someone told me he had planted the garden for his wife."

Danny's mother cultivated a small patch of cucumbers and tomatoes in their backyard, green leaves peeking out of black soil in a tight wooden rectangle. The woman would throw a conniption if a worm bit through any of the plants, let alone an entire fire consume the garden.

The student council never minded the cold and picked up a "fire" themselves through an onslaught of planning new events.

One afternoon over a dissected frog, Michelle informed Danny about the insanity of the student council meetings that took place in a mathematics classroom. "They already started planning for prom—four months out."

Danny chuckled. "Really? Surprised they hadn't started earlier. The slackers."

She sliced her scalpel through the bulging biceps of the frog and pried the skin open with her forceps. The snake in the tank folded itself against the glass, as if waiting for someone to release it to gobble one of the amphibian specimens. It would taste terrible based on the smell. Pungent formaldehyde soaked the room.

Danny placed his shirt over his nose, but it did little to stifle the stench, which churned his stomach. He had insisted on helping, but Michelle had refused.

"You almost puked when we did the earthworm dissection." She motioned to a dissected rat inside a glass display case with its pink organs sprawling over its white fur. "Imagine what a frog would do."

Swallowing a dry taste in his mouth, he relented. For good reason because moments later, his head grew fuzzy. Ah, nausea, his old friend. It had returned after a brief hibernation.

"So prom's four months out, you said." He grimaced, pressing down on his stomach.

"Yeah. Did you know they budget tens of thousands? Yet they still ask students to pay thirty bucks a ticket."

The administrators definitely majored in economics.

The slimy scalpel tore through the frog's midsection, some sort of yellowish liquid oozing past the blade, and Danny nearly retched as Michelle completed the task with a pair of silver scissors. "Great! They gave us a female."

He clutched his stomach as eggs spilled out of the frog's midsection onto the tray. Odds were the frog was going to start crying too.

"Don't see you spooning this stuff out of it." She had already used the prying forceps to dollop the shriveled black spawns onto the tray.

Gagging on the fumes from the frog, he asked, "What other events has the student council planned for January?"

"A winter formal this Saturday night—one of six major events for January, I might add. All council members will have to help set up and tear down—unless they're part of a sport—so that cancels my plans for *Julius Caesar* rehearsal and Bible study."

His chest deflated. There went one member. Might have to close church soon. He could almost hear the pagans rejoice.

"Guess that brings us down to four members."

"Have you tried pinning signs about the study to the bulletin boards around the school, Dan?"

Eyes fixed on the shredded frog, she afforded a small jerk of her head toward a corkboard on the wall. Neon papers advertising organizations such as *Pi People Math Club* and *Ham(let)ing it up Shakespeare Players* overpopulated the small rectangle on the wall.

"If they burn Korans in chemistry, I doubt our sign would last in a science classroom. Besides, Ned has to approve any advertisement before it goes up."

"Thought you had him wrapped around your finger." Michelle slit the frog's throat.

"Probably the other way around."

Of course he didn't want to push his luck with the principal who had just lost his favorite landmark. Not to mention he had no idea when Ned would schedule the next advisory meeting.

Palms growing sweaty in his squeaky gloves, he switched the tête-à-tête to Kim, Michelle's favorite conversation piece that week. It was, after all, the most dramatic.

"Ambitious hardly describes the woman." Michelle crinkled her eyes behind her foggy lab goggles. "Not only did she think she could burn down one school, but she wanted to take over King's, which has a strong leader. Way over her head if you ask me."

A little too ambitious ... even for Kim. Danny frowned as Michelle poked at some bulging blue veins in the frog with her scalpel. "Yeah,

Mitch. It doesn't add up for me either. In Ancient History class, we learned about what world leaders would do to their potential successors. Let's just say it wasn't nice."

"You mean like stabbing them to death, suffocating them in their beds, sorts of stuff Hannah would get giddy about?"

"Well, yeah ... again, not nice. So why would Kim try to take over as principal?"

Michelle stared at the tray for a moment before removing her yellow gloves. They squeaked against her skin as she pulled them off. Danny followed suit.

"I always wondered if she was missing a few gears up here"—she tapped her skull—"but I never thought of her as *this* crazy. How in the world did Emmanuel survive her time there with so many short circuits in her brain?"

Drama, drama, drama.

The sound of water sprinkling the sink and students snapping gloves off their hands and tossing them into the trash bin filled the air for a minute.

"Luckily, they caught her and put an end to it. Right?"

"We can only hope." Michelle sighed as she gathered the tray and headed toward the line of students near the sink at the back of the room to wash their dissection tools.

"Higher." Michelle gripped the base of the wobbly ladder, trying to keep it steady on the smelly red floor. At the top of the ladder, a shiny snowflake streamer dangled from Danny's one hand as he tried to hot glue it to the ceiling. "High as Duke and Dean get on weekends."

Or Hannah's mom for that matter.

Although Danny refused to attend the Winter Formal Dance—after all, he didn't have the thirty dollars to spare for a ticket—he agreed, for Michelle, to hang the decorations in the girls' basketball gymnasium—a squat, stinky room—half the size of the boys' arena a few doors down.

Michelle was the only one out of his three friends assigned to help for student council. Hannah and Rayah both got out of prepping and attending the event because of track and lacrosse workouts. The boys' track team had decided not to meet that day, so Danny had no excuse to not lend a hand.

"It's not really fair." Michelle stared at a basketball hoop strung with balloons around the rim. "King's makes exceptions for sports, but when I tell them I have rehearsal, they say I can't skip this event."

"Welcome to high school"—Danny stretched up on one leg, shaking—"where the arts programs don't matter."

"You could say that again."

"Welcome to high school, where the art—"

"Danny, I'm going to climb up there and punch you."

"Please do. And while you're at it, get this little guy to stay on the ceiling." He strained his leg to reach farther up. At last he wedged the streamer onto the bead of cooling glue.

Back on both feet, he stepped his clunky tennis shoes down a few steps to grab the next streamer from Michelle. The room smelled worse closer to the ground.

"Got lucky online during free period and found a newspaper with Kim's arraignment." She passed him the streamer as a girl behind her spilled a bottle of candy-apple scent, meant to be sprayed on various decorations. "Thought I would peruse it since our school paper is only good for kindling."

"An arraign—what?" He winked at her as he stepped up the ladder. "Orangutan? She does look like a monkey."

"Yes, but no. An arraignment is when a judge reads the defendant all the charges against them, and the accused either pleads 'guilty' or 'not guilty.' They added the charge of arson for the Emmanuel fire, you know. They blamed her for all of it."

"Good for them." The first snowflake from the ceiling broke free, caught itself in a blue streamer someone else had dangled, and then fluttered to the floor.

"Want to know what she pleaded?"

For mercy. "'Guilty,' right? We saw her burn the garden." He glanced down at Michelle to retrieve the fallen snowflake.

She shook her head. "'Not guilty,' Dan."

"What? We saw her torch the thing ... she had a lighter and fluid and everything."

Michelle bent down to grab the errant streamer, her long blue dress forming a bubble when she kneeled. "Maybe she pleaded guilty to that, but we have a definite 'not guilty' for the arson against Emmanuel."

Of course they did. Wouldn't be high school if they didn't make everything complicated.

Giggling from the corner of the gym interrupted the friends as a girl stuffed a handful of white decorative snow down Lawrence's and then another boy's shirt. Across the large room, various student-council members dangled blue crystal-like lights. But once they got their hands on the wires, they spent more time tangling than hanging. Gotta love group projects.

Multiple Christmas trees stood around the edges of the room like spruced-up girls waiting for someone to ask them for a dance. Golden baubles clung to their "dresses" in awkward corners as if those who had strung the trinkets had had a temporary loss of vision. And cerulean and silver balloons hugged so much of the corners, walls, and ceiling of the room that anyone with a latex allergy would convulse instantly upon entry to the dance floor.

A sharp clapping of hands caused all the members to freeze. Valentina's large eyes narrowed at the girl with another ball of "snow" to throw at Lawrence. "Winter formal starts in five hours. You want the students to pay thirty dollars to visit this craphole?" She didn't use the word *craphole*. Valentina's clawed nails clutched at her hips, which were accentuated by her tight green dress.

Wow. She was never that mean in meetings with Ned. Wonder why.

Heads drooped. "No," students mumbled asynchronously.

"All right, then. Stick that fake snow on the wall and get it out of Travis' shirt." She slapped the red bricks on the wall, which clashed horribly with the blue color scheme of the decorations. "Hang those lights on the ceiling. Better look like the Christmas trees in New York when you finish. Ornate, people!" She smacked the back of her hand against the palm of the other.

"And you ..." She rounded on Danny, who dangled from the ladder. And him. Oh, boy. Here they went.

Her lips dripped with shiny lip gloss and relish to give her fellow advisory member a scolding. "One more snowflake falls, and we hot glue you to the ceiling."

He hid a smile at the mental imagery of himself dangling like a spider as couples boogied on the dance floor below. Nothing said winter romance quite like a guy stuck to the ceiling.

Valentina whipped around and disappeared from the dead-fish-scented room.

Following this, grumbles and scurries to complete projects commenced.

Danny stuck a large bead of glue on the ceiling and pressed the streamer into it, burning his thumb. "Believe me"—he winced—"Valentina never talks like that in the PAC meetings. Girl turns on the charm for the principal. Her voice goes up three octaves."

"Amazing what you can do with that amount of influence."

With a swift hand motion, she beckoned Danny down.

He had completed hanging snowflakes and moved onto his next task: hot gluing sticks to the wall for a foresty feel—and to disguise the scarlet of the bricks as best they could.

"Did you know she browbeat every member of the student council to approve a Sadie Hawkins dance this year? Who knows why? She can't ask Dean—the love of her life—to go with her because he's dating—"

The speakers blared "No Diggity" at a volume far too loud for the echoing walls. The DJ decreased the volume and the drums settled into a steady beat.

"I have the solution to get more people for your Bible study, Dan."

"Date Valentina?"

"No, that would scatter them."

Phew. "What, then?"

"Dean!"

He gaped at her for a moment and then returned to the wall, where one of his sticks, despite having the word *stick* in the name, refused to stick. The decoration fell and bounced on the red rubber floor.

"Sure, Mitch. Everyone thinks, *Does heaven exist?* when they see Dean because odds are, the guy'll kill them, and they'll have their question answered." He turned his nose to the wall and breathed the burning glue-gun fumes.

"I meant invite someone who has a lot of friends ... like Valentina or Dean." Michelle frowned for a moment in the steady pulse of the drum. "Well, maybe not those two."

Trails of glue formed spiderwebs by the time he finally managed to cement the stick to the brick. He consulted the bag with extra glue before answering. "Appreciate the gesture considering we're low on numbers, but no thanks."

"How about Duke?" Michelle reached for another stick from the white sidelines. "He piggybacks most of Dean's friends, anyway ... and is less violent."

"Still stands by when others drive hooks into noses." Spittle flew from his lips into Michelle's face as she handed him another stick.

For once in a long time, Michelle fell silent.

Now the gym echoed the footsteps of the other volunteers ... but nothing else. They'd shut off the music.

His heart throbbed in his ears. Crossed a line.

Finally, "You know, Danny, even though your name means 'God is my judge,' doesn't mean you need to play God in that scenario."

"What?"

"Leave the judging to someone else is what I'm saying."

"When did you look up the meaning of my name?"

"Oh, I had some time during free period. Rayah's name means *bitterness* and Hannah's *grace.* I think their parents both messed up during those births."

He couldn't deny it. Danny sighed and faced the wall again. He plucked various flyaway strings of glue. "Mitch, as much as we would like more people to keep the group alive, inviting someone like Duke involves incredible risk. People at this school tear down anything religious. And if he's offended that I even asked him, he might turn to Dean ... and Dean has a fishhook."

"Right, right." She whacked him on the shoulder blade with a stick a little too hard. "I forgot being a Christian meant playing everything safe."

Bible study never took place that week because all but two of its members, Danny and Rayah, had other commitments. Gabe already displayed spotty attendance, going heaven-knows-where during some weeks. This week was no exception as he disappeared off the face of the earth and the grid of technology. Not that he was on the grid in the first place due to the great cell signal at King's.

Hannah canceled due to a heaping pile of homework her Saturday-detention monitor would not allow her to complete, and Michelle explored the world of a blue Winter Wonderland in the scarlet gym.

The next two weeks followed a similar pattern: cancellations due to half or more of the members missing. At this point, they weren't going to have a Bible study until summer. At least Danny wouldn't.

Rayah's and Michelle's parents went to church sporadically. And with all the worry at King's Academy, the Bible study was one of the only ways to de-stress. When they prayed together and spent time studying the Scriptures, reading the verses aloud, all the noise of daily life calmed to a mere whisper. A mental and emotional peace would envelop Danny like a cuddly, invisible blanket, and a feeling of well-being would fill him up that would carry him through the week. Without weekly Bible study, how could he survive King's?

Images from the summer his dad died flashed through his mind. The way the green stairs had smelled of dust. And despite the sunshine, every light in his memory appeared dimmer than Ned's office. One of the hardest periods of his life. He was so mad at God, he had refused to attend church, refused to go to youth group. A few weeks in, he gave up on reading his Bible and threw it against the wall of his room. It smacked a Red Rock Band poster and slid behind his desk.

He didn't pick it up again until someone from church stopped by his house with a homemade lasagna with too strong a basil scent. A mere step up from the "thoughts and prayers" the church members expressed. Just one step up. Holding the lasagna stood a large woman in a floral dress. The pastor's wife.

He remembered the moment so vividly. As he opened the door, in the seeping warmth of the summer breeze, she had drawn him into a tight one-armed hug. Her sweet perfume overwhelmed his nose. "We miss you so much, Danny."

"Yeah. Sorry. Been busy." He smudged his shoes on the *God Bless This Home* carpet by the front door.

Releasing him from the hug, she handed him the warm glass dish. "I know you want to give up now, but this is by far the most important time to come to church."

When he opened his mouth to object, she held up a hand. "Please let me finish. Danny, my husband and I used to run a lot of 5Ks before"—she glanced at her stomach—"before life picked up. I have asthma and his ankles are weak, but we never quit a single race. You know why?"

Danny set down the pasta, which had begun to burn his hands, on the steps. "No, why?"

"Because we wouldn't let the other one stop. No matter how hard the race got." She paused and glanced at her folded hands, fiddling with her wedding ring. "I know you lost someone in your family who you loved dearly."

At this point, Danny had scrunched up his face to prevent tears. Even a month after the death, it was hard not to cry. Cried probably more than his female friends could muster a year's worth of tears combined. He forced himself to focus on the fake potted plants in an aluminum vase by the door. On the yellow fabric flowers …

"But you have another family a couple roads down. Come back to church. We'll help you finish the race."

"You need the Bible study," he told himself now. "You're not strong enough to do life alone."

Desperate and not too afraid of death at this point—after the first few months at King's, he had kind of gotten bored of fearing for his life—Danny approached Duke about joining. Worst case, he'd die and not have to deal with this anymore. A nervous smile crawled up his cheeks. Maybe that was best case.

He cracked open the squeaky door, shoving back a wad of toilet paper and embracing the stale-beer smell. Home sweet home.

Duke kept his eyes transfixed on his phone, his head half sunk into a pillow. "What does the princess want?"

"Hey, man, I was wondering if you wanted to join us for Bible study on Saturday nights."

Duke bolted up in bed, bumping his head on the upper bunk.

Here lies Daniel Belte. Died at age 16. Cause of death: the Duke wanted him dead.

But before Duke could reply or chuck a dagger at Danny's head, his phone vibrated. The device buzzed so much, it sent ripples up the wrinkled brown sheets on the bed. He shoved the phone against his ear. "What do you want?"

Maybe he should leave. Darn it, legs, move. He didn't think "darn it." Nor did his legs budge. No, he had to stay. He needed to finish the race. He gripped his desk to steady himself, crumpled tissues cascading to the soiled carpet. Silence.

Then, "Give me a break. Not like Dad attended either ... fine, tell her to stuff it! I'm serious."

Dagon, he was going to stuff it soon too. Maybe he'd do well as taxidermy. He thought back to the stuffed animals in the science classroom. A headache burned the back of Danny's eyes, and his stomach burbled with nausea. If Duke killed him after the phone conversation, he vowed to come back and haunt Michelle for forcing him into this conversation in the first place.

"Easter?" Duke slammed his fist into the wood on the bottom of his bed. "You know I already had spring-break plans." A pause. "Fine. Thanks for nothing."

He clicked off the phone and chucked it across the room—a great distance away from Danny. It hit the chipped closet door and clunked onto a pile of chip bags. Rough fingers rubbed the bridge of the Duke's nose. After a moment, he glared at Danny with flashing eyes. "What do you do at your Bible-thumping club?"

"Bible study?"

"Whatever."

"We talk about what happened during the week and then read a passage of Scripture and talk about it. Gabe, the guy across the hall, suggested we go through the book of Daniel this week."

"Daniel. The dude who fought off the lions and stuff?"

"Yeah, sort of."

Duke stared at his crumpled sheets, frowning. He scratched his arm, a faint trace of blood trickling down it. Then he drilled the next question, "Who all go?"

Danny ran through the small list in a matter of ten seconds, but after he recited Hannah's name, Duke's face brightened a considerable amount in the shadow from the upper bunk bed.

No, dude, back off.

"Hannah?" Duke scratched his arm again, nails black from blood underneath them. "The girl from the lacrosse team who wears all the weird Japanese shirts?"

The one that Duke creepily stared at? "Yeah."

"The one who gave a player a concussion by hitting her on the head with a stick?"

"Yeah." If Duke wasn't too careful, she'd knock him out too. Oh, the things he never said aloud. Should probably jot them down and write them in a book someday. Like this one.

His roommate chewed on his thin lip for a moment. "Tell you what, Princess. I need to get my mom off my back about missing Mass for Christmas." His square jaw tightened as he nodded to his phone across the room. The cracked screen was visible underneath a Doritos bag. "And she says unless I find a church here, she'll force me to go to Easter Mass to get Grandma off *her* back."

"A lot of backs here."

"So I'll attend your little club for a week or two, and that should satisfy the old women. Understand?"

Danny nodded and made his way toward the door, but a rough growl from Duke held him back. Hand on the cold doorknob, he turned and faced the red-faced roommate.

"One more thing, Princess. Get out of your head any attempts to *save* or convert me. I'm just going so my mom stops calling every five minutes … got it? Just two weeks. In and out."

"In and out, understood." He had meant to duck out of the room before Duke could change his mind, but he found himself staring at Duke's eye. For some reason, it mesmerized him.

Evidently, he took too long a pause because the roommate glared at him. "What, Princess?"

"N–nothing." His blood froze.

Duke jabbed a finger at his bad eye. "Saw you staring at this."

"No, I wasn't." Here lies Danny. Cause of death: stupidity.

"Come on, I've seen that expression a million times. You want to know how I got it."

"I could've been looking at your nose. Since it's really ... ordinary." Great word choice. Wasn't he supposed to be really good at English or something?

A growl. "Everyone always asks. Fine. If you want to know, Mom was a bit of a druggie before she gave birth to me. That's how I got it."

"Oh, OK. Sorry."

Danny passed through the squeaky door, collapsing into a Phrat River lounge couch. His chest released, and he found himself, for once, grateful for his mother—even if she was a little crazy.

Chapter Twenty-Two

CLAUDIA LAY ON A LOUNGE CHAIR IN PHRAT River, shoulders arched back in a tunic dress, reminding Danny of a Roman emperor. The fact that Danny's history class had just covered the beginnings of Rome could have influenced this perception. Granted, the Roman emperors were not huge fans of picking other people's scabs. So luckily, he'd be able to tell the difference between the two. Three weeks into attending the Bible study, Duke had brought the girl with the bob haircut from Danny's graphic-design class.

Week four ushered in four more bodies to the lounge in Phrat River. Danny suspected the three newbies joined just for Rayah's cinnamon-scented snickerdoodles she had made in the Suanna oven. In her defense, they were pretty dang good. She had obtained the ingredients from Duke, who worked in the kitchen. Hence the crowd stuffed into the small brick alcove by the picture of the golden fountain.

Danny never failed to appreciate new faces. This was especially true with rehearsals picking up for Michelle in *Julius Caesar*. The director had reserved all but two Saturdays in the scarlet-curtained auditorium in the coming months for practice. Although Hannah returned from speech tournaments, which were held through the end of April, by the seven o'clock Bible study time, sometimes she arrived much later and missed it.

By the tail end of March, they had run out of seating for all who arrived. Some had to sit cross-legged on the ripped-up carpet. Whenever Claudia sat there, she liked to pick at the holes with her chewed fingernails. Because of this, Danny almost thanked Dagon he had a track meet during the next meeting ... almost.

That Saturday, a chilly rainstorm pummeled the school, turning the red bricks to brown, gold-painted lions glimmering in the water. Power outages broke out in the older academic buildings, the ones unattached to generators. All students who traveled from their dorms to the dining commons found their rain boots drowning in icy sheets of water. Soggy socks and dripping faces left everyone shivering and miserable.

One by one, the announcements tallied the sports that were canceled due to the rain. The "wimps" as Hannah liked to call them.

Baseball and softball went first, with men's tennis to follow. One by one, two by two ... until only lacrosse and track remained in the flood. Hannah had a short practice on the soccer field and could still make the study, pacifying Duke, who had grown anxious about her absences. But when lightning flashed outside the window of Danny's last class, he knew his meet would last for hours because of the delay.

With the hour tolled from the clock tower, he dug through his bag and pulled out a long-sleeve synthetic material his mother had sent him in a cardboard care package. He ran his hands across the smooth fabric. It made a sort of zipping sound when he scratched it. The hand-me-down from Judah at least provided an extra degree of heat in the freezing drizzle.

He peeled off his wet shirt in the locker room and with a lot of effort dragged the elastic, long-sleeved shirt over his skin and the track uniform, still smelling of sweat from the meet the day before, on top of it. He was glad to know he'd be deterring all those fawning ladies with his ungodly scent. Although he would have liked to stuff his uniform in the cramped washing machines on the bottom floor of Phrat River, it was almost impossible. The things were always full like Danny's schedule. Plus the machines smelled moldy and would not have improved any of his dirty clothes.

Coach entered the foot-stench locker room, rubbing his drenched nose with the back of his hand. He banged his fist against a scarlet locker. "They postponed the meet another hour because of lightning." He rubbed his palms on his red-and-gold striped shirt, which had soaked all the way through.

Despite the delays, the coach drilled the team to run laps around the hallways and do complete stretches. Probably wanted to feel like he had some sort of purpose in life. "Stay warmed up. Lydia fights hard in the four by four relay."

Danny pressed his palms to a brick wall during one of the stretching breaks and swung his leg back and forth like a pendulum. "Think we'll run?" He directed the question to a teammate behind him with a lip piercing.

The teammate rubbed his nose against his clammy tank top. "Ned turned Lydia into the new Emmanuel. They would have us do the meet even if a tornado was at the finish line."

After the previous rival, Emmanuel, had been vanquished by fire, the academy had struggled to find a formidable foe from among the few schools in the rolling hills of a poor school district. At last, they landed on the one too far away to be touched by the poverty. A school tucked in a forest of budding pink trees. Equally rich, equally talented. Why hadn't they raced against each other to start?

By five, the lightning ceased flashing in the dark hallway windows, and Coach forced the players outside in a sprint toward the track. Rain pelted so hard, the drops stung Danny's eyes. Lovely day outside. Ahead on the track, an American flag bobbing on the pole in the wind clinked, and the various advertised signs ruffled, especially the one for the statues.

Danny shut his eyelids as a sharp wind gushed over the track and chilled his bones. Goosebumps erupted all over his legs up to where the ridiculously short shorts cut off near his butt cheeks. Already his spiked shoes had filled with pools of cold water as the muffled announcer, almost inaudible amid the slapping rain capsules, called for the 4 x 800 relay, Danny's first event of three.

He waited on the sidelines. As the last leg of the race, he had at least five minutes before they would need him at the starting line. He kicked up his knees in the turf, spraying water with his spikes, trying to keep warm. He rubbed a wet knuckle under his nostrils, trying to keep his nose dry, causing everything to smell like mud and rainwater. Practicing lunges, he stole a glance at the stands at the poor people hunching in their raincoats. No doubt, their pockets must have grown heavy from all the water that filled them.

Of the twenty or thirty attendees, one sat dead center without a raincoat or protection of any kind. It was a tall figure, back as straight as if prepared to defy Pneumonia and Death themselves. Even in the foggy downpour, one could not mistake the curly ponytail, beard, and metallic red tie. *Hiya, Ned.*

The gun cracked, and the first runners bolted around the track. Curtains of raindrops created such a heavy haze, Danny could hardly see the first leg, second leg, and third approach until they reached the final one hundred meters.

Danny in his torn-up neon shoes, which glowed in the storm, made his way to the first lane as King's third leg curved his way into the final stretch. Neck and neck with the Lydia opponent, Danny and the other fourth-leg runners shared a glance of uncertainty as to who should stand in the first lane to retrieve the baton first.

In the last ten meters, the King's runner broke ahead, and Danny began his run with his arm stretched out behind him. He felt the cold metal slide into his palm. Off to the races.

Fingers clutching the golden baton, he broke out into a sprint. Throughout the first lap, the Lydia runner stayed at his shoulder, like a shadow hovering behind him in the gray haze of the storm. Danny whipped his arms as fast as they could go in the cold weather, and he swore he almost jabbed the competitor in the ribs. They were that close. He rounded the first lap and passed the jingling American flag.

The stands erupted with hoarse cheers.

"Come on!"

"Push ahead."

"Pick it up this next lap."

"Don't let him pass you!"

But one voice stood out from the rest, and it bellowed so deep, Danny thought another rumble of thunder cracked in the sky. "Sprint, Danny, sprint!" No mistaking Ned's voice.

Even though his sides burned in agony, lactic acid eating away at his lungs—who needed them anyway—and everything else feeling numb and immovable because of the chill, Danny ran. He ran because he had to. Ran because all the other legs of the race counted on *his* legs. Ran because Ned told him to. And he always followed the rules.

Wheezes overtook him when he was two hundred meters into the second lap. The other runner eased into the second lane to pass him. Danny's mouth formed an O to let out quick spurts of breath to sustain him for the final half-lap. Swinging his arms until his elbows hit eye level, he leaned into the wind down the final stretch. The Lydia athlete continued in the second lane in dead determination to gain an inch or two ahead of him.

Danny doubled over into his abdomen and shut his eyes as they approached the finish line. His arms flew behind him as if he prepared to take flight.

He toppled forward and collapsed onto the polyurethane track. Upon contact, the gritty texture stung his frozen skin. Dang, hurt a lot more than he was expecting.

His head swam and he developed a sudden urge to vomit. What else was new? His eyelids peeled open as he found the three other legs of his race huddled around him.

Neon shoes kicked up rainwater on the glowing white lines on the track. A runner somewhere behind him gripped Danny's shoulder with a cold, wet hand, asking if he needed medical assistance. Every face was beaming at him. Maybe they liked watching people throw up? People at King's seemed to have odd tastes: pulling peoples' scabs, staring for uncomfortable amounts of time …

"We won, Dan"—one teammate jerked his head toward the scoreboard by the sign for the statues—"by zero point five seconds."

Dang. That close?

The huddle around him parted, and the winning time blazed in large orange letters on the scoreboard at the other end of the track: *2:19.26.* Ten seconds faster than his personal record.

"Dagon." His hands wobbled as he pushed himself up onto his knees. "These guys run fast."

One of the others slapped him on the shoulder blade. Pain throbbed everywhere. They ushered him off the track to get out of the way of the second heat of the race and underneath a red-and-white team tent set up by the stands. Looked like something from a circus.

"Don't worry about the meet." Another King's runner swaddled a towel around Danny's shivering shoulders. Didn't help much since it was damp. "We have the rest of the races in the bag."

Mmm, not quite. As the meet progressed, the 100-meter hurdles, 100-meter dash, and 4 x 200 all yielded close results ... that followed with wins for the Lydia side.

"Hear they recruit all one hundred-some they have on their team from other schools," one runner said as she squatted in a patch of grass underneath the tent.

"Hate it when they do that." Another one parked beside her, decapitating the tips of grass with muddy fingers. "It's bad enough that King's recruited so many students this year."

Danny coughed.

By the time the 1600 came, Danny still hadn't recovered from the previous race and could only manage a second place in his best event, nearly colliding with the back fence where a line of trees lay waiting to hug him. Even Ned in the stands had slumped his spine like the rest of the crowd. They all resembled cheerless admirers of a football team that never scored any games. So this is what it felt like to live in Cleveland. One of his relatives was from there.

The rain reduced to a drizzle by the final event, the 4 x 400, sun straining through lines in the slate clouds. But by that point, the other team had outscored them in everything except for the 4 x 800 and the high jump, gained by no other than Gabe himself. Rayah had returned to Phrat River for Bible study. Lucky for her, the girls' team coach allowed those who had finished their events to leave early.

At that point of the meet, Ned had slipped out of the stands along with all but five members of the crowd. Sad day when the Bible study had more people than this.

With one event left to go, Danny and Gabe met at the fence by the track to cheer on the team. Their goose-bump-covered bodies quivered against the chain-link fence as they waited for the meet to end.

"Does anyone know why Ned showed for this? We haven't seen his face for weeks. The man never schedules advising meetings anymore. Then suddenly—*wham*! He's at a track meet in the worst weather of the season."

The official by the starting line cracked his gun, and Gabe's shrug transformed into a surprised jump. "Maybe he wanted something to boost his confidence after the garden-fire incident. If we crushed our new rival in this track meet, he might feel he has a little more control over his school."

"Control?" Did he not have any, or did Gabe forget the five billion cameras around the school?

Gabe held up a finger and shouted at the runners as they bent around into the one-hundred-meter stretch. After they passed, he returned his attention to Danny. "Yeah, control." He stuffed his hands into his angel hoodie. Under the hood, a bit of spiky white hair, slightly darker from the rain, stuck out. "After you told him what that email message meant, he probably thinks his school will have terrible leaders after he leaves."

"But Michelle told me that was a good thing. That principals like to hear that."

"I mean, he would definitely want to hear that he's the best. But if every ruler after him gets worse and worse, what does that do to his legacy? To the school?"

Oh. Following in the footsteps of Emmanuel.

Gabe fiddled with the protective cap on the chain-link fence. "Any principal, knowing his school will go down the toilet, will cling to whatever victory he can. This track meet being the first."

The King's runners trailed slower and slower behind their opponents until, by the final leg of the race, the Lydia team finished half a lap ahead of King's. At least it wasn't a whole lap.

The post-team huddle was by far the most depressing huddle out of all the meets Danny had run. Circled by the jingling American flagpole, Coach only gave them four words of encouragement. "Go get a shower."

Spiked shoes squished in the turf on their way back to the locker room. The sort of defeated squelch that added to the miserable note of the evening.

Luckily, as one of the first arrivals to the locker room, Danny undressed and stood under one of the few faucets in the community shower. The welcome warm water defrosted his numb, blue body from the cold. He was grateful for this luxury here because at Phrat River the water heater had busted some time in December.

With great reluctance, he left the steaming water as the next member in line took his place. Wrapped in the damp towel from the meet, he swung open his locker and put on the cold, wet school clothes he'd worn earlier that day. They felt rather unpleasant against his new, clean skin. This would definitely repulse all the ladies. Too bad he hadn't done a laundry day in a month.

Gabe had already finished his shower and waited for Danny outside the locker room. Together they padded through the sludgy gravel paths on the way back to Phrat River, passing mutilated frogs on the way, half-buried by the mud.

When they arrived at the sullen gray dorm, even more leaden in the sunset skies, his heart stopped. Dagon. What happened?

Rayah bolted toward him, fresh tears streaming down her cheeks, and she collapsed into his chest in a hug. "Horrible, horrible, horrible." All she could get out between sobs. Her hair smelled like campfire smoke.

Dagon. *What happened?*

All of Phrat River, along with the Bible study group, stood on the lawn outside the dorm. Danny spotted the tail end of a scarlet fire truck tucked behind the building.

As Rayah continued to sob into his already wet and smelly shirt, Michelle approached him with a grim expression and crossed arms. "Someone in a ski mask stopped our Bible study." Mud and grass were caked on her heels. "During prayer, he dumped lighter fluid on the carpet, and just as we opened our eyes, he clicked a lighter." She tugged Rayah into a hug, and across the field Duke checked over Hannah as she fought bits of coughing.

Danny didn't even have the energy to tell him to back off. All of it had been drained at the meet. He opened his mouth but no words trickled off his tongue. One moment later, "W–why? Who?"

"No one knows." Michelle wobbled on both feet, sinking into the mud. "Looked like a guy based on his build. But in a dorm like that with no windows ... Lucky we all got out, huh?"

Danny's chin bobbed up and down, but his mind floated a million miles away from his body.

Michelle's hand clapped on his numb shoulder. "Danny, describe to me the lighter and the lighting fluid Kim used that day in the garden."

His eyebrows furrowed. "A yellow lighter, and I think the fluid bottle was the same color with a large red flame on the front."

Her eyes bulged as Michelle's eyes were prone to do.

"Maybe we had the person all wrong for who caused the Emmanuel fire. When you saw Kim at the garden, did you actually see her, you know, set fire to stuff?"

He swallowed with a dry mouth. Everything tasted like metal. "No. But there was no one else aside from her, and she held the lighter and fluid in her hands. She dropped those and wailed a miserable wail. You know the story." He watched the building, expecting gray smoke to billow. Then again, there were no windows. Where could the plumes go?

"Ever thought a student could have framed Kim?" Michelle kicked off her heels, allowing the dirt to bury her pale toes. "Maybe she cried because another person threatened her to stand in front of the garden with the lighter. Guys and guns have incredible influence, you know."

Umm, no. Definitely not. "A bit of a jump, Mitch."

"No. She claimed, 'Not guilty,' remember? Maybe she really didn't set fire to Ned's garden *or* Emmanuel."

Heart throbbing in his chest, Danny looked away to try to absorb the newest conspiracy. Couldn't be right. Then again, nothing here was. His eyes landed on Hannah. She shooed Duke away, like a person trying to wave away a cloud of smoke, so she could cough in peace. Atta girl.

Duke rose, caught Danny's eye, and motioned for him to join him by a spiky elm. "We need to talk." His one eye flickered over his shoulder for a moment.

"Duke, what happened? I miss this study for one day. I feel like a mom who told her kids not to set the house on fire when she leaves."

"Listen, I've seen that ski mask and lighter before. Your other roommate used both when setting his ex's car on fire last spring."

No way. Danny's choked whisper, tasting like sulfur, released a "You mean?"

A grim nod. "Dean tried to set your friends on fire."

Chapter Twenty-Three

DANNY AWOKE IN A POOL OF SWEAT. EVEN though he had piled on two hoodies and three blankets, the chill running up and down his body never went away. His throat burned, and any amount of water swallowed felt like acid spilling down his esophagus. Otherwise, he was doing just fine.

A day or two after the meet and the Bible study incident, a rather nasty virus had attached itself to Danny. Unable to rise from bed or visit the Health Center across campus, he shot an email to all his teachers letting them know he would not be at class that Monday.

During her free period, Hannah sneaked a plastic covered bowl from her room and filled it with the dining commons' tomato soup. She arrived at his Phrat River dorm and forced him to swallow spoonfuls of the salty brew. She wrinkled her nose, ruby nose ring hiding in the crease of her nostril. "Still smells like smoke in here."

"Yeah, well, the fire department said the flames hardly spread across the carpet," he rasped and then gripped his throat, wincing at the pain. "And Ned likes to save money by cramming us into dorms." He coughed. The hack seared his esophagus so much his vision went fuzzy. "So he had no space left anywhere else on campus for us to stay."

"Speaking of our wonderful principal, we tried to have him review the security videos to see a student setting the carpet on fire. 'Cording to Mitch, he keeps telling newspapers some careless student lit a candle warmer or something."

Man, good thing no one read those. Danny's eyes flicked to a smoke detector flashing a red light on the ceiling. "What did he say when you confronted him?"

She ladled the soup at the bottom of the bowl with a crooked spoon. "His *wonderful* secretary, Ashley, intercepted us. Mitch, during her free period, is gonna try to contact him via email, our only prayer with the guy."

Ned checked his inbox almost as much as Dean checked himself in the mirror.

Hannah tore off her fingerless gloves and pressed the back of her hand to Danny's forehead. "Still warm."

Danny shivered. "Doesn't feel like it."

"Your coach's heart will sink. Gabe said the track team keeps trying to get you to run today's meet even though you missed classes." With a hard jab, she forced the soup bowl to his lips.

Danny's weak hand from under the blankets blocked her in time. "Hurts"—he motioned to his throat—"to swallow. Or breathe. Or think."

She rolled her eyes. "Glad Michelle usually does this mom stuff. Stupid *Julius Caesar* rehearsals." She plopped the bowl onto the blanket, spilling some of the rosy liquid.

"You're doing better than my roommates." A chapped-lip smile spread across his clammy face. "Duke tried to make me sleep in Gabe's room so he wouldn't catch my bug. Gabe's roommates refused. Wonder why."

Hannah reached for a dirty T-shirt on the ground to soak up the spilled soup and then paused. "Duke asked me to prom today."

Many "prom-posals" had sprouted in the school since early March. Ranging from the arrangement of pepperonis on a greasy pizza to spell out *prom* to one student hiring a skywriter to spell it out in the sky—which turned out to look more like *RROM* when the pilot tried to make a fancy *P*—every student, it seemed, was trying to snag a partner for the luau-themed dance. Even Michelle, with an iambic pentameter poem, had asked Jeremy if he would go. Jeremy broke down in tears when he read the note and called Michelle to say she cheated by using Shakespeare to win his heart, but he would, alas, accompany her.

"How did he ask you?" Danny thrust off the blanket because the liquid seeped cold onto his skin. He shivered again.

"Just asked." She tossed a strand of frizzy hair over her shoulder. "Not like he wants to marry me. Besides, he knows I hate anything over-the-top."

"What did you say?"

"Told him I would go if he wore a Sonic the Hedgehog hat, my one condition."

Danny tried to picture Duke with blue spikes jetting out of his head as he and Hannah danced to "The Cupid Shuffle." A chuckle rose in his throat, causing pain to sear in his neck. "Why?"

Her eyes flashed at him as if he had asked her why humans needed oxygen. An exasperated sigh. "Wouldn't make sense to go with someone who wouldn't do that."

Yep, Han. That definitely made perfect sense. "And he said?"

"He would even wear a Knuckles the Echidna mask."

Wow. Real gentleman. "Looks like you have a keeper, then."

She cupped the bowl in her hands, and this could have been blamed on the splitting headache tearing into his brain, but he thought she blushed.

"You asking anyone, Dan?" She took a sudden interest in her super-hero-patterned Converse she got for Christmas. They kicked a beer bottle back and forth.

"To wear a Sonic the Hedgehog hat?"

"You know what I mean."

"Ray, I guess. She and I don't really go to these things much, but it seems almost like a capital crime not to attend."

A long silence ensued.

Finally, Hannah rose from the bed. "Feel worse."

Danny let out a half-chuckle, half-cough, which scorched his throat again. Everything tasted like mucus and blood.

"Whenever anyone says to feel better, you always end up feeling worse." She shrugged, refusing to meet his eyes. "Hoped the opposite would work its magic."

She slammed the squeaky door and left Danny under layers of soaked covers and wondering how in the world he had had such luck in meeting a wonderful friend like Hannah.

Tuesday, Danny forced himself out of bed to class.

The night before, his coach had texted him ten times. Of course with the *excellent* cell service at the school, all the messages came in at once. Each of the frantic texts indicated their team had lost to the weak Meede Media, an event unprecedented in the school's history. The weather couldn't even play an excuse as the sunshine blazed outside, or so he'd been told ... no windows.

Guilt building in his gut, he stumbled into his first-period class with swollen eye bags, almost Duke-sized, and a rhinoceros cough.

When he slid into his seat next to Michelle, shivering, she told him that Ned had responded to her emails regarding the video cameras and whether they captured the ski-mask culprit. She showed him the email underneath the lab table when the teacher turned away.

Michelle,

> *Due to the rainstorm that caused massive power outages around campus, several of our cameras went down for the day. The one on the second floor of Phrat River was not an exception. Of course, although I would like to believe your story about the student and the lighter, most of the eye-witnesses had their eyes closed in prayer. With no compelling evidence, it would be a tricky case to convince any authority to investigate and would place a rather nasty name on the school so I would suggest—*

Before Danny could read what Ned suggested—not that he really wanted to—Michelle clicked off her phone as the teacher called on her to recite part of the Krebs cycle. Nothing quite like a mitochondrial matrix to take his nausea away.

Later Danny struggled to walk through the hallways and almost had to take a seat during the pledge because he had grown too light-headed.

Just before her rehearsal for *Julius Caesar*, Michelle made him a cup of honey tea in the dining-commons microwave. The faintly sweet concoction burned all the way from his throat to his stomach, but he thanked her anyway. After all, her rehearsals had picked up in frequency because the upcoming performance was in two weeks, and the fact she had time to make him a drink surprised him beyond belief.

When he arrived at track practice, his coach's expression of delight quickly transformed into one of horror.

"Oh, Daniel, I see you made it out of bed today." He rubbed a sagging jaw. "We have—uh"—he consulted his clipboard, avoiding Danny's bloodshot gaze—"a rather tough workout today for our meet tomorrow against North Sussex. Let me know if you need a breather because I'd like to see you at the starting line."

A breather? The man never even offered water breaks during practice. Throat too raw to speak, Danny nodded and staggered over to the fence to start stretches. Tree branches tickled his palms through the holes as he swung his leg back and forth, head full of cotton.

Their team leader arranged a "ladder workout," which the group had rechristened with a more pleasant name, a "suicide." The runners would sprint a half mile, quarter mile, eighth mile, sixteenth mile, sixteenth again, eighth again, quarter again … and so on and on … on repeat.

One ladder rung in—the first quarter mile—Danny's brain filled with static and his vision faded to gray. All the sounds outside, several rungs in, had muffled until they echoed. His pace slowed as the other teammates whizzed by on the final stretch.

After the final 800, his coach's shrill stopwatch beeped. After that, Danny proceeded to collapse on the track with his palms outstretched, letting the black rubber dig into his skin. He heaved and hacked, throat raw and tasting of bile.

"Thirty seconds and you start the next ladder." The coach bleeped his stopwatch once more.

He wondered what poem Hannah would read at his funeral. Another lap and he was done for.

Hands clawed at his clammy tank top to prod him to rise.

He shoved himself onto his feet and staggered lopsidedly to the starting line to begin the next round.

Agony seared his sides and head so much that during the next lap, blackness coated his vision. What if Hannah read *Goodnight Moon?* He started to hyperventilate, and the runners drifted away as they passed him once more.

Around the two hundred meters, just as he caught sight of the *Up on a Pedestal* advertisement flat against the fence—no breeze—his vision went dark. Oh, eyesight. He kind of needed that but … guess not.

Blinded and very dazed, he plowed forward in a dream state in the slimy afternoon heat, wooliness in his skull.

Then pain. He stumbled into something hard, cold, and jagged and fell back. His head hit the track. His mouth pried itself open as wide as it could go as he gasped heavy, wheezing breaths.

A commotion from the girls' team, which Rayah said would be practicing 200-meter repeats that day, echoed somewhere very far away. He felt a small hand jerk his shoulder.

"Deep breaths, Dan." A soft voice. Rayah's. "Your pupils look huge."

"C ... can't s ... see." He tried to prop himself on his hands, which slipped and scraped on the hot track.

"Don't get up. Just keep breathing deeply. I told one of the girls to grab your water bottle from the stands."

It was at this moment, head fuzzy and not quite altogether with reality, Danny remembered he had to ask his friend something. He would probably die this very instant. As people on death beds were wont to say rash, sweet nonsense, he blurted out his final words, "Go to prom with me?"

He felt a warm liquid rise in his throat as his stomach emptied its contents, followed by screams nearby. A faint rancid smell made his head dizzy again. This went on for a while until someone pressed something hard to his lips and water flooded his tongue. It tasted cool, but the terrible aftertaste of the vomit made it hard to choke down. He swallowed and slowed his breathing. In–out, in–out, in, out. In and out. In and out. In ... and out.

Man, what a wild ride. His vision returned as the blurred images—most of whom had given him a wide berth—sharpened over the next minute with each steady breath. To his left, his coach had buried his face into a thick hand, and at his right by the jingling American flag, a cluster of track-team girls gazed at him with a mixture of pity and disgust. Ah, his admirers.

Facing forward, Danny managed to spot what he had crashed into when his eyesight failed him: a chain-link fence. Right next to the sign for the statues. Now as he remembered the collision, the fence had made a metallic jingle when he slammed into the railing.

Rayah, who sat beside him, rubbed a towel against his chin. He had a sickening feeling that she had received the brunt of his dining-commons lunch. Nevertheless, her lips twitched in amusement, her brow was smooth, and her posture relaxed.

"Have to say, Dan"—she chuckled—"don't think anyone's prom-posal will top that."

Chapter Twenty-Four

FOR THE FIRST TIME ALL YEAR, MICHELLE DITCHED class. Gasp. Horror. Jeremy screams echoing all around.

Dress rehearsals stretched on until well after two in the morning with her creeping past the curfew monitors in Suanna, who supposedly wore all black and smelled like musk. After days of resistance, she finally gave in to sleep.

Danny, himself, had missed a great deal of school to gain enough strength to attend track meets.

After five days' absence, he was called into Ned's office, King's Academy policy. Ned adjusted a potted plant on his windowsill. An aloe. "You can miss class. The track team needs all the help it can get."

Gabe was right. Ned wanted any victory.

Danny managed to place in most of his races but at a throat-searing cost. His sickness—which had sprouted at the beginning of the month—seemed to worsen as they reached the cusp of May, just in time for the sunshine to radiate the campus in unnatural heat. Not to mention the boys' track team only managed to gain a handful of victories and did not qualify for the major meets except to send individual athletes, such as Danny, to States.

Still, on the day of Michelle's first performance, Danny forced himself out of his sweaty sheets to attend classes so he could take notes in the ones he and Michelle had together. For second-period science, his weak arms propped him up as the class rose to do the daily pledge.

"Sit." The teacher remained at his desk, blowing his reddish nose into a tissue. Allergy season. "No pledge for today."

A student in the back let out a whoop, but most of the classmates exchanged puzzled expressions.

Purple in the face, a girl in camo capris shot her hand into the air.

"Yes, Miss Murabi?" The teacher used the students' last names as he always did.

She tugged a strand of green hair behind a sharp, square ear. God made the girl out of angles, no soft curves. "Is the school doing the pledge later in the day?" Her tone came out hard and fast like a drill sergeant. She had mentioned to a classmate, once, that five of her family members served in the army, and she planned to join one of the forces when she graduated.

The teacher banged a stack of papers against his desk and rose to hand out the cellular-respiration worksheets for that day.

Danny's own cells were having difficulty respiring as his breaths came out ragged, interspersed by coughs. The perpetual scent of form-aldehyde didn't help.

Murabi repeated her question, louder this time.

The teacher licked his finger to hand Danny's leaf to him and another one for Michelle. "Trust you'll deliver that to your friend." He sniffled, reaching for the tissue he'd placed in his pocket.

"Mr. Radon!" The girl had risen to her army-boot-shod feet and banged her fist against the table. A strand of emerald hair fell in front of her burning stare.

"Miss Murabi, the principal wishes to disband the practice of a school pledge until further notice."

Wait, what? Why? Danny was too dazed to think straight.

Murabi's nostrils flared as the teacher continued, ambling past a fake human skeleton dangling at the edge of the front rows of tables. He handed out papers along his weaving path. "He plans to institute a new practice for the school come mid-May, during the school spirit week, I believe, but until then, he offers no further news on the subject."

His wet thumb plucked the last sheet and set the paper on the desk in front of Miss Murabi. "And I trust you can take it up with him when you meet Mr. Rezzen after class because of your disruption." He took a golf pencil out of his pocket, right next to the tissue, and scribbled an office note. As Mr. Radon slapped it on her table, the corners of his mouth twitched as he whipped around. "Fill out those cellular-respiration sheets on your own, class. I want to cover something a little different today."

"Ridiculous." Fresh tears sparkled in Murabi's eyes. She collapsed into her seat, the wood shrieking against the tile floor.

Mr. Radon continued, "Although we're studying biology, we had an extra day in our curriculum to cover your upcoming science class: chemistry. As a sneak peek, we'll discuss the noble gases." He clicked his next slide on the PowerPoint. "The most honorable of all the elements."

Amid the groans of the other students at the lame joke, Danny whipped around to the seat next to him and mouthed, "I'm sorry," to Murabi.

She flipped him off and pulled out her cell phone when the teacher rambled on about krypton, having to clarify that, no, you could not use this element to defeat Superman.

By the way Michelle had described how the play's tickets would sell out, Danny and Rayah arrived an hour early to an empty ticket office on opening night. For once he wished he'd followed in Hannah's footsteps in waiting until five minutes before the performance started. At least this building smelled nice, unlike all the rest, like old popcorn from concessions.

Parked on a remote plush bench by huge windows sat an acne-scarred student. Arms and legs had folded themselves in like a box, almost as if Jeremy hadn't wanted anyone at King's Academy to notice him.

"Hi, Jeremy." Rayah waved at him underneath a poster of a man holding an umbrella. *Singing in the Rain*?

Jeremy's shoulders relaxed when he realized who called to him, and a nervous tongue rolled over a pair of silver braces. This time, purple and gold rubber bands decorated them. "Like these?" He flashed a smile. "Wanted to match Michelle's prom dress. Can't believe your school dance happens in two weeks."

With limited shopping options around the school, most of the students bought their prom outfits during spring break, which occurred in late April. Michelle and Rayah scavenged a secondhand store near their homes, and each bought a gown for under forty dollars. Danny's date, Rayah, would wear a sky-blue dress, and that's all Ms. Abed would allow her daughter to reveal to him about the matter.

Dipping into the $2,000 Ned gave his family, Danny's mother used a small portion of that to fit her "little boy" into a new tuxedo. Of course, he had protested that she save the money for something else. After all, Judah had a tux that was a near shade of Rayah's dress. Like a typical mother, she had refused his request and bought him a pricey tux he'd use just once. Maybe parents got financial advice from school administrations. At least when it came to prom.

To pass the time, Danny and Rayah asked Jeremy about homeschool and the world a thousand miles away. He leaned against a wall underneath old hanging lights like the ones above movie theater seats from the 1920s. He groaned about his isolation from most of his school friends and how he *had to* join community theater and begin book-writing projects to occupy his time.

"I have four novels in mind." He rubbed his acne-scarred face, which always smelled like eczema cream. "All very sad and depressing stories. Coming to see this play will help the writing process. Nothing like a good tragedy to spur on other tragedies."

Students began to spill through the glass doors to the atrium twenty minutes before the play's start time. Glass doors to the ticket booth swung wide open, and the two friends bolted to step in line as Jeremy described the main character of his books as an "angsty, misunderstood type of guy."

So all main characters, then?

A squat woman with smeared brown lipstick handed Danny his ticket with a bag-eyed glare. The group hobbled upstairs as an usher handed them a program that read in bleeding scarlet letters, *BEWARE THE IDES OF MARCH*, and in tiny text that followed, *Julius Caesar*.

"They needed a graphic designer to fix this." Danny nudged Rayah with the program. They entered the auditorium, which fanned a strong scent of plywood and paint. "Just at a glance, no one would know the name of the play."

As the crowd filed into the weak orange lighting of the auditorium, the three followed an usher in a scarlet vest who led them to their places in the center, fourth row back.

"What a steal!" Jeremy collapsed into his folding chair. Dust particles swirled in the air. "I thought for sure they would give us nosebleeds because we bought the tickets so late."

Rayah placed the blue shawl that had been draped around her shoulders on the seat next to her to reserve it for Hannah. In her other hand, she held a bouquet of fresh, scented wildflowers she had picked by the track. Because no stores near campus sold flowers, she made do with "buttery agrimonies, frost asters, and bluebell bellflowers" wrapped in a plastic bag for Michelle's bouquet.

Danny didn't know what any of those names meant. Flowers. They meant *flowers*. Pretty yellow, white, and blue ones.

He scanned his program to pass the time, reading the actors' bios. To his surprise, the melodramatic Michelle did not have the longest description in the bunch.

__Michelle Gad__ is excited for her first performance at King's Academy Theater. When she's not trying to save Julius Caesar, she plays for the tennis team and takes part in student council meetings. Past credits include Mary at the Christmas pageant held at Grace Brethren Church.

Auditorium now half full, additional students or teachers dressed in wrinkled oxfords stumbled through the theater doors. Jeremy's gaze hovered over the empty seats, and his jaw sank. "Terrible theater etiquette." His head was outlined by the carpeted red walls as he shook it. "Everyone showing up right before the play starts."

Danny winced. "Jeremy, I don't think a whole lot of people are going to come. Our school tends to place sports on a higher pedestal. And in complete honesty, no one wants to go to a depressing play."

The lights dimmed five minutes before the performance began and illuminated the bloodstained set on the stage. Lovely. Scarlet paint spattered the columns and the Roman arch that spanned the proscenium.

Besides the bold splashes of crimson, the rest of the stage was gray, accentuating the spots of gore.

"My kind of play." Hannah slumped into the spot Rayah had reserved for her, wearing ripped jeans and a ripped T-shirt. "Everyone dies at the end of this, right? Shakespeare and I would've been friends."

The auditorium faded to black and the director, dressed in a Roman-style gown, approached center stage with shadows underneath her eyes.

"Good evening"—grim smile, grim voice—"and welcome to our production of *Julius Caesar*. Please shut off all cell phones and"—her lip twitched—"beware the Ides of March." She stepped behind a pleated curtain to half-hearted applause.

Danny soon discovered most of the members of the "Ham(let)ing it up" club also participated in this play, because they all overacted. The soothsayer took a whole minute to get through his "Beware the Ides of March" lines because his character kept wailing and breaking down into tears.

The audience members audibly exhaled when Julius Caesar shooed the soothsayer away with the line, "He is a dreamer; let us leave him: pass."

At last Danny could release a slew of coughs he had been suppressing through the first couple of scenes.

All the actors projected so forcefully that when Michelle—Calpurnia—entered the stage in a sheer silk gown, her voice paled in comparison. For once her tone sounded unglamorous and restrained. Yet she conveyed slight crackles of speech and a deep-seated desperation for Caesar to stay in their house instead of venturing out into public during the Ides of March. She described her nightmare of Caesar's blood serving as a fountain in the streets.

Nightmares had plagued Danny all during the school year. Growing more and more frequent. Of fires and tar-covered demons and every horror imaginable. One bad dream repeated throughout the year: his friends trapped in a burning room with no windows or doors to escape.

Calpurnia grasped Caesar's elbow in a fierce grip. She carried herself like a proud woman, shoulders arched and neck high and regal. "When beggars die, there are no comets seen. The heavens themselves blaze forth the death of princes."

A glimmer of tears rolled down Jeremy's face.

Oh, come on. "Caesar hasn't even died yet."

Someone shushed from behind.

"I know." Jeremy knuckled the tear away. "But when you know what will happen and what could have been prevented, you can't help but cry."

Mmm, clearly one could. Look at Hannah. She was bouncing up and down in her seat with a creepy grin.

Calpurnia buckled onto her knees, silk dress rippling. She looked odd with her head bowed when it had been raised so erect a minute ago. "Let me, upon my knee, prevail in this."

Out of pity for this act of humility, Caesar agreed to stay at home to appease his wife. But another character, Decius, said Calpurnia had interpreted the vision all wrong. He gave some sort of bogus explanation, but Danny couldn't tell with all the ancient language. Buttered up like a roll, Caesar liked this version better and left the house.

Wow. Were Caesar and Ned all that different?

Fast forward to the conspirators kneeling around Caesar as he sat on a fabric-cushioned throne. They begged him to change his mind about banishing Publius Cimber, one of the reasons they wanted to kill him. Caesar arched his back over the purple seat and cackled. Seeing he would not be moved, the senators advanced with sharp knives drawn.

This would be Hannah's favorite part.

One by one, they plunged a sharp vessel into the dictator's side. Blood capsules burst underneath the actor's pure white clothing, spraying the other cast members. As Caesar collapsed on the dusty platform, he reached out a feeble hand to his best friend, Brutus. The man turned his head away as he dug his dagger into the ruler of Rome.

"Et tu, Brute?" With a rattling breath, he collapsed.

Tangerine lights flooded the auditorium as the carcass remained on stage. How pleasant.

Only one audience member gave an enthusiastic clap at the end of the first half: Hannah. "Please tell me someone recorded that. I want to watch it on repeat." Her knees bounced up and down in anticipation of the long fifteen-minute intermission to end.

Danny was suddenly very eager to sit at the end of the row, far away from Hannah as possible.

Jeremy turned to Danny with red-rimmed eyes and a quivering lip. "Beware the Ides of March."

"Yeah, the soothsayer dude said it, like, five times. It's on the program in large caps. Can't miss it."

"No, Danny. Beware the Ides of March."

Danny cocked his head, hair stroking his temple, his heart thumping hard in his rib cage. "What?"

"I have a bad feeling your March fifteenth is coming soon."

Chapter Twenty-Five

"SO MANY PEOPLE SAID THEY LIKED THE PERFORMANCE."
Michelle grinned and clicked her mechanical pencil on the black table. "Even Valentina said, 'Well, you didn't screw up.' Might as well have given me a Tony."

Michelle arrived at their second-period science class in high spirits despite the weekend's lack of sleep. Besides the inverted Roman-arch wrinkles under her eyes, she appeared happy, as if school had already ended.

Danny offered a weary smile.

She deserved a chance to brag. Her parents hadn't even shown up for the play. Now that was the true tragedy.

He had also arrived sleep deprived to class. But unlike Michelle, he came in a less-chipper mood. Nightmares and throat-searing coughs had kept him up all hours. Even his track times suffered under the never-ending sickness and lack of rest. At the last meet, he had only placed in one of his events.

"Might have to bench you if you don't improve." Coach thrust a water bottle into Danny's chest when he reached the white finish line.

At this point, ending track season didn't sound like the worst idea in the world.

An energetic *bong-bong-bong-bong* sounded from the speaker on the wall, far too excited for that time. Morning announcements. The class still fought the urge to rise for the pledge, and several students hovered an inch above their seats before remembering and plopping back down.

"All in good time." The teacher cradled the usual stack of papers in his arms as the announcements droned something about prom ticket sales. Mr. Radon slid two leaves onto the tables, one piece of paper for each student.

Danny rubbed his eyes and glanced down, expecting another diagram of a cell's parts. His vision remained blurry, and all he could spot at first peep was a wet thumbprint from where the teacher had licked his finger. Gross. Once his eyesight adjusted, he realized the teacher had not handed out anything class-related at all. What the—?

"A new pledge?" Miss Murabi's voice piped from next to Danny. Today she wore her green hair whipped into a messy bun, pinned back by two dragon chopsticks.

"Yes, Miss Murabi." Mr. Radon inhaled a sharp whiff of air as if preparing for a football player to crash into him. "Your principal handed out this new school pledge. With some students and employees betraying the school, the principal wants to ensure he has everyone's loyalty."

Looking down at the paper, the title itself set off fire alarms in Danny's head. He visualized the red beams whirling to the sound of a shrill *beep*. Oh, Dagon, this looked bad.

Pledge of Allegiance (to King's Academy)

I pledge allegiance to the statue
Of the King's Academy school
And to its principal for which it stands,
One school, under Rezzen, forever loyal
With tolerance and equality for all.

Dagon, he couldn't do that. This couldn't be legal.

Sniggering came from a student with an underbite grin in the back corner of the room. He sat right next to the snake in the glass case. "He sent this as an April Fool's joke, right? Poor Ned printed this off a month too late."

"Statue?" Michelle's eyebrows scrunched at the paper. "What statue? Did he mean the golden water fountain on campus?"

Danny answered with a noncommittal grunt. After all, the only statue he associated with Ned came from the email with the spliced figurine of the principal.

Mr. Radon cleared his throat, and the mutters of confusion dissipated like a worn-out chemical solution ceasing to bubble. "Principal Rezzen requested I read this email transcript along with the document:

"Dear students and faculty,

"With great distress and sorrow, I must announce lax loyalties have caused many harms on this great campus. The fires in the gardens come first to mind when mentioning such tragedies. As a school, we must unite to prevent any further damage to an institution with such an illustrious history.

"The pledge in front of you ..."

Mr. Radon motioned with an indistinct gesture, motioning by accident to the skeleton in the corner.

"ensures disasters will not strike again. I must ask you to read this pledge in the most sincere manner as through speaking it, you place your allegiance far above family, above religions, and, yes, even above your country—"

At the sound of this, protests erupted throughout the classroom. Already on her feet, Miss Murabi banged her spiked metal bracelet against the lab desk, scratching the charcoal surface. Others had pulled out phones to document their frustrations. Not that the texts or Snapchats would send.

Danny continued to blink at the paper. Ned had snapped. There was no other logical explanation. "Can he get away with this?" He flicked the paper at Michelle. "We have physical evidence against him. What if we just walked out of here and showed this to a police officer?"

"I don't know, Danny. Someone could argue a student wrote this. It's not in his handwriting, you know."

"What about the email? It came from his inbox."

"He could've been hacked. Remember they have incredible lawyers here. And I don't know how many kids are going to risk their future at college to turn in someone for a pledge."

"I still think we should try—"

A quick jerk of the head. "I mean, other schools have school pledges. Ned could argue this is one of those. I don't think this is a war you can win, Danny."

Dagon, she was right. For once.

Mr. Radon's dry fingers snapped against his hand, sounding like a gas stove igniting with flame. "Silence." Hush. He continued to read the principal's speech.

"Some students may dislike this strong commitment ..."

"No kidding." Murabi still stood, clawing at her skin with her fingernails. Her burning eyes flickered back and forth between the teacher and the American flag hanging by the whiteboard.

"but the members of this body must understand how much King's Academy provides for their futures, unlike their country. America will not lead you to a six-figure job like we do. Uncle Sam offers no connections to future employers that will ensure financial security for you and your families. The sweet land of liberty has fewer liberties than you think, students and faculty. If you want the freedom to pursue your happiness, say the pledge.

"I will give you the opportunity to recite this oath at the Spirit Week Pep Assembly.

"As many of you know, spirit week takes place right before the ever-so-popular prom, and the week's activities conclude with a pep rally at the football stadium.

"When the marching band enters and plays the King's Academy school anthem, they will take a pause. During this moment, all students will rise and recite the pledge. We will post monitors to ensure every student and staff member takes part in this new tradition. Also, we expect and will ensure that every student and faculty member attends unless the person has a dire medical condition, for which we will have nurses determine that person's fitness to attend. No field trips, tests, or academic pursuits of any kind will take place during the assembly."

And if we don't? popped the question into Danny's head. Waterboarding? Lethal injection? Forcing them to listen to a Justin Bieber album?

The letter replied:

"Failure to comply and say the pledge will result in a terrible punishment, worse than a mere expulsion. We take loyalty very seriously at this institution, and the school body ought to do the same."

Saturday Bible study convened in Rayah, Hannah, and Michelle's room, a squat square enclosed with gray bricks with far too much hair clumped on the carpet.

The group had decided to move the meetings there to throw off any more pyromaniac attempts from Dean. And the Suanna dorm blew air conditioning, a luxury for those in the sweltering Phrat River lounges. Despite the change of location, all but four of the members scattered after the most recent fire incident.

Even Gabe had disappeared again, not only from the Saturday night get-togethers but from the school in general, or so it seemed. On Tuesday he didn't show up for the track meet, causing the bright-red letters on the scoreboard to suffer even more without his winning high jump. Maybe the pledge had scared him away from campus.

But Ned had foreseen the potential for students to try to evacuate the school before the assembly day. At every entrance and exit of the school, he stationed guards in jet-black ties and eggshell oxford shirts. Each was equipped with a holster, stocked with a taser, gun, and any other weapon the student body imagined they saw, which was a lot of crazy stuff. With these new security protocols, Danny had to trust that Gabe had ascended to heaven to escape the madness of the school.

"Can't those guards blocking the entrance to the school count as evidence?" He motioned to one of them on his walk with Michelle to her dorm. "A reason to sue Ned?"

Michelle pulled out a keycard and slid it through the door reader with a beep and a click. "Sorry, Dan, but a ton of public schools have police officers stationed on the premises for protection. This isn't really out of the norm."

A flush of AC, along with the smell of feet, cooled his cheeks. Better than sweat, he guessed. "Well, I don't like the norm. Both the thing and the person. My Uncle Norm is a really obnoxious Cleveland Browns fan."

His friend didn't reply but her heels echoed up the concrete steps of her dorm.

The Bible study continued, but the students dispersed throughout the room, Bibles in front of them, unopened.

Each friend bathed in silence. Danny distracted his mind with the various elements of the room. At one corner the girls had triple-stacked their wooden bunks with a ladder leading up to the second level for Rayah. Hannah, according to her two roommates, tried to ninja crawl up to the highest bed and often succeeded, even in pitch-black conditions from the lack of windows.

On the peeling-paint walls, various pictures hung on thin white strings. When Ms. Abed had seen the naked walls on her visit during Thanksgiving, she printed every picture in her arsenal of Rayah and her friends. These included embarrassing photos of her little girl as a child when she had placed her frilly bathing suit on backward to a shot of Danny scrunching up his face before a healthy sneeze. At least until Rayah stuffed those photos into her desk drawer. The Command hooks used to support the strings had withstood the humidity for the most part except for one or two pegs that draped lifelessly, forming spiderwebs on the other strings.

Across the room, Hannah had taped various sketches to the wall. She favored the scarlet element of blood as her muse for most of the illustrations. Surprise, surprise. They seemed odd interspersed with Rayah's watercolor canvases that were dappled with tulips and soft sunsets.

Michelle's wall remained rather bare. Besides the hung *Julius Caesar* program signed by each member of the cast, the blank bricks brought forth a convincing case for police to ticket them for public indecency.

The fourth wall held a loud, ticking clock, which the girls had forgotten to adjust for the end of daylight savings.

At last Hannah cleared her throat. "So the stupid assembly happens in less than a week."

They had meant to speak about this subject together sooner. But conflicting track and lacrosse meets prevented such an interaction. Although they had finally planned to talk about it after Danny's meet on Friday, their plans were cut short when he blacked out on the fifth lap of the 3200 and crashed into the chain-link fence in front of the stands. He came to in the campus health clinic after a purple-faced coach informed him he would not run for the rest of the season. So much for running at state.

Michelle glanced at the chipped wooden door and sighed. "Too bad they lock those from the outside. Otherwise, I'd shut us in until the end of next Friday."

"Ned would call in the fire department to break down the door with an axe." Hannah rolled a piece of lint on the ground in her fingertips. "By this point, he must have them on speed dial with the number of fires at this school."

"Anyone want to break my leg so I can't attend?" Michelle dangled upside-down from the first bunk, her cheeks and forehead flushed from the pooling blood.

Danny shook his head and hacked into his sleeve. Spots coated his vision as he gestured to the fire alarm on the ceiling. Like the one in Phrat River, it blinked red.

"Might want to—*cough*—take this talk—*cough*—somewhere else."

Rayah nodded. "Besides, if the cameras watched someone break your leg on purpose, they would suspect foul play."

"And make you attend the assembly anyway." Hannah sucked the blood from a recently bitten hangnail.

Michelle slumped against her desk in the bloody-illustration side of the room and craned her neck toward the smoke detector. Beads of sweat sparkled in the hair coating her neck. "Danny's right. We should take this conversation outside."

Danny tottered as he rose, dizzy as he hobbled from foot to foot, ignoring the black crawling up the sides of his eyes. What else was new?

"Oh, stop trying to be so brave, Danny." Michelle forced him to drape his arm around her to help lead him outside.

Even if their rooms had windows, the girls lived three floors up, and a free-fall escape from the room would have entailed certain death. Off balance down the many, many steps, Danny shuffled his clunky sneakers one stair at a time. Long after ten minutes had passed, they finally reached the bottom floor and outside.

"Visited the clinic today?" Michelle's sweating intensified in the humid air.

He crumpled onto the dry grass and shook his head, hair cold and dripping. "Nurse Nintin said my symptoms ranged all over the place and only to return if they got worse. She placed the diagnosis anywhere between a cold and mono. WebMD says I'm dying. So that's fun."

"You've had this sickness for over a month, and she won't let you come back unless you're at death's door?"

He rolled onto his back, eyes drooping from continued lack of sleep. "Nintin said lots of students have come to her with 'dire medical conditions' to avoid the assembly next Friday. One guy even claimed to have lost his hearing. 'Can't say the pledge if I can't hear the marching band.' Bet now Ned wishes he hadn't included the medical exception in the letter."

"Who knows?" Hannah clawed at a dry anthill by the concrete doorstep. "If you keep up the illness, you might get out of doing the assembly."

Yeah, right. His head stirred, rubbing itself in the parched dirt. "Unless someone stabs me thirty-three times like Caesar, Ned'll make no exceptions. Even in that case"—his voice sunk low like thunder—"'Come on, Danny,' he'll say. 'Back in my day, we said our pledges even after they shot us forty times.'" The roaring rumble in Danny's ears faded into a series of coughs that sprayed clouds of dust everywhere.

Rayah brushed off her maxi skirt, which received the brunt of the dust storm. "Assuming Ned makes us all go, should we say the pledge?"

Never.

Each member eyed one another as if anticipating a traitor to reveal themselves. After the dramatic pause and a series of bird chirps, a resounding "no" echoed throughout the group.

"Agreed." A slow nod from Rayah. "Because this pledge means something different than normal school pledges."

"Right." Danny scrunched his face, preparing for a sneeze that failed to follow through. "Because Ned placed himself above our families, our country, and our *God* ... means he made himself into *a god*." And there was nothing funny about that.

A morose ripple of assent passed through the group. No eye met another one. Hannah scooped a clump of dust and poured it onto her hair like a pile of ashes.

Something like a squeak sounded from Rayah. "What do you think he meant by a punishment *worse* than expulsion?"

Warm summer breezes swished through the question. The air smelled of sunshine and a freedom so close ... but so far. Crickets chirped, quite unaware of the tension tightening the chests of four very frightened students.

"I guess it means he'll give you a bad name no matter what college or job you apply for." Michelle shrugged as a group of giggling girls passed them on bicycles. "Your future"—she snapped her fingers—"gone. Just like that."

Just like that.

"But expulsion already includes all those things." Hannah's fingers moved from the anthill to a patch of sprouting dandelions. "He said he'd give something *worse*."

Michelle's answer was cut off by a Frisbee smacking against the Suanna building. By the look on her face, even if she had opened her mouth, no words would have spilled out.

The student council assigned themes for each day of spirit week, including some of Michelle, Hannah, and Rayah's choices.

Schedule:

Monday: Future-job day. All of campus wears what future occupation they would like to pursue (Rayah).

Tuesday: Superhero day. Students sport their favorite hero or villain (Hannah's choice, obviously).

Wednesday: Twin day. (Valentina's idea. She pushed for this one hard.)

Thursday: Decades day. Students can dress in whatever period of clothing they want to revamp themselves in (Michelle's pick).

Friday: School-spirit day. Students must wear the scarlet-and-gold colors of the school for the pep assembly (Ned's instituted day).

On Thursday, Decades day, Michelle arrived in her sheer *Julius Caesar* dress she borrowed from the theater department after haggling with the seamstress for fifteen minutes. Hannah forgot a getup and came in a T-shirt and cut jeans, and Rayah arrived in a form-fitting forties dress, topped with red lipstick she borrowed from Michelle.

Danny found himself quite flustered when he saw Rayah in her outfit. He wanted to tell her she looked "nice" or "wonderful," but then he realized neither word was quite nice or wonderful to the four friends.

As for Danny, he donned what he called a futuristic outfit, made of tin foil and his Kermit the Frog pajamas for when he'd return from class to fight his fever with a nap. His symptoms had gotten worse throughout the week, but the line trailed so far into the Health Center that Nurse Nintin refused to see anyone for the rest of the week unless their "leg has fallen clean off."

Also, seeing that most of the men's outfits in history included a suit and tie, he thought he'd save that outfit for prom on Saturday—if Ned hadn't expelled him and his friends after the Friday assembly. Oh, joy. Glad to be reminded of that every five minutes.

But as it turned out, tin foil and fevers made terrible twins, like Valentina's spirit day of the week. By his second-period class with Michelle, his whole body was caked in sweat as his feeble, shaking hands tried to tear off the foil, which bit into his skin. Darkness crawled up his vision even though he had torn off the insulating elements of the costume. The paper DNA helix dangling from the ceiling blurred until it looked like a single line.

"Danny?" Michelle's laurel wreath in her hair shook at him to the backdrop of a table with microscopes all in a row.

"Doing fine, just can't see, that's all."

"You can't see?"

"Yeah, everything went b–black. And I k–kind of need to p–puke. But it's all good."

"Do you need to visit Nintin?"

"She won't s–see anyone th–this week. Oh, Dagon, I need to vomit."

As he started to hyperventilate, Michelle ushered him out of the building into the thick humidity toward the Health Center. But the effort to walk became too much. Head growing light, he kneeled on the grass and tucked himself into a ball, head dissolving into wool.

"Danny!" Michelle gripped his fuzzy pajamas with her nails, probably choking Kermit. "Get up, you have just five yards to go."

"Just need to rest ... Dagon, I really need to throw up."

He shut his eyes before they went completely dark to the tune of Michelle banging her fist against the glass Health Center doors. "We need an ambulance, right now! Dial the hospital!"

Chapter Twenty-Six

BEFORE DANNY COULD PEEL HIS EYELIDS OPEN, SOMEONE hoisted him onto a hard bed covered with thick parchment paper. Clawing hands forced him to lean forward as other, gentler ones placed a thick pillow behind his neck. A familiar, sterile smell mixed with urine flooded his nostrils.

Dang it. He'd hoped for heaven. Health Center would have to do.

Someone dialed a phone number, the keys beeping with each number.

"Calling an ambulance?" He squinted and saw Michelle cross her arms in front of a burlap curtain. The beige paint slowly came into view.

Nintin raised pencil-thin eyebrows, ear glued to the phone. "Ned won't allow for any students to leave campus until after tomorrow, even for a hospital."

What a nice principal.

"But we have an emergency here!"

"Following orders, dear. I have his secretary on the phone right now. They're sending Ned over."

"What for?"

"Goodness, what a barrage of questions! ... I want him to come and confirm that we can call an ambulance for your friend."

Danny's eyelids unfastened all the way, despite their heavy weight. The harsh lights stung his pupils for a moment, and his headache intensified. His heartbeat rattled in his ears.

Nintin waddled to the cabinets. Her pruney hand froze in the air, seemingly unsure of what medication bottle to pluck from the wooden shelves. Her raisin-like fingers removed one, and she poured two pills from it into a plastic cup.

Danny wanted to protest because his mother had only agreed to Pepto-Bismol on his medical forms, but he imagined he needed something stronger than the bubblegum-pink medicine.

Wheeling around on her heels, she saw he was awake. "Let me grab you something to down this." She placed the plastic cup on a table beside his angled bed.

Michelle slid onto a rolling chair and scooted toward Danny. She pestered him with questions about how he felt and whether he saw one or two of her. But most of what she said didn't register as the room faded to a blur once more.

Nintin returned, equipped with a large bottle of orange Gatorade. "Small sips." She put the bottle beside the medicine cup.

He groaned as a woozy feeling assaulted his stomach.

The nurse pursed her lips. "I expect you to get through that whole thing by the time the ambulance arrives."

He expected to disintegrate into vomit, but sometimes things didn't go according to plan. He swallowed, glancing at the liquid. Dagon, he was going to puke all this if he downed it.

Michelle bolted out of her seat, the chair rolling back against the wall beneath a sign with a cartoon cell phone with a red X marked over it. "So you did order an ambulance?"

"Out, out!" Nintin motioned to the door. Instead of her usual squat, hunched self, she stood erect and bolder than ever before. Michelle's jaw sagged, but before a well-worded protest came out, the nurse smoothed her pruney fingers against her scrubs. "Mr. Rezzen will arrive at any moment, and I would hate for him to think you and Danny put on a big show so one of you wouldn't have to attend the assembly."

Smart lady.

Wide-eyed for a moment, Michelle registered the meaning and turned to Danny, who sipped the sweet-salty liquid that tasted like orange sweat. "Stay sick. I mean it."

She stared at him long and hard as if she would never gaze upon his face again, then disappeared behind the loud thud of the shutting door.

Nintin eyed the smoke detector on her ceiling once Michelle had departed. "Will return in a moment, dear, with a crossword puzzle to keep your mind off the pain."

Danny wanted to tell her how much the corners of his eyes throbbed and how he didn't think he could complete a crossword puzzle with such a splitting headache. But the nurse's clunky white shoes vanished before he could say a word.

The door groaned when Nintin returned five minutes later, according to the big cat clock on the wall. "To ease your pain." She slipped the sheet onto his lap.

Before he could object, he glanced at the paper and noticed the nurse had already filled in most of the squares to the puzzle—all the horizontal ones, anyway. Top to bottom the words read, *ACT, SICK, MORESO, THAN, EVENNOW, WHEN, NED, ARRIVES.*

Dagon, she really was smart. It was like she had gone to nursing school or something.

Nintin eyed him over her pair of thick-rimmed glasses. When she saw he'd scanned the document, she snatched it from him.

"Dear, oh, dear"—she clucked her tongue—"I forgot you had a splitting headache. Your blonde friend mentioned it to me." As she said this, she tore the paper into several pieces and crumpled them into the waste bin by the door. "Better hope the strain didn't harm you." She winked at him.

As if on command, Danny's stomach twisted itself into sour pretzels. The fresh urge to vomit fell over him once more as it had throughout the year.

He didn't *need* to act sick. Right as the thought passed through his mind, a tall figure that contained a stern face and a thunderous voice emerged from the doorway. "Well?" A pause. "Well?"

"Quite the opposite, Mr. Rezzen." Nintin's lips twitched. "Our patient does not look well at all."

Well-played. She reached into the cabinet and pulled out a thermometer. Once she replaced the mouthpiece, she thrust the flimsy plastic covering under Danny's tongue.

Up to this point, he'd tried to prevent himself from puking, and the cold metal object in his mouth aided little in this process.

Ned squinted at Danny. "The boy looks fine to me!" Still he managed to keep his distance.

"His skin is two shades greener than when he entered this office."

"His skin always had a green-like quality to it."

Wow. Danny cringed at another sharp pain in his head.

Nintin yanked out the thermometer when it gave a shrill *beep*. "102.4."

The principal took a step forward as if to take away the thermometer. He passed just in front of Danny for the student to catch an incense whiff, which turned his stomach more. "I went to school with a 105 fever as a child."

She held the thermometer above her head. "Good thing institutions have become less barbaric since then."

A glower from Ned, then he rounded on Danny. "Stomach problems again?"

Danny clutched his abdomen with his fist. He pinched his skin to distract him from the nausea.

"Goodness, this kid must have puked into every toilet bowl on campus. Get him some TUMS, and he'll whip into shape. Here, I'll find them."

Determined, he advanced to the cabinet, chucking various bottles over his shoulder in search of a stomach reliever. Plastic containers littered the floor, rattling each time another one hit the deck. What happened to the principal who hated messes? Definitely had blown a fuse. Maybe two.

The nurse lunged forward and tried to shut the door on Ned's probing hand. "The kid blacked out during class. Flintstones Vitamins won't help him."

"He can stand through a pledge, Kara."

Ned excavated a bottle of aspirin and scanned the ingredients. With a rosy-cheeked face and pure fire in her eyes, the nurse slammed the cabinet with a raucous *wham*!

The principal jerked and kicked a pill bottle on the floor—the same one from which Nintin had given Danny pills in the cup, minutes before Ned arrived. As the container tumbled near his bed, he miraculously managed to read, *To induce vomiting*, before the label trundled beyond his vision.

Dagon. She gave him pills so he would puke.

"He needs to visit a hospital, Ned." She balled her thick fists and stood resolutely with her legs apart like a football player.

Ned froze at the small act of defiance before collecting himself with a stoic expression. "We do not permit students to leave campus, especially this close to the assembly tomorrow." He spoke each word through gritted teeth.

Nintin inhaled a deep breath.

Over in the corner, Danny let out thick exhales to prevent himself from upchucking. His mouth flooded with saliva, a sure sign of an oncoming storm.

"So!" Nintin unclenched her fists, smoothing her hands on her outfit. "If a student comes to me with his arm chopped off, you still expect him to attend your assembly tomorrow?"

He shrugged in his ironed suit jacket. "You need one arm for a pledge. I don't see why not."

Wow. He didn't have words funny enough *or* serious enough to capture how he felt about Ned in that very moment. *Wow* seemed to fit the bill.

"As if you never had the stomach flu as a child! If you send him in this state to the stadium tomorrow, he'll puke and ruin the ceremony."

Danny arched his neck on the pillow, sweat glistening on his arms, legs, and face, and he let out a soft moan. Ned shot him a glance of annoyance that quickly faded into one of pity.

"Danny's a good kid. Never bluffs about anything, straight As, good athlete. A *great* kid. But"—he rounded on the nurse—"I will send my assistant tomorrow. If she sees that your patient has improved in any way, she will escort him to the football stadium."

Ned eyed the trash can—which Nintin had tossed the crossword puzzle in—with great suspicion. More suspicion than even a good Michelle ought to give garbage. He inched toward the bin for a moment but seemed to think better of it. He swiveled on his dress shoes and clicked the door shut, a bit too hard for the boy with the headache.

Well, that was nice. Oh, Dagon ... so was this. Danny mentally swore as hot vomit launched up his throat.

The nurse lunged onto the counter, grabbing a square plastic bin. She placed the container in front of her patient as he leaned forward and emptied all his stomach's contents. The fire-tasting bile came out a scarlet red. Hannah would approve.

A sickening smell filled the room, which seemed to grow several degrees hotter. Danny curled into a ball as the war in his body raged on.

Nintin fled the room for a moment and returned, sprinkling her hands with water in the sink. "My, oh my"—her silver-streaked hair swayed from side to side—"what terrible timing. If Ned had stayed a minute longer, he might have phoned an ambulance."

She scooped the various pill bottles off the ground and returned them to the cabinet. Squatting down to the retrieve the vomit-inducing container underneath the bed, she held it up and mouthed "sorry" to Danny.

He had puked in vain, after all. "Plenty more where that came from." His chest heaved up and down. "My body seems to have practiced that very thing all year."

Fretful fits of sleep haunted Danny throughout the night. He faded in and out of feverish dreams, sprinting away from a ten-foot leopard with wings right into an even larger ram with bloody eyes that blocked his way. The creature bowed its head as its foot pawed the dirt, ready to charge. Right before the two beasts plunged at Danny, something hard jerked his shoulder and pull him out of the dream.

"Time to take your pills." Nintin emptied a few capsules into the plastic cup, the same one as before. The rattling of the medicine boomed in Danny's ears. She placed the cup on the table with three tablets in the goblet instead of two. Puke Up Your Guts, extra strength. Buy it at your local boarding school today.

His abdomen tightened at the thought of how much more he would retch, after freeing himself from the nausea the night before. "Please, no." Sleep clung to his voice, causing his tone to barely come out as more than a weak rumble.

She ignored him and slid the cup closer till it almost reached the tipping point of the tabletop. "Time for pills."

"Time for more sleep." His heavy eyelids fluttered. The beige room slipped in and out of darkness.

"Remember, Ashley Penaz will arrive in half an hour to see if your symptoms have gotten weaker. I imagine unless a sudden fit of sickness attacks you she will deem you better than before."

Dang it, his sickness *had* improved. No longer did queasiness plague his stomach or sweat cake his body from a raging fever. His body had the worst timing in the world. All that remained was a throbbing abdomen, splitting headache, and chills from a minor fever. Although miserable, none of these symptoms would prevent him from going to the assembly.

And expulsion on top of sickness, the day before prom, would qualify as one of the worst days of his life.

But maybe he should go to the assembly. He was a coward otherwise.

Nurse Nintin cleared her throat. Thick heels tapping once, twice under the medicine cabinet. "Your blonde friend dropped off a note to my assistant this morning. Perhaps that will help persuade you."

She handed him a slip of paper, which he squinted at, still battling the headache.

Danny,

Rayah said you might try to come to the assembly anyway. Because you're a rule follower by heart and want to put on a brave face.

Don't. Don't you dare, Daniel Belte.

Let me dare, Michelle. Let me.
The note continued:

Did you think that maybe God allowed you to get sick, so you could keep going to King's instead of getting expelled? If you want to be a martyr and all that, I'm sure the school will give you plenty of opportunities in the next two years to get hurt.

You'll have lots of chances to be brave. And it's not like you haven't shown courage before. You've already had to do that with so many things (the cafeteria food situation, the initiation, asking Duke to Bible study, etc.).

Hannah's in the room as I'm writing this, and she says the best kind of heroes sacrifice themselves only when there is no alternative. Until then, they do everything to stay alive.

So, stay alive. Stay sick. And for Dagon's sake, do not go to the assembly. We'll at least have some hope that one Emmanuel student was able to survive King's with his head held high and future intact.

Michelle

Fine, Michelle. For his friends ... time for pills. If he refused them now, he would sentence himself to death. Which would probably not fit well into his four-year high school plan.

Cringing, he tilted his head back and swallowed the three capsules, dry. They tasted bitter and got stuck in his esophagus until enough saliva pushed it down. He refused to drink the Gatorade on the table to down the pills because he didn't want to hate the taste of the beverage after he threw it up so many times.

While he took the medicine, the nurse switched around the pills in the cabinet in dizzying arrangements until Danny couldn't tell one container apart from the other—almost all looked the same anyway. Why was she doing that?

Nintin also dumped a few bottles into the garbage bin along with the crossword-puzzle evidence and Michelle's ripped-up note. Danny thought of this gesture as a rather odd one considering his mother always insisted they flush bad pills down the toilet, not in a trash can.

Then again, his mother also thought butter was a useful agent for healing burns. It wasn't.

Nintin plucked out an orange container that resembled the vomit-inducing bottle, but when she held it up to his face, the label read, *For upset stomach.*

"I gave you this pill yesterday and today." Her winking eye was turned away from the smoke detector on the ceiling. "If you feel sick at all, I will place it at the front of the cabinet for you to grab."

She swung the small wooden doors and put the bottle where the vomit-inducing pills had been before. Sneaky, sneaky.

Fifteen minutes after the medicine dissolved in his stomach, all his symptoms returned. His skin prickled under the heat of the room despite the AC running behind the burlap curtain, and he kicked off the sheets to relieve himself of the stifling heat, to no avail. The headache pierced his temples so much, he couldn't keep his eyes open because the light stung them. Heart thundering in his chest, he buried his face in his hands and let out a loud whimper as he rocked back and forth.

"Dear, do you feel all right?" Nintin cocked her head in an innocent sort of manner. "My, oh my, you look dreadful."

Danny was afraid to open his mouth for what sort of horrors would spill out. So, instead, he continued his pendulum swing back and forth for what seemed like forever. Back and forth. Forth and back. Back and forth and ...

"Bin!" he gasped. "Nurse, I need the plastic bin to throw up into!"

He cracked open his eyes to the woman scanning the room in an unhurried, casual manner. "Dear, oh, dear. I think I left the plastic container in the sink when I washed it out yesterday. Too late to grab it now by the looks of you." She thumbed her chin. "Gee, what should we do?"

A clack of heels echoed down the tile hallway. Ashley.

"I'm going to vomit my contribution all over the floor." Danny hugged his knees tight to his chest.

Nintin snapped her fingers and grabbed the trash can, in which she had discarded the crossword puzzles, Michelle's letter, and the vomit-inducing pills. She thrust the bin in front of Danny, and he vomited right as the sound of heels stopped in the doorway.

He retched four separate times with only a mere gasp in between the burnt-tasting breaths. When the dry heaving at the end ceased, Nintin fetched him a towel to wipe his face.

While she did this, Ashley whipped a crumpled tissue out of her purse and shoved it under her nose.

"Sorry, Ashley." Nintin returned from removing the trash can from the room. "Bad timing."

The other's voice came out stiff, as usual. "What pills did you give him half an hour ago?"

Nintin scooped the stomach relieving bottle from the table by his bed. She handed it to Ashley who squinted at it.

"We saw you rearranging the cabinet." She clacked the pills against the table, hard.

"Yes, that." Nintin flung open the cupboard to display the many prescription pills. "Yesterday, I noticed quite a few expired bottles in here and wanted to keep my storage up-to-date. With the large number of patients in my office until this morning, I had no time until today."

"Ned sent me to investigate that bin and collect Danny for the assembly."

Danny's chest emptied just as his stomach had. All that pain for nothing.

Nintin motioned to the trash can in the next room with gloved fingers. "By all means. I can grab you a pair of gloves to rummage through that can. I imagine you wouldn't want to mess up that fresh manicure with the vomit splattered on the trash bag. Fair warning, several of the bottles look the same in that cabinet and bin, so one can easily mix up one and another when investigating." She eyed Ashley with a look that declared, *You have nothing you can prove against me, woman.*

Nurse Nintin approached Danny, laying a thick hand on his shoulder. "As for this little guy, I imagine he would love to join his friends at the assembly. However, given his present state, a puking incident during the pledge will spoil Ned's special day. Perhaps we shouldn't risk it."

Ashley licked her sweaty lip, and Danny almost wanted to declare victory in that moment. Ned's secretary would do anything to make sure he was happy. She held up a finger as she pressed her phone to her ear. "One moment, please."

She stepped out into the hallway and the nurse beamed at her patient. "My, how terrible you look."

He cracked a smile. "I woke up like this."

Stern faced, Ashley returned and wrinkled her nose at the stench upon reentrance. "For today, Danny may stay here, but Mr. Rezzen expects him to recite the pledge on Monday morning before his first-period class."

The heart that had soared in his chest plummeted a moment later. Michelle was right, he would have a chance to be brave, after all, when he refused to say the pledge on Monday. Just sooner than he'd hoped.

"Mr. Rezzen also wishes for your patient to watch the event on a phone, as we have arranged for him to watch a live feed."

Nintin reached into her scrubs to pull out a phone, but Ashley raised a hand.

"*My* cell, Kara." She gazed sternly over her glasses at the squat woman. "I don't want the password to the private website saved on your phone. And remember, he wants all faculty at the event too. I will stay with Danny as I have recited the pledge about five times in Ned's office before this."

"Of course." Nintin straightened the stethoscope draped around her neck and strode out the room, chest puffed with dignity.

Ashley maintained a wide berth from Danny, but she dropped her phone on his lap with the video playing.

The cameras, in the ten minutes before the event began, panned across an empty field and students slowly filing into the stands. A pole tinkled in the wind, but the thing was stripped of the American flag.

As the marching band and color guard formed a lion shape on the field, a large object stood cloaked in a scarlet curtain. Before the band started to play, Ned strode into the lion shape and grabbed a fistful of the crimson cloth. He tore it off, revealing the object on the field, as the school's theme tune commenced with the sounding of trumpets.

Danny's heart plummeted so far it reached his toes.

Chapter Twenty-Seven

A GIANT GOLDEN STATUE OF NED SITTING ON AN oversized chair glittered in the mid-morning sun amid a honking clarinet solo. The kid on the woodwind needed some more practice. Sounded like a dying cat. Ashley winced as she watched the screen. During a flute flourish before the chorus, Danny looked carefully at the small phone screen and turned up the volume, shoulders relaxing when Ashley leaned back to watch from afar.

The image resembled the picture that the principal had received in the email months before. This time, instead of just a gilded head, the entire image glistened gold. Three times Ned's size, the sculpture must have consumed the entire school's tuition for the year. No way that thing could've been all gold. Maybe it was painted to look like it.

The tuba blasted a note that sounded like a thunder peal, concluding the song. At this time the camera panned the scarlet stands, where hundreds of students and faculty members rose to their feet, the platforms groaning under the weight of the school body. Even Nurse Nintin in her white scrubs stood among a crowd of teachers in front of the announcement booth with the lion painted on the front. In their Sunday best for Friday's worst event.

Hands clung to chests as they recited the new mantra:

"I pledge allegiance to the statue

Of the King's Academy school,"

The live stream on the phone screen shifted to a group of students in the center row who remained seated. His three friends held their spines ramrod straight. Hannah, Michelle, and Rayah. The last of the land of the free. Last of the brave ...

"And to its principal for which it stands,

One school, under Rezzen, forever loyal,"

Others around them cast quick glances at the trio that refused to rise. One jabbed Rayah in the back with a free hand and motioned for her to stand.

She shook her head and faced forward.

"With tolerance and equality for all."

Ashley clicked a button on her phone, and the screen turned black. She stared at it for a moment, forehead crinkling. Then she looked at Danny.

"Hope you said *goodbye* to your friends recently." She rose. Her sharp heels clicked on her way to the door. She stopped in the doorframe and allowed for a brief glance of pity at the sick patient. "I will see what I can do."

Ashley's *excellent* solution consisted of a second opportunity for the friends. According to Hannah, who met up with Danny the next day when the Health Center released him, Ned had spotted the three in the crowd during the pledge and called them into the office right after. Ashley had intercepted him in the carpeted hallway.

Hannah gave Danny a blow-by-blow account in the Suanna lobby downstairs.

"Told Ned we were good kids. That King's earned thousands because parents liked how there was healthier food in the dining commons. Ned just jerked his chin at us to follow him into the office."

Danny envisioned the dark room, smelling the strong incense fumes.

Hannah scratched a scab on her arm. "Ned sat but made us stand. Gave us one more chance to say the pledge. Each of us stepped forward and gave our reasons against it. About how it went against our religion and first amendment rights. He wasn't having it."

Hannah stopped and glanced at her bitten nails.

"Seeing he wouldn't budge, we all sat in his office until he turned us out."

"Did he tell you what your punishment is?" Danny tugged at his tight suit collar.

Hannah smoothed her corseted leather dress with her black fingertips. "No, he didn't."

"I mean, he let you go to prom today, so it couldn't be that bad, right?"

She shrugged, her leather straps made a *scrunch* as she raised her bony shoulders. "No expulsion, either. At least, not yet. Michelle bets he'll make us go through finals before telling us we no longer go to this school. She assumes that's what he meant by something worse than expelling students. Exams."

The best torture device in the whole, wide Earth.

With nothing to do for the next two hours as the other two friends prepared themselves, Danny and Hannah whipped out a game of War in the Suanna lobby.

He was grateful for the air conditioning because his suit jacket packed a lot of heat, and he had just recovered from his medical episode the day before. Still queasy, Danny considered sitting the day out, but he couldn't let Rayah down—it was basically a felony to skip prom—so he carried anti-nausea pills to sustain himself through the night. He decided to shrug off the suit jacket until Rayah arrived, just in case.

As Hannah slapped down a king of hearts with one hand, playing with her messy bun in the other, she eyed the medicine bottle. "You plan to carry that thing around with you all night?"

He plucked at the fake "pockets" of his jacket. "Pants can't hold anything either."

Hannah grabbed the pills and stuffed the container into her torn leather bag. "If you need these during any part of the night, I'll be with the dork in the Sonic the Hedgehog hat."

Oh ... Duke. What a sight that'll be.

Jeremy arrived an hour before the dance and joined them in their game of War. He picked his spot on a lumpy green chair, which clashed with his suit. Rather competitive in nature, the poor, Old Spice-doused boy realized the game operated on pure luck and slapped his cards on the table after the third round. "Play something else." He scowled, crossing his arms over a thin lilac tie, which kept escaping his matching suit jacket.

A blue spiked head entered as the door clicked open: Hannah's date. Duke joined the group but sat on another brown couch at least five feet away from the nearest member. The triangle ears and cobalt barbs stared Danny down as if to say, *Laugh at my Sonic hat. I dare you.*

It was really tempting. But Danny would rather not die the day of prom.

Hannah waved Duke over to join the game of War. He did so with reluctance, staggering over his words when he saw his date. That was right, buddy. She was beautiful.

"You look wonderful." Hannah smirked at the hat.

He frowned. "At least this hat will get people's attention off my eye."

Hannah wrapped an arm around him, pulling herself closer to his hip. "Duke, I never notice it. The other eye is so many different colors, it takes all my attention."

Although Duke just grunted in reply, a blush crept up his cheeks as a smile tore across his face.

All right. Danny approved but just for tonight. Tomorrow they would sign her up for the convent.

The time came for the rest of the girls to descend the stairs, their raucous peals of laughter bouncing off the cement steps. Most of the giggling came from Michelle, who emerged in front of a gray brick wall in a purple mermaid-encrusted dress with golden designs at the bottom. The dress hugged her wide hips, accentuating her figure.

For once Jeremy lost his speech and looked on with open mouth.

Rayah followed in a modest navy-blue—an Emmanuel blue—dress "with petal sleeves and wisps of transparent chiffon trailing behind." How she had described it. Danny thought the dress blue and pretty. Golden, sparkly eyeshadow glittered each time she blinked.

Dagon, he was glad he was going. "Beautiful, Ray." Onto her small wrist Danny slipped a corsage with frostbitten roses, the sort of blue dead lips would be. Dang it. Why did he always think of the creepiest images? Hannah was rubbing off on him too much.

Rayah stared at the wristband with a sad smile, as of someone looking at flowers in front of a tombstone. "You look nice." She turned away, fanning her welling eyes.

Hannah yanked Danny into a small kitchenette that smelled of ramen noodles while Jeremy yelled at Duke about Sonic versus Mario. "Ray worried herself sick all last night about Ned's punishment. Because he left us dangling on a noose, we've no idea what's waiting for us Monday. Imagination punishes more than people can, you know."

He nodded and returned to his date, arm wrapped around her in a side hug. Her cinnamon scent far surpassed the smell of the kitchen. "I won't let him touch you on that dance floor." By her ear, he inhaled a strong whiff of hairspray.

Jeremy interjected a "How can a respectable man such as yourself appeal to the nonsense of a fast, fat hedgehog as a hero?"

"None of us will let Ned get near you, Ray. Not tonight."

She let out a sigh and mouthed a quick, "Thank you."

"Mostly because he's probably a terrible dancer and that would just be embarrassing."

A chuckle bobbed in her throat. "Right, that's the reason."

The group members posed for pictures in front of the gray, windowless building, one couple at a time. Their parents had begged the school board to allow them to stop by and snap photos of their children, but the academy would not allow it with the event's proximity to the infamous assembly. Wonder why.

With phones stuffed full of memories and correspondingly diminished storage, they ambled toward the men's basketball gymnasium, where the school was holding the dance. They passed various couples along the cobblestone path with gaudy, glittering dresses and mops of hair drenched in sweat from the muggy evening. A heavy bass beat sounded from half a mile away at the large brick building.

A wall of sound blasted them when they reached the glass doors. Before they could enter, they were subjected to breathalyzer tests and signed in with a lady at a gray table.

The smell of feet stunk the gymnasium as they entered the room, which was twenty degrees hotter than the weather outside. Paper palm trees and balloons coated the sides of the room, covering red-painted letters that read, *WELCOME TO THE DEN.* Chaperones patrolled the edges in grass skirts and leis. Each looked more miserable than the next, and the teenagers grinding off to the sides didn't seem to faze them.

Each couple split off the second they dove into the sound wall. Hannah dragged Duke to the center of the dance floor, where most of the students left very little room—physically and for the imagination. Jeremy stayed on the outer rim and broke out his newest "moves," which reminded Danny a lot of a middle-aged man starting a lawn mower. Michelle laughed.

Rayah and Danny lurked somewhere in the middle where couples teetered on gray half-court lines, barely covered by a see-through tarp. It must have been to catch all the sweat. Rayah's dance moves started off as a mere pumping of the arms, like a tentative weight lifter. But by the third song, "We Didn't Start the Fire," she thrust her arms into the air and flung her neck back as if she floated in a pool of calming water. Glad to see her mind was off Ned. She and Danny danced to almost every song, loitering on the sides for just two to catch a breather.

He considered grabbing her a plastic cup of punch from a table off to the side, but Dean lurked nearby that display too often for comfort. He had, after all, spiked the punch during the Sadie Hawkins dance too. Solid guy.

Instead, the two escaped through the hallway, bridging the girls' and guys' courts, and grabbed drinks from a fountain after waiting in a snaking line. Even though the water tasted like metal, Danny would've drunk mud by that point. Afterward, Danny took off his jacket and placed it on a pile of reeking suits at the corner of the gym by a cardboard cutout of a lei dancer.

After the last song, "Don't Stop Believing," they headed back to Suanna with Michelle and Jeremy. According to Michelle, Hannah and Duke had left early to grab dinner from the dining commons. Duke apparently didn't mind because people kept tearing off the Sonic hat from his head and playing games of catch with it.

"Guess the cubes of cheese they served at prom didn't fill Hannah." Michelle clutched at the sides of her tight dress, breathless. "Who could blame her? She eats like five football players combined."

They filtered into the foot-scented dorm with what seemed like the rest of the prom crowd. When they entered, each let out a satisfied "ah …" as they refreshed themselves in the Suanna AC. The crowds filed up the stairs and thinned out by the time they reached the third floor.

Rayah and Michelle arrived at room 315 and knocked on the door. A drowsy Hannah, in a panda onesie and makeup smudged on her face, answered. "Wish we could lock the doors on the *inside*. You all just interrupted the season finale of *Naruto*." She slammed the door, sending a tumbleweed of hair that was on the carpet in their direction. Gross.

Michelle gave Jeremy a hug, from which he staggered backward, unprepared. Rayah followed suit in a gentler fashion, thanking her date for the wonderful night. Even though caked in sweat, she still smelled wonderful. The two women entered their room and shut the door behind themselves.

The two men split off at the lobby doors as Danny headed back to Phrat River. He dreaded entering the building without any AC.

Nausea struck him as soon as he returned to his room. In the windowless darkness and Duke snoring off in the corner, he probed his desk for his stomach meds. Cans crashed onto the floor, thudding on the carpet. Then he recalled that Hannah had stuffed the bottle of pills into her purse. He clicked the light on his watch to read the time. Five minutes till curfew.

Suanna was seven minutes away, but if he sprinted, he could get the medication without a monitor catching him. Look at him, living life on the edge. Next he would turn in his library books late. What a heathen.

His thick dress shoes clunked down the stairs, oxford dripping in sweat, as he raced outside into the cooling night once more. His head grew fuzzy on his run just as it had toward the tail end of track season. The pills would make the journey worth it.

But when he reached the girl's dorm, the building a black silhouette against a red-and-yellow backdrop, he stopped dead in his tracks.

Dagon, no.

The smell of fire, the second most common scent of that year, saturated the air, thicker than ever before. Outside the dorm, clusters of inhabitants—half in pajamas, the others in prom dresses—huddled hundreds of feet away, staring at the building with frowns, tears, and screams.

He scanned the crowd for a panda onesie or the prom dresses of his friends but found none. "Oh, God. Please tell me they made it out."

A girl nearby crumpled to her knees and wailed while another comforted her. Danny rushed over, knees crackling in the cold, rustling grass. "What happened?" The force of his voice scared him, but it didn't matter now. He needed to know his friends were safe.

She motioned to the sobbing girl. "She came from the third floor, where the fire started."

His heart thundered. "Third floor?" No, no, no, no, no, no, no ...

She nodded. "Happened right as the monitors started locking the rooms. Right before they were going to lock hers." She motioned to the weeping friend. "A smoky scent woke her up. To think, they could have trapped her in a room without windows."

"What room did the smoke come from?"

She shrugged her shoulders and gestured to the sniveling girl. "She knows."

He placed a hand on the girl's arm. "Please, tell me what room."

Between gasps, she got out, "The–one–next–to–mine ... 315." Then she melted in a stream of tears.

315. Rayah, Hannah, and Michelle's room.

The wind knocked out of him. Danny clenched fistfuls of grass, paralyzed to do anything else.

A hand clapped on his shoulder, and he glanced up stiffly at the giant figure of Ned in a disheveled suit and fresh tears streaming down his face into his knotted beard.

In Ned's free hand, he held lighter fluid, and in the one on Danny's shoulder, a lighter.

The adventure continues ...

In Book Two of the Blaze Series:

Den

Acknowledgments

TO CHRIST, MY LORD AND SAVIOR, WHO SAVES ME FROM the den every day.

To the Dannys in my life: Mom, Dad, and Cyle, your levelheadedness has helped me to have hope for my future, even when circumstances look bleak.

To the Hannahs: Daniel, Ellen, and Alyssa, your carefree spirits encourage me to embrace the unknown and take a few chances.

To the Michelles: Grace, all writing mentors, and Sonya, your no-nonsense sense has whipped me into shape and made me determined to conquer my fears.

To the Rayahs: Tessa, Jeanette, James, Katie, and Carlee, your encouragement gave me something to keep pushing forward, even when I felt like I was smooshed against a wall.

Made in United States
Orlando, FL
08 September 2023